Seasons of Magick

SUZAN HARDEN

This is a work of fiction. All characters, organizations and events in this novel are products of the author's imagination and are not to be construed as real. Any resemblance to persons, living or dead, is entirely coincidental.

SEASONS OF MAGICK
The Seasons of Magick Anthology

ISBN-13 – 978-1-938745-72-0

Published by Angry Sheep Publishing
Findlay, Ohio

Cover Design by For the Muse Designs
Interior Design by QA Productions

More books by Suzan Harden

Bloodlines
Blood Magick
Zombie Love
Zombie Confidential
Zombie Wedding
Amish, Vamps & Thieves
Blood Sacrifice
Love, War & a Bulldog
Zombie Goddess
Ravaged
Sacrificed
Reality Bites
Ghouls in the Grocery
Resurrected

Seasons of Magick
Spring
Summer
Autumn
Winter
The Seasons of Magick Anthology

Justice
Sword and Sorceress 28 ("Justice")
Sword and Sorceress 30 ("Diplomacy in the Dark")
Justice: The Beginning
A Question of Balance
A Modicum of Truth
A Matter of Death
A Touch of Mother

888-555-HERO
Hero De Facto
Hero Ad Hoc
Hero De Novo
A Very Hero Christmas

Miscellaneous
Sword and Sorceress 31 ("Pig-Headed")
Sword and Sorceress 32 ("Unexpected")

For more information or to be added to her mailing list, visit Suzan's website at www.suzanharden.com

*To Angie P., who has been a wonderful friend
though we have yet to meet in real life*

SPRING

Chapter 1

Tessa McClain shoved the mass of blond curls out of her face and glared at the tarot card lying on the cloth in front of her. Early morning sunlight poured through open windows, highlighting the white stars on the deep blue fabric. The day already held a hint of more unseasonably warm April weather for Manhattan.

Tessa closed her eyes and opened them. Nope, the same card still lay there, an accusation of how messed-up her life had become.

The Five of Coins.

She tilted her head and regarded her neighbor, Rain Bean, seated on the other side of the coffee table. "Money problems, huh? The freakin' cards can't tell me something I don't already know?"

Rain sighed, a long dramatic sound Tessa knew was calculated to annoy the crap out of her. Her friend fingered one of her oddly designed hoop earrings. "If you don't like the answer—"

"Try a different deck." Tessa couldn't stop herself from blurting the words. Maybe her smartass attitude wasn't properly respectful of Rain's beliefs, but the electricity that shot across Tessa's nerve endings bothered her. The weird feeling occurred whenever Rain tried to read her fortune. It excited her and scared the shit out of her at the same time.

Rain cocked an eyebrow, the fine dark line at odds with her shoulder-length silver hair.

Tessa swallowed what was left of her pride. "Please?"

Without a word, Rain collected her everyday Rider-Waite deck and set it aside. She turned to pull another deck out of the carved wooden box sitting beside her on the floor. The sunlight streaming into her apartment caught on the gold earrings she wore.

Heat flooded Tessa's face as the intricate design of the hoops resolved into a man and woman intimately entwined in the throes of passion. She wasn't sure what bothered her more, that she didn't have the guts to wear something blatantly sexual like the earrings or that a woman three times her age saw more action than she did.

But then Rain looked and acted decades younger. Tessa chewed on her lower lip as she realized she didn't know Rain's real age.

It's not your business, young lady. Amazing how she could still hear her grandmother's disapproving tone years after the funeral.

The soft rifling of the cards jerked Tessa's attention from her wayward thoughts. Rain caressed the dark, eerie second deck, treating the cards as if they were her lover's body. Okay, maybe if her lover was of the feathered persuasion. Reddish orange crows against a black background covered the backside of this deck. The black birds promised doom and freedom at the same time.

Tessa sneezed, a loud obnoxious sound in the tiny apartment. The heady, musk incense Rain burned only accentuated Tessa's allergies. Yanking a tissue from the pocket of her shorts, she blew her nose. Life truly sucked when she couldn't even afford over-the-counter meds.

Finally, Rain stopped shuffling and nodded at her to pick a card. Tessa bit her lip before pulling a card from the middle of the fanned deck Rain held.

"What the—" Tessa dropped the card. It landed face up, and once again, Tessa stared at the Five of Coins. The picture on this card was far more unnerving than the other deck. A lioness perched on tiny geometric shapes in the middle of black space, peering at something off to the side. The big cat's expression was both welcoming and wary.

Rain tapped the card with her index finger. "Errors occur."

"Yeah, letting Jimmy move in was one big error," Tessa muttered.

Pity flared in Rain's deep brown eyes. "He's gone. Your money's gone—"

"My job's gone thanks to that asshole using my company AmEx card." No one but her friend, Brady Morrison, had stood up for her in the aftermath of the accusations of fraud and theft. Because of Jimmy's bullshit, Tessa had been blacklisted throughout the tristate area. All her job search efforts and living expenses over the last six months had chewed through her emergency fund, the one bank account Jimmy had not discovered. And New York City wasn't a cheap place to live to begin with. What she needed was a job, not Rain's pity.

Rain sighed again and shook her head. "When are you going to let go of your anger, Tessa?" She tapped her index finger on the lioness. "This can also mean you're unable to give up control."

"Giving up control to Jimmy is the reason I'm about to lose my apartment." And anger was pretty much all Tessa had left thanks to that asshole. Her family had given her so much grief about moving here. The last thing she wanted was to flee back to Indiana with her tail between her legs.

"Giving up control may be what we need to do to find our heart's desire. And I said you're more than welcome to move in with me." Rain smiled. "You'd only have to move boxes across the hall."

The hard knot of fury in Tessa's chest loosened. It wasn't fair to take her anger at Jimmy out on Rain. She had been nothing but nice to Tessa from day one, even if the old gal did have some freaky hobbies.

Tessa blew the wayward curls out of her face again. "I might have to take you up on that." She rose from the floor, stretching the tense kinks in her back. "Let's see how job hunting goes today."

Rain looked up from putting away her tarot cloth. "If you don't find what you're looking for today, let me know. I know a place that's looking for a full-time person."

Tessa placed her hand on the doorknob. "Thanks, but you've already been helping me so much." Guilt gnawed at how much she owed Rain as it was. Owed the lady things that had nothing to do with money. Okay, maybe stock in Proctor & Gamble for all the tissues she'd used while curled up on Rain's couch the first month after Jimmy had left the country with all her money along with the funds he'd stolen from others.

Rain gave her a soft, sympathetic smile. "Just keep it in mind, and good luck."

Tessa nodded, not trusting herself to speak around the moisture that threatened to pour from her eyes. She dived through Rain's apartment door, closing it behind her, only to have her heart lodge in her throat. Across the hall, tacked to her own apartment door was an eviction notice. With shaking hands, she ripped it off. She was now officially out of time.

Chapter 2

By three-thirty in the afternoon, the blister on Tessa's heel had burst. The acid-burn sensation topped off a lousy day. Hell, she couldn't even nail a counter position at the freaking coffee shop two blocks ago.

She limped to a bus stop bench and sat down. Easing off her shoe, she examined the damage to her heel. A hole in her hose matched the hole in her skin. Yanking open the zipper on a side compartment of her purse, she pulled out an adhesive bandage and a tiny bottle of clear nail polish.

Jimmy had made fun of her Midwest "be prepared" mentality, so she'd tried to be the nonchalant person he wanted. She shook her head at her own foolishness. She had let the asshole play her like a violin.

Gritting her teeth against the pain, she applied the bandage through the stocking hole then dabbed polish along the torn ends of ruined hose to keep the run from spreading. While she waited for the polish to dry, she checked the classified section of the *Times*. The print-out of job listings she pulled from the neighborhood library computer had been exhausted an hour ago.

Reading one of the few ads where she wasn't overqualified for the position, she groaned. Even with the bandage to cushion her raw and seeping skin, there was no way in hell she'd make it on foot to the company holding the open interviews fourteen blocks away. They closed at four. And no money meant no taxi, no bus and no subway.

Closing her eyes to the despair seeping deeper into her soul, she leaned back and inhaled a lungful of air. Car exhaust mixed with garlic and soy from the Chinese restaurant behind her. Folks could bitch all they wanted, but the scents of this city had exhilarated her the moment she had stepped off the plane five years ago. New York held the smell of promise. She didn't want to leave.

Traffic hummed and the sun's rays caressed her face. Maybe Rain's gods would listen if she asked them for help. Religion wasn't a big deal in Tessa's life, but right now, she had nothing else left to lose. And Rain always said all Tessa had to do was ask. To compose her thoughts, she took another deep breath.

Her giant sneeze nearly knocked her off the bench.

Blinking her watery eyes, Tessa reached for the tissues inside her purse and froze. A crow perched next to her on the back of the bench. The bird was freakin' huge. Black feathers shone with iridescent highlights in the bright afternoon sun. Its head cocked as it regarded her with one yellow eye.

Damn. If it were a pigeon, she'd know what it wanted. This thing stared at her like it expected something besides peanuts or bread crumbs.

Caw!

She jumped in her seat at the crow's cry, but it made no motion toward her. Instead, the head swiveled to peer across the street. Tessa didn't move a muscle. Wild animals were unpredictable, and New York was no exception. When she failed to move, the crow looked at her and squawked again before turning its attention back across the street.

Turning very carefully so she didn't startle the bird, Tess looked in the same direction. Inside the store window on the corner, red lettering on stark white poster board caught her eye.

Help Wanted.

Maybe Rain's gods were listening after all. She eyed the bird. "Thanks."

The crow gave a quieter cry that sounded suspiciously like "welcome." Wings spread and the bird shot off into the sky.

Tessa blew her nose and slipped her sensible black heel back on her abused foot, but crossing the street when harboring a limp took more effort than usual. Cabs in particular seemed to aim for her as she dodged insane drivers. Maybe they were as psychic as Rain and knew she couldn't pay their fares.

Once on the other side in one piece, Tessa glanced at the neat gold lettering stenciled across the big picture window. Morrigan's Cauldron. Probably some New Age type place, but right now, she couldn't afford to be choosey. Tessa willed the butterflies in her stomach to calm down and ran a hand over her hair before she pushed open the door.

The wind chime above the frame tinkled as she entered. She sneezed again at the spicy herbs that dusted the air inside of the store. The exotic odor swirled around her, no doubt the intention to entice the unwary to explore a little further. It only made her long for the cleaner car exhaust outside.

Examining the dark wood shelves, she discovered her assumption about the store was correct. An odd assortment of modern books, antique journals and loose paper in bins littered the shelves of the left wall. A small table carried a number of large black leather-bound tomes. One volume stood on a tripod at the top of the pile.

Curious, she flicked it open. A painting of a man and woman illustrated the page. The colors flared with life, the ancient Hindu style vibrant with detail. What the painted couple were doing sent heat flooding through her cheeks. The woman had her skirts hiked to her waist, and she straddled her lover, facing away from him, her attention solely on guiding his well-endowed penis into her. It was all Tessa could do to close the book without slamming it. Did the entire universe have to rub in the fact she hadn't had sex in the last six months?

Taking as deep a steadying breath as she could without setting off another round of sneezing, she glanced to the right. A beaten, manual, century-old cash register held court on the scarred counter. Standing sentinel on the shelves behind the register, ancient apothecary jars contained the fragrant herbs that had set off her allergies. More shelves lined the middle of the long store, the objects sitting on them too numerous and too odd to mention.

"May I help you?"

A man stepped from behind a myriad display of carved crystals. Tessa gasped, not because he startled her, but from the sheer force of his masculinity. Easily over six feet tall, he dressed in black. Tight black t-shirt over a sculpted chest, black jeans that hugged him in all the right places and black moccasins that simply looked comfortable. Somehow, she had the impression he dressed to suit himself, not out of any sense of Big Apple fashion chic. His burnished gold locks curled slightly around his ears before they brushed his powerful shoulders. The same artist who had created the quartz pieces behind him could have sculpted the sharp planes of his face.

"May I help you?" he repeated.

Dizziness threatened to overwhelm her.

That's what you get for skipping lunch.

Ignoring her internal voice's smartass remark, she sucked in a shallow breath. "I'm here about your 'Help Wanted' sign." She jabbed a thumb over her shoulder in the direction of the window.

His frown pulled the corners of his mouth down in a look reminiscent of the bouncers she had encountered when she first moved to the city. The slow sweep of his eyes raked her from top to bottom, taking in her classic gray interview suit, modest white blouse and oh-so-sensible one-inch heels. Reflected in his eyes was the uptight financial planner she'd been for the last five years. Five years minus the last six months of hell.

His lips pursed a moment before he said, "I don't think you're what I'm looking for."

Yep, she was getting turned away before she ever got past the velvet rope.

Not sure if it was desperation driving her or the irritation at his condescending tone, she squared her shoulders and marched over to him until she was nose to, well, chest. Arching her neck, she glared into his gray eyes. "If you're looking for someone who's good with numbers and has an excellent rapport with her clientele, I am the person you are looking for." She gave a disdainful glance around the shop. "And you don't exactly seem to be swimming in customers." She turned her attention back to the man. "I have a double major in finance and marketing, and I can put together an advertising campaign that will double your client base in three months."

The silence dragged on for an eternity, but one lesson she'd learned long ago was when to stop talking and let the client make his decision. Not breaking eye contact, he stepped closer, his presence taking over her personal space.

"What if I need something from you other than your business expertise?" A hint of a smile curved his full lips.

Ignoring the sensual promise in his voice, she raised her chin a notch further. "I seriously doubt someone like you could possibly need anything from someone like me, other than I show up on time and I'm prepared to work." She gave him her most "hands-off" smile in her repertoire. "Besides wouldn't your boyfriend object?"

Instead of getting pissed off as she expected, he threw back his head and roared with laughter. When he got his mirth under control, he stepped back and waved at her to follow him. "Maybe you'll do after all." He strode over to the counter and bent over it.

Her leeriness didn't stop her from admiring his ass as he fished for something underneath the counter. She should have walked out of the store at his suggestive question, but desperation made a woman do stupid things.

Yeah, desperation and lust.

Great. All she needed was to take up with another bad boy who'd leave her high and dry.

A bad boy with a trim waist meant for wrapping her legs around as he entered her. Slow. A tickle of moisture seeped at the direction of her thoughts.

Okay, maybe not dry as Jimmy left me.

He popped up with an application in his hand, his attitude all business. "Fill this out. We're open from noon until eight. Come in at eleven tomorrow. You can fill out the tax and insurance forms while we eat lunch." He named a figure for her starting wage. "But that's for your thirty-day probation period. Once I see how things work out, we can discuss a raise."

The rush of information tossed her out of her erotic daydream. She shook her head, curls bouncing wildly. "Wait a minute! I didn't say I accepted the job."

His right eyebrow disappeared under his thick bangs. "Why are you still here?"

It was a question she couldn't answer.

Steeling her nerve, she fired back. "A sewer rat couldn't survive on what you're paying." She named a number thirty per cent higher than his original offer. It still wasn't enough to pay the back rent on her apartment, but it'd be enough to live on while she stayed with Rain and searched for something else.

By his frown and his long pause, she was sure he'd toss her out on the street. His eyes bore into her as if reading her soul. Then something in his manner shifted and he nodded.

"Agreed, but no raise until your annual review."

She wouldn't be here for a year but no sense telling him that. She held out her hand. "Deal, Mr.?"

"Adrian Holloway." He smiled and took her hand.

Tessa stifled a gasp at the warm rush that filled her at his touch, a flow of energy that both soothed and excited. She looked into his eyes. The soft gray irises darkened, and he slowly withdrew his hand. To cover the flush heating her cheeks, she yanked a pen out of her purse.

"How about I fill out that form?"

Chapter 3

Adrian leaned against the front window of the shop, admiring the sway of Tessa McClain's hips as she sashayed down the street. The woman had a fire that set him on edge. He swiped a hand over his face. Maybe it'd been too damn long since any woman had warmed his bed. And a new employee was probably not the best place to start looking either.

Still, he couldn't pull himself away from the window until she disappeared among the pedestrian traffic. He walked back to the counter, snagged the phone receiver and punched in the owner's number from memory.

"Hello, Adrian."

"Dammit, Rain, you know that freaks me out," he said. "Especially when I know you don't have caller ID."

Soft laughter chimed over the receiver. "How else do I keep my manager in line?"

He smiled even though she couldn't see him. Two years ago, he'd stumbled across Morrigan's Cauldron during one of his many sleepless nights in the horrible months after he'd lost Jennifer. Rain's group had been celebrating an esbat after store hours, and the light from their candles had been inviting, comforting. Surprisingly so, given how his staunch Presbyterian parents would have viewed the Wiccan full moon ritual. His encounter with Rain and her friends had been like coming home to a place he didn't even know he missed.

For the first time in over two years, the horrific, all-consuming grief didn't swallow him whole at the memory of Jennifer. The pain was still there, like the scar from some god-awful wound, but bearable.

Putting his personal shit aside, he said, "I have a new employee starting tomorrow." He glanced at the application form in his hand even though he'd already memorized the information. "Tessa McClain. I want to run a criminal background check on—"

Laughter rang through the receiver.

Suspicion snuck through him. "Shit, Rain. Is she one of your strays?"

"Yes." She continued to giggle between words. "I hope you don't mind."

Adrian held the receiver away from his ear as she dissolved into another round of uncontrollable laughter. He didn't share Rain's beliefs, but after some freaky coincidences, he had learned not to question her ways.

Yet, his reaction to Tessa had been so intense. His cock jerked at the image of peeling off that damned suit of hers to find what lay beneath. Somehow, he didn't think she was the granny panty type despite the conservative image she tried to project.

An image far too similar to the one he'd once hidden behind.

He'd rip off the pewter wool she wore like armor to discover the soft flesh beneath it. Pink lace, the same color as the lipstick slicked across her mouth, would grace her generous curves. Except she wouldn't bother with any panties at all. Framed by the lace of her garter, dark gold curls would wink and beckon between her thighs. And when he knelt before her, the rich scent of peonies would fire his senses as he buried himself in her—

"Adrian? Adrian, are you still there?"

Rain's voice yanked him back to reality. God, he was seriously losing it.

"Yeah, I'm still here." He placed Tessa's application on the counter and backed away. Five minutes with the woman and he had a hard-on to rival Ron Jeremy. Two minutes alone with the application she'd filled out, and he wanted to follow her and fuck her until neither of them could walk. He stared at the accusing piece of paper with her number and address. She was toxic. Everything she touched was toxic. Toxic to the carefully constructed peace of mind he'd built over the last two years.

Too bad he didn't have a biohazard container.

"Play nice with Tessa. She's had a hard time."

Rain's admonishment fired another image of the lovely Tessa bent over the counter, her pert ass in the air as he plunged into her. He ground his teeth to rein in his libido.

"Don't worry, Rain. I'll take good care of her." He clicked off the receiver before something more inappropriate popped out of his mouth. He was going to need a raise himself to pay for all the cold showers he'd need for the rest of the week.

Chapter 4

Tessa blew an angry huff at a wayward curl dangling in her eyes as she stacked boxes containing ceramic fairies. Muscles ached from moving and unpacking merchandise. Damn, she had thought she was in shape. The ache in her biceps and thighs said otherwise. Thank God, she only had an hour to go until closing time.

She jerked at the large heated palm on her shoulder.

"How's it coming?"

She turned to find Adrian standing close. Way too close. "Just fine. Almost done." She flashed him a smile that she didn't feel.

He stared at her, a twist to his mouth, but he didn't say anything. He nodded, squeezed past her and continued down the tight aisle in the storage room.

She sighed and broke down the shipping containers for the recycling bin. It wasn't his fault that she was as jumpy as a cat in a roomful of rocking chairs. She smiled, a genuine one, at Grandma's old saying. Grandma had been full of them. And Grandma would have loved Rain.

Learning that Rain owned Morrigan's Cauldron started her pissy mood last night. The old woman had confessed over their celebratory dinner of chicken lo mein. Bad enough that she had to move in with Rain. She had offered to lend Tessa the money to cover the back and current rent until she found another roommate, but her upbringing forced her to say no. Rain's charity at letting her rent the older woman's spare bedroom had been hard enough to accept. And part of her wondered if Adrian was one of Rain's lovers, but Tessa hadn't conjured the nerve to ask.

Electricity sizzled in the air giving her ample warning the boss was headed her way again. Adrian murmured, "Excuse me," before he slid past hauling a box of handmade soaps, his arm brushing hers in the narrow space. Every little insignificant touch of his body sent hers tingling.

It wasn't his fault he exuded sex appeal the way other people breathed. The problem was his sex appeal seeped into her pores until she was one big raging hormone. And that pissed her off to no end.

The work itself wasn't that bad. Phylicia and Tom, the two other full-time employees who had joined them for lunch, were sweet, and Phylicia's son, Jamal, who worked part-time after school, kept her in stitches. In fact, they acted like one big, happy family with Rain as the matriarch.

Tessa had been relieved to discover that Phylicia and Tom would be at the store the entire day. For some stupid reason, she had believed their presence would take the edge off her intense attraction to Adrian.

No such luck.

She had been able to concentrate on work when Adrian had walked her through the entire operation at the beginning of the day. She was amazed at how much of the store's business consisted of online orders. He had asked her opinion on some improvements he was considering. What amazed her more was that he had actually listened.

She dragged the flattened cardboard out the back door and dropped it into the recycling bin next to the dumpster. It had been a long time since anyone listened to her business advice, and dammit, it felt good.

Maybe that was the real problem. She was so hungry for male attention after the Jimmy fiasco she read too much into Adrian's actions. Was that why she snuck glances at him when she thought he wasn't looking? Good grief, was she that desperate? Sucking in a deep breath, she steeled herself and went back inside.

She grabbed the next box of merchandise off the stack by the back door and stumbled from the deceptive weight of the smaller package. Her elbow nailed the corner of a metal storage shelf when she fought to gain her balance. Biting her tongue against the pain and numbness, she desperately fumbled with the cardboard. In the slow motion horror of any accident, the box slid between her hands and crashed to the floor with a sickening crack, sending a plume of Styrofoam peanuts into the air.

For a long moment, she couldn't move. Foam bits drifted through the stifling air.

"What the hell!" Adrian stood in front of her, foam clinging to his hair and t-shirt.

Tessa's vision blurred. First day on the job and it'd be her last. There was no way she could pay for whatever she'd just broken.

"Are you okay?" Dodging the mess, he grasped her upper arms and pulled her close. The heat from his touch burned her in a way that had nothing to do with the embarrassment at her klutziness.

Phylicia poked her dread-locked head around the corner. "Everything okay back here?"

"Nothing the rest of us haven't done." Adrian waved her back. "Move along. Nothing to see."

Phylicia laughed and disappeared.

Adrian turned back to Tessa and bent to look into her eyes. "You sure you're okay?"

His touch was disconcerting, but she nodded and raised a hand to swipe away the sweat and tears from her cheeks. "I'm so sorry."

"Hey, it was an accident." He picked foam bits out of her curls. His fingers combed through her locks to shake out the remaining pieces, and it was all she could do not to sink her face into his palm.

She stole a glance at his eyes to find they had turned the same dark smoky color as yesterday. Her breasts tightened under his gaze until the scrape of her lace bra across her nipples was agonizing. The animalistic part of her wanted Adrian to push her up against the naked brick wall and have his way with her. He shifted closer.

A loud crunch under his heel made them both jerk away.

"Shit." Adrian swore something else under his breath that she didn't catch.

"I think it was just a peanut," she offered, but the spell was broken. She wasn't sure who moved, but their bodies were now feet apart instead of millimeters.

He chuckled and shook his head. "Let's pick this up and put it on the bench. It's almost eight. We can deal with the damage after the store closes."

Forty-five minutes later, a nervous energy coursed through Tessa as Adrian locked the front door and slid the steel gates into place. Phylicia and Jamal offered to stay and help, but Adrian had shooed them out the door.

Tessa couldn't help rubbing her arms when Adrian turned to her. "So what do we need to do?"

"Let's load the box onto the dumb waiter and take it upstairs."

Upstairs? There was an upstairs? Alone with him? She didn't trust herself not to jump him.

He must have sensed her nervousness. His expression stilled, but his eyes reflected nothing of his thoughts. "You don't have to stay."

She sucked in a lungful of air. The nag champa incense Phylicia had burned earlier lingered, but Tessa's nose didn't so much as tingle. The same couldn't be said for the rest of her.

What am I so afraid of?

Except it wasn't fear that fired her senses. It was raw desire for a man she'd met only yesterday. What the hell was wrong with her? She'd always made sensible choices. Well, until Jimmy anyway. And did she really want to go down that road again with some hunky New Age store manager?

She shook her head and said, "It's my fault for dropping the box. The least I can do is give you a hand in dealing with the damage." And keep her jeans zipped in the process.

Adrian gave a curt nod and stalked back to the cramped storeroom. She followed, mesmerized by the fluid motion of his back and legs. His movements were possessive and predatory, a big cat stalking his domain. Maybe she did have an ulterior motive in staying late. One she hated to admit to herself. *If you fell off a horse,* Grandma would have said, *you climb right back on again.*

Grandma hadn't stated she couldn't trade her missing pony for a stallion in the process. No one said she had to make a lifetime commitment to the Cauldron or to Adrian. Maybe Rain was right. Maybe she should give up control for once in her life and go with her instincts.

And her instincts said Adrian Holloway would be one wild ride.

Bracing their arms under the damaged box, they shuffled across the storeroom to what Tessa had assumed earlier was a couple of storage closets. Adrian elbowed open the smaller door to reveal an ancient dumbwaiter. They slid the box into the tiny elevator, and Adrian motioned Tessa to follow him up a set of dimly lit, narrow stairs hidden behind the second door.

Nerves made her pause for an instant. Maybe this wasn't such a bright idea. Adrian wasn't the one she mistrusted. He'd given her an out, and she hadn't taken it. No, she could behave herself for the, what, maybe half-hour it would take them to check the contents of the box. She started up the stairs, unable to stop herself from admiring his backside as they climbed.

Adrian opened the second floor door and stepped aside. "Home, sweet home."

A riot of color blasted her optic nerves. Every single square inch of the plastered walls were covered in free-form splashes of scarlet, amethyst, royal blue, black and white. Only the naked brick in the open kitchen had escaped the mad painter. Flooring and furniture further sectioned the loft, and her vision adjusted to drink in the sight.

White plush carpet cordoned off the living area. Small jewel-tone pillows in red and purple graced the black cloth-covered couch and two bulky over-stuffed chairs. An entertainment center painted black held the requisite large screen TV and stereo system, standards of every man she'd ever met. To her left was the well-apportioned kitchen. Black cabinets framed stainless steel appliances. The breakfast nook sheltered a black stone and steel table. Scarlet cushions padded the matching steel chairs. A short hallway disappeared behind the entertainment center.

Apprehension grabbed her. The loft could have been designed by the same SoHo decorator who had done Jimmy's. Or at least the one Jimmy claimed to own. Just another lie in a long string.

"So what do you think?"

She looked up at Adrian. She couldn't imagine someone like him needing approval from anyone, but he had an air of . . . expectancy.

Tessa shot him a wry smile. "It's amazing. And no offense, but it's not the style I pictured for you." But then, what had she pictured? A tree-hugger, like Rain? With lots of beads, hemp and bean bags? Not Mr. Practical Business Man. The loft was the work of a serious graphic artist. Had he designed it himself?

Before she could ask, he raised both eyebrows and one corner of his mouth twisted upwards. "I'm afraid to ask what you pictured." He held up his hand when she opened her mouth. "That was not an invitation to analyze me. Let's grab that box and see what we can salvage."

After pulling the box from the dumbwaiter and setting it on the carpet, they knelt on opposite sides of the ruined cardboard. Adrian pulled out the first bubble-wrapped item and handed it to her.

Her breath hitched in dread of the damage she would find. Carefully, she unwound the air-filled plastic from the hefty object. An eight-inch carved stone penis dropped into her waiting palm.

On an esthetic level, she could understand the artist's desire for this particular stone. She ran her fingers across the cool, smooth surface. Creams, beiges and pinks shifted and swirled through the length of the piece ending in a deep rose at the head.

The back of her neck itched, and she slowly lifted her head to find Adrian staring at her. He sat crossed-legged, his back propped against the couch. Smoky gray darkened his eyes, the same predatory look he had earlier in the storeroom below. A shiver ran down her spine. Her hands squeezed the object, a physical response as she tried to corral her emotions. Heat flared in her cheeks when she realized she was fondling the stone penis.

No wonder he stared at her. He must think she was a total pervert.

She handed it to him, electricity sparking at the touch of his fingers on hers. "No chips or breaks on this one." Her attempt at cheer rang false when her voice cracked with a husky sound. She cleared her throat. "I didn't think the store carried, um, adult products."

Reluctant to release his contact with Tessa, Adrian forced himself to take the sculpture and set it aside. "The statues are used in fertility rites. Beltane is coming up. I was beginning to wonder if we'd get the shipment in time."

She reached in the box for another piece. "Beltane?"

He grinned at her confused expression. "It's a Wiccan holiday held on May 1st."

White teeth nibbled her bottom lip as she unwrapped another stone penis. "You mean May Day?"

"Yeah." He took the proffered statue and check it off the inventory sheet. It took all his willpower not to pull her next to him and guide her soft hand to his own erection. He gave a silent prayer of thanks that bubble-wrap covered the bulge in his jeans. From what Rain indicated on the phone and the hesitant look in her eyes, Tessa had been burned so bad that she'd bolt if he didn't take care, didn't reassure her that it was all right to desire.

And for the first time in over two years, he wanted, too. Wanted Tessa McClain.

They continued to work in silence, and he gauged each piece's effect on Tessa as she gingerly unwrapped and examined the soapstone sculptures. He found himself envious of a bunch of rocks.

She bit her bottom lip again, the flesh pinking under the tips of her perfect white teeth. She traced a long slim finger over what appeared at first glance to be a delicately fashioned flower in rose and cream soapstone. Her face flushed again when she realized what the carving was. The image of her tracing the slick folds of her own body in the same manner nearly sent him over the edge.

Another sculpture of two woman entwined merited only her cursory check for damage. Good. He wasn't the sharing type.

Her pupils dilated when the next bundle revealed a man and woman. The soapstone woman straddled her lover, her head thrown back in ecstasy. Tessa's fingers lingered on both the statue and his skin when she handed it to him, and he relished the contact.

More carved penises and flowery vulvas followed. Her face remained flushed as she unwrapped each piece with care, but no longer in embarrassment. Her lips parted, the rose lipstick she used long since chewed away. He gritted his teeth with the effort to remain sitting still, the press of the zipper into his erection on the edge of pain.

"Oh, no." He looked up from the inventory sheet at Tessa's soft murmur. She held a carved lock of hair that had broken off the statue she'd unwrapped. The loss of the broken piece didn't affect the erotic scene of the stone man kneeling between the stone woman's spread legs, buried to the hilt. Tessa tilted the piece, looking for additional damage. The artist had carved every detail, including the man's sac pressed against his lover's ass.

That view was the last straw. All self-control broke as cleanly as the female statue's hair. He had to taste Tessa. Tonight.

"Let's set this one aside." Adrian took the broken statue and placed it on the couch before he grabbed her hand. His thumb stroked across the soft flesh of her palm. Her breath hitched at his touch, but she didn't pull away.

She blinked, her long lashes sweeping against her pale cheeks. "I'll pay for it."

"Wait. You might find a piece you like better."

She broke eye contact at his gentle teasing, but she didn't jerk out of his grip. Her hand slid from his and reached into the box for another item. He wasn't sure, but her breathing seemed to take a faster pace, not quite panting but close. He wanted to hear her pant, moan, scream his name when she came.

The remaining foam peanuts fell away as Tessa removed the last statue, and she unwound the bubble-wrap. The kneeling woman leaned against her lover's chest, her back arched. The man explored her left breast with one hand while his other hand delved into her folds, stroking her. The woman's mouth formed a delicate "o". Tessa's index finger traced the soapstone faces as her tongue flicked along her bottom lip. Her actions enticed him by the sheer unconsciousness of them.

God, he wanted to lick the moisture off her mouth, taste everything about her. His body shook but he forced himself to remain seated.

"Would you prefer that one, Tessa?" He kept his voice low, fearful of breaking her trance. For all her sophisticated pretense, an air of innocent sensuality surrounded her.

With obvious effort, she dragged her gaze away from the statute and up to meet his. She shook her head. The fear and wariness no longer shone from her eyes. Something heated peered out instead. Something that made his own lust yowl in frustration, demanding to be released.

He held his hand out and she gave him the statue. This time there was no physical contact, a deliberate move on her part.

She climbed to her feet and brushed off dust and Styrofoam peanuts off her jeans. "I need to get going."

Damn, maybe he'd been too patient. "Why don't you stay?"

Chapter 5

Tessa's heart skipped a beat at Adrian's question. She should leave now before she did something stupid, but she couldn't deny the desire coiled thick in her belly. Desire for the man sitting in front of her.

"Rain will be waiting for me."

He stood. "Let me at least buy you dinner for staying and helping with this mess."

His expression wasn't pleading, but it did hold a hint of hopefulness. "Then I'll walk you home."

This is such a bad idea. But she found herself nodding. "All right."

They quickly divided the packing materials into their respective recycling sacks. Now that the spell was broken, she found they worked well together. As they placed the last bag in the dumbwaiter, her Midwestern sensibility required she make one last offer of reparations.

Adrian shook his head. "Like I said this afternoon, we've all had accidents. You should have seen the carnage when Jamal went through a growth spurt two years ago. All arms and legs. I swear something broke every five minutes around that kid."

The image Adrian painted made Tessa laugh. Really laugh. And that was something she hadn't done in a very long time.

Tessa was still laughing an hour later as they left the diner. The sexual awareness of her new boss was still present, waiting in a dark corner of her mind. She ignored it. "You don't have to walk me home. It's just a couple of blocks."

Something passed across Adrian's face. "Yes, I do. Rain would have my head if something happened to you." His mouth set in a grim line.

If Tessa had any money, she'd bet his determination had nothing to do with Rain. But it didn't seem to be related to the magnetism between them either. The creature in the corner of her mind sighed with disappointment. "Really, I'll be fine."

He locked a hand on her elbow, not hard enough to hurt, but a bit alarming nonetheless. "No arguments."

She had to jog to keep up with him, but he finally slowed after the first block. Beneath the streetlights, the line of his jaw relaxed, but he still had a look like he was in some other place.

The growing silence between them sent a tickle of unease up her spine. "How 'bout them Yankees?"

He stopped, released her arm and stared at her. "What?"

"What do you think about their chances this year?"

"You hate baseball."

Now where had that comment come from? Tessa smiled to chase away the weird feeling. "I didn't say that. I just don't follow it as closely as basketball." She shrugged.

Adrian blinked. "Oh, sorry." More blinking. Then a wry grin. "Let's get you home."

This time, instead of pulling her along the street by the elbow, he threaded his fingers between hers. She found she didn't mind that so much as they headed for her building. Jimmy never liked to hold hands. She'd always assumed he was a secret germophobe. Now she knew better.

Adrian insisted on walking her up to her floor. Was he going to insist on a nightcap as well? She wasn't sure she was ready for any kind of relationship. Where did the r-word come from? Damn, she was losing it all right.

In fact, she was so lost in wondering about how to handle the end of the night with Adrian that she automatically headed for her former apartment. The key slid in but the lock refused to turn. *Crap.*

Heat flared in her cheeks. She glanced at Adrian, who had a bemused expression on his face. "Old habits." She jerked the key out of the door, did an about-face, and jammed the offending stainless steel into the lock on the opposite side of the hall. This time, the deadbolt slid back with a *snick*.

"Thanks for dinner. I'll see you tomorrow." Tessa opened the door and eased inside.

A cocky grin lifted the corners of Adrian's mouth. "Tomorrow then. G'night, Rain."

From inside came a "Good night, Adrian."

Tessa closed the door to find Rain propped on the couch, a book in her hands and a sly smile on her face. Butterflies twirled through the patty melt in Tessa's stomach. Why'd she feel like she'd been busted for something?

Rain inserted a bookmark at her page and laid the paperback on the coffee table. "How was your first day?"

"Fine." Tessa crossed the living room and sat at the other end of the huge couch. "I broke a statue. Adrian wouldn't let me pay for it, so can you dock my pay check?"

The older woman waved her hand. "Oh, please. Do you know how much merchandise Adrian broke in his first week?"

Tessa plucked at the hem of her plain t-shirt. "You're not exactly filling me with confidence."

"So what do you think of him?"

Tessa raised her head to find Rain peering at her with an intense expression. She shrugged. "He seems okay. I haven't been around him enough to form an opinion."

Liar, her conscience said.

Disappointment dulled the look in Rain's eyes. "Really? He couldn't say enough good things about you. In fact, he called me this afternoon wanting to implement a couple of the changes you suggested."

"Oh, um, thanks." The heat from earlier returned to her cheeks. "I think I'll turn in." She wasn't the least tired, but she couldn't deal with Rain's scrutiny.

"You know, he's lonely, too."

Tessa turned to find Rain peering at her over the tops of her bifocals. "I'm not lonely. I just don't need any more complications in my life."

"Oh. Well, good night, then, dear." With a last quizzical look, Rain picked up her book.

Heading for her new bedroom, a thought smacked Tessa's brain. Did Rain have an ulterior motive in pushing Tessa to work at Morrigan's Cauldron? She shook her head. That gave the old woman too much credit.

Her hand hovered above the light switch when she spotted the yellow eye staring at her through the window. A bird, no, a crow, perched on the ledge. If she didn't know better, she would have thought it was the same one from the bus stop yesterday. *No, that's just ridiculous.* The crow cocked its head to examine her with its other eye. Then it cawed once before it dropped from the window ledge. For an instant, black wings were silhouetted by a streetlight before the crow disappeared.

A silhouette far too similar to Rain's tarot cards.

Chapter 6

The next week passed in a quiet rhythm. Tessa gave up on finding a consultant position in the tristate area. Mornings were spent contacting college classmates and business associates outside of New York. Rain knew what Tessa was doing, but she was pretty sure that wasn't why the older woman shot disapproving looks her way.

It was Tessa's refusal to have another dinner with Adrian. Even worse, Rain must have pulled Phylicia into her little scheme. Every time Tessa was alone with her co-worker, the woman extolled Adrian's virtues and his availability.

Tessa highly doubted the second part. A decent-looking, heterosexual male lacking companionship in Manhattan?

Except he was more than just decent-looking.

For his part, Adrian took her rejection in stride, even agreeing it was best not to mix business with pleasure. So why wouldn't Tessa's hyper-awareness of the man go away? Especially on the occasions she was alone with him.

Like tonight. Tom had the day off, and Phylicia had left early for a function at Jamal's school.

The air lay thick on her skin as she restocked candles. The ancient A/C unit three feet away didn't seem to make a difference with the oppressive humidity. She swiped at the sweat on her forehead.

Lightning flickered above the tenement across the street that housed the Chinese take-out place. She watched dark clouds roll over the Village and counted the seconds silently. At "five-Mississippi," a resounding boom rattled the windows in their frames.

Adrian set down another box next to where she knelt, but the weather consumed his attention. "This front's moving in faster than the weather folks predicted. We won't have much traffic tonight. If you want to beat the storm home, go grab your stuff."

Tessa leaned back and checked the time on the antique mantel clock perched above the apothecary jars. Only a little past six. She looked out the window again. Way too early for street lights, which were flickering on as the sky turned from dirty cotton gray to a sickly blue-black. "Don't we have to finish prepping those packages for shipment?"

"I can do it." The answer seemed an afterthought as he continued to stare at the angry-looking clouds. Another round of grumbling thunder shook the glass panes.

Tessa shoved damp curls out of her eyes. "That hardly seems fair. I'll stay." She needed the money too much to lose two hours of pay. At least, that's what she told herself.

Adrian looked down at her. "Thanks. It'll be easier with two of us. Besides, as fast as the storm blew in, it'll be done by quitting time."

His attention held more than gratitude for her offer of help, and she swallowed hard. She was only doing the job she was hired for.

Yeah, right, her conscience mocked. Tessa licked her dry lips and waved at the two boxes. "Let me get these put away."

He nodded. "All right. But I'm running across the street and grabbing us some food." When she opened her mouth to protest, he held up a hand. "No objections." He flashed her a heart-stopping grin. "And no catches. I'll be right back."

Another, louder crack of thunder drowned the tinkling of the chimes when Adrian pulled the door open. She couldn't help admiring the view as he jogged across the street, expertly dodging the evening traffic. Tessa forced her attention back to the box of candles he'd set next to her, but she stole constant glances out the front window.

He'd just reached the curb on their side of the street with their dinner when the clouds made good on their threat. Within three steps, rain soaked through his red t-shirt. Nothing was left to the imagination. Tessa jumped to her feet and swallowed her desire as she raced to open the door for him.

Stepping inside, Adrian laughed and shook droplets from his hair.

"Hey!" Tessa leapt out of the way of the spray, but she couldn't help joining his good humor. "I already took a shower today."

"I know." His eyes darkened, the emotion having nothing to do with the weather.

To cover her discomfort at his words and change in mood, she grabbed the damp bags from his hands. "Let's get these open before the paper tears."

"I'll be right back." Adrian disappeared behind the door to the storage room.

Probably going up to his apartment to dry off and change. Which meant he was upstairs. Naked.

Tess shook her head. Why did her imagination persist in torturing her? She opened cartons to distract herself. Scrounging through the disintegrating paper bags produced a plastic fork and chopsticks.

By the time Adrian reappeared in a dry t-shirt and jeans, her mouth watered with a normal type of hunger. Steam rolled from the rice and mixed with the garlic, spice and soy filling the air. She waved the fork at the white boxes neatly lining the counter. "I call dibs on the cashew chicken."

He laughed, and she tried to ignore the pull of emerald green cotton across his chest. "Figured you might."

He bought my favorite. Tessa squelched the wave of pleasure he'd noticed two days ago when Phylicia did the lunch run. She blew a wayward curl out of her face as she scooped rice into the container. A forkful of tender chicken entered her mouth, and she was in heaven.

Adrian reached for the remaining carton, but a dark blond eyebrow rose. "How long have you been living in New York?" He eyed her choice of utensil.

She glared at him while she chewed and swallowed. "Do you want sauce and chicken bits all over your merchandise, Mr. Holloway?"

He held his hands up in surrender. "Sorry." He pulled the garlic beef closer and sat across the counter from her. The slight distance didn't lessen the electricity in the air that had nothing to do with the lightning searing the skyline.

They ate in companionable silence, broken only by the clicks of Adrian's chopsticks. Outside, pedestrians had disappeared under the storm's rage. Even the auto traffic lessened, an occasional car sloshing through puddles, but the two of them could be the last living things on earth for all the activity outside.

The lights dimmed. Tessa's attention jerked to the antique fixtures hanging over their heads. Again, the bulbs flickered. "I think we're—"

Illumination faded at the same time the streetlights went dark.

"—about to lose power," she finished.

Sound shuffled nearby and moved away from her. A darker silhouette appeared at the front window. "Looks like the entire neighborhood is down," came Adrian's voice from the shadow.

"Great," she muttered. That's all her libido needed—stuck in the dark with someone she shouldn't be wanting.

Chapter 7

Adrian couldn't help a chuckle at the total disgust in Tessa's voice. The woman protested a little too much. When he'd finally pried Tessa's story out of Rain, an urge to throttle her ex had filled his blood. The idiot didn't know how good he'd had it. And Tessa didn't deserve such shit.

Not that she'd ever accept sympathy from him. More likely she'd start throwing the erotic statues they'd unpacked last week at his head rather than admit she was attracted to him.

The sound of wood-on-wood came from the direction of the cash-wrap. A sharp, metallic crack was quickly followed by Tessa's muttered curse.

"You okay?" He tried to keep the humor from his voice, but failed miserably. According to the rest of the staff, Tessa's clumsiness only appeared when he was present.

"Yeah. Nailed the register with the other elbow."

"You'll have matching bruises." He strode back toward her. They needed some light before he had OSHA writing him up for her klutzy behavior.

With a snap, a small flame appeared. Apparently, Tessa had the same idea. Some of her usual efficiency took over, and she lit the four sample candles on the back counter.

"That's better. She looked across the counter at him. Blue eyes sparkled in the candlelight. "Just one little problem."

"Oh, what's that?"

"How are you going to do invoices and mailing labels without power?"

He grinned at her wry look. "Way ahead of you. Everything's already printed and waiting for us."

Once again, Tessa glanced out the window. True to Adrian's word, no customers braved the dark, wet streets. Flashlights and candles flickered in the restaurant across the street. The only people she'd seen for the last hour were the poor delivery boys. Dressed in their yellow slickers, they ran out with bags every few minutes, then raced back for more take-out. The gas stoves must still be working.

Unfortunately, traffic was Adrian's only correct prediction. Though the thunder and lightning had eased, the rain poured as heavily as when the storm started.

She reached for the packing tape only to have a warm, masculine hand close over hers. What was wrong with her? Even though she'd kept to the opposite side of the counter, every move brought her in contact with his skin.

This is not good.

He paused for three very long heartbeats before he pulled away. "Sorry." Except his voice didn't sound any sorrier than his lingering touch had felt.

She slapped the tape dispenser against her box harder than necessary. Tape screeched in protest as she pulled it over the flaps. With the tension in the atmosphere, she wanted to wail along with the cellophane.

"It's eight. Do you want me to call you a cab?"

It's your chance. Leave now!

She looked at him and paused. Despite his neutral expression, desire flared deep inside her. Her reluctance to take a taxi home had nothing to do with her limited funds. Candlelight flickered, and tiny rays touched his hair. Sunlight. Antique gold. Honey. She wanted to run her hands through those strands, sure they were softer than the thread Rumpelstiltskin had spun.

But she'd sworn to herself and to him that she didn't want anything. So why did the thought of walking out the front door, away from him, make her chest ache?

Maybe that's what Rain's tarot card had been trying to tell her. Maybe her control issues were the reason Jimmy found it so easy to manipulate her. Maybe it was time to let go and take a chance.

"Not yet."

He exhaled and relaxed a fraction. The smile that tilted his lips was almost shy. "The least I can do is offer you dessert."

Stupid woman!

For the first time in her life, she ignored the tiny voice in the back of her head. The one that told her to be a good girl and not do anything foolish or inappropriate. Well, screw that. She'd done everything right and still been fucked over. This time she wanted for the sheer pleasure of wanting.

"That sounds wonderful." Her determination didn't stop her voice, or her hands, from trembling.

He locked the door and pulled down the ancient iron gates as she set the last boxes on the outgoing package shelf behind the counter and blew out most of the flames. With a wave, he gestured for her to proceed. Picking up the last candle for illumination, she headed for the back room and its narrow staircase.

She sucked a deep breath. The staircase that led to Adrian's apartment. And his bed.

Laughter from the nervous energy surrounding her expelled the air she held. "So what are you going to tempt me with?"

"I have lots of things you might enjoy." His words seemed a simple statement of fact, but their connotation sent a ripple of anticipation through her.

You know nothing about this man.

She tensed as she reached for the doorknob to the narrow staircase, her body going rigid as all her trust issues broke the surface of her consciousness. But then, she'd thought she knew everything about Jimmy. Look how wrong she'd been about him.

Rain knows I'm here, she reminded herself. So does Phylicia, and both women couldn't say enough good things about Adrian. The way the two of them practically pushed Adrian into her lap, she doubted either one had done the mattress mambo with the man.

But things could change in the bedroom.

We're just having dessert.

As if reading her mind, Adrian's breath warmed her ear, and he whispered, "Nothing's going to happen unless you want it to, Tessa."

She didn't know he was telling the truth. She *felt* it. The heat of him pulsed against her back, but he didn't touch her. Letting her set the pace. God help her, she wanted him to grab her, press her against the wall . . .

A small laugh didn't drive the image away, but it lessened the logjam at the back of her throat. "What I want is something cold. You got any ice cream?"

She started climbing. The tiny candle made the pitch-black staircase look like a tunnel into oblivion.

"Strawberry, but there's also cheesecake in the fridge."

"Cheesecake sounds—" Tessa stumbled, expecting another stair where there wasn't one. A strong arm kept her from falling flat on her face as Adrian's hand grabbed the candle.

"You okay?"

He wasn't releasing her. The hand splayed across her belly sent a current of electricity straight to the core of her being.

"Yeah, just klutzy." Thank goodness, he couldn't see her face. Her pale cheeks would have given everything away.

The warm hand on her abdomen slid around her waist and across her lower back before his fingers twined around hers. A gentle tug urged her in the same direction the candle led. He set down the jar in the kitchenette and let go of her hand.

A chair scraped against the hardwood as he pulled it out for her. She sat gingerly, half-afraid of knocking the candle over and setting the place on fire.

"Is turtle cheesecake alright?" He didn't look at her as he stepped over to a drawer.

Part of her was glad. She wasn't sure her nerves could handle eye contact. "Yeah."

Adrian pulled out a flashlight and flipped it on. The harsh illumination broke the spell the candlelight had woven around her brain. A sigh whispered past her lips at the sense of loss.

He pulled two bottles of water from the refrigerator and a white box and placed them on the table. Plates and forks quickly joined the cheesecake and drinks. With a click, the harsh glare of the flashlight disappeared. The dim glow of the candle beckoned the shadows closer.

"How long do you think the power will be out?" Tessa wanted to kick herself for the inane question, but the silence was unbearable.

"Hard to tell." Adrian sat across from her and dug into the box with a crystal server. A server far too fancy for a single man. So where had it come from?

No, it didn't matter. She didn't really know him. Didn't want to know him. Didn't want to get dragged into something she had no control over.

He set the plate in front of her, then frowned. "Is something wrong?"

She shook her head to dispel the past. "No." The stainless steel fork gave her some measure of stability. She scooped a bite with the tines and raised it to her mouth.

Her tongue exploded under creamy cheese, silky chocolate and rich caramel. "Oh, my god," she said when she could speak again. "This is incredible! Where did you get it?"

"A little place called Bruno over on LaGuardia. We used to—" He stopped and an apologetic smile crossed his face. "I used to go there a lot with someone."

"Used to?" Now, why the hell had she asked that? *Thought you didn't want to know him*, her internal voice mocked.

"Used to," he said firmly. "I had a craving the other night."

She giggled, more at his confirmation than his words. "I thought only women had cravings."

He grinned in return. "Are you questioning my manhood?"

"No, I—" Air caught in her lungs. Time seemed to halt under his hypnotic gaze as his expression grew serious. The only sound above the rain hammering on the windows was their harsh breathing. This silence wasn't uncomfortable, more like a promise.

Adrian pushed back from the table and stood. He bent over her.

Tessa knew she could have leaned away, could have simply said, "No." Instead, she closed her eyes.

Lips brushed hers. Hints of caramel lay in the caress. The touch tempted her more than the delicious dessert. Stainless steel clattered against ceramic. Her hand wove through his hair, pulling him closer for more. Her inner voice faded along with the rain. Every ounce of willpower focused on the kiss.

He coaxed her lips apart, her reservations swept away by his gentle insistence. Hands that were equally insistent pulled her to her feet. She sank into the embrace. A soft moan of protest filled her throat when his mouth left hers. Much to her skin's delight, his lips traveled across her jaw line, testing and tasting in ecstatic nibbles.

She tilted her head to give him better access to the soft spot behind her ear. With her eyes closed, she became acutely aware of her rapid pulse and the steady thump of his heart. His scent, rich and earthy and wholly his own, filled her head.

His sure, steady hands stroked her arms, her neck, her back as his mouth found new areas to tease. Hot liquid pooled inside her, and her muscles throbbed in time with her pulse. He grabbed her waist, pulling her tight against the length of his body, his erection pressing against her belly.

"Last chance, Tessa."

Something deep inside her shattered the walls she'd erected around her psyche over the last six months and demanded release. She pressed against him, eliciting a low moan from him. "I'll stay."

His chuckle rumbled against her hair. Nibbles followed by soft licks flowed across her bare skin. He inched her t-shirt up from her waist. Cool air raised goosebumps, but they were soothed away by calloused fingers stroking her belly. The contact drove her wild, and she wanted, no, she needed more.

She reached for his hands, desperate for him to touch her full, aching breasts. The lace scraping her sensitized nipples was already driving her crazy, but skin on skin would be oh-so-much better.

A quick move captured her wrists, and he pressed her palms flat against her denim-covered thighs. "Pushy, aren't you? This is my turn to explore." A wicked laugh vibrated next to her ear, then he added, "Or do I have to tie you up?"

Her eyes flew open, and his question sent a pulse straight to her core. She considered herself open-minded, but never once had she suggested any games to Jimmy. Maybe because deep down, she had known she couldn't trust him. Not the way she trusted Adrian.

She stared up at him. Dancing candlelight reflected in his eyes. "I'll behave." She pressed herself against Adrian once again. "This time."

Another groan rumbled against her ear. Her laugh turned into a gasp when strong fingers pulled and plucked her hardened tips through her bra. She fought for breath, the sensation centering until—

"Not just yet," he whispered.

A gasp escaped her throat. No one had ever brought her that close by just touching her breasts.

Huge palms kneaded and massaged her flesh, the fit perfect. His magic hands kept her at the plateau when she was almost at the peak of the mountain.

She opened her mouth to protest, then snapped it shut. If she were truly going to give up control for tonight, she needed to let him lead. Her nails dug painful furrows into her thighs in her effort not to reach for him.

He raised her arms. With a gentle tug, her shirt slid up and over her head.

A soft click and her breasts sprang free from the confines of her bra. Adrian dragged the straps down, his hands in constant contact. His pampering intoxicated her, sending a gentle, caring warmth through her that had nothing to do with the sexual heat driving her insane.

Cool air whispered across her naked flesh. A whimper escaped her throat, but then he bent and took her nipple in his mouth, followed by his tongue, his fingers, his palms. They all seemed to be everywhere at once, nipping and tugging her peaks before laving the tender underside. She grabbed his shoulders to stay upright in the onslaught of sensation. Skin danced against skin as he skimmed her belly and waist. She closed her eyes, drinking in each caress. Then came the unmistakable snap of her jeans.

He slowly pulled the zipper down. She shivered with the anticipation zooming along her nerves and back. Fingers slid beneath her panties, touching, exploring, discovering how wet she was. He penetrated her, and breath hissed from her mouth. Her hips thrust of their own accord. With no sight to distract, her body remembered the age-old rhythms. She ground against his hand, seeking release from the terrible pressure building inside her. Once again, Adrian pulled his clever fingers out of her when she was oh-so-close to coming.

She cried out in frustration.

"I want to be inside you the first time you come for me."

The hoarse words forced her eyes open, to face him. No, not the words themselves. It was the passion behind those words.

Hands shoved clothing down her legs, out of the way, before he lifted her onto the table.

"The cheesecake."

Adrian paused in yanking off his t-shirt. Gray eyes peered over the neckline. "Seriously? You're worried about the cheesecake?"

Tessa snatched the box from where it teetered on the edge. "It's very good cheesecake."

He tossed the shirt over his shoulder. "Yes, it is." She didn't like the mischievous glint in his grin as he pulled the box from her hand. "It'd be a shame to waste it."

Before she could say anything, he'd cleared the table of the candle and their utensils. "What are you doing?"

Two fingers dug a scoop of cream cheese and caramel out of the container. "Exactly what you said. Not wasting the cheesecake." He proceeded to smear the chilled dessert around each breast.

His tongue traced a path around the cream cheese. He took his time, carefully licking her skin clean. Lips sucked the caramel and chocolate off each nipple. She shuddered at the sensation. Adrian pressed her back until she lay across the stone surface, his mouth eating with a slow, hot sensuality.

Her muscles were tight, straining. She wanted the torture to go on and on until she exploded. Then the sharp zip of his jeans sounded before the crinkle of foil tearing. She looked into his eyes as his length nestled between her spread thighs.

He shifted and the round, pulsing head pressed against her opening. "What do you want, Tessa?"

"I want you." Her voice was a choked whisper.

"You want me where?" His voice held amusement, that same condescending tone he'd used when she first came into the store. His shaft slid across her slick folds, making rational thought nearly impossible.

Tessa gritted her teeth. She hated begging, but dammit, she was going insane.

Swallowing hard, she whispered, "I want you inside me."

The last word hadn't faded from the air when he thrust into her. Hard, long, filling her so completely she couldn't breathe, couldn't think. His mouth swallowed her cry of delight.

His eyes were no longer pussy willow gray, but the dark blue-gray of the fierce thunderheads. And Adrian Holloway was just as unpredictable and dangerous. He withdrew his cock inch by agonizing inch before he plunged into her again, so hard she would have slid off the table if not for her legs wrapped tight around his waist.

Reaching for him, she raked her fingers through his locks, stroked the harsh planes of his face. She matched his pace, drawing strands of energy until all her points of contact with his body formed one gigantic circuit. His harsh pants matched her own rapid breaths.

The pressure built for a third time, in her belly, in her whole body, in her soul. It was too much. Her orgasm ripped through her. She couldn't see, couldn't reason, as she shook with the force of it. All she could do was feel. And scream.

The grip of her slick walls tightened around Adrian, the convulsions sending him over the brink. With a hoarse shout, he bucked against her, ramming deep and hard. The pulses of his orgasm added to her own.

Tessa's hands continued to grip his arms. She blinked, realizing for the first time that wetness streamed down her cheeks. She swiped at her face with the back of her hand. Tears. Where the hell had tears come from?

"Are you okay?" Adrian's voice was husky and as unsteady as her trembling limbs.

"Yeah," she said. "That was . . . amazing."

He nuzzled her neck, the sensation sending delicious aftershocks through her. "You're amazing," he murmured against her skin. He withdrew from her, the slow motion overloading already hypersensitive nerves, but he didn't break any other body contact.

Now Tessa knew what her girlfriends meant by feeling boneless. Sex with Jimmy had been okay, but comparing him to Adrian was like comparing a firecracker to a nuclear bomb. And she definitely suffered from the effects of fall-out.

"Would you like to clean up?"

Her body tensed at his words. Had she misjudged him? She palmed his cheeks and met his eyes. "Job's done and you're throwing me out?"

He chuckled at her words, pulled her upright and hugged her against his chest. "Actually, I had something else in mind."

Chapter 8

Adrian tugged Tessa to her feet, and the brush of her tight, heart-shaped ass against him sent another wave of lust through him. Damn, he acted like a horny teenager around this woman. After the last couple of years, he'd begun to wonder if the damn thing still worked.

Clasping her small palm in his, he grabbed the candle and led her back to the tiny bathroom. When Rain had turned the loft above the store into an apartment, she hadn't bothered with a tub. He'd been pleasantly surprised to find a double-sized shower with a ledge when he'd moved into the place. The shocked gasp from Tessa as they entered the bath indicated an equal delight.

He set the candle on the toilet tank lid, and still held her hand as he flicked the shower knobs. The ancient pipes took several minutes to deliver hot water, and they shared a laugh over the vagaries of New York plumbing. Being here with Tessa felt right. More right than his life had been in a long time. His cock stirred again. Okay, maybe lust was overriding everything.

Once hot water flowed, Adrian followed Tessa into the spray. Grabbing the soap, he lathered his hands and proceeded to wash her. He paid special attention to her breasts where sticky caramel still clung. She was soon moaning at his ministrations. Never had he been with a woman who came just from him playing with her nipples, but Tessa fell apart under his slick, soapy fingers. And damn, if his cock didn't roar to life and want to take her again.

Turning her to face him, he held her until her trembling slowed, and he was sure she'd keep her footing on the slippery shower floor.

Blinking droplets from her dark lashes, she stared up at him. "How do you do that?"

He frowned, unsure of her meaning. "Do what?"

"Make me come just by touching me."

He brushed dripping curls away from her face. "I can't take all the credit."

A sly smile crossed her face. "And I can't take all the rewards." She knelt before him, not breaking eye contact.

Anticipation raced through him. Her soft lips brushed against his shaft, making it jerk and throb. Her tongue traced a path along the underside before she took him into her mouth. Bracing one arm on the shower wall, he stroked her hair and face as her mouth danced its magic up and down his cock.

One soft hand cupped his balls, testing their weight. Then Tessa bent further, pulling his sac into her hot, greedy mouth and sucking with delicately intense motion. Her fingers traced the curve of his ass.

Pressure built under her careful attention. He blinked away the water dripping into his eyes, the need to watch Tessa's face overwhelming. Her eyes closed against the spray of the shower, her expression intense, concentrating.

Her attention switched, and her soft lips played along the length of his cock. She covered him, took him, worshipped him. Her tongue wreaked havoc as it swirled around the head, and he could no longer hold on to his self-control. His hips jerked, and he lost it. She swallowed and licked until every last drop was gone.

He drew her to her feet and wrapped his arms around her. He wanted to keep her here, safe with him. Forever.

The depth and power of the feeling shook him. He barely knew this woman. He had no right to be thinking such things.

Tessa's shivering drew him back to the here and now. And the sudden drop in water temperature.

He chuckled and turned off the cool stream. "Sorry about that." Grabbing a towel, he stroked and petted her dry, laying kisses on each body part as he went. He knelt, lavishing a long slow lick along the small of her back. A soft moan rewarded him. Rising, he wiped his own body off with short, quick motions before sweeping her into his arms and heading into his bedroom.

He kissed her, a deep, penetrating kiss that left them both breathless when he deposited her between the cool sheets. He couldn't get enough of this woman. Nuzzling her neck, he inhaled the indefinable scent that was just Tessa and let it fill his head. He hadn't relaxed his grip on Tessa when she fell asleep in his arms without a word.

He kissed her half-dry, haphazard curls. No, he wasn't about to let go of Tessa McClain any time soon.

Chapter 9

At six the next morning, with an apology breakfast in hand, Tessa eased her key in the lock and turned it. Rain's deadbolt slid back with a resounding boom that echoed down the empty hallway. At least, that's what it sounded like to Tessa's guilt-ridden conscience.

The door swung open to the sight of Rain on her knees surrounded by buckets and rags strewn across the floor.

Tessa's head swept from side to side taking in the mess. The brightly colored living room rug had been rolled up and was sitting across the length of the couch. The sofa itself was pushed back against the breakfast table. Anything that had been at floor level had been piled on the table. "What the hell happened?"

Rain grimaced as she dumped a soaked towel into the metal pail next to her. "A spell backfired, and the apartment flooded." She looked up and a sly smile filled her face. "How was your night?"

Tessa swallowed any comment about Rain and magic. It wasn't any of her business what her new roommate believed. There had been enough problems in Tessa's old apartment for her to think this was anything but a leaky pipe. A drop plunged from the damp ceiling plaster and splashed into the purple plastic bucket.

"Let me set these down, and I'll help." She juggled the tray of hot Styrofoam cups and bag of pastries as she crossed the slick floor. So much for sneaking in before Rain woke up. And Rain had the same smirk on her face Grandma had the morning she'd caught Tessa sneaking in from a night out with her boyfriend in high school.

Rain nodded toward the pastry bag and tray. "You didn't have to bring breakfast."

Heat crawled up Tessa's face. Only a week living here, and she was catting around like some co-ed. Rain must think she was a complete slut. Yet, an erotic thrill shimmered up her spine at the thought of Adrian and the things he'd done to her last night.

Including the after hours dessert. She'd never be able to look at cheesecake the same way again.

She set the pastries on the pass-through window to the kitchenette before she handed the first cup to Rain.

Rain took a sip of her tea before a bemused smile crossed her face. "Honey, I'm your roommate and your friend. I'm not your mother. Or your grandmother."

Tessa shook her head, unsure of whether to be unnerved or pissed. She slung off her backpack and laid it on top of the table pile.

Rain set her cup down on the coffee table. "You miss her, don't you?"

"Miss who?" Tessa asked, but deep down she knew.

"Your grandmother."

Tessa nodded. "Yeah." She swallowed the old grief that welled up with a healthy swig of her coffee. Shaking her head, she met Rain's eyes. "You know, you really freak me out when you do that mind-reading shit."

Rain laughed, a musical sound that matched the wind chime at the store. "Adrian has the same complaint." Her slim black eyebrow cocked upward. "I trust the two of you had a pleasant evening."

The warmth in Tessa's face flared hotter. She grabbed a dry towel from the pile sitting on the rescued rug. "I'm sorry. I should have called—"

Rain held up her free hand. "You have nothing to apologize for. You're both adults, and it's your personal business." She waggled her eyebrows. "Now, if you want to have a girlfriend chat about the hot guy you were with last night . . ."

Tessa grabbed the pastry bag and flopped down on a dry spot next to Rain. The rich scent of cinnamon drifted through the air when she opened the sack. She handed a scone to Rain before taking a bite of her own.

"Well?" Rain stared at her expectantly.

A nervous giggle erupted from Tessa, nearly causing her to choke on the scone. She swallowed the hard lump before she answered. "I'm sorry. This is like talking to my mother."

Rain grinned in return. "Honey, I may be older than dirt, but I'm not dead." She leaned over to pat Tessa's thigh. "As it is, I'm happy for you. It's about time you both rejoined the living."

Tessa eyed Rain, the weird comment setting her nerves aflame. "What's that supposed to mean?"

Rain shook her head and sighed. "It's not my place to say, but Adrian's been hurting just as much as you have." She rose and stretched. "Why don't you get some more sleep while I finish here? I doubt if you got much last night." Another knowing smile crossed her face, one that said she knew exactly what Adrian and Tessa had done all night. She popped the last bite of scone in her mouth.

Tessa couldn't meet Rain's gaze any longer. "How about I finish the mopping while you take your shower? I don't think I'll be able to sleep after all this coffee."

The older woman didn't say another word, just patted Tessa's shoulder as she passed on her way to the bathroom.

Instead of mopping, Tessa picked at her scone, sure her face glowed like a neon light. One night of wild sex did not a relationship make. Okay, one incredible, fantastic night.

She sighed and popped a piece of crumbled pastry into her mouth. Why the hell was the r-word even crossing her mind? Hadn't she learned her lesson already?

She reached for her coffee, gratified that steam still wisped from the hole in the lid. This thing with Adrian was a rebound fling. From what little Rain had hinted out, it was probably the same for him. Yeah, that's it. She sipped the coffee, rich hazelnut flavor swirling over her tongue. Just a rebound fling. She took another bite of scone.

So why did she care so much about who had hurt Adrian?

No, she didn't. She just needed to get Adrian Holloway out of her system. She devoured the last crumbs of her scone and started wiping up the last couple of puddles. Maybe, just maybe, she could scrub away her emotions as well.

Later that evening, Tessa stood in front of Adrian, holding up her skirt as he had commanded. She twisted her mouth in a wry smile. "So is this why you sent everyone home early?"

She'd lost the battle with her own desires the moment she'd walked into the store and saw him. The devastating kiss he laid on her in the back room when she was putting away her purse hadn't helped.

Adrian didn't answer, just stared up at her from his office chair with a look that could have melted steel.

Breath hissed between her teeth as he slid his palms beneath the edges of the cotton gauze and caressed his way up her thighs. Just the skin-on-skin contact was enough to send her libido into overdrive. Hooking his thumbs in the side strings of her thong, he pulled her into the vee of his legs. She let go of the skirt and clamped her hands on his shoulders to stay upright. Instead of yanking her thong down as she half-expected, he traced his fingers underneath the flimsy underwear until he reached her already soaked intimate curls.

Two fingers thrust in, stroking all the right places, and her muscles clenched at the sensual onslaught. Her eyelids fluttered shut against her will. Her entire being focused on the sensations caused by his magic touch.

"Look at me. I want to see your eyes when you come."

She couldn't resist his harsh order. Deep down, she didn't want to. Sucking in a breath, she forced her lids to open. Adrian's thumb started to stroke her clit the moment her eyes met his. His other hand massaged her ass, adding to the push and pull of his fingers inside of her.

This man was quickly turning into an addiction. An addiction she wasn't sure she could give up anytime soon. Especially when he made her feel so feminine, so alive.

The orgasm ripped through her and left her shaken. She wasn't sure if she fell or was pulled into Adrian's lap, but his fingers continued stoking the fire inside of her. His mouth swallowed her whimpers in a devastating kiss. He slowed his strokes but did not stop, and another explosion of pleasure followed.

One of his hands remained beneath her skirt, caressing away the tremors. His other hand played with the curls at the nape of her neck as she nuzzled his chest. And his very erect penis poked at her hip.

"You should wear skirts more often."

Her laughter bounced around the walls of the store's tiny back office. "The only reason I wore it was because of this stupid heat wave."

His chuckle rumbled through his chest, and he kissed the crown of her head. "Maybe it's our fault for last night's activities. Want to see if we can get the mercury over ninety?"

She squirmed in his lap, eliciting a male groan. "What did you have in mind?"

His hand surfaced from underneath her skirt, and he tugged her chin up until her eyes met his. "Do you trust me?"

She examined him, but his storm-gray eyes revealed nothing of his intentions. She didn't know why, but some part of her knew that Adrian Holloway would never deliberately hurt her. Maybe Rain and her tarot cards were right, and she really needed to release her insane obsession for total control. After a moment's hesitation, she nodded.

A wicked grin lit up his face. One that promised her another evening of sensual delights.

He set her on her feet and rose from the office chair. Lacing his fingers with hers, he led her up to his apartment. When they reached the living room, he motioned for her to kneel on the rug and disappeared down the little hallway leading the bedroom.

An idea flashed. She bounced back up and slid off her thong. The ballerina flats were kicked off in the process, and she stuffed the flimsy material in the toe of a shoe before she resumed the kneeling position. Adrian reappeared with a silver and emerald striped tie in his grip and knelt behind her. When she twisted to face him, he looked at her with a passion that no man ever had. The feminine thrill tamped down her qualms but didn't quite eliminate them.

Eyeing the silk, she giggled with the nervous sexual tension that filled her. "I didn't picture you as a suit kind of guy."

"There's a lot of things you don't know about me." His words weren't a threat, simply a statement of fact. He reached around her and slipped the tie over her eyes.

He was right. She knew almost nothing about him, but he was a lesson she wanted to learn. She tensed, her body going rigid as all her trust issues crashed into her psyche. No, if there was something wrong, Rain sure as hell wouldn't have encouraged her. Come to think of it, Rain hadn't exactly warmed to Jimmy.

Adrian pulled the silk snug across her eyes. His breath tickled her ear and drove any memories of the past right out of her mind. He whispered, "We won't do anything you don't want."

She stifled a groan. The hard length pressed against her ass gave her a pretty good idea how much he wanted her. And, god, how she wanted him. Wanted him to make her feel good again.

Hell, to just feel again was enough. The soft silk of his tie across her eyelids. The heat of his chest against her back. The rasp of stubble as he nuzzled her neck.

His hands slipped beneath her light cotton shirt. Fingers traced the curve of her waist, brushed the tender skin under her breasts, teased her in every way possible.

His touch sparked a daring in her that she hadn't known existed. "Adrian?"

"Hmmm?" The vibration tickled the soft spot behind her ear.

"Take off my clothes."

"Excuse me?" The haughty voice was back.

Some instinct said it was part of his game. "Take off my clothes, please."

"And what makes you think you're in charge?" More teasing lay in his words. Those magic fingers rose upward and tweaked her nipples until a whimper filled her throat.

"Don't make me beg."

Laughter rumbled against her back. "You didn't have a problem last night."

Frustration welled when his hands slid from beneath her shirt. Her breath caught in her lungs. Was he serious? Would he really make her plead for his touch? The tug of cotton across her chest was followed by a breath of air, then wet kisses on her shoulder. Material slipped down her arms as each buttoned was released.

Calloused fingers tracked the edges of her bra. Despite the heat, shivers rippled along her skin. She waited for something, anything more, but he seemed content with light strokes and gentle kisses on her exposed areas.

The slow torture was killing her. Fine. Two could play that game. Tessa shifted her hand behind her back and grasped the hard ridge protected by rough denim.

"You simply cannot follow orders, can you?"

She gently squeezed in response and felt rather than heard his sharp intake of breath.

He yanked her wrist away from his erection. "Not to mention you're totally shameless."

Before she could answer, both hands were trapped in his firm grip and pressed against her chest. "Hey!" Gauze brushed her thighs, rising higher. His free hand shifted under her skirt. She bit her lip and waited for his reaction.

A low chuckle filled her head as he touched the wetness seeping from her. "Definitely naughty."

Air whispered across her naked flesh. The pressure on her wrists disappeared. Arms held her close, both hands exploring her intimately.

"Touch yourself."

Her breasts tightened at his command. She'd never done anything like that in front of someone. Her hands slowly dropped to where his played. One tentative touch, then another. The act was so wanton . . .

"Yes." The word hissed in her ear. She swallowed the lump in her throat. Her fingers found their own boldness, stroking, touching, but they were no substitute for him. Never before had she put on such a show for her man. The power in pleasing herself and Adrian at the same time intoxicated her.

Behind her came the ruffling of cloth on skin, followed by the rasp of a zipper. Corded muscle pulled her against a hard masculine chest. A very naked chest from the crisp hair brushing her back. A thigh thrust between her legs and shoved them apart. Smoothness pressed against her opening. And he stopped.

Tessa waited. Neither of them moved. Harsh breathing filled the room, but nothing else. She licked her lips at the anticipation. "Please. Adrian?"

Her muscles quivered. Plush carpet tickled her shins. Then pressure and he entered in slow, agonizing millimeters.

"Say it, Tessa."

She whimpered. No control over him, no control over herself. All that was left was raw desire. "I want you."

Silence met her demand.

"Adrian." Her voice broke. "Please. I need you inside of me."

One hard thrust was all it took for her ache to explode into a million stars.

A few more pumps and a guttural cry signaled his climax. He collapsed against her, his weight comforting. Limp and satiated, a new kind of pleasure flowed through her. Simple happiness. An emotion she hadn't experienced in so long, she barely recognized it.

He tilted her chin. Lips pressed against hers. Unlike the seductive kisses before, this one was possessive, demanding. He released his hold and tugged the silk from her eyes.

Tessa let her head fall against Adrian's shoulder. This game gave her more pleasure than she'd ever imagined. Maybe Rain and her crazy tarot cards were right. Maybe she did need to let go in order to discover more about herself. And maybe, no definitely, Adrian Holloway could show her how.

Chapter 10

Tessa reached under the sink, but the tiny cabinet was devoid of towels. She grinned. Most of the dry linens had sacrificed themselves in the name of ice melt.

"Adrian! Do you have any more towels?"

"Closet. Left side, fourth shelf up," he shouted from the kitchen. From the heavenly smell drifting on air, he was in the kitchen, whipping up one of his wonderful concoctions.

Still grinning to herself, she padded into the bedroom. The man was sex personified and could cook like nobody's business. She must have died and gone to heaven.

Sliding open the left closet door, she found towels right where he said they'd be. Plucking one off the top, she jumped when something white and fuzzy tumbled from the shelf and landed on her feet.

Tossing the towel over her shoulder, she bent over and picked up a teddy bear. Shiny, black button eyes stared at her from the white fur. A huge, baby blue bow decorated its throat.

She peered at the back of the shelf. Was that a bottle of whiskey behind the other towels? Puzzled, she tried to put the innocuous pieces together. Why would anyone hide stuffed animals and a bottle of whiskey behind their towels? It made no sense whatsoever.

"What are you doing with that?" Adrian's sharp voice made her jump a second time.

She whirled to find him standing behind her clad only in his jeans, the look on his face unreadable. "Sorry, your bear fell out when I grabbed the towel."

He snatched it out of her hands and placed it on the top shelf, well out of her reach without a step ladder. "Don't ever touch it again."

What the hell? He wasn't half as upset when she dropped the box of statuary. Irritated at his manner, she held up her hands. "Sorry. It *was* an accident. By the way, you might want to hide your bottle of whiskey so I don't drink it either."

Whirling on her heel, she stomped back into the bathroom. She bent over and towel-dried her hair, rubbing hard until her scalp tingled. Damn him, he acted as if she'd been snooping on purpose. Okay, so she didn't know a whole lot about him. Did she really want to? It wasn't like she expected a permanent commitment.

A whisper of air let her know Adrian stood in the doorway. She stood upright and glared at him. "What?"

The look on his face wasn't exactly repentant, but it wasn't the weird half-anger of a minute ago. And the way he looked at her, she became very aware of just how naked she was. He shoved his hands in the front pockets of his jeans. "I'm sorry. Maybe I . . . overreacted a little."

"You think?" She couldn't stop her snappish tone, but she felt so damn vulnerable. Much more so than when he had blindfolded her.

"Look, it's something from the past that I can't let go, but I don't want it to come between what you and I have."

The sadness in his expression tore at her. Jimmy hadn't been blue when she first stumbled across his secrets. No, he'd attacked her verbally, vicious with no attempt at understanding or apology. Adrian, on the other hand, stood in front of her offering an olive branch, as Grandma would have said. She sucked in a deep breath. "I'm a good listener if you want to talk."

He shook his head. "It's best to leave it alone."

She didn't want to push, but now curiosity consumed her. Why would someone like Adrian keep a teddy bear hidden in his closet? She licked her lips, choosing her words carefully. "If you change your mind about wanting to talk, I'm here."

"It's the past, Tessa. Leave it alone." A strange glint shone in his eyes. "Unless you want to talk about your last boyfriend?"

Heat rose in her cheeks, and she couldn't face him any longer. "Not really."

She finished toweling off her body. Dammit, why was he still standing in the doorway?

"Let's make a deal then."

Her head jerked up at his throaty voice, and she met his eyes. "What kind of deal?"

Fool me once, shame on you. Fool me twice, shame on me, came one of Grandma's sayings.

"Neither of us wants to talk about our pasts. Let's just focus on what we have here and now."

She considered his proposal before she said, "That means no pumping Rain or fellow co-workers for information."

He nodded and stuck out his right hand. "Deal."

She took the proffered hand and shook it. "Deal."

Except he didn't let go of her hand. He tugged her to him and laid a deep, wet kiss on her that made her nerves sizzle. So delirious from the kiss, she barely registered when his huge hands grabbed her ass. His palms massaged and fondled, and she sank against his chest, his denim-covered erection rubbing against her belly.

All thoughts of their argument disappeared when his fingers traced her crevice, parting her ass cheeks. His strokes circled her puckered hole. She never particularly thought of her rear as an erogenous zone, but his touch had her shaking with desire.

Then he lifted her. She shrieked when hot flesh contacted cold ceramic. Wiggling to get off the edge of the sink did no good. He pinned her in place with his massive body. Just as she'd fantasized about him on her first day at the store. And it whet her appetite. He unzipped his jeans and rammed into her. Hard. Rough.

Tessa gasped in surprise. God help her, she loved it. The passion. The desperation. The need. She was full of him, complete, and the cold sink suddenly didn't matter. Adrian's pace so fast, so demanding, and yet so intoxicating, all she could do was wrap her legs around his waist and hang on for dear life.

She wasn't just a receptacle for his all-too-male possession. She sensed there was something else behind the obvious lust. Something beyond his claiming, beyond his marking her as his. Like he needed her beyond mere physical release.

"I'm sorry. I can't—" His hoarse voice broke, and gave one more violent thrust.

And the sensation of him pulsing inside of her sent her into oblivion as well.

The next day, Tessa murmured her thanks when Phylicia handed her the extra-large cup of coffee. She rolled her head to ease the tightness in her neck. The caffeine was a welcome break from printing out orders and shipping labels.

"*De nada,*" Phylicia said, waving her hand nonchalantly as she resumed her seat next to Tessa. "I'm just happy I have someone who shares my vice. Everyone else here drinks *herbal tea.*" She gave a dramatic shudder before taking a sip from her own cup.

Tessa took another drink as she clicked to print the last label. From the corner of her eye, she noticed Phylicia watching her with a thoughtful expression on her face.

Tessa swiveled on the chair to face her. "Am I doing something wrong?"

Phylicia shook her head, a sheepish smile appearing. "No, no. I can usually pick out accents but I have to admit yours has me stumped."

"Really?" Suspicion flared that Adrian had put Phylicia up to this. Tessa wanted to kick herself. It was her own damn fault for not being more specific in the terms of their agreement last night. She hadn't said a damn thing about the staff acting on his behalf. She cleared her throat, not wanting to alienate the other woman. "So where do you think I'm from?"

Phylicia shrugged. "You don't have the clipped or nasal tones of the East Coast or a Southern drawl."

Tessa grinned. "That only leaves three quarters of the country."

Phylicia's warm laugh filled the tiny office. "True, but it's indistinct enough you could be an Air Force brat like Adrian."

"Excuse me, ladies."

The tiny bit of triumph at the morsel of information faded when Adrian's voice came from behind Tessa. She and Phylicia both turned to find him leaning against the doorframe.

"Phylicia, can you cover the register while I take a quick break?"

His words would have been totally innocent if he weren't staring at Tessa with a laser-like intensity as he spoke. So why did she have a guilty sensation like she'd broken their agreement?

"No problem." Phylicia rose but gave Tessa a quick smile. "Why don't you take the orders to the back table and start pulling the items? I'll help you finish up when I'm done up front."

Once Phylicia had disappeared, Adrian's mouth quirked into a wry half-smile. "Couldn't even make it twenty-four hours before you broke your word, could you?"

"Excuse me?" She rose to face him. "I'm not the one who sent Phylicia on a fishing expedition."

He frowned. "Fishing expedition? What fishing expedition?"

Folding her arms over her chest, she tapped her toe in frustration. "Phylicia's questions about my accent? Come on, I'm not that stupid."

A puzzled expression replaced his frown. "I didn't tell Phylicia to ask you anything. You're the one asking about my childhood."

"No. Phylicia made the comment that my accent was similar to yours, and she volunteered the info. I didn't ask." She jabbed an index finger at his chest. "Which you should know since you were eavesdropping."

"I wasn't eavesdropping." His bouncer voice was back, but his hooded eyes told a different story. "And by the way, your accent isn't indistinct."

She dropped her hand to her side and shuffled a step closer until their bodies touched. "Really?" She bit back her smile when his breath hitched at the brush of her breasts against his chest. "So you have an expert opinion?"

His eyes turned storm dark, but he made no move to touch her. "It's lower Great Lakes Midwestern, so you're probably from Ohio, Indiana or Illinois."

She had a serious problem focusing on their conversation when her pussy was soaked just from his nearness. After a deep, shuddering breath, she said, "How can you tell?"

An evil grin spread across his face as if he knew exactly his effect on her. "My dad was stationed at Wright-Patterson in Dayton, Ohio, for a year." He leaned a hair closer until his hot breath brushed her ear. "That's the only freebie you'll get, sweetheart. The rest you'll have to pay for." He stood straight again, the grin not leaving.

She licked her suddenly very dry lips. "How will I have to pay for them?"

"I'm sure we'll come to an equitable arrangement." An eyebrow cocked upward. "After work hours." He stepped back but not before she felt the unmistakable bulge of his erect cock against her belly. "You'd better get started on those internet orders." With those words, he turned and sauntered toward the mini-fridge that Rain kept stocked with soft drinks for the staff.

Tessa sank back into her chair, every nerve in her body on edge. They were both too professional to do anything stupid during store hours, but damn! She gulped in air to cool off her over-heated flesh. What the hell did he have planned for tonight?

Chapter 11

Over the next two weeks, Tessa settled into a different routine. Work, passionate sex most of the night with her amazingly talented boss with dinner somewhere in between, and a catnap at his loft before breakfast with Rain. Then Tess would grab another nap at the apartment. Rain had even insisted that Tessa and Adrian take a day off together last Friday to go to a Yankees game or the Met. Anything, Rain said, to get them out from under her feet while she audited the books.

"In other words, you two need to go on a real date," Phylicia had added with a mock finger shaking.

And Tessa and Adrian had a terrific time doing a normal couple thing. Of course, the Cleveland Indians clobbering the Yankees had helped her spirits immensely. And their bet on the game had been oh-so satisfying.

Yep, life was good.

Except she hadn't gotten any further information on Adrian's past. At lunch one day when it was just the three women, Phylicia had mentioned she'd turned down the manager position two years ago in order to fit in her college classes. Both she and Rain added that Lady Fate had blessed them by dropping Adrian in their laps. Unfortunately, neither woman was more forthcoming. They guarded Adrian's privacy as zealously as he did. Rain refused to even clarify what she'd hinted at earlier about Adrian being in pain. Had his wife or lover stabbed him in the back like Jimmy had done to her?

She sighed and dunked her head under the shower spray to rinse. Did her lack of knowledge matter though? She'd thought she knew everything about Jimmy, only to find out his entire life was a carefully crafted lie. Besides, she reminded herself, Adrian's just a fling.

Wasn't he?

She stepped out of the shower to be greeted by the snappy notes of "New York, New York." So her cell's ringtone was hokey, but she always heard Frank singing in her mind, an invitation to excitement and adventure. Just getting her service reinstated went a long way to restoring her peace of mind.

Snagging the phone off the counter, she checked caller ID, but the number wasn't one she recognized. Some instinct told her to answer the call anyway.

"Hello?"

"Hey, Curley! How's it going?"

She breathed a sigh of relief when she recognized the voice. "Well, Brady Morrison, to what do I owe the pleasure?" She propped herself on the edge of the sink. Brady had been the only co-worker who'd been sympathetic when she'd been fired last October. For that alone, she owed him one.

"I've quit the firm, and I've got a proposition for you, girlfriend." His excitement practically made her phone quiver.

Tessa jerked upright. Her breath lodged in her throat. Brady had always joked when he came into his trust fund he'd open his own financial planning business, and he'd steal her away from their employer. At least, she had assumed he'd been joking about the trust fund.

"Are you telling me what I think you're telling me?" After seven months of career hell, her change in luck couldn't be this easy.

"Damn straight, girlfriend. How'd you like to become partner of Morrison and McClain?" Brady almost sounded like he was dancing in glee.

She couldn't speak. Hell, she couldn't breathe from the lump in her chest.

"Don't tell me you've accepted another position, Tessa. Come on, sweetie, don't break my heart."

She laughed at the abrupt switch to pleading in his voice. "I don't know what to tell you." She sighed again, disappointment thick in her gut. No, things definitely weren't going to be easy. "I'm sorry, Brady. I can't. I don't have the cash to bankroll my share of the firm."

"I'm loaning you the money for your share." He cut her off before she could make more than a token sound of protest. "I've already got enough clients lined up for you to pay me back in the first quarter of operation."

She did the math in her head and whistled. Brady had been a busy boy to line up that many people in such a short time.

He continued, heading off another objection from her. "Plus, my dad finally retired so he and Mom are spending the next year in Europe. They're letting us use their apartment for our initial office. We'll have plenty of time to build up the business and scout out an appropriate location. Their place is on Central Park West, and you can live there for the year rent-free as part of your compensation."

Tessa raked her hand through her dripping curls. Brady was throwing too much information at her too fast, and his phone call was way too good to be true. She'd had to fight and scratch to get everything in her life. Suspicion rang through her even though she knew Brady didn't have an ulterior sexual motive.

"Tess? You still there?"

"Yeah, I'm still here. I don't know what to say."

"Say 'Thank you, Mr. Morrison. I love you, Mr. Morrison. I accept, Mr. Morrison.'"

She laughed. "I'll skip the 'love you' part. Chad would kill me."

Brady's chuckle rippled through the receiver. "Nah, he's too busy auditioning for the *Grease* revival. Come on, Tessa. What do you say?" When she didn't answer right away, he added, "Ten of our patrons are your former clients who were pissed off by how the firm treated you, and only came with me because I said you were on board."

"Brady, you didn't!" She dropped to the floor in hysterics at his audacity.

Brady's voice dropped. "I didn't think I'd have to work this hard to convince you. You used to love your job. What's going on?"

"I'm helping out my roommate at her retail store. I can't leave her in a lurch."

"Talk to your roommate tonight about an exit strategy and call me tomorrow morning." He rattled off the same number displayed on the caller ID. "You're the best financial whiz I know, Tessa. I can't do this without having the best on my team."

She clicked off the phone and slumped back against the wall. The cool tile against her back relieved the heat that flooded her. She wanted back in the game. So bad she could taste it.

But she couldn't abandon Rain, Phylicia, and Tom by cutting out without any kind of notice.

No. The admission slammed her hard, but she had to face it. She didn't want to leave Adrian. Even though they both focused on Morrigan's Cauldron during business hours, afternoons were an exquisite form of foreplay. The teasing and subtle touches left her breathless and needy by the time they locked the doors.

She shook her head, exasperated with her maudlin mood. Leaving Morrigan's Cauldron did not mean she and Adrian couldn't continue their . . .

Not sure how to label what she had with him, she climbed to her feet. Any moisture on her skin from her shower had long since dried. She settled for toweling the remaining dampness from her hair before she combed and scrunched her curls. The orange-mango scent of her favorite lotion usually soothed her agitation, but now the citrus smell only reminded her of the decision she needed to make.

Really, there was no decision. This was the opportunity she been waiting for. Tomorrow morning, she'd meet with Brady to hammer out the details of their partnership. Rain would be ecstatic for her. She just prayed Adrian would take things in stride.

If Adrian looked down, he knew his still-beating heart would be pulsing in Tessa's hand. Part of him was happy for her getting her career back on the path she wanted. The other part wanted to drag her upstairs by her hair and fuck her until she changed her mind about leaving him.

Not me. She's only leaving the shop.

And he couldn't blame her. She was young, brilliant, and could do a lot better. Because he'd thrown away his career after Jennifer didn't mean Tessa had to give up her life plans, too.

Her forehead creased in a worried frown. "Aren't you going to say anything?"

He leaned back against the counter and folded his arms over his chest, attempting to assume an air of nonchalance that he sure as hell didn't feel. "I suppose Brady needs you to start right away."

She nodded. "But he understands my situation here. I'm not leaving Rain in a lurch, especially not after everything she's done for me."

His breath hitched in his lungs at her choice of words. Rain. Not him.

He shrugged. "This will work out for Jamal. He graduates next month and needs something full-time for the summer to help with the college bills. If you can finish this week and come in on Saturdays and Sundays until then, we should be fine."

Her face went blank. "Oh. Okay then. I guess that should work for all of us."

He plastered on a smile and stuck out his right hand. "Best of luck on the new business."

She took his hand in a tentative grip and licked her full lips before she said, "Thanks."

He released her burning touch and stalked back towards his office before he did something really stupid.

Like begging Tessa to stay because he loved her.

Tessa wasn't sure how Adrian accomplished it in such a small shop like Morrigan's Cauldron, but he managed to avoid her for the rest of the afternoon and evening. She closed and locked the gates behind Phylicia and Jamal then marched back to the tiny back office.

Adrian shot her the briefest glance before he returned his gaze to the spreadsheet on the computer.

The blatant dismissal pissed her off more than his fake smile and blasé good luck wish earlier. She reached over and yanked the swivel chair around until he faced her. "You want to tell me what the fuck your problem is?"

He slowly rose from the chair until all six-foot-three-inches of him towered over her. "I don't like being played. You never had any intention of staying through your probation period, did you?"

Something didn't ring right with his words. The man who seduced her and held her enthralled with pleasure every freaking night wouldn't be this petty. She narrowed her eyes and folded her arms across her chest as she stared up at him. Striving to keep the snideness from her tone, she said, "Nice try. Care for some truth this time?"

He looked away and raked a hand through his hair before his eyes returned to hers. "How do you know this Brady of yours doesn't have an ulterior motive?"

She shook her head in disbelief and laughed. Adrian's problem couldn't be as simple as jealousy, could it? She reached out and laid a hand on his bicep, the female in her enjoying the hardness of muscle beneath her fingertips. "Brady's in a committed relationship."

He stiffened and opened his mouth, but she laid a fingertip on his lips and added, "Besides, I don't have the parts he's interested in."

His body remained tense, and he slid away from her touch. "What do you know about the neighborhood?"

She blinked at both the tactile loss and the abrupt change in topic. What the hell did he want her to do? Nothing he was saying made any sense.

"It's fucking Central Park West, and it's as safe as you can get in New York. Now, answer my question. What the hell is your problem?" Anger shook her to the core.

He grabbed her arms and shook her, the motion so swift fear rose in her throat. The man she'd known for the last three weeks had been replaced by a wild-eyed maniac. "You know damn well, there's no place safe in this city. Dammit, Jennifer! For once, would you—"

"Jennifer?" Tessa jerked free from Adrian's hold, an ugly suspicion seizing her. "Who the hell is Jennifer?"

Adrian froze, and the blood drained from his face. "Tessa, I'm sorry." He reached for her, but she stepped back.

"Who's Jennifer?" Her voice sounded cold and ugly, even to her own ears.

His nostrils flared as he took a deep breath. "I overreacted, Tessa." He took another step toward her, raw pain and pleading on his face.

The betrayal was happening all over again, and there wasn't a damn thing she could do to stop it.

"So not only do you have my work replacement picked out, but your new bedmate as well." She laughed, a sound so high and bitter it hurt her ears. "Thanks for everything, Holloway."

She whirled, snatched her purse off the coat rack and fled out the back door into the muggy May night. It wasn't until she was three blocks away that the realization hit her, and she cursed herself. She'd fallen for the wrong guy.

Again.

Chapter 12

When Tessa walked through the apartment door, Rain looked up from her book, shock smeared across her face. At least, that's what it looked like through Tessa's unshed tears.

Rain laid down her novel. "Sweetie, what are you doing home so early?"

Rain's concern tore through Tessa's fragile control and she dissolved into sobs. She wasn't sure how, but she found herself curled up on Rain's couch, Rain's arms wrapped around her and rocking her gently as the tears poured out of her. Just like Grandma would have done, which only made her cry even harder.

When the tears slowed to a trickle, Rain's soft voice asked, "What happened?"

Tessa sat up and wiped away the gunk that collected in the corners of her eyes before she turned to face Rain. "Who's Jennifer?"

Rain's face stilled, an old sadness leeched from her eyes. The look froze Tessa's blood.

"Rain, who's Jennifer?"

A long sigh escaped from Rain's lips. "Let's make some tea." She rose from the couch and started for the tiny kitchen.

Fury scorched its way through Tessa. She jumped up from the couch and stalked toward Rain. "Damn it, Rain! Why's everyone avoiding my question!"

Rain held the kettle under the faucet. She turned to set the kettle on a burner and flipped the switch to heat the water before she faced Tessa. "Jennifer was Adrian's wife."

Tessa leaned against the counter, needing the support against the shock. "Is she—" She licked her lips, not wanting to deal with this. She had been right when she spoke with Brady that morning. Things were too good to be true.

It's just a rebound fling, remember?

She cleared her throat and tried again. "Does she want him back?" Or even worse, did he want her back?

Rain reached into the open cupboard for two mugs and set them carefully on the counter. Tessa dug her nails into the palms of her hands, wanting desperately to force the answers from the older woman.

Rain placed two teabags in the mugs before she faced Tessa again. "You have to understand I'm violating a confidence. I thought he would have told you as close as the two of you were becoming." She turned away and rubbed her temples as if a terrible headache assaulted her. "Jennifer died almost three years ago, Tessa."

Tessa's heart skipped a beat. Things slipped into place. "She died somewhere near Central Park West, didn't she?"

Rain whirled to face her, eyebrows raised in shock, and nodded.

"No wonder he freaked out when I said I was moving there," Tessa whispered. But his reaction was still out of proportion, which meant there was more to the story. "It wasn't an accident, was it?"

Rain shook her head before she laid her hand on Tessa's forearm and gave it a squeeze. "You should go talk to him."

Tessa hugged the older woman. "Thanks for telling me." She turned and headed for the door. Everything was such a jumble in her head. Snagging her purse from where she'd dropped it on the floor, she slammed the door shut and jogged down the stairs. What the hell *was* she going to say to him? And how the hell could she compete with a ghost?

Adrian sat on the floor of his loft and stared at the shot of Kentucky bourbon he had poured. The amber liquid winked and sparkled, mocking him for screwing up his life a second time. The white teddy bear with its jaunty blue bow leaned against the bottle, once again a silent witness to his personal misery. His fingers itched to call Tessa one more time, but he'd already left three messages on her cell phone's voice-mail. She'd obviously turned off her phone, and after the way he'd acted all day, he didn't blame her one bit.

So why don't you call the apartment, the bear's black bead eyes accused.

Because he didn't want Rain to know what a shit he'd been. He wasn't sure what would be worse, never seeing Tessa again or Rain's disappointment in him for driving Tessa away.

He jerked at the soft knock at his door, sloshing bourbon over his hand and jeans. Okay, now Rain's freaky mind-reading act went too far. He didn't know who else would be at his door. The glimmer of hope that it might be Tessa was squelched when he saw the VCR clock. More than enough time had passed for Tessa to return to the apartment and Rain to come flying down and read him the riot act.

He marched over to the door. Might as well get it over with since he knew Rain wouldn't leave until she said her piece. He yanked the door open, and his mouth dropped. Tessa stood there, her hand poised to knock again. Red rimmed her swollen eyes, and he wanted to kick himself for causing her tears.

"Um—" She bit her lower lip in that adorable way of hers and glanced around him at his living area. "Mind if I join you and Teddy for a drink?" She gave him a tentative smile.

He nodded and stepped out of the way, not trusting himself to speak.

She strode past him and into the kitchen where she pulled a tumbler out of his cupboard. Before he could get past the wonder that she was actually here in his loft, she had marched to the living area, flopped down on the floor next to the bear and poured several ounces of bourbon in her glass. She took a healthy swig and started coughing.

"You might want to be careful. That stuff's one hundred-twenty proof." He walked over and sat down across from her, aching to touch her but not daring until he knew why she came back.

"This is some good stuff." She took another sip before she met his eyes. "Forget the deal. If this thing between us is going to work, you need to be straight with me."

Bile rose in his throat at her look, the same sympathetic one that hundreds of people had given him before. The look he never wanted to see on Tessa's face. He swallowed hard. "Rain told you."

"Not all of it. Only that Jennifer was your wife and she died." She leaned over and rested a hand on his knee. Her touch burned, but not with the usual lust between them. This touch was tender, caring. "If you don't want to tell me what happened, that's fine, but you can't use me as a replacement. It just won't work, Adrian."

"Is that what you think? That you're her replacement?"

She shrugged. "I'm not sure." She picked up the bear and stroked the soft white fur, much as he'd done for several days after the funeral.

He sucked in a breath. Maybe he needed to release his demons to start fresh with Tessa. "Did Rain tell you we used to live a couple of blocks from where you're moving?"

Her eyes widened in surprise before she shot him a wry smile. "No, she didn't." She hugged the bear to her chest and waited for him to continue.

He downed the contents of his shot glass and poured another before he could continue. He couldn't look at her, not if he wanted to get the words out.

"I used to be a stockbroker." He rolled the glass between his palms. "The bright, rising star at the firm." Bitter laughter at his past self-delusion erupted before he could stop it. "I thought we had it all. The day I got the corner office, I called Jennifer to tell her the good news. She told me she had some news of her own, but she wanted to surprise me when I got home. When I walked into the apartment, the bear was sitting on the kitchen table with a card saying 'Congratulations Daddy!' Dinner was half made, but she—"

He swallowed the second shot. The burning in his throat matched the burning in his eyes. "The police figure she was mugged coming back from the store and struggled with the guy."

Tessa, to her credit, didn't move, didn't try to touch him, didn't comfort him. The last thing he wanted was her pity. He was so tired of everyone's pity.

"Sucks, doesn't it?"

He frowned, unsure of her meaning. "What sucks?"

She was no longer looking at him. Instead, she examined the face of the bear, toying with the bow. "Everyone telling you that you need to get on with your life when all you want to do is curl up and die, too." She lifted her eyes to meet his. "That's why you quit your broker job, isn't it?"

He leaned against the couch. It was almost as if she understood, but the context didn't fit. "I don't see how this compares to you getting fired because of that asshole."

Her brows knitted into a frown. "So Rain blabbed about me, too."

He smiled in wry sympathy for Rain's penchant for "helping" her strays. "All she told me was that you'd been fired for someone else's wrongdoing."

She returned his smile. "You're right, but I wasn't talking about my departure from my last place of employment." Her smile faded, and she blew a wayward curl out of her face, a gesture he had quickly learned meant she was irritated or uncomfortable. "My grandmother survived cancer only to die from an aortic aneurysm a year later. It happened so fast." She sighed, a soft, sad sound that released her pent-up pain. "She was gone before she hit the floor. It sucks when you don't get the chance to say good-bye, doesn't it?"

For once, the ache in his chest had nothing to do with the past. "Yeah, it does." He climbed to his feet, feeling free for the first time in an eternity. The only unknown was whether Tessa still wanted him. He held his hand out to her.

She gave his hand a wary look before turning her huge, blue eyes up to him. "Stay." When she didn't say anything, he whispered, "Please."

Chapter 13

A week later, Tessa elbowed Adrian in the ribs. "Quit messing with the blindfold!" Despite her stern command, she couldn't keep the giggle out of her voice.

He stopped tugging at the scarf but still fidgeted inside the elevator. "It itches."

She snorted. "It's cashmere."

"I'm allergic to wool."

"Cashmere comes from goats."

He grumbled something under his breath she couldn't make out.

Standing on her tiptoes, she pressed her breasts against him and whispered in his ear. "Sometimes, you need to let yourself lose control, Holloway."

"It still itches."

She ignored his complaint because damn! He looked delicious in the gray suit he wore, the silver and green tie from their second night knotted neatly at his throat. The elevator dinged and she led him forward. Flinging open the penthouse doors, she shuffled him inside. The sandalwood and citrus candles she'd lit before racing down to meet him in the reception area of the building filled the room with their intoxicating scent.

She closed the doors and whipped the scarf from his eyes. "Voila!"

Candlelight illuminated the room. She'd left the drapes wide open so the city skyline beyond Central Park glittered against the black velvet night sky. He blinked then gave a low whistle of appreciation as he took in the sunken living room and the wide marble staircase that led to the second floor. He looked down at her and grinned. "I'd say you hit the jackpot."

She couldn't suppress the shiver of excitement at both her good fortune and the aura of the man next to her. "I'm just a glorified housesitter for Brady's parents until next May." She stepped away and twirled, the flowing skirt of her new dress caressing her naked legs. "But until then I plan to enjoy every minute of living in a multi-million dollar apartment."

He stepped closer, wrapped his arms around her and pulled her against his chest. She sank into his embrace, luxuriating in the press of her back against his hard muscle.

His breath warmed her ear when he leaned close and whispered, "What else do you plan to enjoy?"

She pulled away and turned to face him, a mischievous smile tugging the corners of her mouth. "The look on your mug when I tell you I'm not wearing any panties." Gray eyes darkened by lust rewarded her.

He loosened his tie. "Prove it."

She waggled her index finger at him. "Uh-uh-uh. Your place, your rules. My place, my rules." She smiled, awareness curling through her. "Now we could play strip poker if you want to find out or—"

Tessa's breath caught in her throat at the wicked glint in his eye. He stalked toward her. Feeling very much the prey, she backpedaled until she hit the foyer wall, the textured paint digging into her back. Not sure how the tables were turned, she found she didn't care under the thrill of anticipation that ran through her.

Adrian pinned her against the wall with his body, his erection evident through his trousers. His eyes never left hers as he jerked her skirt up to her hips. She'd never felt so helpless and so wanton at the same time. He ran his fingertips along the length of her pussy, and a shudder took her. Then hands and lips skimmed, stroked and caressed her until she turned into one big knot of arousal on the brink of exploding.

Just when she was about to fall over the edge, he stopped. A frustrated whimper rose from her throat at the loss of his touch. An evil grin spread across his face in response to her irritated glare. He grabbed her hand, tugging her toward the living room.

Once next to the largest couch, he stopped and swooped down to kiss her. And this kiss was nothing like his previous ones. This time he kissed her like she was the only woman in the universe, like their souls depended on it, like he couldn't survive without her.

With a few deft flicks, he unbuttoned her dress. His hot palms slid the soft cotton over her shoulders and down her arms, igniting a firestorm in her nerves. The material pooled at her feet. Breathless, she waited to see what he'd do next.

She didn't have to wait long. He eased her down onto the couch, the smooth leather caressing her ass, her back, her shoulders. A brief kiss and tongue swirl around her clit left her wanting to scream in sexual agony. Instead, he stood and shed his own clothing before he knelt between her spread legs. The tip of his cock brushed her swollen flesh, and she closed her eyes against the exquisite torture.

"Tessa, I want you to look at me."

Her eyes snapped open at his husky voice. Inch by inch he eased into her, filling and stretching, until she couldn't take anymore. Her legs wrapped around his waist, and she threaded her fingers through his thick locks, keeping him close. Spice and citrus mingled with his indefinable male scent. She concentrated on each slow thrust, squeezing her walls as he withdrew. His eyes glittered, and she knew his own control was slipping.

"Let go," she whispered. "For both of us."

And there was no holding back as they both shouted their climaxes into the candlelit night.

Outside the French doors, a dark form watched them with a yellow eye. She made a single satisfied squawk before she leapt from her perch. For an instant, the moon silhouetted black feathers before the crow disappeared into the night.

SUMMER

Chapter 1

Jamal Washington watched the crowd milling in front of the Wongs' restaurant across the street. Most of the kids he recognized from the neighborhood or high school. Most of them were trouble only when teachers and parents weren't looking. All of them were friends of Mark Li. Or had been.

He looked over his shoulder. "We should call the cops, Rain." The elderly Wongs wouldn't. It wasn't in them to make a fuss. By the time they did, it would be too late.

At the ancient wood counter, Rain Bean looked up from her paperwork and peered over the tops of her reading glasses. Her eyes narrowed when she caught sight of the mob. "What's going on over there?"

Jamal blinked in surprise. The owner of Morrigan's Cauldron was usually plugged into the Greenwich Village gossip network. "You didn't hear?"

She turned her sharp gaze on him.

He shrugged. "Shan's ex-boyfriend Mark hung himself last night."

Her expression turned quizzical. "Really?"

Jamal didn't say anything. No reason to since Rain's freaky ESP probably already knew he was involved. Sort of.

Her dark eyebrows knitted a frown. "Did you tie the knot on the rope?"

His eyes widened. "Shit, no!"

A wicked smile lit her face. "Then quit feeling guilty. Mark Li was a bully and a—"

Someone banged on the delivery door of the store. Rain inclined her head toward the back. "Go let Shan in." She resumed staring at the crowd.

Threads of unease wiggled their way up his spine. It wasn't that Rain knew things. He'd learned from the time he could walk that he couldn't get away with anything around her. No, it was the anger sparking in Rain's eyes. It took a lot to piss off the old woman.

Shan had begged him not to tell anyone about what Mark did to her. And he hadn't. At least, not to anyone who didn't already know. He had the sinking feeling Rain had just pulled the truth from his brain.

Jamal jogged to the back door and yanked it open. A gust of hot air boiled into the already stifling storage room. Shan stood there, shivering despite the late July temperatures. He squelched the urge to wrap his arm around her.

She gave him a tentative smile. "I was supposed to work at the restaurant today. My grandmother called while I was still on the bus and said to come here instead."

He waved her in, not trusting his tongue. Damn, she looked fine despite the red rimming her amber eyes.

Anger seeped through his blood at the sight of her puffy skin and forced words into his mouth. "Please tell me you're not crying for that asshat."

She shook her head. The motion sent her high ponytail swinging. Glossy, black hair he wanted to run his fingers through.

Her throat bobbed. "Mark's parents called mine. They said some awful things. That it was my fault."

God, how he wanted to hug her. Sooth away her pain. She was too beautiful, too sweet for this kind of shit. "It's not."

She jumped at the sharpness in his voice.

More rage poured through his nerves. The bastard had definitely done a number on Shan. Damn, why hadn't he seen what was happening until it was too late? "Look, you did the right thing breaking up with him. I still think you should have pressed charges."

She glanced around, obviously checking for the older members of the staff. "He left a message on my voice mail last night. He said he'd get us both. What did you do, Jamal?" Her voice was little more than a hoarse whisper.

He suppressed a snort of disgust. Like the asshat could do anything if he were lying in the city morgue. "Nothing that I shouldn't have done a long time ago." Just the memory of Li standing over Shan in the high school band room drew a circle of rage around his heart.

But he wasn't stupid enough to land his own butt in jail. Of course, his growth spurt the last year of high school helped. Mark wasn't such a cocky little fucker when someone towered a good six inches over the bastard.

The look in her eyes became suspicious.

He raised his hands. "I swear, Shan. I didn't touch him. All I did was tell him to leave you alone."

The wary expression on her face didn't go away, but she didn't press the subject. "What's going on at the restaurant?"

Again, he shrugged. "Just some of Mark's toadies trying to cause trouble."

Shan pushed past him and marched toward the storefront.

Jamal followed, admiring the swing of her hips under her shorts. Pink looked good on her. Always had. Ever since kindergarten.

When they entered the showroom, Rain stood before the huge plate window, peering past the gold lettering that spelled out the name of her store. Her lips moved, but she didn't say anything.

Anticipation raced along his nerves. He knew that look on Rain's face, had seen the same look on his mom's. He didn't have to wait long. Across the street, the joints on the fire hydrant at the corner cracked. The teens gathered in front of the restaurant stared at the bright red fixture. He imagined the groan of metal on metal freaked them out as much as the bolts on the hydrant twisting without help. Then water exploded from the fixture.

The high-pressure spray nailed Bill Mailer in the face. He stumbled back and tripped over his girlfriend. They both toppled to the concrete sidewalk. The blast of water followed, dousing the rest of the group. Kids scrambled out of the way, but water arched from the top of the hydrant. Shouts and cries filled the street as they tried to evade the steady gush.

One girl ran for the front door of the restaurant. A black shape plummeted from the sky and intercepted her. Her shrieks filled the street, and her arms waved wildly as the bird continued to dive-bomb her every time she took a step toward the eatery.

Jamal snickered. Served them right for trying to intimidate the Wongs, and Shan in particular. His humor died when he realized where the gush from the hydrant and the crazy bird guided the group. They made a beeline for Morrigan's Cauldron. "Rain?"

The hydrant faltered, then sputtered to a stop. Rain blinked. She turned and smiled. "It'll be all right."

While he respected the old woman's peculiar abilities, they were outnumbered. The last thing he wanted was to see these idiots trash her store. He leaned close to Shan and tried to ignore the sweet scent of jasmine in her hair. "Got your cell?" he whispered.

She nodded, but her attention remained on the crowd as they crossed the street.

"Get in the back and call 9-1-1."

"No." The answer came from both women at the same time.

His gaze locked with Shan's. Damn, a man could get lost in those eyes.

She shook her head and laid a soft hand on his bicep. The world stopped at the feel of her skin on his. She gave him a brave smile, though real fear shone behind bright amber irises. "I can't keep running away, Jamal."

The tinkling of the bell that hung on the door broke the spell. Bill Mailer stepped into the store and dripped on the ancient oak flooring. As Mark's right-hand man, Bill had no problem occupying the power vacuum created by his friend's death.

Except this wasn't high school anymore.

The others followed Bill through the door and spread out. Red flared on Bill's pale face when he spotted Shan. "There's the whore."

Jamal stepped forward, shielding Shan from the crowd. It meant losing her exhilarating touch, and a part of him whimpered to get it back. But he wasn't about to let Mark's gang lay a finger on her. "Go home, Mailer."

"Get out of the way, Washington. You know what she did."

A not-so-nice smile tightened the muscles along Jamal's jaw, and he took another step forward. "I know what Mark did to her. For all I know, you held her down while Li beat on her."

Unease flickered on Bill's face. Damn, the bastard knew!

Jamal searched the expressions of the rest. Most looked confused. But a couple of others, including Bill's girlfriend—yeah, they knew all right. Jamal clenched his hands into fists to stop the shaking. Damn, how he wanted to smack the shit out of Bill and his cronies.

"I suggest you all leave now." Rain's crystal voice echoed through the store as Jamal and Bill stared at each other. "I don't think Princeton will look too kindly on you threatening an innocent girl, William Howard Mailer."

Bill's attention darted from Jamal to Rain and back. Jamal didn't dare take his eyes off Bill. An occasional *plink* of water hitting hardwood broke the silence.

After a few seconds, a sneer twisted Bill's mouth. "Hope you enjoy her, Washington. Mark said she was a lousy lay." He turned and stomped out of the store. After some pointed muttering, the rest of the group followed. The last girl tried to slam the door, but a gust of wind softened the gesture. The bell tinkled, sounding like an angry fairy.

Rain shook her head. "What a bunch of twits."

Jamal pivoted to check Shan. Her lips were a tight line, and her normally golden skin appeared pasty in the sunlight streaming through the front windows. "You okay?"

She nodded, but she stared at the floor. "I'm sorry they—"

"Hey." His right hand moved of its own accord and tilted her chin until he could see her eyes. Wetness glimmered but did not fall. "You have nothing to apologize for." When she didn't respond, he said, "You hear me?"

"Why don't you two clean up that mess?"

Jamal looked over at Rain whose head tilted in the direction of the puddles spreading across the front of the store. "Can you watch the front while we get the mops and buckets?" Rain's gaze fixed on Jamal, even though her words were aimed at Shan.

"Yes, ma'am," they both replied.

Jamal tapped Shan on the shoulder. "Owe me a coke." One of her sweet smiles rewarded his attempt at humor. Then he followed Rain to the back.

Rain reached the washroom and handed him a mop. "After you clean up the mess, I want you to take Shan home."

Jamal took the bucket she held out. "Her bus doesn't come—"

The old woman raised a wrinkled hand. "I'll give you the money for a cab from petty cash."

His heart thumped at the thought of a little time alone with Shan. In the backseat of a taxi. So close. But guilt took hold of his overactive imagination. Rain had done far too much already for Mom and him. "I can't take your money."

A brilliant smile lit her face, making her look decades younger. "Save yours. You'll need it for college this fall." She winked as she passed him a mop. "And I'll give you a little extra to buy her a coke."

Crap. Was Rain actually trying to play matchmaker? Perspiration slickened his grip on the bucket handle and wooden staff. "Actually, she owes me."

Rain shook her head as she dumped a roll of paper towels in the plastic bucket. "Men."

An hour later, Jamal handed a few bills to the driver and slid out behind Shan. The cab peeled away from the curb, reggae blaring from the open windows. He turned to find Shan staring at him with a quizzical look.

"My apartment is another two blocks."

He shrugged and nodded at the grocery behind her. "Figured you might want to get something cold to drink before heading home."

She crossed her arms and glared at him. "Why are you playing me? What's really going on?"

He held up his hands and spread his fingers. "It was Rain's idea."

"You told her about the prom, didn't you?"

"No, I didn't. I swear." He held a hand over his heart.

"Uh-huh." Suspicion didn't leave her expression.

"I went along with it because we need to talk."

Her gaze dropped to the cracked sidewalk under their feet. "Don't start with me, Jamal. Not now."

Hot air fried his lungs when he sucked in a deep breath. Maybe he should have beaten the crap out of Mark Li when he saw what that asshat was doing to Shan on prom night. Maybe it would have been worth going to jail just to get the truth out. "Okay. Fine. But I still want something cold to drink."

Jamal pressed his hand against the small of her back. Dampness met his palm, and he wondered what she would taste like if they—

No, he couldn't think about her body parts or one of his would give his feelings away. At least he could blame this damn heat wave for his own sweaty palms. She didn't resist his urging, and together they entered the blessed A/C of the grocery.

Once their purchases were made, they sipped from their bottles as they walked the last couple of blocks. He tried to keep the conversation light, but something had plagued him for a while.

"I thought your parents were pushing for Columbia or Harvard. Why'd you decide on NYU?" Even the traffic noise died as if waiting for her answer. When the silence continued, he stole a glance. Pink flared in her cheeks. God, he was so stupid.

"You've got to be kidding me," he muttered under his breath.

"It wasn't because of Mark," she snapped. "I had . . . other reasons."

"Like what?"

"Like none of your business, Jamal Washington." She stomped up the three steps to her building's main doors. Did she realize her hips did a cute little wiggle when she was pissed?

When she reached the top step, she flashed a blinding smile at the building's doorman. "Hi, Tyson."

"Miss Shan." Tyson pulled the main door open with a flourish. "Hey, man." He reached out with his free arm to fist-bump Jamal.

Jamal hung back a few steps so Shan wouldn't hear. "Has anybody been here looking for her today?"

Tyson sobered. "Li's posse this morning. Had to threaten to call the cops to get 'em to leave." He shot a quick glance at Shan, who stood by the elevators. "So he really committed suicide?" At Jamal's nod, he shook his head. "His parents showed up about ten minutes ago. I didn't want to let them up, but Dr. Wong insisted."

"Shit." Worry skittered up Jamal's spine. "Thanks for the warning, Ty."

Tyson shrugged. "*De nada*."

Jamal strode over to Shan. He couldn't let her walk into that mess alone.

Her lips pressed into a thin line for an instant. "I think I can find my own apartment from here."

"Rain will give me hell if I don't walk you to your door." And maybe Mr. and Mrs. Li would leave with him there.

Shan's eyes narrowed, but she kept silent and stabbed the already lit button again. Once the car arrived, her irritation was a palpable thing in the tight confines of the elevator. When they reached her floor, she arrowed straight for home.

With two strides, Jamal caught up with her. If she wanted to ignore him, that was fine. She jammed her key in the lock, shoved the door open, and froze.

In the tiny living room, Mark's parents sat on the couch across from the

Wongs. Mrs. Li had tears streaming down her face, but red suffused the cheeks of both men. On the other hand, Mrs. Wong was as pale as fresh snow.

Mr. Li rose and glared at Shan. "Murderer."

Protective instincts kicked in. Jamal stepped in front of Shan once again. "You need to leave."

The rest of the group stood as well.

"Yes, that would be best." The tightness in Dr. Wong's voice contradicted his polite words.

Mrs. Li pointed a shaking finger in Shan's direction. "Mark died because of her." The statement was more sob than words.

Crimson filled Jamal's vision, but before he could form a coherent sentence, Dr. Wong said, "That is enough. I will not tolerate any more accusations against my daughter in my home."

Jamal couldn't remember Shan's dad raising his voice. Ever.

Mr. Li shot a nasty look at Dr. Wong. "Your little bitch—"

In two steps, Jamal was in Li's face. "Shut the fuck up!" He leaned over the smaller man, just like he had when he'd confronted Mark at the Fourth of July party. "You wanna know why Shan broke up with your precious son?"

"Jamal, no," Shan said from behind him. "You promised." Her voice sounded so small. But he was so damn tired of seeing Shan jump at everything since that night.

He stared deep into the senior Li's eyes. "Mark tried to rape Shan at prom."

The red drained from Mr. Li's face. "You lie."

"The only reason he didn't succeed is because I pulled him off of her. And it wasn't the first time he'd hit Shan." He looked over his shoulder. Shan stared at the tiled floor. Tears trickled down her cheeks.

Mrs. Wong crossed the room and laid a hand on Shan's shoulder. "Is this true?"

Shan gave a single nod. Then she raised her head. Fire burned deep within amber. The anger aimed solely at Jamal.

Damn. In all the years they'd been friends, he'd never broken his word to Shan. Maybe she'd hate him forever, but her parents needed to know the truth.

Jamal jumped when Dr. Wong roared, "Get out! Get out now!" He waited for another insult from Mark's folks, but Mr. Li guided his wife out the door.

Her face was buried in tissues and she wept in earnest. Despite the blazing emotion flooding the room, the door closed quietly behind the couple.

Dr. Wong didn't say another word. He headed for the balcony, his body so rigid he walked with a jerky motion. The French door closed behind him. The look on Shan's face was awful. She turned and raced down the hallway, and disappeared into her room. This time, a door slam followed.

A lump formed in Jamal's chest. He'd made things worse, but he'd been so damn mad at the insults Mark's parents had flung at Shan.

"Jamal, you should leave too."

He looked at Mrs. Wong. Sadness filled her eyes, but unlike everyone else, anger was absent from her gaze. He glanced at the balcony. Shan's dad wasn't in sight. It didn't feel right leaving things the way they were.

Mrs. Wong patted his arm. "I'll make sure she calls you later."

"She won't. She's pissed at me." The lump grew larger, heavier. What would he do if he never saw her again?

"Yes, she is, but we needed to know." Then she shocked the shit out of him by giving him a huge hug. Mrs. Wong wasn't exactly the touchy-feely type of mom. "Thank you."

Awkwardly, he wrapped his arms around her and hugged back.

Jamal jogged down the stairs, needing to burn off some of his own anger. When he hit the lobby, Tyson said nothing, just gave him a single nod and another bump. Good. Tyson'd let him know if there were any more problems.

Even though Rain had given Jamal enough cash for a return cab ride to the shop, walking seemed a better option despite the heat. How was he going to get Shan to forgive him for narcing?

He dodged people, his strides eating concrete. His brain churned through ideas, most of which it tossed aside. Hands jammed in his pockets.

Maybe something grand was needed. This was his chance, wasn't it? To show her how he felt? That not every guy was like Li? How about something girls thought was romantic? Roses? Nah, that's what Mark had done when he tried to suck up after one of their fights. Maybe he could ask Rain. She knew the meanings of all the flowers. He'd just have to swear the old woman to secrecy . . .

The hairs on the back of Jamal's neck rose. Someone was watching him. He pivoted, but none of the pedestrians paid any attention to him. People bustled by, intent on their own errands. He resumed his path back to Morrigan's Cauldron, but as he passed an alley, the feeling grew.

A bird flew in front of him, so close he felt the breeze of its passage. A huge, black thing, not a pesky little pigeon. It screeched as it entered the alley.

Jamal looked down the shadowed way. White flashed and disappeared behind some dumpsters. Just some homeless person. Damn overactive imagination. Now Shan had him going with that talk about the last cell message from Mark. Next thing he'd be seeing would be Li's ghost.

Chapter 2

When Shan's bedroom door squeaked, she looked up from her damp pillow. A tea tray was balanced in Mom's hands as she nudged the door open. In addition to the teapot and cups, a large pile of Double-Stuf Oreos graced a plate.

Things must be bad if Mom had dug into her secret stash of cookies, the only junk food she brought, and hid, in the apartment. Dad would have a royal fit if he knew.

Speaking of which. "Where's Dad?"

Mom sat the tray on Shan's desk. "He went to the park." White wisps steamed from the cups despite the stuffiness in the room as she poured.

Shan toyed with the fringes of one of her pillows. "He's furious with me."

Sad eyes flicked in her direction at her statement. "No, honey." Mom abandoned the tea and came to sit next to her. "He's angry with Mark and with himself."

Maybe her brain was fuzzy from the crying. "Mad at himself?"

Her mother laid a manicured hand over hers. "We knew something was wrong." Were those tears in Mom's eyes? "We should have—"

"It was my problem. Jamal shouldn't have—"

"No!" The fierceness in her mother's voice made Shan lean away. "Jamal did the right thing. We needed to know. I wish—" A deep sigh whistled past her lips before she said, "Why didn't you tell us Mark was hurting you?"

Shan couldn't meet those sad eyes any more. The old mixture of guilt and nausea swam through her stomach. "I—" She swallowed hard to keep the ugly mess from erupting. "I didn't want to disappoint you and Dad."

"Disappoint us?"

"Heritage, culture. It's important to you and Dad. And Grandmother and—"

A soft hand cupped her cheek, the touch gentle and . . . surprising. Mom wasn't one for affectionate displays. "Not at the expense of your safety." Coldness filled Mom's voice.

The second surprise forced Shan to look up. Scarlet seemed to blaze from Mom's coffee-colored eyes. So not like the calm facade she maintained for court. The anger disappeared as fast as it appeared, only to be replaced by an analytical expression.

"You thought we would not approve of a relationship between you and young Mr. Washington." It was a statement, not a question. A ghost of a smile tugged at Mom's lips.

Shan blinked. "Jamal? What are you talking about? We're just friends." Her protest sounded hollow even in her own ears.

Mom ran her hand over Shan's hair before dropping it into her lap. The ghost smile became wholly visible. "Then you are even more blind than me. NYU? Really, Shan?"

"It's a great school!" The odd tickle in her chest started again. The same one she'd felt all summer. The one that had started last spring when she really believed Mark would do horrible things to her before he killed her, and Jamal appeared like some warrior of old to rescue her.

That night had been the first time he hadn't been the scrawny kid from kindergarten who shared his crayons with her after Bill Mailer had stomped hers to bits. The first time she really saw the man he was becoming. And the first time she had admitted to herself the real reason why she had chosen NYU.

Because that was where Jamal was going.

Jamal jerked the store door open, causing the bell to echo his pissed-off mood. He only caught a few words between Shan's grandmother and Rain, enough to know they were speaking Chinese. Both women turned to stare at him. The silence grew to uncomfortable proportions before he reached for the top of his head and said, "What? Did a pigeon poop on me again?"

Rain rolled her eyes before returning her attention to the eldest Mrs. Wong.

More Chinese spilled between the two of them, but two phrases were repeated a few times. One was "Mark Li." The other "*kiang shi*."

He'd lay money that *kiang shi* meant "asshat."

Crossing the floor, he noticed the tarot cards spread on the counter. In a swift movement, Rain collected them. But not before he saw the ragged red figure that looked like the half-rotted corpse of a bird of prey. Death.

Who was the subject of Rain's reading? Could it be Shan? Despite his obvious stare, Rain ignored him and continued her conversation with Shan's grandmother.

Finally, Mrs. Wong gave a curt nod. She bowed deeply to Rain, then turned for the door. Before she reached it, she stopped before Jamal and gave him an even deeper bow. The bell hanging on the door tinkled softly as she left.

What the hell? Shan's grandmother's usual behavior consisted of towel snapping when he filched a fortune cookie or when Shan slipped extra egg rolls in his take-out bag. Not . . . respect.

He looked at Rain.

She shrugged. "Tom, Jamal and I will be in the back."

"Okay." The muffled voice came from the bookshelves to the left.

Jamal suppressed the shiver threatening his spine. Tom was okay, but the man's ability to appear out of thin air gave him the willies. Well, not out of thin air, which was ridiculous, but he was so damn quiet. You didn't know Tom was in a room unless he wanted you to.

Rain crooked her finger, and Jamal trudged after her into the storage room.

"Why were you doing a tarot reading for Mrs. Wong?"

Rain said nothing, just walked with a determined air towards the teeny store office.

Jamal tried again. "Was it about Shan?"

Instead of answering, Rain stopped in front of the dumbwaiter that went to the upstairs apartment. An apartment currently not occupied since the store's manager Adrian had taken a few days off to vacation with his fiancée.

Rain opened the door and yanked on the pulley that moved the dumb waiter car out of the way and locked the mechanism. She reached inside. Wood groaned when she slid the rear panel up and out of her way.

A secret compartment? Jamal shook his head in disbelief. Saying Rain was eccentric ranked up there with saying the sky was blue.

She pulled out a long object wrapped in dusty white fabric and handed it to him. It was over a yard long and much lighter than it looked. She shot him a curious look before she closed the compartment and lowered the dumbwaiter back into place.

Jamal carried the bundle over to the table they used for unpacking vendor shipments. Something about the object almost seemed . . . sacred. He set it gingerly on the wooden surface.

"Unwrap it."

He unwound the soft cloth, trying not to stir the dust more than necessary. The material felt like the handspun cotton from one of Mom's artsy-crafty periods. He uncovered a scabbard. Runes were stamped into the darkened leather. He'd been around Morrigan's Cauldron nearly all of his eighteen years. Long enough to know this definitely wasn't a replica. He swallowed hard and looked at Rain.

She smiled and inclined her head. He pulled away the rest of the material to reveal a tarnished pommel. A deep red stone was set in the hand guard. Something that large should have been a fake, but he'd bet his college fund that the gem was a real ruby. The slightest effort tugged a foot of sword from its sheath. Unlike the hilt, the blade was shiny. Sharp. And very real.

His eyes met Rain's.

This time her expression was all too serious. "You'll need it to protect Shan."

"Are you fucking nuts?" He pushed the sword back into its scabbard and stepped back from the table. "I can't carry live steel on the street."

She picked it up and held it out to him. "Mark Li will come after Shan. You'll need a weapon."

This was too freaky even by Rain's standards. "Right. And when I get stopped by the cops for carrying an unlicensed sword, I'll tell them my boss is psychic, and I'm guarding my best friend from her dead ex. Yeah, getting a mental health evaluation is so much better than getting gang-raped in the jail shower."

She said nothing. Blue eyes bore into his. Then she turned and headed back into the main part of the store, yelling for Tom.

Jamal left the sword on the table and took a step toward the beaded curtain, but . . .

A soft hum called to him. Not quite music, not quite singing.

No, it had to be his imagination. He took another step away.

The hum rose, an insistent trill.

Rain must have hypnotized him. That was it.

He strode back to the table and grabbed the scabbard. The hum disappeared. Maybe that psych evaluation wasn't so far-fetched after all.

An hour and a half later at Tom's gym, a cramp stitched in Jamal's side. Only his heavy panting broke the silence. Most of the men had stopped whatever they were doing to watch the two of them hack at each other.

"Keep your guard up." The flat of the older man's wooden practice sword slapped Jamal's wrist. The gray at his temples was definitely misleading. Even with the sheen on his face, Tom still looked like he could go a couple more hours.

Despite the pain and numbness deadening the nerves in his hand, Jamal tightened his grip and parried Tom's next slash at his head. This was nothing like the demos they'd trained for. Tom treated this session like it was for real, not for some Ren fair show.

Too bad Shan wasn't here. She loved this kind of stuff. And dammit, between the mysterious tarot session with Mrs. Wong, then Rain giving him the secret sword and pushing Tom out the door to train him, he'd forgotten to ask her about what flowers—

His feet flew into the air. He landed on his back. Hard. The force drove what little air he had out of his aching lungs. A whistle stopped just millimeters from his neck. He looked over the wooden sword and up at Tom.

"You're dead, kid." Chocolate brown eyes peered down the length of pine. "You've gotta concentrate." The sword snapped back and Tom held out a hand.

Jamal grabbed it and hoisted himself upright. Maybe he needed a guy's opinion. "Can I ask you something?"

A wary expression crossed Tom's face. "Depends."

"Have you ever pissed off a woman?"

The older man stared at him for a second before he howled with laughter. Waving for Jamal to follow, he left the practice area and collapsed on the nearest bench. He fished in his gym bag, then tossed a bottle of water to Jamal.

Jamal snagged it and dropped next to Tom, who took a long swallow from his own container. The group that had been watching them broke up. Several muttered to each other. Guess a brother with a sword was still gauche in New York. He smiled to himself. On the streets, a black man wasn't supposed to know the definition of "gauche" either.

He glanced at Tom. The older man rarely spoke and almost never about his past. A friend from his unit who showed up one time on Tom's day off was the only reason Jamal knew the guy was a vet from the first Gulf War. It didn't sound like he would open up now either.

Tom finally stopped chuckling. "I don't think there's ever been a man in existence who hasn't pissed off a member of the opposite sex." He took another drink. "Why?"

Taking the opening, Jamal told him everything. The prom, the promise, what had happened at the Wongs' apartment. "How do I make things right with Shan?"

"Geez, kid, you don't ask the easy ones, do you?" Tom grabbed the hem of his t-shirt and swiped at the sweat on his forehead, before he chugged the rest of his water. "I'm the last person to ask."

"Why? What did you do?" Jamal sipped his bottle, not really expecting Tom to answer.

"I rejected someone. A very powerful someone."

Jamal nearly choked on his water when Tom spoke. He twisted the cap on the empty plastic. "She took it bad?"

Tom's second round of laughter filled the area. "You could say that." Then something like pain spilled from Tom's expression when he faced Jamal. "I could have handled things better. I didn't have to be cruel when I said no."

"Oh." Well, damn. That was totally no help at all.

"Mind if I ask you a question?"

Jamal shook his head. This had to be the first time he'd had a conversation with Tom longer than a minute that didn't involve the shop.

"What do you know about the Sword of Lugh?" Brown eyes stared with an intensity that unnerved Jamal.

He leaned his head against the concrete block wall, trying to pull the old tale into focus. A slight hum came from under the bench where he'd stowed Rain's gift. Tom had found a canvas bat bag to carry the damn thing in.

"Lugh was one of the Tuatha de Danann." Jamal wiped the sweat dripping in his eyes. "His sword was one of the most powerful weapons ever created. The story of Arthur and Excalibur is supposed to be based on Lugh and his magic sword." He tilted his head to eye Tom and grinned. "You telling me Rain's the Lady of the Lake? 'Cause I don't think a dumbwaiter qualifies as a body of water."

A funky look crossed Tom's face. "Nah. Just talking fairytales." He clapped Jamal on the shoulder. "Let's call it quits. You've got a long night ahead of you."

Thank God, her parents had some medical association dinner to go to tonight. Shan didn't think she could handle anymore of her dad's moping or her mom's sly looks. It didn't help when Mom whispered, "I put condoms in your nightstand drawer," right before they left. When Shan protested, Mom shook her head and said, "You're eighteen. You need to act responsibly if you plan to have a relationship."

Shan yanked off her *Wong's Take-out* t-shirt and tossed it in the hamper. A relationship. Right. After all today's drama, a nice quiet evening was what she really needed. Popcorn, a movie . . .

Jamal loved action flicks. She eyed her phone on the nightstand. Her anger at him had evaporated after her talk with Mom. Maybe she should call and apologize. He'd been right about the whole Mark thing. Maybe if she told him how she really felt . . .

Shorts followed the t-shirt.

But Jamal had never seemed interested in her. Oh, sure, he was his usual kind, sweet self, but he acted more like a brother. His behavior didn't stop her from wondering. Wondering what it'd be like to kiss him. Wondering what it'd be like to touch his chest. To run her hands over all that muscle.

Oh, God, she really needed a cold shower. With a flick of the knob, the shower spurted to life, but a tepid spray was the best it could do in this July heat wave.

She ditched her undies and stepped under the water. A quick lather and she started washing away the stress. But as soapy hands slid over hot, slick skin, a different image rose in her mind. It was Jamal's hand stroking her belly, moving up, brushing the tender underside of her breast. Her head tilted back, and she closed her eyes.

Her nipples perked as his fingers circled the tips. One hand slid down her hip, touched her thighs, brushed her curls. He teased her, knew what she wanted, where she wanted his hand to go next, but he wouldn't comply. Not just yet.

Instead, he returned his attention to her breasts. Palming them, testing their weight. Tweaking and rolling the tight buds while whispering sweet nothings in her ear as she leaned against his chest.

"Please, Jamal . . ."

He pulled her against him, and his erection pressed against her ass. One huge palm lay against her stomach, steadying her as the other traveled south. He touched her intimate curls, feather-light strokes encouraging her to open up to him. So gentle and patient knowing this was her first time.

She gasped when one finger entered her. The sensation sent tremors through every nerve. Her hips thrust against his hand, demanding more. A second finger joined the first, and together they found that certain spot—

Crash!

The sound jerked Shan out of the fantasy, and she turned off the water. "Mom?" After a second of silence, she called, "Dad?"

Another *bang* filled the apartment's quiet.

Tyson wouldn't let anyone up without calling first, but Gavin, who worked the night shift, wasn't known for his common sense.

Shan wrung out her hair and grabbed a towel. Wrapping the terry around her and tucking the ends, she strode into the hallway and listened. Silence. It could be something as stupid as a pigeon that had rammed a window in the glare of the sunset.

Except a bird wouldn't account for the muffled swearing coming from the direction of her bedroom.

Chapter 3

"Goddamnit!" Jamal jerked the pommel of the sword from between the steps of the fire escape ladder. Tom and his bright ideas. Strapping the bag across his chest with a small opening unzipped so he could reach the sword was so fucking brilliant.

He was finally getting the hang of his stupid-ass height and not banging into everything in sight. But he forgot about the extra inches peeking over his shoulder until the sword got caught in the ironworks, threw him off balance, and nearly sent him plummeting fifty feet. He was going to have a nasty bruise on his shoulder from hitting the railing, in addition to the ones Tom had dealt out during their afternoon practice.

Good thing her grandmother told Rain that Shan and her parents would be out tonight. Shan was already pissed enough at him. He didn't want to explain to Shan why Rain thought he should be guarding her from a ghost.

Oh, hell, he had no idea why he was even going along with Rain's crazy shit. Except he'd seen some of the weird stuff she could do. The same weird stuff she'd taught Mom. And deep down, he believed.

He knelt on the landing and pulled snacks out of the bag for his all-nighter. The faint whiff of jasmine drifted by when he saw the shadow of someone behind him. He threw himself to the left, smacking his already sore shoulder against unyielding brick.

The aluminum bat nailed the railing where his head had been with a resounding *bong*.

Shan whirled around, bat raised for the next swing. The anger in her face fell for an instant, but only an instant. About the same instant the towel she wore slipped to display the most perfect golden shape he'd ever seen.

Not that he'd seen many breasts. But Shan's real one definitely beat the ones in Tyson's nudie mags. Now if the towel could fall the rest of the way . . .

"Jamal Washington, what the hell are you doing out here?" She glanced at her open window, then back at him. Outrage sent amber eyes sparking. "Were you peeping at me?" Muscles tightened, the prelude to another swing.

"No! I just got here!" He held up his hands, fingers spread. More an attempt to catch the bat if she swung again than a gesture of surrender.

"What are you doing out here?"

"Why aren't you with your parents?"

The bat lowered. Her eyes narrowed. "They're at one of Dad's medical association dinners. Why would I go? And what the hell are you doing?"

"I swear I wasn't looking." Not that he could help looking now. In addition to the tight nub of her nipple winking at him, a nice slit in the towel showed an expanse of supple thigh. A millimeter more and he'd see . . .

He licked his lips and forced himself to meet her eyes. "I didn't think you were home."

The bat rose an inch. "You snuck up here when I wasn't supposed to be home? What were you planning to do?" Her toe brushed against cellophane, and she looked down to where he'd started his pile.

When her gaze returned to him, the bat lowered all the way. "You brought me Twinkies?"

"Actually, your box is sitting downstairs with Gavin."

"You left *my* Twinkies with Gavin?"

"Don't worry. I wrapped them in a plain brown wrapper so your parents wouldn't know."

"Then I'd better go get them." A long leg stepped through the open window, giving him a flash of the most perfect round ass.

He groaned. Good thing he wore knit shorts. A zipper would be digging into some sensitive parts about now.

She poked her head back out. "You okay?"

He closed his eyes and shifted the bag across his lap. Her towel had slipped farther. Not that he didn't want to look, but he really shouldn't without permission. "I'm fine. Just please put some clothes on before you go downstairs."

A giggle escaped from Shan as she and her box of very bad snacks rode the elevator back to the fourth floor. Maybe her display had been unintentional, but now she had no doubt that Jamal wanted her. His little efforts didn't hide some very big evidence. And the apology note he'd included with the Twinkies was so sweet. But first things first . . .

When she returned to her bedroom, he sat on the edge of the pale lavender duvet, the sports equipment bag still draped across his lap. He hadn't even moved to flick on the lamp against the deepening twilight.

She closed the door and dropped the box inside a dresser drawer. The last thing she needed was Dad to come home early and see the Twinkies. She turned, put one fist on her hip and waved at the now-closed window with the other hand. "You going to tell me what you were doing on my fire escape?"

He ran a hand over his short black curls. She'd learned years ago the gesture was his "embarrassed" tell, since his skin was dark enough that his cheeks didn't give anything away. "You wouldn't believe me."

"Try me."

He stared at his size 13 feet. "It's stupid."

"Try me," she repeated.

"Your grandmother and Rain think a *kiang shi* is after you."

She dropped to the bed and stared at him. "A hopping corpse?"

He shrugged. "Rain said it was a Chinese zombie."

She smirked. "Or a con job to get out of paying travel and death taxes, depending on the source of the story." Her humor fled at the memory of the voice message she received last night. The one that threatened to rape her and slit her throat. After he made her watch as he killed Jamal. "They think it's Mark?"

Jamal's non-answer spoke the truth.

She stood and started pacing. "That's so stupid."

"Told you." He leaned back on his elbows.

"He's dead."

"Yep."

"Has it occurred to you that Rain and my grandmother are setting you up?"

"Oh, yeah, it has."

At his irritated drawl, she stopped pacing and really looked at him. The hard length of his body. The wry amusement in his eyes. The full lips that promised so much. *How could I have been so blind all these years?*

Maybe not so blind. At least, not her subconscious, which made the decision to attend NYU. Or her body, which still tingled from her fantasy of him in the shower with her.

Maybe she needed to let him know. How she really felt. Who she really wanted. And what she wanted from him.

She yanked the bag away from his legs. It landed on the floor with a muffled *thud*. Then she crawled in his lap, her thighs straddling his, and laid a deep kiss on him.

Jamal was dreaming. He was sure of it. One of his favorites where Shan finally returns his feelings. A questioning tongue slipped between his lips, then turned demanding. All he could do was give her what she insisted on having.

Her breath hinted of cinnamon as he began his own exploration. She shifted a fraction, the pressure on his dick an exquisite counterpoint to her lips.

He lay down, drawing Shan with him. His hands massaged her hips as her mouth followed his. The sweet weight of her breasts drew a groan from deep in his throat.

Hands slid under her t-shirt and soft skin met his fingers. They followed that trail of skin until they met lace. He paused, waiting for her to protest. Expecting her to tell him to stop.

Especially when she broke their kiss.

She smiled at him, that sweet smile that had his blood churning. "Don't stop," she whispered.

"Shan." His voice sounded gruff, like he'd forgotten how to speak. With her kissing him like that, maybe he had. "Are you sure?"

Instead of answering, she sat upright. His erection fit between the V of her legs oh-so-right. It was all he could do not to swallow his tongue. God, he wanted her so bad. But he didn't want to push her into something she didn't feel.

In one swift motion, her thumbs hooked the hem of her shirt, and she swept it over her head. White lace gleamed in the faint streetlight streaming through the window pane. White lace that cupped her perfectly.

"Touch me."

That was all the permission he needed. With his index fingers, he traced the patterns in the lace. Her nipples budded under his touch. Her soft pants encouraged his exploration. Tremors shook her thigh muscles, clenching his waist in a comfortable tightness. Her body rocked against his, a slow rhythm that promised so much.

"Jamal." His name was a word, a prayer, a command all at once.

His hands clasped her waist, tugging her closer so he could reach her bra clasp. Lace slipped from her breasts, revealing her perfection.

He sat and his mouth dipped to take the golden flesh offered. A soft moan was his reward. A hint of salt and the sweetness that could only be Shan filled his taste buds. Her body arched, offering him everything he'd dreamed of.

His attention turned to the other nipple, a long, slow lick tracing the hard bud. The motion of her hips grew more urgent. God, he wanted to bury himself deep in her, but dammit, he wanted this first time to be special.

He pulled away, more to keep himself from exploding prematurely, when a flash drew his attention to the window.

A white face framed by white hair. Crimson eyes stared at them. A lipless mouth pulled back in a snarl, revealing sharp white teeth. Ice gripped Jamal when he recognized the face.

Mark Li.

Chapter 4

Shan's blood-curdling scream split the night.

Jamal tossed her off his lap. He'd apologize later. Right before he apologized to Rain for not believing her freaky story.

He rolled off the bed, pulling the sword through the slit Tom had insisted he keep open. When he gained his feet, the ghost face was gone. But a flash of movement and the clang of iron said, whatever that thing was, it headed for the roof.

It took precious seconds to open the window and climb out. Long enough that he only caught a glimpse of a foot at the top of the fire escape. Thigh muscles caught fire as he clambered up the steps.

When he reached the roof, a figure in dark rags stood at the opposite edge. It looked over its shoulder at him.

Definitely asshat's face, but now he looked like something out of a horror flick.

Crimson eyes shot hate. A growl thrummed under the sounds of traffic. And through it all, the blade hummed a deep bass note in Jamal's hand.

Sword raised, he took a step toward the thing Mark Li had become. The growl turned to a hiss of frustration. The *kiang shi* seemed to shrink inside itself.

Then it leapt.

The hand holding the sword dropped as Jamal waited for the sickening plummet of the thing to the pavement below. Instead, the *kiang shi* landed on the roof of the next tenement. It glanced back and gave another odd hissing growl. Then it ran. Another graceful leap.

Jamal watched as the thing hopscotched from building to building until the white hair disappeared. He shook his head. "What the fuck" didn't come remotely close to dealing with what he just saw.

When Jamal climbed back through Shan's window, she huddled against the headboard in a tight ball. She'd had the presence of mind to turn on a light, but her lithe body shook violently. The pupils were so wide that her eyes looked black under the bedside lamp.

Damn, she was in shock.

"Shan."

Nothing.

He whispered her name again. Still nothing.

After closing and locking the window, he crossed to the bed and stowed the sword back in the bat bag. This was bad. Should he call an ambulance?

When his hand touched her shoulder, she jerked. The look of fear tore at his heart. "Shan, we've got to get you to a doctor."

"No."

Her cell phone lay on the nightstand. Mrs. Wong's number was programmed in the speed dial. He reached across Shan, only to have her hand clamp on his.

"No. They won't believe us," she whispered.

"Shan . . ."

"Just hold me, Jamal." She licked her lips and looked at him. "Please."

The pleading was too much. He managed to pull the covers over her semi-naked body before lying on top of the duvet next to her. She huddled close to him, her head in the crook of his shoulder. Damp hair tickled his neck as he held her. As many times as he dreamt of Shan in his arms, this was so not how he'd pictured it.

Slowly, the violent shaking calmed and stopped. Neither of them spoke. And they were awake long after Jamal heard Dr. and Mrs. Wong come home and go to bed.

"What the hell are you doing in my daughter's room?"

Jamal blinked gummy eyes and tried to identify the male voice that woke him.

Someone's fist grabbed his t-shirt and yanked. He landed ass-first on hardwood.

"Dad!"

Shan's shriek increased the pounding behind his eyes. He'd stayed awake until the first rays of dawn had lit her room. If the *kiang shi* had been the figure he'd seen in the alley yesterday, then daylight was obviously not its friend. But grabbing a few minutes of shut-eye had been a mistake, judging from the tight grip Dr. Wong had on his shirt.

Okay, he hadn't wanted to disturb Shan. Enjoyed the glorious spread of ebony hair across his chest a little too much.

"You come into my home throwing accusations at a dead boy, and then I find you here? With my daughter practically naked?" Dr. Wong's other fist drew back.

"Dad, no!"

Jamal closed his eyes and waited for the blow. Damn, he knew how this looked. How close he and Shan had actually come. If it were his daughter, he'd be kicking some ass, too.

"Chen, *tingzh*."

At the sharp command, one eye popped open. Shan's mother and grand-mother stood in the doorway to Shan's room. More rapid fire Chinese issued from Grandmother Wong to her son. Disbelief replaced the fury in his face.

Then she turned to Jamal and switched to English. "It came last night, did it not?"

He nodded as best he could with Dr. Wong's clenched hand under his neck. "Yes, ma'am. About sunset. It jumped to the next apartment building before I could catch it."

Grandmother Wong gave a curt nod and left the room.

Shan's dad looked a little dubious at whatever story he'd been given, but he released his hold on Jamal's shirt.

Mrs. Wong wasn't fooled at all from the gleam in her eye. "Why don't you two wash up, and I'll make you some breakfast."

"What were you thinking last night, boy?"

Another smack landed on the back of Jamal's head as he knelt by the bookshelves. God, what he wouldn't give for a customer to come into Morrigan's Cauldron just so Mom would stop hitting him every time she walked by. Not that the blows hurt, but they didn't help his sleep-deprivation headache.

"I thought I taught you better."

Smack.

"You did, Mom." He checked off a few more items on the book inventory. Just his luck that same morning of the fiasco at the Wongs' apartment, he opened with his mother. And of course, Shan's grandmother had come over once Mom had flipped the sign, spilled the truth and ruined his carefully constructed story of spending the night at Tyson's place.

"The last thing you need is to knock up a girl." *Smack.*

"I know, Mom." He gritted his teeth and checked off the last reference guides on the bottom shelf.

The door bell tinkled in greeting. He looked up hopefully, but it was Tom's grinning face that met him. He'd seen more humor from Tom in the last two days than he had in the last two years. Crap. Did everyone in the store have to know what happened?

Jamal rose and stretched, ignoring Tom.

Mom hadn't even acknowledged the other man's entrance, her wrath still focused on something he hadn't even had a chance to do. "With you both starting college this year, the last thing either of you need is a baby."

He gently caught her arm in mid-swing and gazed into her eyes. It'd been a long time since he'd seen that hurt look. And he knew most of it had nothing to do with him.

"I'm not my father. And nothing happened last night."

A soft rumble of masculine laughter came from the register. "Not for lack of trying, I hear," Tom said.

Mom's eyes squinted as she looked up at Jamal. He released his hold on her. For a second, it looked like she'd smack him anyway, but her arm lowered.

Jamal shot a glare at Tom. "You're not helping." The older man seemed to find the situation even funnier.

"It's the lying that bothers me." Old pain laced Mom's voice.

Damn. He'd promised himself years ago that he'd never make her sound like that. "I'm sorry, Mom. I shouldn't have."

Tom's cough interrupted the uncomfortable conversation. "Aren't you going to miss your class, Phylicia?"

She glanced at her watch. "Oh, crap. And I've got a test too." An index finger shook under Jamal's nose. "Don't think this conversation is over, young man."

"Wouldn't dream of it."

A fierce hug enveloped him. "Just make sure you use protection," she whispered.

"Mo-o-om." It was bad enough when he'd found the foil packs Tom had slipped into the bag with the sword. Thank god Dr. Wong hadn't seen them, or he'd be in the morgue with Mark.

That thought sobered him from the token embarrassment. Both he and Tom watched as Mom slung her backpack over her shoulder before she charged out the door and down the street.

"Tell me about last night." Tom's gruff voice broke Jamal's guilt over hurting his mom.

He turned to the older man. "I think you know enough."

"No. The *kiang shi*. What happened?"

He spilled the story, well, the edited version. The version where Shan still had her clothes on, anyway. But Tom seemed more concerned about Zombie Mark. He kept asking specific questions. Teeth, claws, speed, strength.

Damn, by the time Tom was done, Jamal felt like he'd taken a beating.

Tom ran a hand over his jaw a couple of times before he said, "As soon as Rain gets here, we'll head over to the gym. I know a few tricks that might help."

"Do you really think he'll come back?" Worry nibbled under Jamal's headache. Shan had been so freaked-out last night.

"You were making out with the woman Mark considered his." Tom's hand continued to rub his jaw line. "If I were a betting man, I'd say his appearance tonight is a sure thing."

❖

Hours later, Jamal knocked on the Wongs' door. The canvas bag shifted, almost like the sword knew where it was, what was expected. He hoisted the strap back in place and knocked again.

After Tom had put him through his paces at the gym, including a round with live steel in guards, Rain had marched him up to the apartment over the store for a shower and a nap. When he woke, she had dinner for the three of them ready. Steak, new red potatoes, greens. He wasn't sure if he was supposed to be a hero on a mission or a condemned man.

Mrs. Wong opened the door with a big grin and another hug. Was the woman possessed?

As he stepped inside, Shan's smile of greeting faded when she caught sight of the bag slung over his shoulder. God, how he wanted to kiss away that bleak look, but her father stood behind her. Instead, he settled on "Hi."

Then Jamal realized what was wrong with Dr. Wong. Scrubs. Shan's dad may have been the top heart surgeon in the tristate area, but he never wore scrubs in public, much less his home.

Between Zombie Mark, her mom's affectionate turn, and her dad's weird state of dress, it was a wonder Shan hadn't gone off the deep end.

Dr. Wong crossed his arms and continued to glare at Jamal. "You know I don't believe your story."

The jolt at his word being questioned was squelched by common sense. He hadn't believed Rain's story either. Not until the evidence peeped at him and Shan, and he chased it to the roof last night. "What about Shan's or your mother's? Are you willing to bet your daughter's life that we're wrong?"

His quiet certainty sent a glimmer of unease through Dr. Wong's eyes.

Mrs. Wong closed the door. "Would you like a soda, Jamal?" Her question broke the tension in the living room.

"Sure."

She'd only taken a step when the intercom buzzed. She twisted and punched the button. "Yes?"

A tinny version of Tyson's voice rattled through the speaker. "Mrs. Wong? There's a couple of cops down here to see Shan. Something about a body missing from the morgue."

Chapter 5

Jamal clenched his jaw to keep from laughing at the incredulous expression on Dr. Wong's face.

However, anger clouded Mrs. Wong's features. "Do they have a warrant?"

The speaker crackled, then another voice spoke. "This is Detective Jensen, ma'am. I need to ask your daughter about Mark Li."

Mrs. Wong jabbed the button again. "Send them up, Tyson." She turned to Shan. "Do not say a word while they're here. Understand?" Then she eyed Jamal. "If I or the detectives ask you a question, answer only the question. Do not embellish." Even though she was as tiny as Shan, Mrs. Wong stepped forward, tilted her head and gave him a look that should have burned out his retinas. "Do you understand me, Jamal Washington?"

He swallowed hard. "Yes, ma'am." Shan's mom gave new meaning to the term, "tiger mom."

Dr. Wong's arms dropped, but his fists clenched at his sides. "Jennifer, you can't—"

She stepped to him and laid a hand on his shoulder. "Chen, let me handle this. If you can't hold your temper, I need you to leave. You won't be helping Shan by berating the police." She smiled, a look that would have fit on a tiger mom about to eat a baby. "This is my area. Trust me."

Shan's dad stared at a blank spot on the wall for a few seconds before he gave a curt nod.

Shan leaned on the balcony railing and sucked in a deep lungful of air. Despite the setting sun, simmering heat still hung over the city. Heat that matched the anger that still simmered in her belly. Anger at herself for not standing up to Mark and his bullying months ago, for not telling her parents what he did to her, and—worst of all—for not acknowledging her feelings for the man next to her. All of this craziness could have been avoided if she'd just been honest with herself.

"Holy shit. Remind me to never get on your mom's bad side." Jamal glanced through the French doors to where her parents sat on the couch, talking.

Mom had lit into the two detectives from the minute she'd opened the door. By the time she was finished, she had a complaint filed against Mark's parents for harassment.

"She means well." Shan gave a sad, ironic laugh. "I know this sounds bizarre, but I actually understand Mark a little better now."

Jamal shot her that irritated look he always did whenever her former boyfriend came up in conversation. "Sympathy for the dead ex? The one who's now stalking you, by the way."

She leaned a little closer. As much as she wanted to kiss Jamal, she didn't dare with the poisonous looks Dad kept shooting at him through the window. The last thing any of them need was for Dad to push Jamal over the edge of the balcony.

"Think about how Mark's parents are reacting to all this. Can you imagine the pressure they must have put on him?" Since Grandmother had told her to stay home until the *kiang shi* had been dealt with, she'd spent the day on the internet researching Chinese lore. "Suicide over a break-up is bad enough, but to kill yourself in order to become a monster? That's twisted." She shook her head. "He needed therapy when he was still alive, and I was too scared to admit that."

Jamal reached over and smoothed a lock away from her cheek. "He doesn't deserve your compassion."

She reached up and held his hand to her face. A different kind of heat spread along her nerves and pooled deep inside her. "I didn't do him any favors by keeping silent. If I'd stood up to him, maybe he could have gotten some help."

The grimace on Jamal's face told her exactly what he thought of that idea. She didn't want to dwell on her own shortcomings. A change of subject was needed.

"At least, Dad agreed to you spending the night here." She grinned.

Jamal rolled his eyes. "Yeah. On one of the couches." He glanced through the French doors. "Your wa-a-ay too small couches."

The heat in her belly turned to fluttering butterflies. "After Mom and Dad are asleep, come to my room."

An answering flame ignited behind his espresso eyes. "Shan . . ."

The French door creaked, and Mom's voice interrupted the delicious tension. "Time to come in, you two. We need to lock up for the night."

The kitchen light sent a dim glow into the living room as they followed her inside. Enough light to reflect off white hair in the hallway. The ragged figure clung to the ceiling. Crimson eyes fixed on Shan.

Panic grabbed her by the throat, but this time it was Mom who screamed.

Everything turned into a blur. Jamal dove for his canvas bag behind the couch furthest from the door. The *kiang shi* crawled into the living room and dropped to the floor. Fear froze Shan in place.

Until Dad stepped between her and the creature.

"Dad, no!"

The *kiang shi* launched itself, claws extended. Blood exploded with its strike. Hot, sticky drops hit Shan's cheek. Dad crumpled, an ugly gash across his neck leaking his life.

The sight broke the spell. Hurting her was one thing. But not her family . . .

Mom's manicured hands grabbed her wrist and yanked. Shan had never raised a hand against anyone, but now? Now wasn't the time to be gentle. Mark would kill everyone she loved to get to her.

Shan shoved her mom. Hard.

Between the surprise and the stilettos on polished hardwood, Mom stumbled and slid into the ugly antique chair by the fireplace. Apology later. Shan raced for the closet. The bat. Dammit, she needed her baseball bat.

She whirled around, aluminum solid in her two-handed grip. Jamal had the sword out, but Mark ducked under the blade. *Dammit, it's not Mark. Not anymore.* He leapt straight for Jamal's face. Jamal swung.

The *kiang shi* contorted in ways no human body could to avoid the sword. Shan's stomach churned at the sight. It landed on the back of the couch, then leapt straight up. Claws dug into the ceiling plaster. Crimson eyes met hers once more. The thing scrabbled across the ceiling toward her. Fast. Like something out of a horror movie.

Keep you eyes open. No different than a 90 mile per hour pitch. Just like practice.

The thing that used to be Mark dropped from the ceiling. Hips swiveled and she swung with everything she had. The bat connected with its head. It flipped in mid-air with the force of her strike and landed with a thud. Was it dead?

Crimson eyes blinked open. Sharp, white teeth shone as it grinned at her with terrible humor.

Then Jamal was next to her, the sword swinging down. The *kiang shi* threw up an arm to block the blow. A godawful screech rent the air.

Shan let go of the bat and slapped hands over her ears to block the inhuman sound. Except the cry didn't come from the *kiang shi*.

No, it couldn't have possibly come from the sword.

Then the ragged figure was up, running, the damaged arm dangling behind. It jumped through the glass of one of the French doors and disappeared from sight. Shards tinkled as they fell.

"Chen?"

Mom's tear-filled voice broke through Shan's adrenaline-charged thoughts. *Dad?*

Mom already had her blouse off and wadded it against Dad's neck. Night had fallen, but there was enough light to see the dark, dark stain on the rug by Mom's knees.

Shan took a step forward. "Dad?"

A fierceness filled Mom's face despite the tears streaming down her cheeks. "Shan, hand me the phone, then I need you to leave."

Leave?

"Jamal, take the fire escape. Get her somewhere safe." A sob escaped from Mom. A matching lump filled Shan's throat. "B-before the ambulance and police get here."

Jamal stepped closer. A warm, reassuring palm rested on Shan's shoulder. "Mrs. Wong—"

"I'm not losing both of them, Jamal. Do as I say!"

Shan felt Jamal jump at the same time her body jerked. She snatched the portable phone and crossed to hand it to Mom. Blood had already soaked the white cotton blouse pressed against Dad's wound.

"Good girl," Mom whispered. "Now, go. I'll call when I can."

Shan ran for her room, Jamal on her heels. The sword was already back in its canvas bag. From the living room, Mom's voice rattled off the address to the 9-1-1 operator. Shan grabbed her phone and followed Jamal to the window. He raised the sash and looked around before he helped her through.

They scrambled down the three flights of ladders. The clanging of metal couldn't drown out the pounding of her heart. Dad couldn't die. He just couldn't. Not like this.

Jamal caught her when she jumped from the bottom rung. Her body slid against his as he lowered her to the pavement. *Please, please let Dad be okay.*

A few blocks away, sirens wailed. The sound grew steadily closer. Jamal grabbed her hand and tugged her toward the opposite end of the alley.

She glanced up at him as they jogged. "Where should we go?"

A determined look filled his dark features. "The safest place I know."

Chapter 6

Jamal paced Adrian's living room as he relayed the night's events over the phone to Rain. Given the shop owner's peculiar abilities, the apartment above the store was the safest place to stay and still keep innocent folks out of harm's way. He should be exhausted as hell, but the rush of energy he'd felt when he picked up the sword and tried to kill the *kiang shi* refused to leave him.

Rain made a clucking sound over the receiver. "I doubt it makes another appearance tonight. Sounds like between the two of you, it'll find a quiet hole to recover before it tries for Shan again."

Jamal glanced at Shan, who curled up on the black couch with a purple pillow clutched against her chest. Damn, he was so proud of her. She hadn't frozen like she had when the *kiang shi* showed up last night. That swing of hers should have taken its head off.

His eyes met hers. Her intense gaze meant she was paying close attention to his conversation.

Too close. Last thing he wanted was for her to think he was a fruitcake.

He turned away from her and lowered his voice. "What about the *special* protections?"

A sigh whistled through the receiver. "I'll come in early and reinforce the building's wards, but you should be fine tonight as long as you stay in the apartment."

"You sure?"

Rain's soft chuckle filled his ear. "You don't trust me with your life?"

"It's Shan's life I'm not taking chances on, Rain," he bit out. "That thing already got into the Wongs' apartment."

"Don't take that tone with me, young man." The reprimand cut, but not deep enough to penetrate through the black ball of fear in his gut. His memory replayed the *kiang shi*'s claws slicing Dr. Wong's flesh like an overripe peach. It could be Shan lying in that operating room.

Or worse.

Jamal took a deep breath and squeezed his eyes shut. "I'm sorry. It's just . . . you didn't see what this thing did to Shan's dad." The replay of events in his own head sent fear rippling through his gut. He could only imagine what Shan was feeling.

"Mark had been welcomed into their home while he was alive. Since his soul hasn't left his body, the invitation was still valid. Trust me, the *kiang shi* can't get into the store or apartment unless one of you asks him in."

There were voices in the background, but Jamal couldn't make out the words. Then Rain spoke again. "I'll stay with Jennifer until Chen is out of surgery. Call your mother, Jamal. And don't lie to her this time." The other phone clicked and a buzzing filled the receiver. He thumbed the red button to end the call, set the phone on the coffee table, and flopped on the couch. The thought of dealing with his mom right now appealed about as much as a full-body wax.

Shan nudged him with a bare toe. Pink polish. He liked it. A lot.

"And . . ." she prompted.

"Rain and your grandparents are already at the hospital with your mom. Your dad's still in surgery."

She nodded, a sad look on her face. Nope, definitely not freaking like she had last night. His practical Shan was back.

He stretched an arm along the back of the couch. As much as he wanted to touch her, he wasn't sure if it was the right thing. He didn't want her to think he was pressuring her. Not with an undead ex stalking her. Not with her dad fighting for his life on an operating table.

His gesture must have been good enough. Shan scooted across the cushions to cuddle against his ribs. His arm automatically fell around her, and her head nestled in the crook of his shoulder.

The soft scent of jasmine tickled his nose. He pulled her tighter and kissed the top of her hair. "He'll be fine. Your dad's a fighter."

Silence filled the small apartment for a long time. He wasn't about to move if she'd fallen asleep, but her small hand reached for his chest.

"We need to stop this thing," she whispered. "Before it hurts someone else."

A bitter laugh rumbled in his throat. "It's not like we didn't try tonight."

She twisted to face him. "What's that sword of yours made of?"

He frowned, not sure how much to tell her. It's not like Rain or Tom said not to, but... *What do you know about the Sword of Lugh?* He shuddered. Tom couldn't have been serious, could he?

"Some sort of silver alloy, I think. The handle was tarnished when Rain gave it to me." But the blade itself? Silver couldn't cut through skin and bone the way this weapon had. And he was pretty sure, even with the lack of light in the Wongs' apartment, that only a sliver of flesh kept the arm connected to the *kiang shi*'s body. And what the hell was that sound when he'd struck the monster? It seemed to come from the sword, not the thing that used to be Mark Li.

Shan's eyes lit up the same way they did when she chased the answer to a calculus problem. "I did some research today. According to Tao tradition, you need a wooden sword or one made of copper coins connected with red thread to stop a *kiang shi*."

"Get real, girl! How are a bunch of pennies going to cut through that monster?"

She smacked his chest lightly. "At least I was trying to do something constructive." The hand on his chest made a fist, and she shifted until her chin rested on it. "Supposedly, a *kiang shi* can also be cremated or buried. Water can't destroy it, but it can't cross a river or a stream." She grinned up at him. "Not that I'm advocating a swim in the Hudson."

With more of her delicious weight on him, he swallowed a groan. Dammit, he was trying real hard to be a gentleman. If he didn't do something soon, she'd find out how much he wasn't thinking about the *kiang shi* or her dad.

Instead, he concentrated on what she was saying. "So a *kiang shi*'s vulnerable to the five elements of Chinese lore?" Five elements. A thread of something Rain had said once teased the back of his mind.

She blinked in surprise. "Yes." Then her eyes narrowed. "How did you—"

"Scooch over." When she sat upright, he stood. "Let me go find something. I'll be right back."

✦

Minutes later, Shan tensed when she heard the lock on the door leading to the apartment *snick* open. Nothing was in reach she could use as a weapon.

A bunch of throw pillows wouldn't hurt the *kiang shi* no matter how hard she threw them. Her eyes fell on the canvas bag by the coffee table. There was always the sword. Maybe she couldn't kill it, but it may think twice if it saw she was armed.

She reached for the bag. A relieved exhale followed the sound of the door relocking and the familiar thump of Jamal's footsteps.

He appeared at the top of the steps. In his hands was a book, something that qualified as an antique, judging from the worn leathery cover. Gently turning pages, he crossed back to the couch and dropped next to her again. The pensive look on his face worried her.

She laid a hand on his shoulder. "What's wrong?"

He ran a hand over his hair.

"Jamal," she whispered, "there's nothing to be embarrassed about."

Worry flickered in his deep brown eyes, but she had the distinct impression it had nothing to do with the *kiang shi*. "Shan, I—"

The book was open to a picture. The method looked like a wood stamp technique, but the item itself was all too familiar.

Jamal's sword.

She sucked in a breath. The writing used the English alphabet, but none of the words made sense. "What language is this?"

"Irish Gaelic."

A wry smile tilted her lips. "And you're embarrassed because you can read this?"

His small chuckle shook his shoulder underneath her palm. "You gotta admit it's not a normal talent for a brother."

"I don't think of you as a brother." The deliberate misreading of his words slipped out before she could stop it. God, what did he think of her? Coming on to him while her dad was in surgery? To cover, she tapped the page with her free hand. "So, what does this say about your sword?"

"Western lore has its elements too. Earth, water, fire, air and spirit. When I was little, Rain told me a story once that the Tuatha de Danann—" He must have recognized the confusion on her face. "That's the Celtic gods. Anyway, they can't lie, but they gave humans the wrong order and symbols for the elements. That's why humans haven't mastered the magickal arts."

She cuddled close to him once more. The rise and fall of his deep voice was almost hypnotic.

He pointed to the woodprint. "In modern Wiccan practices, the sword represents air. But Rain showed me this book and said the element for the sword is actually fire." He shook his head. "I can't believe I forgot about this."

She ran her fingertips across his forearm, enjoying the prickle of his skin. Yeah, he couldn't hide his feelings anymore than she could. "Remember that field trip to the Museum of Natural Science our junior year? Didn't the Celts use bronze, too?"

"Bronze?" She could almost see the lightbulb clicking on over his head. "Yeah, maybe there's enough copper in the blade to affect the *kiang shi*." Then he shook his head again. "The blade's the wrong color for it to be bronze. Rain may have some daggers downstairs that have copper—"

She leaned closer to him, letting her breast brush his bicep. Touching wasn't enough. The need to kiss him grew. *Stupid hormones.* But the hormones overpowered the rational side of her brain. His warm breath brushed her skin as he tilted his head. So close.

Some Beyoncé song crashed through the mood. Jamal's cell phone.

He jumped up and snatched the phone. "Hey, Mom." A palm ran across his short hair.

Shan smothered her snicker in a pillow. Not soon enough from the irritated look he shot her.

"I was going to call you. We were scrounging something to eat." A pause. "Yes, Mom, I'll replace Adrian's groceries. I've got a question—" Jamal glanced at Shan and paced away before he raked a hand across his hair again.

She sucked in a deep breath. Why the hell was he being so secretive? Everyone in the Village knew Rain was a witch and Jamal's mom was her apprentice. He worked in an occult store, for cryin' out loud.

Leaning over the coffee table, she examined the book. The only word she could make out in the caption was "Lugh". There had been a sign down in the store about some festival with the same name tomorrow night. She flipped to the beginning of the book, but there was no copyright date. Of course not. Had Rain's family brought the book and the sword to the United States when they immigrated?

Her own pocket started warbling. She stood, pulled it out and checked the caller ID. Mom. Trepidation surrounded her heart and squeezed. *Please let it be good news.*

"Hey, Mom."

"Rain said you and Jamal are at her store."

"Yeah, we're fine." Shan hugged herself. Despite the heat, chills ran across her skin. She was sure she didn't want to hear the wrong answer, but she had to ask. "How's Dad?"

"He's out of surgery. They're keeping him in the critical care unit overnight because of the blood loss." A hitch like a swallowed sob echoed through the receiver.

Shan closed her eyes. *I should be there with her.*

"He'll be fine, honey." More sniffling sounds. Mom was crying.

Tears welled in Shan's eyes. "I'll come to the hospital. You shouldn't be alone."

"No!" came the sharp reply. "Your grandmother and Rain say it's safer for you to stay there tonight."

"Mom, I—"

"Stay where it's safe, Shan. Do you understand me?"

"Yeah, I understand." Muscles gave out and she collapsed on the couch. "Will you call me in the morning?"

"Yes," Mom whispered. A slight cough sounded tinny in the connection. "Get some sleep."

"I love you, Mom."

"We love you, too."

Shan thumbed the "End Call" icon and shoved the phone back in her pocket. Swiping away the tears that escaped with one hand, she pulled the book closer. Something about the sword looked familiar, and not just because Jamal carried the real life version.

"Mo-o-om!" Jamal's voice drew her attention away from the illustration. He shot her a nervous look. "I'll call you in the morning." He shoved a thumb against the screen to end the call.

Shan released the air she held. "What's wrong?"

"Nothing." Again, with the tell. "Rain called Mom." He snorted. "Mainly to make sure I spoke with Mom, but also to let her know your dad's out of surgery." Jamal sat down next to Shan and slid an arm around her. "I take it your call was your mom."

"Well, duh." The smile she attempted lasted less than a millisecond.

Another chuckle shook him. "You know, I've only heard you say 'I love you' to your family."

Is that what he wanted from her? She buried her head against Jamal's solid chest and closed her eyes. His arms enveloped her again, making her feel safe. Admitting she liked him a lot, even lusted after him, was one thing, but after her ex, could she really trust her feelings?

"I never said it to Mark." It was still hard talking about him, no matter how much she tried to push him out of her head.

"Not that I ever heard." There was a trace of skepticism in Jamal's voice.

"I *never* said it. I never felt it either. He was . . . convenient." Prickling burned behind her eyelids, but she swallowed hard and forced the fear down. Dammit, she was through crying because of her ex.

"Convenient? Convenient how?"

It was so much easier to confess her issues if she kept her eyes closed. "I thought he was more acceptable to my parents."

His exhalation ruffled her bangs against her forehead. "I know your parents expect a lot, but I never got the impression they were . . ."

"Racist?"

"Yeah."

An ironic laugh escaped. "Thanks. Mom also pointed out how stupid I was being yesterday." Wetness escaped from beneath her eyelids despite her best efforts.

"Hey, you okay?" he said. His fingers toyed with her hair.

She nodded and inhaled what should have been a cleansing breath, only to drown in another set of emotions. The herbal spice of Jamal's soap, along with the scent that was just him, filled her nose, her mind, her heart. The combination brought her back to her original plan for the night. And the circumstances were far more private than she expected.

Except she'd never seduced a guy before.

Last night had ended in disaster, and she hadn't even gotten as far as taking off any of her clothes when the *kiang shi* had shown up at her parents' apartment tonight. She finally got a clue about her own feelings, but the chance she wouldn't have an opportunity to act on them sent a sharp jab in her soul.

"I don't want to die a virgin."

His muscles beneath her cheek quivered. Then Jamal's chest shook in earnest and the laughter exploded.

Ah, crap. I said that out loud. Heat rushed to her cheeks. So much for subtlety. "It isn't that funny." She gave his stomach a light slap.

"That's supposed to be my line," he said between bouts of chuckling.

What? She sat upright and stared at him. "But you and Amy Crawley..."

He shook his head, eyes still twinkling. "She has a thing for Madison Fisher, but her parents would have a fit if they knew she was a lesbian. Amy would lose her trust fund." A shrug lifted his shoulders. "I didn't mind being her beard."

"So you mean you're..."

He twined the fingers of his free hand through hers. Seriousness and passion filled his expression. "I want my first time to be with the right woman."

Her heart skipped a beat. He had waited for her. Somehow that meant more than the flowers or stuffed animals she received from past boyfriends.

Shan didn't resist when he cupped her head and drew her closer. The kiss started as a gentle exploration. Maybe they both expected another interruption.

Then boldness seized her. She ran her tongue between his lips.

That was all the invitation he needed. The kiss deepened. Electricity arched between them, sending all kinds of interesting signals south. His fingers tangled in her hair, tugging her closer.

Somehow, she climbed into his lap without breaking contact. His hand released hers and she laid her palms against his chest. The rapid beat of his heart matched the throb deep inside of her.

Palms slid under her t-shirt, stroked her waist, her back, her stomach. God, how she wanted them higher, but he seemed to take his dear sweet time. She pressed closer. The hard length of his erection intensified the need to feel him, all of him.

Jamal's hands stopped their exquisite exploration, grabbed her thighs, and pushed her back a fraction of an inch. Teasing distance. "Whoa, girl."

Mortification replaced the pleasure in her synapses. "Wh-wh-what? Did I do something wrong?" The bad kind of heat flooded her cheeks.

"No, baby." He grinned at her. "It's just . . . if you keep that up, I'll be done before we get started."

"Oh." Relief released the hold embarrassment had on her muscles. She giggled. "Sorry."

He leaned his forehead against hers. "Nothing to be sorry about. Let's go to the bedroom and take our time." He kissed her. "We've got all night." More kisses trailed across her cheek, down her neck, hitting a spot that made her shiver in delight. "I want you to enjoy this."

She nodded and climbed off his lap. He slipped his fingers between hers once more. They had only taken two steps when the rational side of her brain pointed out a necessary fact.

"Oh, fuck!"

He looked over his shoulder. Both eyebrows rose as he peered at her. "I was actually going to refer to this as something else."

"No." She squeezed her eyes shut in irritation. "I left the condoms Mom gave me at our place."

At his laughter, her eyes popped open. "This isn't funny either. We shouldn't have sex without protection."

He shook his head. Between deep throaty chuckles, he said, "The funny part is your mom giving you rubbers."

His laughter stopped abruptly and the anti-Mark expression returned. "She didn't get them because you and . . ."

She blinked. He couldn't be serious. "No!" His jealousy and her mom's sudden turn-around hit her own funny bone, and she smiled. "No. She didn't even bring sex up until she . . ." A giggle escaped. "Until she made me admit I liked you."

"Your mom knows." He palmed his face.

Another giggle. "It could be worse. Rain and Grandmother could have supplied us."

He pulled her gently to where the canvas bat bag lay on the carpet. "The only reason I don't have any from Adrian is because he's on vacation."

Heat flooded everything, not just her cheeks. "Rain and Grandmother didn't actually . . . ?"

A wry smile tugged the corners of his mouth. "No, but only because they're making sure your parents are okay." He picked up the bag. "The ones in here are courtesy of Tom."

It took some effort to close her mouth. "Tom? Seriously?" The man was so freaking quiet, rarely joked, and just . . .

"Seriously." Jamal's smile faded. "Look if you don't want—"

Shan stepped closer. Heat radiated from him, surrounding her, pulling her into him. Wrapping her arms around his waist, she smiled up at him. "I want."

He bent, and if the first kiss tonight had been hot, this one was positively volcanic. Sensation and anticipation created a delightful tingle across every nerve ending. A soft whimper filled her ears. Hers. She pressed closer, and he edged backward, drawing her further down the short hallway.

There was a dull thud and then they were falling. She landed on top of him with a gentle bounce that broke the kiss. She took in the surroundings.

Oh yeah. The bedroom.

His warm hands stroked her waist, her back, distracting her from anything else but his skin on hers. And that's what she couldn't get enough of.

His lips traveled to her neck, little nibbles that set every nerve ending on alert. His fingers slid up the front of her tee. He brushed the hardened tips of her breasts through her bra. The satin did nothing to dull the sensation. His touch was almost enough to send her over the edge . . .

The heated caresses disappeared, and she almost cried out in protest. He sat, pushing her upright. A soft *click*, a tug, and her t-shirt and bra disappeared. Cool air stroked her back. Nipples tightened, demanding relief.

Except he did nothing. His eyes roamed over her exposed flesh.

The urge to cover herself hit Shan hard. "Jamal?"

His large palm cupped her cheek. His eyes so filled with emotion, they appeared black. "You are so damn beautiful."

Relief and desire swirled through her. All doubt disappeared when his head dipped. Warm and wet, his mouth covered her nipple. His tongue swirled the tip, and the sensation jolted straight to her core. Her back arched. She'd do anything for that feeling to go on and on.

A *snap* followed by *zzzz* of the zipper. Then his huge hands slid beneath her shorts and . . .

Jamal broke their kiss and leaned back. One of his eyebrows climbed his forehead. "A thong?" A finger traced the thin line of fabric along her crevice.

She let a sly smile cross her lips and she kneaded muscles through his gray t-shirt. "You don't like thongs?"

A smoldering look filled his eyes. "I'd like to see you in it." She climbed to her feet and slid off her shorts. This time no weirdness intruded. Standing before Jamal, clad only in a pink satin thong and matching nail polish, she felt wanton, desirable. Loved.

Her heart gave a funny leap. Yes, she could finally admit it. At least to herself. She wanted the first time to be with someone who wanted *her*, not for the power he had over her. Someone who loved her.

He slipped his thumbs under the thin strips of fabric at her waist and tugged her between the vee of his legs. Slowly, gently, he eased the wisp down her thighs, her calves. She stepped out of them and stood before him. Naked. There was no embarrassment, no shame.

His fingers clenched on his jeans-clad thighs. Almost like he was afraid to touch her. Was that the reason for his question in the living room? Was he scared?

She rested her palms on his face. Stubble tickled her skin. "We don't have to do this. Not now. Not if you don't want to." Despite her attempt at rationality, her heart froze.

A hoarse laugh erupted from him. He pulled her right hand from his cheek and rested it on the large bulge under the zipper of his jeans. "You think I don't want you?" He swallowed hard. "I've been dreaming about you, about this..."

"Then touch me." She licked her lower lip as she saw passion and hesitancy war in his eyes. "Please."

His hand moved, paused, then an index finger brushed her lower lips.

The bolt of sensation ripped through her. She clutched his shoulders to stay upright under the onslaught.

Jamal continued his exploration of her slick folds. Each stroke raised the energy level flooding her nerves. Then he hit her clit and everything exploded.

Muscles shuddered and collapsed. He caught her, pulled her back onto his lap, and all the time, he continued stroking that button of pleasure.

"Jamal, oh god, please... don't... stop..." He didn't, and another orgasm sent a tidal wave of pleasure shooting through every nerve ending.

When the trembling finally slowed, she watched his cocky smile through half-lidded eyes. "Rather proud of yourself, aren't you?"

His smile widened. "A little. Reality is usually different than what the book says. But from your reaction, I think I did okay."

"Book?"

With his hands full of her, he couldn't run a palm over his hair. "I snuck out a copy of the Kama Sutra that Rain sells."

Dang, he did all that for her? She ran a finger down his aquiline nose. "I think you studied enough. Now you're making me feel inadequate."

"Well, it said, uh, that . . ."

The heat coming from his arms rose an appreciable notch. His eyes zoomed all over the room. And here she thought she would be the nervous one. She nuzzled his neck to break his mood. Otherwise, this was over before they had begun.

His soft moan when she slicked her tongue around the rim of his ear said her plan was working.

"You mean, you wanted to make sure this was good for me," she whispered. She placed her hand over his and guided it back between her legs. "But you already know how wet I am." She pressed his fingers against her slick folds and traced circles with them. "This is what you do to me. I want this to be good for you, too."

When he continued the strokes, she lifted his tee out of the way and unbuttoned his jeans. The length of him stretched the elastic of his dark blue briefs. "I need you naked."

He met her gaze this time, all trepidation gone, and nodded.

She slid from his lap and stood. Jamal followed suit, but she realized her mistake as soon as she reached for his tee. There was no freakin' way she'd get it over his head while standing now that he was nearly a foot taller than her.

He grinned. "Why don't I take care of this?" His shirt disappeared while she pushed his jeans and underwear down.

Only to be stymied by his shoes when she knelt down.

Shan couldn't help it. The giggles just rolled out of her.

"You know a woman laughing when she's eye-level with a guy's equipment does not instill confidence."

She shook her head. "It's not that. I'm really bad at this seduction thing."

His touch brushed the top of her head. "You're just fine."

The twinkle in his eye made her bold. She ran her fingers along the vein that traveled his erection from base to tip. His sharp inhalation made her decision. Her tongue traced the same path her fingers had.

"Shan?"

The tip of her tongue swirled around the head. His grip on her chin stopped the second round.

"Seriously, girl, I need to get my clothes off."

Jamal pulled her to her feet, then shed what was left of his clothing in record time. She crawled into the bed while he reached in the canvas bag.

"May I?" She held out her hand as he slid in next to her.

White teeth flashed. "Ladies first."

She hesitated as he handed her the condom and took a really good look. Damn, his erection was as big as the rest of him.

His now-free hands touched, caressed, made her feel so good. "Shan?"

What if the reality didn't live up to her vivid imagination? A few rapid blinks and a deep breath. She ripped the foil packet. No, this was what she'd wanted for longer than she cared to admit. Carefully, she rolled the latex down the length of him

She reclined on the bed as he positioned himself between her legs. An odd mixture of hard and soft pressed against her opening. His hands braced on either side of her.

"Shan, look at me."

Her eyes met his chocolate brown ones.

Pressure.

She gasped. He filled and stretched her. It was scary. It was incredible. All at the same time.

"You okay?"

She nodded, blinking away the threatening tears.

He withdrew, inch by inch, teasing the pleasure out of her. Then, in again, just as slowly.

Her legs wrapped around his waist of their own volition. Her hands stroked his skin, his hair.

In. Out.

New pressure built inside of her. A familiar heaviness filled her, growing. And every time he withdrew, he hit a spot that ramped the tingling that raced along her nerves and muscles.

"Shan, honey, I can't—"

She cupped his face. "Let go, baby. Let go."

He plunged into her once. Twice. On the third, he stiffened, groaned, and the pulse of his release set off her own explosion. She shuddered as the orgasm seized every muscle with pleasure. Oh god, this was so-o-o much better than her imagination.

His weight crumpled around her like a comforter. Not too heavy. Warm. Cozy. Someone she wanted to curl up with forever.

Jamal raised up on his elbows. "You okay?"

She nodded. "Yeah."

His hand brushed a lock of hair from her face. "I didn't hurt you?"

The worried expression on his face melted her heart. "I'm fine, baby. Just fine."

A grin lit his face. "How fine?"

Her smile answered his. "Fine enough that I want to do this again."

He rolled his eyes. "I don't mean to be rude, but I gotta take care of this condom first."

At her nod, he withdrew. She already missed the feel of him inside of her. "Shit!"

Her languid mood disappeared. "Wha—"

But he'd already swept her into his arms. "Oh, god, I'm sorry. I wasn't thinking."

She wrapped her arms around his neck and giggled as he strode into the bathroom. "You're not supposed to do a lot of thinking during sex."

He deposited her on the counter. When he stepped back, she saw the reason for his anxiety. He removed the blood-stained condom and grabbed a washcloth from the shelf above the toilet.

"Jamal." She laid a hand on his arm as he turned on the faucet and ran the washcloth under the water. "I'm okay."

Worried eyes met hers. "You sure?"

"Yes." She shrugged. "It sometimes happens the first time."

No words answered her. Instead, he spread her knees apart. Cool, wet terrycloth met overheated flesh. With gentle strokes, he cleaned her inner lips, stopping every few minutes to rinse the washcloth with cold water.

Except each touch only inflamed her nerve endings. Everything swelled with desire until she couldn't keep her hips still.

He jerked back. "What is it? Am I hurting you?"

She reached for his hands and pulled him closer. "No, baby, just the opposite."

His face lit in a wicked-ass grin. "So I turn you on by bathing you?"

She couldn't help returning his grin or remembering her fantasy in the shower yesterday. "If you only knew, sweetie. If you only knew." She inclined her head at the stall behind him. "Wanna get clean?"

Chapter 7

A funky smell tickled Jamal's nose. Eyes blinked open to the haze of sunshine peeping around the edges of the curtain. Not his room.

He ran a hand across his face. Adrian's apartment. This time the warmth curled at his side wasn't Mom's cat. One of Shan's legs was thrown over his thigh. Her hair fanned across the pillow and sheets, like a sail caught in time. Face muscles tightened into a grin as he remembered last night.

The smell that had woken him grew stronger. Incense burning. Rain must be downstairs.

As much as he didn't want to, he eased away from under Shan's touch and climbed out of the bed. She murmured softly and rolled onto her back. He held his breath, not from fear that he disturbed her sleep, but from simple joy.

How'd he get so damn lucky?

Her lithe body stilled, deep asleep once more. He pulled the sheet over her before snatching his clothes off the floor and heading for the bathroom.

Fear and love played tug-of-war with his heart. He couldn't let the *kiang shi* get close to Shan again. He needed to kill the creature. Tonight.

And once that was done, he and Shan could focus on the future.

Ten minutes later, Jamal jogged down the stairs and headed for the storefront. Rain sat crossed-legged in the middle of the showroom floor, but she was already collecting her paraphernalia and storing the pieces in a deep blue velvet bag. The last ashes from the incense cone in the open silver crucifer crumbled to the sand.

"Good morning." She nodded at a knapsack and plain brown paper bag on the counter. "Shan's grandmother dropped off a change of clothes, and there's some other things I thought you two might need."

From the twinkle in her eyes, he had a pretty good idea what the "other things" were. Ignoring Rain's bait, he crossed the room and reached for the white bag from the bakery down the block instead. "What's for breakfast?"

She grunted as she climbed to her feet. Jamal hid his smile. The sound indicated she was more perturbed about not being able to tease him this morning than any extra effort due to her age. "Donuts."

Rain walked over, dropped her bag on the counter, and reached for the drink holder. "Here's your green tea and Shan's vanilla latté." She handed him a Styrofoam cup before she grabbed the third, popped the top off, and took a deep drink. "I take it she's still asleep."

He nodded. "Neither of us got much sleep the night before last."

A frown creased her forehead, and she tapped an index finger on her cup. "Your mom, Tom and I will be busy with tonight's ceremony. Think you'll be okay here for a couple of hours?"

"You reinforced the wards." He shrugged. "I don't see how it'll get in."

She snorted. "Doesn't the monster kill the teens right after they have sex in those stupid horror movies you watch?"

He scowled at Rain. "That is not even remotely funny."

"In this case, running upstairs would be the smarter decision. It won't get past the apartment threshold." She took another drink of her tea. A pensive look settled wrinkles deeper in her skin. "Maybe we should cancel the Lughnasadh."

"No, don't." He tried to put more confidence in his voice than he felt. "We hurt it pretty bad last night. Maybe it'll think twice before it tries something again."

The look Rain gave him over the rim of her cup said exactly what his gut told him. Whatever was left of Mark Li in that thing would track Shan here. It wouldn't give up until Shan was dead. And Jamal couldn't, *would not*, let that happen.

Jamal rattled the metal grates covering the front windows and doors. Nope, they weren't budging. He flipped off the lights as he headed back to the storeroom. Both locks on the back door were engaged and the heavy steel cross bar was in place. The *kiang shi* wouldn't be getting in through conventional means. He prayed Rain's unconventional means would also keep the damn thing out tonight.

Heading for the narrow staircase, he figured he might as well enjoy the two or three hours he'd have alone with Shan. Rain, Tom and his mom decided to go to the Lughnasadh after all and closed the store early. The three promised they'd be back at the store for guard duty as soon as the Sabbat ceremony was finished.

He jogged up to the apartment. Shan already had steaming cartons open and spread all over the coffee table. The smells of old Mrs. Wong's donations to the "Save Shan" effort triggered grumbles in his stomach.

Shan offered him a bright smile and a pair of chopsticks as he dropped to the pillow on the floor next to her. "I think you impressed Grandmother."

"How so? By getting caught in bed with her topless granddaughter?" He snagged the carton of beef lo mein in front of him and dug into the noodles.

"She sent you six egg rolls. And a box of condoms."

"Great. We'll add them to the rest of the collection." The image of Shan, naked, willing, made it difficult not to drag her to the bedroom right this second.

Shan giggled. "Yeah, I think your mom is the only one who hasn't contributed."

Jamal chuckled. "She was pretty adamant those expenses were coming out of my paycheck."

She picked up the carton of white rice and scooped some of the contents into her container of kung pao chicken. Settling on her pillow, she let her chopsticks hover above her dinner as she gave him a more serious look. "Thank you again for taking me to the hospital this afternoon."

Jamal shrugged. "*De nada.*" Rain had figured noon would be safe as long as they stayed in brightly lit areas.

"Mom called while you were locking up. The hospital might let Dad come home tomorrow."

His chopsticks halted in mid-air and the noodles slithered off and back into the carton. "Is that a good idea? I mean, with everything going on . . ."

She shoved her own chopsticks into her dinner and set it on the coffee table. "Haven't you noticed the *kiang shi* is fixated on me? Our apartment's safe as long as I don't—" Pain caught in her throat.

Jamal set his lo mein down and pulled her close.

Her audible gulp invaded the tiny living room. Shan's fist clenched against his chest. "No, dammit. I'm not crying over this any more."

The tickle of wetness soaking into his t-shirt said something else entirely.

"Hey." He cupped her chin and tilted her head up until their eyes met. "You will go home again." A swipe of his thumb took care of the tears that hadn't been absorbed by his clothing. "I promise."

A weak smile tried to emerge on her face, but fear shone in her eyes. "Don't get me wrong. I love being here with just you, but . . ."

"Well, Adrian coming home tomorrow *will* put a crimp in our style."

That got him a giggle. Then a shy seductress peered from between Shan's eyelashes. "Maybe we should take advantage." Her tongue traced a wet line across her bottom lip. "While it's still daylight." Elegant fingers reached for him. Not that he needed her touch to get a hard-on. Just thinking about her was enough.

"Far be it for me to ignore a lady's wish." He grinned. "But are you sure we have enough condoms?"

She stopped in the middle of unzipping his jeans and climbed to her feet, an impish expression on her face. "Maybe I should go check?"

It didn't take much to throw her off balance. She landed with a *whoof* on the couch. Her shirt slid up, displaying an expanse of flat stomach and her cute little belly button.

He rose on his knees and stroked that soft skin, edging the blue cotton higher until he found his prizes. "Never mind. I think we've got enough."

The white lace covering her breasts left nothing to the imagination. Dark areolas stood out against her golden skin through the flowery design. A breathless gasp rewarded him when he gently nipped the bud teasing him through the skimpy cloth. Her body arched, and soft little whimpers of pleasure filled the room. Light jasmine filled his nose along with the fragrance that was purely Shan.

He kissed his way south, pausing to swirl his tongue around her belly button, before he slid her knit shorts down those long, long legs. This time she wore bikinis that matched her bra. And the delicate black triangle under the lace beckoned.

One swift move and the panties disappeared somewhere over his shoulder. He slid his hands under her tight ass and pulled her to the edge of the couch. Musk teased him, and liquid glistened along the swollen pink flesh. He lifted her legs to rest on his shoulders and dipped his head.

The second the tip of his tongue touched her, Shan cried out. Another long, slow lick and her hips bucked. Then a swirl around her clit. One finger entered her as he repeated the licks. She tasted salty, spicy, heavenly. He added another finger and stroked her hot, wet passage. Then she screamed.

Her body jerked, and the muscles in her pussy clamped around his fingers. The tremors went on and on, and he didn't stop. He wanted to wring every last ounce of pleasure out of her. He'd waited too damn long not to make this count.

Her trembling subsided. She raised her head, and glazed eyes looked at him. "I swear, Jamal Washington, you'll be the death of me."

"I take it you liked?"

Her head flopped back the couch though her eyes didn't break contact. "Oh, yea-a-ah . . ." After a few seconds, she rose on her elbows. A sly smile promised more wickedness. "Take you pants off."

He climbed out of his jeans with record speed and tossed them over his shoulder.

Shan shook her head. A mock frown tilted her lips. "Underwear."

Like he need to be told twice. When he stood before her, his dick proudly declaring his excitement, she wagged her finger. "Shirt, too."

"Man, you're bossy." But the tee flew in the same general direction of his jeans and briefs.

She sat up and patted the couch next to her. "Sit here."

What kind of game was she playing? Anticipation made his whole body throb. He did as he was told.

Shan stood and bent over, ostensibly poking through a bag on the coffee table. Except with her legs slightly spread, he had a perfect view. And from the little glances she knew exactly what she was doing and how it was affecting him.

He leaned forward to touch her ass.

She straightened, whirled and slapped his outstretched hand. "Behave yourself." The drawn-out rummaging continued.

Jamal groaned but swallowed the sound. Damn, the girl was driving him crazy. Finally, she produced a foil packet.

Shan straddled him and tore the package open with excruciating slowness. She paused, an eyebrow raised, like she waited for him to do or say something to disobey her.

As impossible as it was, his hands remained on the couch and his mouth shut. He stared back. Warmth encased him as she rolled the condom over his dick. She must have had it sitting on top of the egg rolls the entire time.

She rose up on her knees, positioned her body and sank down over him. The feel of sweet tightness freed the groan locked in his throat. Shan braced her hands on his shoulders. She slid up and down with an agonizing little wiggle.

Two could play that game. He leaned forward and captured one of her dark nipples between his lips.

"Hey, I didn't say you could touch." Her protest came out in short little gasps.

Jamal released the hard bud and rested back against the couch. "Do you really want me to stop?" He didn't wait for an answer. Instead, his hands slid up from her hips until they reached her breasts. His fingers gently rolled both nubs.

Her eyes closed. Her nails dug into his skin. Her hips rocked their own little dance in time with her breathing. Internal muscles squeezed and released his dick every time he gave a slight tug.

God, he needed more. He let go of her breasts and pulled her head to his for a searing kiss. He tasted cinnamon and spice on her tongue. Her little cries filled his mouth, urging him faster and higher. She ground against him, the friction creating a different kind of fire in his skin, his blood, his soul. When he didn't think he could take any more, she stiffened. Her hot passage clamped around him. Every muscle in his body contracted. Fireworks exploded behind his eyeballs.

He didn't think he'd ever be able to move again.

Shan collapsed against his chest, her body quivering, her skin slick.

He brushed her hair back from her cheek. Could hearts break from feeling this much emotion for one person? "I love you. I always have."

Her body stiffened, and his gut said this was not a good thing. What had he done?

She pulled away, not meeting his eyes. "I'm hungry."

What the hell? How could he have totally misread things?

Shan stood, leaving him feeling cold and defenseless. "We should eat before it gets too much darker."

Agony and anger warred inside him. Jamal stood as well. "That's all you have to say? I tell you how I feel and you respond with 'I'm hungry.'"

Fear flashed in her eyes. She stepped back, away from him. She wrapped her arms around herself. "You're laying a lot on me."

Guilt shoved all the other emotions aside except one. Of course. Asshat. Understanding didn't negate the hurt though.

"Shan, look at me." He counted silently. He'd reached twenty before she finally met his gaze. "I. Am. Not. Mark."

Her eyes found a sudden interest in her toes. "I-I know that. It's just—" A sound caught in her throat. "I need some time."

"Okay." He took a deep breath and released it. "Okay."

But it sure as hell wasn't okay. He stalked across the carpet to retrieve his clothes. Looking at her, feeling her presence, trusting his feelings to her left a gigantic hole where his heart had been a minute ago. By the time he yanked his t-shirt over his head, he felt he could trust his voice again. "I'm not hungry. I'll start cleaning up."

"I'm not either."

He looked over at her. She'd been silently dressing as well. "Fine."

They gathered boxes and utensils without another word. The camaraderie, the joy, the attraction had disappeared. When he woke up next to Shan this morning, he'd truly believed this was it. That he finally had the woman of his dreams.

It wasn't the zombie ex-boyfriend that had ruined everything. No, his premature use of the L-word nuked the relationship all by its lonesome.

Maybe he had been stupid, but there was something that didn't make sense. He shoved leftovers into the fridge, slammed the door shut, and turned to face her.

"Shan."

She looked up from rinsing their glasses.

"Tell me one thing. If you don't care about me, why did you sleep with me?"

She turned off the water. Jaw muscles clenched as her eyes looked everywhere but at him. "Jamal, it's not that—" A gurgle filled her throat.

He followed her eyes up to the kitchen skylight.

In time to see a dark figure with a shock of white hair lift an arm.

Jamal grabbed Shan and pulled her down, shielding her body as he did. Glass shattered and rained down followed by a loud *crack*.

Fear grabbed his heart and squeezed. He glanced over his shoulder. A brick lay in the middle of the splintered hardwood floor where Shan had stood. His gaze shot up to the smashed skylight. White hair flashed and disappeared. Clanging came from outside. The bastard was on the fire escape.

He jumped to his feet. "You okay?"

She nodded. Sparks flew from her amber eyes.

Jamal didn't wait. He was already running for the living room. "Follow me down and lock up behind me in case he doubles back."

The sword sang as the pommel met his hand. Almost like it knew what they needed to do.

He took the narrow stairs two at a time and raced past shelves and Adrian's office. Footsteps pounded behind him. "Lock it and get back upstairs," he called over his shoulder.

It took too many precious seconds to release the steel door. He shot outside. A shock of white hair disappeared around the corner at the end of the alley. Jamal took off at full speed after the *kiang shi*.

Shan slammed the door shut, flipped both deadbolts and raised the bar into place. The adrenaline rush spent, she leaned against the steel and slid down until she sat on the floor. Breath came in gasps from running. The trembling from the short sprint.

Liar, her conscience whispered. Her inner voice was always more honest in the dark. And other than a couple of faint security lights, it was pretty freakin' dark in the storeroom.

She'd froze in kitchen when she'd seen Mark's arm lifted. A flashback to the band room the last time he'd hit her. Except . . .

The *kiang shi*'s eyes had glowed red every other time it had appeared. This time they were dark smudges in the middle of the pasty face. Had she and Jamal hurt it bad enough last night that its powers were weakened?

The thought eased the lump of guilt sitting in the middle of her fear. Jamal had a chance to get rid of it this time.

She climbed to her feet, only to have the guilt grow. Jamal was out there, chasing the hell-damned thing, and here she was, safe in the locked and magickally protected store. Jamal, who'd said he loved her upstairs. She'd frozen then, too. What the hell was wrong with her? The guy had offered his heart, and even though she'd stomped on it, he was still protecting her. What could she do? How did she make things right?

Maybe she should give Rain a call. Yeah, that was a good idea. She headed for the stairs to the apartment. Warn the old woman that the *kiang shi* was roaming the streets tonight so it couldn't jump her and Jamal's mother when they returned. And maybe Rain would know how to fix things with Jamal, too.

In the meantime, I can clean up the broken glass. Yeah, that was definitely a plan.

Her foot landed on the first step when someone pounded on the back door. "Shan, let me in." The voice was muffled. *Jamal?*

More hammering. "Shan! Let me in before he kills me!"

Claws and blood swam in her vision. Dad falling to the floor . . .

She raced for the door and struggled with the security bar. *Too long. It's taking too long!* Was the *kiang shi* shredding Jamal to bits because she was too fucking slow? The last lock released and she yanked the door open.

"Get in here—" The words clogged the back of her throat.

Crimson eyes gleamed and sharp teeth shone between a lipless grin.

"Why thank you, Shan." The *kiang shi* stepped into the storeroom.

Chapter 8

Lungs burned as Jamal gained on the *kiang shi*. The way it had moved two nights ago, it shouldn't be possible for a human to match its supernatural speed. Was it a trick to get him in range of its claws?

The creature dodged down another alley. This was his chance before anyone saw them and called the cops.

Forcing a burst of energy through aching muscles, he took two strides and jumped.

He crashed into the ragged figure. They fell, tumbling into a set of garbage cans. Limbs flailed as they both fought to remain on top. A pommel strike to the monster's temple produced a grunt of pain.

The blow gave Jamal the room he needed. A roll to the left and he gained his feet. He raised the sword above his head.

"Shit, Washington!" It threw its arms up to protect its head.

Recognition splashed across his awareness. Not an it. He. A wig. Some kind of costume. Jamal cursed himself for a fool. The eyes of the figure at the skylight hadn't been glowing red.

Lowering the sword, he grabbed the fabric at Bill Mailer's neck. "What the fuck kind of game are you playing?"

"Y-you wouldn't believe me."

"Try me." The growl in his voice sounded alien even to his own ears.

"M-mark came to my place last night. He was hurt. Said you tried to kill him."

Ice formed in Jamal's gut. "Mark's dead. Why are you acting like the bogeyman? Thought you'd get your jollies scaring the shit out of Shan? How'd you know where she was?"

When Bill didn't answer, Jamal aimed the tip of the sword at the jerk's left eye. "Tell me. Or I'll start slicing."

Silence.

He lowered the sword point to Bill's crotch. "Starting with your dick for calling Shan a whore."

"Mark! Mark told me." Mailer's voice rose an octave. "Where she was. How to dress. To distract you. He said if I didn't do what he said, he'd kill me!"

The ice in Jamal's gut shattered.

Shan.

Shan edged back, away from Mark. Or the thing that used to be Mark. "How'd you get in here?"

It slunk toward her, its movements alien, almost reptilian, but not quite. "You asked me inside."

"Did not."

"No. Technically, you told me to."

"Since when have you ever done *anything* I said?" *The stairs.* If she could get up to the apartment, lock herself in, and call the police . . .

No. No stairs. That's how stupid girls die in horror movies.

"Well, since I did something you told me to, you must do something for me." The *kiang shi* stalked after her, much slower than last night. Was it because it was still injured or because it was playing with her?

Dummy, if it still holds part of Mark, then he's just playing. And she sure as hell didn't feel like portraying the mouse. She licked her lips, trying to think. "And what's that?" Another step back. The office and bathroom were out of the question. No windows and the *kiang shi* would probably be able to smash in the doors.

It laughed, a horrible screech that made her want to cover her ears. "I want you to sit on *my* lap. I want you to fuck me, just like you did Washington. And if you make me feel real good, I'll let you live."

"Really?" No, he wouldn't. But if she said that, she was as good as dead. *Think, girl!* Five elements. Water, wood, metal, fire and earth. Burying the *kiang shi* wouldn't work. It wouldn't stay still long enough for her to dig a hole. The Hudson was too far away.

It sidled closer. "Of course, Shan. You're my girl." The last came out with an odd rolling of the "R".

Two more steps back. Any wood downstairs was solid: shelves, floors, counters and tabletops. Nothing stabby. There were boxes of candles and incense cones, but god only knew where the staff kept the butane lighter for the testers. She couldn't afford the time to search the drawers.

That left the showroom. Another step back. Maybe she could hold it off with something. At least until Jamal realized he'd been tricked and came back. Because she sure as hell wouldn't last long enough for Rain and the others to return from their festival.

"What if we do it by the front windows?" She swallowed and inched back. "So everyone in the neighborhood can watch? Would that make you happy?" It took everything she had not to gag on the last part.

"Why, Shan, you little exhibitionist."

She could have handled the sibilant sounds except its tongue darted from its mouth. The purplish-pink appendage tested the air and retreated just like a snake's. Except it looked like half-rotten flesh.

"You'd like that, wouldn't you? Showing that you could make me do anything." Another step.

Metal? Jamal took the sword with him, but his words echoed in her head. *Rain may have some daggers downstairs that have copper.*

"Maybe you should blow me first." Anticipation ran hungry in its voice.

It didn't like light. Could she hit the light switches fast enough to reach the display case with the ceremonial knives and smash it open?

"Sure." Beads swirled around her as she stepped past the psychedelic curtain. "Whatever you want."

She slid right, hand outstretched. The *kiang shi* parted the bead curtain, and she slapped the switches.

An unholy screech rent the air. Shan grabbed a statue and whirled. The heavy figure of some goddess shattered the antique glass. She reached for a knife with the orange-ish patina of pure copper.

Pain fired along her scalp and she flew backward. Her head cracked against something that refused to yield to bone. Colored balls flashed in her eyesight.

She blinked away tears. The thing with Mark Li's face stood over her, hands raised. Claws gleamed under the old-fashioned incandescent fixtures.

She was about to die and the thing that surprised her most was that she felt no anger. No terror. Just an overwhelming sadness that she'd been too chicken-shit to say, "I love you, too," to Jamal tonight.

Beads clattered. The *kiang shi* whirled. Shan's attention followed suit.

"Get away from her." Jamal growled the words. Just like he had nearly four months ago.

Chapter 9

Déjà vu didn't come close to what Shan was feeling. But dammit, she wasn't going to be a victim. Not anymore.

She drew a leg to her chest.

"Come closer and she dies."

Good grief. The *kiang shi* sounded like a villain in one of the sucky Hong Kong flicks Mark insisted they watch. Well, she wasn't the helpless heroine.

Her foot shot out, heel straight into its knee. The monster howled. Shan scrambled toward the cash register as Jamal rushed the *kiang shi*.

Despite the damage to its leg, the creature jumped on top of the counter. Jamal swung his sword. The *kiang shi* leapt for the shelves behind the sales counter. More glass hit the floor and shattered as jars of herbs and powders were knocked over in its mad scramble.

White hair flashed behind Jamal. Raw panic shot Shan's heart into over-drive. *Two of them?* No, the face was wrong, the eyes not glowing.

It wasn't worth taking a chance. She pushed herself to her feet and charged the second figure. The tackle pushed them through the doorway to the store-room, ripping strands of beads off their hooks. They slid along the floor and crashed into a metal shelf unit. Boxes tumbled down on top of them.

Her fist cocked behind her ear before it smashed into the second *kiang shi*'s nose. An audible *snap*, then bright red blood spurted.

"Shit, Wong! What da ell's wong wit oo?"

She reared back. "Bill?"

He shoved her off him and clambered upright. "E've gotta stop Washington. E'll kill Mark."

A weird scream echoed from the showroom. The same sound the sword made in her apartment. Bill ran toward the fight.

Damn, she couldn't let them both jump Jamal. She climbed to her feet once again and followed.

The *kiang shi* leapt from bookshelf to bookshelf to stay out of range of the sword. From the thick, black liquid dripping from its left cheek and arm, Jamal had barely missed taking its head off.

Bill rammed Jamal from behind and together they crashed into one of the antique bookcases. Mortars and pestles fell to the floor in a series of cracks and bangs. The handmade soaps and candles landed with softer thumps. The bookcase started to tilt, then came down against another set of shelves against the wall. Wood groaned as the piece leaned at a precarious angle.

Jamal reared up and shoved Bill aside. Bill took a wild swing that connected with Jamal's temple. Then they started trading punches in earnest. Above it all, the *kiang shi* clung to one of the ancient light fixtures. It smashed the bulbs before leaping for the next set. Judging from its cackles as it swung, it was more than willing to let its former friend take the punishment Jamal was dishing out.

The sounds of the creature got Jamal's attention. He heaved to his feet and took one step toward the *kiang shi* only to have Bill hook an arm around his ankles. The wrestling began again.

The showroom grew darker as the *kiang shi* swung from fixture to fixture, smashing bulbs.

Shan licked her lips, trying to think past the growing headache. The sword lay on the floor, shoved over by the shelves holding occult books. All it would take was a few steps . . .

She got as far as two when she ran into flesh so cold, so awful, she felt it in her marrow. The *kiang shi* grabbed her upper arms, and its death rictus grin widened. The realization it was about to bite her kicked survival instincts into overdrive. A stomp on its instep did nothing, but a head butt knocked it back a few paces.

The blow made Shan want to vomit. She swallowed the bile and backpedaled. The hard lumps under her heels registered a split second before her feet flew up in the air.

Stupid beads.

She landed on her hip, and the impact sent a wave of agony through her abdomen. She looked up. The *kiang shi* made a sound. It took her a second to realize the weird chirp-hiss was laughter. The bastard was enjoying her suffering. Just like every other time he'd hit her.

Fury shook her limbs. Or it might've been the pain. At this point, she wasn't sure of anything.

Slowly, she pulled herself backward with her hands. The beads actually helped her progress. Not that the *kiang shi* really cared. It toyed with her, enjoying the game until it decided to kill her.

Glass sliced into her right palm, and she cried out. The monster jumped on top of the counter once again and crept in her direction.

Shan reached behind her for something, anything, to throw. Her fingers closed around stone. The statue she'd used to smash the display case.

Despite the pain, she threw the tiny goddess figure. The pitch wasn't as good as her best fastball, but it caught the *kiang shi* by surprise. The creature emitted a metallic shriek when the stone connected with its head.

Agony screamed through her hip and head as Shan used an unbroken section of the display case to pull herself to her feet. She reached inside. Fingers curled around greenish orange metal.

"You'll pay for that, bitch."

Both fiery rage and liquid calmness flooded her mind, body and soul. Shan whirled, her aim true. The copper knife plunged into the chest of the *kiang shi*, right where its heart should be. Just as the silver tip of Jamal's sword protruded a hairsbreadth above her strike.

"I'm no one's bitch."

The monster stumbled back when Jamal pulled the sword free, a look of shock twisting its features. It tried to pull out the knife, but the metal seared its hands from the smoke that wisped from its blackening fingers.

The sword hovered in Jamal's hands, but the *kiang shi* silently collapsed to the floor. Its skin turned from a ghastly white to mottled blue and gray. Hair darkened to a dull black. The crimson glow faded until milky white orbs stared at the ceiling.

Then whatever energy that had filled Shan left just as suddenly as it had appeared. Her knees collapsed, but before she hit the floor, strong arms caught her.

"It's okay, baby. I've got you."

She blinked and looked up. Blood trickled from Jamal's mouth and nose. Already, the skin around his left eye was swollen.

Reaching up, she gently cupped his cheek. His wince at the contact twisted her heart. "I'm so, so sorry."

"Nothing to be sorry about, baby." He glanced at the still form of Mark Li. "It's over."

"Y-yes, there is." Her tongue felt swollen twice its normal size. "I-I love you, Jamal. I should have said it before. Wanted to. I was just so scared."

He said something else. Something about calling an ambulance as he settled her on the floor. It didn't matter. She'd told him. Said how she really felt. Damn, her eyes felt so heavy.

"C'mon, baby, you got to stay awake for me."

It hurt to open her eyes. And whenever she did, some stupid bird stared at her through the huge plate glass window. One yellow eye peered through the security gate, then it swiveled its head so the other eye could watch.

Caw!

"Tell the bird to shut up, Jamal. I want to sleep."

Caw!

"What bird, baby?"

Caw!

Her head ached so bad. Why couldn't she just curl up in Jamal's arms and get some rest? She'd earned it after the last three days, hadn't she? "The big black crow sitting on the window sill. It keeps cawing."

"Shan, baby." His voice sounded odd. "There's no bird. But the ambulance is here. I've got to let them in."

"Sure."

Except that stupid-ass crow rode in the ambulance all the way to the hospital with her. And it never shut up.

Chapter 10

Jamal and Tom had just righted the last bookcase when Adrian strode through the front door of the store.

"Why aren't we open—" He stopped, his gray eyes sweeping across the chaotic mess. "What the *hell* happened?"

No one said anything. Not Mom who had been sorting through the spilled soaps, or Rain who had been sweeping up broken glass. Tom just looked at Jamal.

This totally sucked but he had to come clean. Jamal cleared his throat. "There was a fight." Something grated along his vocal cords, and he coughed before he tried again. "I'm sorry. I'll pay for the damages."

Adrian shook his blond head in disbelief. "You? In a fight?"

Rain dumped the dustpan of shattered jar pieces in the trash can. The glass fell with an angry tinkling. "I told you twice already, Jamal. Mailer and Li's parents will be paying for this mess."

Adrian stared at Jamal. "You got into a fight with Bill and Mark?" He gestured at the mess. "Inside the store?"

Jamal plunged his hands into his pockets to keep from fidgeting. "Well, there's damage to your apartment. I'll pay for that, too."

"My apartment?" Adrian's expression grew more incredulous. The small suitcase dropped from his hand.

"No, you won't, Jamal." Rain's voice was as sharp as the glass she was sweeping up. She turned to Adrian. "Mark Li did something stupid and tried to kill Shan Wong. Jamal was protecting her. And the contractor will be here in an hour to put together an estimate for both the store and the apartment."

Heat flooded Jamal's face and hands. "Rain, if I hadn't let Mailer con me, none of this would have happened, and Shan wouldn't be—" He'd royally fucked up. He should be paying. God knew Shan was. *Please, PLEASE let her be okay.*

Supposedly, she only had a mild concussion along with some nasty cuts on her hands and feet, but with brain injuries, anything could happen. The police had dragged him out of the ER for questioning shortly after 2 a.m. Mrs. Wong said she'd call, but it was already noon.

Adrian raised his hands. "Would someone please start at the beginning?"

"Jamal . . ." Mom's voice held a frightened note. "Whose blood is this?"

He looked around the other side of the bookcase. Mom knelt on the floor, a statue of the Morrigan in her hands. In the fight, he vaguely remembered Shan throwing things at the *kiang shi*. Then there were the slices on her palms. "Shan's, I think. Why?"

Mom looked at Rain, who strode around the counter and took the stone figure.

Rain's face was totally unreadable. The non-emotion was more frightening than her anger. She shook her head and said, "I'll clean this up."

Once she disappeared into the back room, Mom and Adrian exchanged perplexed looks before she started giving him a run down of the damage and an estimate of when they'd be able to open.

Jamal's attention went to Tom.

The older man wiped a hand over his mouth. A concerned expression creased the crow's feet at his eyes. "Well, that explains last night."

"Explains what?"

"Rain passed out at the bonfire."

"What?"

Tom shook his head. "Nothing, kid. Go get the stepladder. I'll check the wiring of the light fixtures that the *kiang shi* played jungle gym on before we screw in new bulbs."

When Jamal trudged past the tattered remains of the bead curtain, he could hear water running in the bathroom. He peered in to find Rain scrubbing the statue with a brush. Even though the blood had dried, the water rinsing it ran bright red, as if the blood were fresh.

"Rain . . ."

She raised her head. His heart jolted at the tears streaming down her face. "Yeah."

"I-I'm sorry. I—"

She lifted her shoulder to wipe away the wetness. "No, I'm the one who should apologize. You're so damn young and inexperienced. I shouldn't have left you two alone last night. I was being selfish . . ."

Maybe it was the lack of sleep, but Rain wasn't making any sense. "For wanting to go to the bonfire? That's stupid."

A wry smile tilted her lips. "Guess we were both stupid last night. Go get the ladder for Tom. Shan's mother will call you when you get to the showroom." She started to scrub again, then paused. "Lilacs. The florist a block south of the hospital. Get Shan lilacs."

Warmth hit him. Shan would be okay. For once, he was glad about Rain's freaky precognition. "What do lilacs mean?"

A real smile lit her face. "First love."

Shan's grandmother sat beside the hospital bed when Jamal arrived. She glanced at the sleeping Shan, held a finger to her lips, and motioned him into the corridor.

He set the vase of purple flowers on the stand next to the bed and followed the old woman out of the room. His heart stuttered. On the phone, Shan's mom had said she would be fine.

Grandmother Wong patted his arm. "The nurse just checked on her. She's fine, Jamal. Only tired. They kept her up most of the night running tests." She shook her head. "They weren't necessary, but Chen insisted. And they are keeping her for another night, more to please my son than because Shan needs additional care."

"Dr. Wong? Shouldn't he have been—"

"One of the third shift nurses came to his room and told him Shan had been brought in last night." A smile creased the old woman's face. "He may not be able to talk right now, but he can still order the residents around with nasty notes."

She turned serious again. "Have the police talked to you?"

"Yeah." The second round with Detective Jensen had been even more fun than the first. Not.

Mark's last message on Shan's phone had helped, but Jamal had a sneaking suspicion Jensen knew neither he or Shan's mom had been entirely truthful. How the hell could they explain Mark committing suicide in order to turn himself into a monster? "Is Bill still here?"

Mrs. Wong nodded. "They have him in—" She paused, obviously searching for the right word in English. Finally, she pointed her index finger at her temple and made little circles.

"The psych ward?"

She let out a deep sigh. "Yes. Poor Bill told too much of the truth. The doctors gave him drugs to quiet him."

He couldn't think of a damn thing to say to that. The cops would latch onto the more plausible explanation: that Bill, in his grief, had stolen Mark's body and had attacked the two people he blamed for his best friend's death.

Mrs. Wong fished in her purse, drew out a wad of cash and pressed it into his hand.

He pushed the bills back at her. "I can't take this."

"Stay here with Shan tonight. You need to eat. She needs to eat. This hospital food is shit."

Mrs. Wong using profanity startled him more than the gift. "But—"

She shook her head, a stern look on her face. "Jennifer is caring for Chen at home. I must return to the restaurant before supper hour. My husband will burn the seafood, and we are not a Chinese-Cajun place." Her eyes twinkled before she pivoted and marched toward the elevator.

Jamal started to shove the bills into his pocket, but something crinkled with a metallic sound. He pulled the folded bills apart, and there lay a foil packet. At the end of the hall, a giggle sounded before the elevator doors slid shut. *Crazy old woman.* He wasn't about to ask why Grandmother Wong kept condoms stashed in her purse.

Instead, he shoved open the door to Shan's room.

"Hey, cutie."

His heart lifted at Shan's sleepy greeting. Enough that he didn't mind the lame nickname. "Hey there, yourself. How're you feeling?"

She raised her bandaged hands. "Other than a headache and my mummy imitation, I'm fine." A wry smile lit her face. "And, thanks to Mom, I won't be charged with mutilating a corpse."

He lowered himself onto the chair next to her bed. "Sorry about that. The cops were right on the heels of the paramedics. What I can't figure out is how they couldn't see the sword?"

She gave a careful shrug. "Maybe it really is a magic sword."

Silence fell, and neither of them could look at the other.

He wanted to ask about last night, but . . .

"Jamal, I—" she said.

"I don't want—" he said at the same time.

She blushed. "Go ahead."

"No, ladies first." Because gods help him, if she was going to break his heart, if what she said last night was a delusion from her concussion, if she didn't love him . . .

Her hands twitched, like she needed to fiddle with something but couldn't because of the stupid bandages. "I'm sorry I hurt you last night. I—" She swallowed hard. "I didn't trust myself. Didn't trust my feelings."

She was ripping out his heart, and still he wanted to protect her. "Shan, it's okay—"

"No, it isn't!" She swiped at an escaping tear with the back of her arm. "Mom and I had a long talk last night. And she's right."

Finally, Shan faced him. "I compared every guy I dated to you. I wanted you to ask me out, but you never did. So I thought I wasn't good enough. I'm not blaming you. It's definitely my problem. And then Mark—" She sucked in a deep breath. "Then Mark fed my insecurities and twisted everything until I didn't know which way was up."

Jamal blinked in surprise. "What do you mean you weren't good enough? I loved you. I always have. You're everything."

Sadness filled her eyes. "Then why didn't you ask me out?"

"Because . . ." He scrubbed a hand over grainy eyes. "Because I didn't want to lose you. I was afraid if I did and you said no, our friendship would be over. I'd rather have you as a friend than not at all."

A weak laugh filtered through Shan's tears. "Guess we were both stupid, huh?"

His chuckle answered her humor. "I've gotten a lot of that today." He looked deep into her amber eyes. After the last three days, it was all or nothing. "I meant what I said, Shan. I love you. I have ever since that first day in kindergarten."

This time there was no hesitation in her voice. "I love you too."

Jamal leaned over her. The kiss was meant to be gentle, tender, but quickly turned scorching.

When they parted, Shan scooched over and lightly patted the mattress with the two fingertips peeking from the bandages.

"You sure?"

She gave a careful nod, and after a little maneuvering, she snuggled in the crook of his shoulder. And having Shan this close sent signals south. The girl was in the hospital, and yet his dick was raring to go. *Focus on something else, man.*

"Your grandmother gave me some money for real food."

"Thank goodness." She groaned. "All I've had is tapioca pudding and applesauce."

"She also gave me this." He slid his hand in his pocket and held up the foil packet in two fingers. So much for distracting his libido.

Shan giggled. "Not that I'm adverse to the idea, but I don't know how much pounding my head can take right now." She raised a gauze-clad hand. "And I'm not sure what else I can do."

He kissed her hair. Underneath the antiseptic smell of hospital lay the faint hint of jasmine. "Why don't you let me worry about the doing?"

His hand slid under the blanket. The soft skin of her thigh met his touch. Inch by inch, he eased the hospital gown upward, over her hip, her flat stomach.

Another giggle shook her. "Jamal, what if someone comes in?"

He had a sneaking suspicion there was another reason Grandmother Wong told him when the nurse had last been in Shan's room. "How often do the nurses check on you?"

"About every two hours. Why?"

He smiled. "Then we've got plenty of time." His hand brushed her curls, eliciting a moan from her. Damp curls. His fingers stroked slick flesh, prompting Shan to lift her hips ever so slightly.

"Jamal, we really shouldn't—"

Another gasp as he entered her, and her eyes closed. So hot. So wet.

"Do you want me to stop?" Not that he was going to give her a chance to answer. One stroke. Two. Three. The slightest pressure of his thumb on her clit as his finger slid in and out one more time. Her body stiffened, and he swallowed her cry with a kiss.

She panted in his ear as her trembling eased. He removed his hand, slowly, reluctantly. *We'll have plenty of time later.* Spreading her gown back in place, he kissed her eyelids.

"Why don't I get us some dinner while you sleep?" Damn, he didn't want to leave. Wanted to stay next to her forever. But he forced himself out of the hospital bed.

"Jamal." Her eyes blinked open. "I love you."

That simple statement squeezed his heart. "I love you, too, baby."

Her eyes fluttered shut and a couple of seconds later, her breathing eased into a slow rhythm.

Jamal headed for the door, but the feeling of someone watching made him look back. A black bird perched on the outside windowsill. One golden eye peered through the glass. *Shan's imaginary crow from last night?*

It bobbed its head once and winked at him. Then it spread its wings and dropped from sight. An instant later, its form appeared, silhouetted by the lowering sun.

AUTUMN

Chapter 1

Phylicia Washington leaned against the counter, rolled her eyes and count-ed to ten before she sent a prayer to the namesake of the store for patience. But like every other time lately, the goddess remained silent.

On the other hand, Jamal continued his nagging. "Come on, Mom. You're not even thirty-five yet. You're too young to be sitting at home on a Friday night."

"It's Thursday." She glanced out the giant plate glass window, past the gold lettering that spelled out "Morrigan's Cauldron". No hope for a customer on such a blustery October afternoon to interrupt Jamal's harangue. The delivery boys at Wong's Take-Out were the only ones on the street because anyone with sense stayed home in this cold wind and spitting rain.

"Mom. Tomorrow night. Halloween. Samhain. Rain will cut you some slack this one time." He flung his arms up to emphasize his point, sending wisps of incense smoke curling through the air. "Besides the party won't be in full swing until after ten. You'll have plenty of time to change into a costume if you insist on going to the Sabbat ceremony first."

Phylicia glared at her one and only child. She was beginning to under-stand the parental urge to commit infanticide. "I appreciate the offer, but your friends sure as hell don't want you bringing your mama to their Halloween party."

"You just graduated from college yourself. We'll tell 'em you're my older sister."

Phylicia started to shake her head in disbelief, but for the first time, she noticed her baby boy's arms no longer held the lanky thinness that had plagued most of his teens. Instead, hard muscle defined his body in a way she was sure caused the heads of the NYU girls to turn and drink in the sight. Somewhere she'd blinked and missed that her baby was now a grown man.

"You're a fine looking woman, Mom," Jamal said, oblivious to her discomfort regarding this particular conversation. "I don't want you sitting at home alone giving up on men just because of my father."

She bit her tongue in an effort not to badmouth Isaiah. No matter that she'd let herself get knocked up at fifteen despite taking precautions. No matter that he'd abandoned her and Jamal a year later. No matter that she ended up homeless and begging on the streets with a baby in her arms. Things had changed so much since those dark days, but part of her clung to the old fear.

Jamal turned to the older woman who entered the shop from the back storeroom. "Rain, talk some sense into Mom."

Rain Bean set the box she carried on the counter and leaned her elbows on the antique oak scarred from decades of use. She favored Phylicia with a wicked smile. "If you don't want to go to the party, why don't you conduct the Sabbat, and I'll go with Jamal to check out the hard bodies."

Jamal slapped his hand on the wooden countertop and laughed.

One of Rain's slim, dark eyebrows cocked upward as she eyed Jamal. "Are you saying I can't fit in with your friends?" She held a pale, veined hand to her chest in mock dismay,

Even Phylicia had to chuckle. She wasn't sure of the store owner's exact age, but with her gorgeous silver braid, Rain more than qualified for AARP membership. But her notorious libido outstripped any teenage boy's. "His friends would never survive a night with you, girl, and you know it."

Rain grew semi-serious. "If you don't want to party with the kids, come with us."

Phylicia swallowed another sigh. Rain and her latest boyfriend were headed upstate to his farm after the coven's Halloween celebration. While Phylicia appreciated the thought, being the fifth wheel for the weekend was the last thing she wanted.

An excuse flared in her brain. "We can't leave the store unmanned on one of our busiest nights."

Rain snorted. "Adrian and Tessa already volunteered to work, and you know business dies by six pm."

"That's not fair," Phylicia protested. "I'm sure they've got plans."

"So what if they do?" Rain's evil smile promised repercussions if Phylicia continued to argue. "Who owns this store?"

"You do," Phylicia and Jamal said in chorus.

"Damn straight." Rain nodded sharply at their acquiescence. "Now about your weekend—"

The bell over the front door chimed furiously. Phylicia turned to find a god stepping into the store.

Okay, maybe not a god, but oh, sweet Morrigan!

The broad shoulders of the man carried a well-used backpack on one side and a couple of garment bags slung over the other. The scarlet Henley he wore defined his chest before disappearing into the narrow waistband of his jeans. White, perfect teeth gleamed against mocha-colored skin. His smooth, shaved head gave a whole new meaning to bald is beautiful.

She blinked to find his warm, chocolate eyes twinkling in amusement at her blatant stare. Heat bloomed in her cheeks and grew to an inferno when Jamal said, "Dante, 'bout time you showed up." So this was the famous Dante Jones, the junior who'd taken Jamal under his wing at NYU. The ex-marine that Jamal thought was the greatest thing since Michael Jordan.

And damn if she wasn't eyeing her son's friend like he was a choice hunk of prime rib. She should be royally ashamed of the images running through her head. Like the one where she turned him into her own personal hot fudge sundae, licking chocolate off his . . .

". . . and this is my mom."

Dante's smile blossomed wider, as if he knew what she was thinking. He held out his hand. "Pleasure, Ms. Washington."

She blinked again, struggling to catch up with the introductions. Wiping her damp palm discretely on the leg of her khakis, she forced a smile and reached across the counter. When Dante's hand engulfed hers, electricity shot across her nerves. For a brief instant, she would have sworn heat flared in his eyes.

No, her imagination was running wild. There was no way someone like him would ever be interested in someone like her. Not when he had his pick of the campus honeys. Not when she was a worn-out older woman with a son close to his age.

Dante swung the hangers off his shoulder. "So where are we stashing our costumes?"

"We'll leave 'em upstairs in the apartment until after class tomorrow." Jamal waved his friend to follow him to the back of the store.

"Ladies." Dante nodded at both women.

When his gaze seemed to linger on Phylicia a second longer than necessary, shivers ran down her spine and straight to her core. The heat in her pussy didn't abate when he turned and followed Jamal. She really needed a session with her vibrator tonight if she was imagining a college boy coming on to her. Her self-doubts didn't stop her from admiring the play of Dante's ass and powerful thighs underneath denim before he strode past the bead curtain. Those thighs between hers, grabbing that magnificent ass as he plunged into her hot, wet—

"Yoo-hoo? Anybody home?" Rain waved a hand in front of Phylicia's face.

The motion jerked her back to reality. "I'm sorry. Did you say something?"

"You need a costume for tomorrow night." Rain smiled and tapped an index finger on her cheek.

The older woman's smirk sent a shudder of a different kind through Phylicia's body. Rain was coming up with one of her cockamamie plans. The only problem was the last two had resulted in Adrian's engagement and Jamal losing his virginity.

"You've already lost your virginity, and I'm not planning on getting you married, dear." Rain's smile grew wider. "Just laid."

"You know you irritate the shit out of the rest of us when you do that mind reading crap." Phylicia ran a hand over her dreadlocks. "And I'm way too old for that boy." She shook her head. Rain couldn't be serious. "For crying out loud, woman, he goes to school with my son."

"He looked pretty full grown to me. Especially in all the important places." Rain leaned closer. "And he definitely checked you out. The only question is—do you want him?"

"He did not! You're imagining—" Phylicia clamped her jaw shut when Jamal and Dante's chatter preceded the two men into the store.

Jamal ducked behind the counter to grab his own backpack then planted a kiss on her cheek. "I'll see you tomorrow. We'll be back at eight to pick you up and change into our costumes."

She opened her mouth to protest once again, but Rain jumped in and said, "She'll be ready."

Dante gave Phylicia a smile that sent electric tingles to places where she had no business feeling electric tingles. "Until tomorrow, Ms. Washington." He followed Jamal out the store's front door.

When the bell attached to the door gave its last cheerful tinkle, she realized she hadn't said one word to Dante Jones the entire time he was in the store.

Chapter 2

The following night, Phylicia held as still as possible as Tessa McClain stroked liquid eyeliner across the edges of her lids.

"There. Take a look." Tessa stepped as far back as the tiny apartment bathroom would allow.

Phylicia stared at her reflection in the mirror above the sink, not sure which was more impossible—that she had let Rain talk her into going to the costume party or that Rain and Tessa had transformed her look so completely.

Metallic gold ribbon wove through her dreads, pulling them into a style that was part updo and part crown. Matching gold eye shadow and black mascara gave her eyes a mysterious Egyptian air. The gold-spangled halter pulled her breasts to a height they hadn't seen since high school.

She padded into the bedroom and took another look in the full-length mirror on the closet door. A gold belt studded with carnelian and turquoise held in place the pleated white gauze panels that could barely be called a skirt. And for once, all the damn exercising seemed worth it since her tummy didn't roll over the belt too bad. She sucked in her gut and looked again. She was going to have to breathe sometime tonight.

Rain's reflection grinned at her from where the older woman sat on the bed. Rain pointed at the bathroom. "You need lipstick. Get back in there."

"Bossy," Phylicia shot back.

"That's because I sign your paychecks."

Tessa chuckled as Phylicia marched back into the bathroom. "I don't know why you're bothering to fight her. You know she always gets her way." The blonde slicked a layer of cinnamon-colored lipstick across Phylicia's mouth.

Phylicia rolled her eyes. Tessa was right. When Rain got her mind wrapped around something, the gods themselves couldn't stop her.

"I can't go to a party in underwear," Phylicia protested for the fifth time when the two women returned to the bedroom. And damn, if she didn't feel naked. A good stiff breeze and everyone at the party would be able to count her pubic hairs.

"You're in a costume, not your underwear. And we both know that errand you ran this morning was a bikini wax. Put these on." Rain held out a pair of gold sandals with stiletto heels in her hands.

Phylicia groaned. Her tendons would be cramping long before they got to this party on Long Island. Besides, she knew the type of people who lived, or vacationed, there. More discomfort prickled her skin. She didn't fit in their class. Never would.

She slid the things that could only be marginally called shoes on her feet, her balance precarious at best. How the hell did someone in her sixties wear these things without breaking a hip?

"Because Harry usually has me on my back three seconds after I walk out in them," Rain said.

Phylicia held up a manicured hand while Tessa laughed outright. "TMI, girl, and stop reading my mind. If I really wanted to know, I'd ask out loud."

"Sorry." But the grin on Rain's face said she wasn't sorry at all. She stepped back to survey her handiwork. Then she smiled and nodded in satisfaction. "Damn, you're an ancient queen come to life. Let's go see if the boys are dressed."

Phylicia yanked on Rain's arm to stop her from charging into the living room with no warning. She wobbled over to the bedroom door and yelled, "You guys decent?"

"You ruin all my fun," Rain whispered, her lips twisting into a pout.

"Yeah!" came the joint reply.

From the short hallway, Phylicia entered a scene from *Pirates of the Caribbean*. If Dante's shirt earlier hinted at muscle, the leather vest he now wore displayed a perfect set of pecs and abs with more ridges than her favorite potato chips. Tight white pants that left nothing to her imagination were tucked into calf-high black boots. A red handkerchief covering his head and a pair of small gold hoops set off his roguish pirate to perfection.

And if he dragged her off to fuck her, she'd only give the most token of struggles. He'd laugh at her weak attempt as he pinned her down on the wooden deck of his ship. And his crew would watch while he ripped off her clothes and impaled her with his huge cock, telling his men without words that she was his. . .

"So what do you think, Mom?"

She blinked as Jamal's voice dragged her back to reality. Clearing her throat to cover her embarrassment at her fantasy, she examined Jamal's outfit. He dressed in a British navel uniform, complete with the tri-cornered hat and sword strapped to his belt.

Sword? Phylicia took a harder look. That wasn't a costume version of an officer's saber, but the real ancient broadsword Rain had given him. No one else but Rain, Tom and herself would know the difference. The weapon seemed to exude a glamour that fooled most folks. Was he expecting trouble tonight?

"You look great, baby." She smiled in an attempt to cover her emotions. And damn, if he didn't look great. His girlfriend, Shan, would be fighting off the other girls all night.

"What? I don't get any compliments?" Dante flashed a smile that could have melted the spangles right off her breasts.

Which would be nice considering the way the tiny metal circles dug into her painfully erect nipples. She didn't remember to breathe until Rain pinched the delicate skin on the underside of her arm. "Oh, um, you look very nice too, Mr. Jones."

"Nice?" He laughed, an uproarious sound that filled the loft. "Oh, sugar, that's what you tell your grandpa."

Heat filled her cheeks. "Let me get my coat."

"Nope. Not that raggedy thing you need to burn." Rain waggled an index finger.

"Rain, it's freezing outside. I need more than un—" Phylicia bit off the word. For some reason, "underwear" could have been a synonym for "naked lust" when Dante Jones was in the room. Hell, she could practically feel the heat rolling off him.

"You're wearing this instead." Rain reached over the back of the couch. The cloak she shook out was immense. The volumes of fabric looked sable, but iridescence shimmered under the lamp light. Almost like the feathers of a raven. Or a crow. "Tessa, help me."

Her friends dressing her sent a wave of unease through the pit of Phylicia's stomach. They acted like ladies-in-waiting. So why couldn't she just enjoy the pampering?

Dammit, she was a self-sufficient woman. Had been for the last seventeen years. That's why. She depended on no one. Hell, she'd paid Rain back every cent the old woman had given her to obtain her GED and college degree.

Except . . .

From the corner of her eye, she could see Dante's frank male appraisal. And intuition said he'd give her a whole 'nother type of pampering. A type that would leave her limp and satiated. A type she wouldn't forget.

"Shall we, Ms. Washington?" With a flourish, Dante swept a hand in the direction of the narrow staircase.

She brushed past him, not touching, but his body heat penetrated the cloak. Going to this party was such a bad idea. She'd barely slept last night, and when she did, Dante starred in very explicit dreams. Like the one where he knelt in front of her, his tongue running over her . . .

Phylicia bit the inside of her cheek to interrupt that train of thought. What the hell was wrong with her? Maybe, she should call her doctor on Monday. Maybe her hormones were out of whack.

With the rest of the group trooping behind her, she exited the staircase and strode through the storage area, too aware of the man following her. When she parted the beaded curtain and entered the front of the store, tension lay thick in the air between the three men in the room.

Then again, maybe the problem was that the entire staff of Morrigan's Cauldron spent too much time around Rain and her libido.

Like the owner had said, no customers browsed this late on Samhain evening. The store manager, Adrian Holloway leaned against the counter. His attempt at small talk did nothing to deter their co-worker, Tom Laoch from glaring at Rain's boyfriend Harry.

On one hand, Phylicia respected Rain restraining her sex drive when it came to the males who worked for her. On the other, the older woman was blind not to realize Tom's feelings. Or maybe she deliberately ignored him.

The fact remained that Harry wasn't much older than Tom's mid-forties, so the issue definitely wasn't the age difference.

"Hey, lady." Harry's face split into a wide grin when Rain walked in. "Ready to go? I'm double-parked."

"Just a moment." Rain retrieved her large bag and her coat from behind the counter. "Thanks for giving Tom a ride tonight."

Harry's smile faltered for a moment. Phylicia smothered her own grin at the obvious second-guessing that flitted across his face. "Uh, sure."

Tom, as usual, said absolutely nothing.

Rain stopped next to Phylicia and leaned close. "Don't do anything I wouldn't do."

Phylicia wanted to sink into the floor. The woman didn't even bother to whisper. Tessa buried her head in Adrian's shoulder. Adrian covered his mouth with his hand to hide his own smile. If it were possible, Tom scowled even harder at Harry.

Once Rain, Harry and Tom walked out and the front bell had stopped tinkling, Jamal said, "When is that guy going to grow a pair?"

Tessa lifted her head from her fiancé's chest. "It's not always that simple."

"Should I ask?" Dante's warm breath caressed Phylicia's bare neck.

She turned her head. Eyes the color of milk chocolate stared into hers. She wanted nothing more than to sink in those depths. Had he said something?

"Tom's got a thing for Rain, and he's too chicken-shit to say anything," Jamal said.

Her son's voice broke the spell Phylicia was under. She eyed him. "Watch your language."

"Besides, isn't that like the proverbial pot calling the proverbial kettle a certain color? Exactly how long did it take you to tell Shan you were interested?" Adrian grinned.

"Shan and I are a totally different situation," Jamal protested.

The byplay made Phylicia smile. "And if we're going to speak in clichés all night, it takes one to know one, Holloway."

"Ouch." Adrian slapped his hand over his heart. "At least I don't need my mom to fight my battles."

Tessa stepped between the verbal combatants. "And we're stopping right there." She gave Phylicia a meaningful look. "You've got a party to go to."

Phylicia glanced toward the back of the store. "I need my bag."

"No, you don't," Tessa said. She rounded the counter and produced a little evening bag that matched the gold sequins on Phylicia's costume. "I packed your driver's license, some money and a couple of extras like your lipstick."

The way Tessa said "extras" made the butterflies in Phylicia's stomach start fluttering again. She had a sneaking suspicion what the "extras" consisted of, but she wasn't about to open the bag in front of Dante, much less Jamal, to confirm her hunch.

The bell on the front door jangled. Jamal's girlfriend, Shan strode into the store. "Aren't you ready yet?"

The girl had the sense to wear a much warmer costume. A cream-colored Stetson sat on Shan's head. Her brown leather duster swirled around her boots. Spurs jingled with each confident step.

For the second time in as many days, the realization hit Phylicia hard. The planes of Shan's face were sharper. Her make-up more sedate, not the strawberry lip gloss she'd favored years ago as she and Jamal bent over homework at the kitchen table. Shan was no longer the shy little girl begging for Oreo cookies, but a woman with an entire life before her.

A tiny snake of jealousy reared its head in Phylicia's heart. Shan hadn't screwed up her future by getting knocked up in high school like Phylicia had.

She quashed the feeling. She'd made her own choices. Maybe they'd been the wrong ones, but she wouldn't have Jamal otherwise.

Phylicia smiled. "I believe so. Shall we hail a cab?"

Shan blinked under the brim of her hat. "Ms. Washington, the car's waiting for us. The driver sent me in to find out what's keeping you."

"Car? What car?" Phylicia looked at Shan, then Jamal, and finally Dante. "What car?"

"Don't sweat it, Mom. Jason sent his parents' car to pick us up." Jamal crossed the floor to wrap an arm around Shan. His hello smooch went awry when their headgear collided. Amid the kids' laughter, he picked up both hats and pecked Shan on the lips. "Let's go."

Heat radiated next to Phylicia. Dante extended his arm. "Shall we, Ms. Washington?" The smile he gave her was brilliant, charming. And a similar smile was the reason she was pregnant at fifteen.

But not to take the proffered arm would be rude as well. Tentatively, she slid her hand around his elbow.

"I don't bite," he whispered in her ear. "Unless you want me to."

She should have pulled away. She wanted to pull away. But it'd been too long since a man touched her. Once again, hormones overrode good sense. "I prefer something gentler, Mr. Jones."

If it were possible, Dante's smile went up a couple of watts. "I'm sure I could accommodate you."

Amid the flurry of good-byes, Tessa yelled, "Remember what Rain said." It took everything in Phylicia not to march over and deck the blonde. She prayed the subject would drop on the way to the party.

Jamal and Shan must have been in on Rain's plan. They made a point of climbing in first and grabbing one of the bench seats for themselves. Which meant Phylicia had to sit with Dante on the second seat, or she'd appear totally asinine cramming herself next to the kids.

She paused before entering the car, the flutter of movement across the street catching her attention. Crows lined the back of the bus stop bench in front of the Wongs' restaurant. She blinked. It was her imagination. A trick of the light. But the bird on the end looked like the crow that lived on the roof of her apartment building. The grizzled veteran with a blind eye she sometimes fed on her windowsill.

"You all right?" Dante's deep voice broke her trance.

"Yeah." Her nerves were in overdrive thanks to Rain and Tessa. She was definitely losing it if she thought a bird was following her. She ducked and slid onto the seat.

Once everyone was ensconced in the limo and it pulled into the Greenwich Village traffic, Dante leaned closer to Phylicia. "So . . . is there anything Ms. Bean won't do?"

Phylicia closed her eyes, more to control her own libido though disgust over Rain's behavior ran a close second.

Shan giggled. "Rain is a . . . rather active senior citizen."

"That's putting it mildly," Jamal added. "Just be glad she didn't set her sights on you, man." A whistle pierced the compartment. "I swear that woman has stock in Trojans—"

"Jamal!" Phylicia's eyes snapped open, and she stared at her son. "That is no way to talk about our employer."

Jamal shrugged. "Rain would be the first one to admit it's the truth."

"Still." Phylicia struggled to find the words. Dante Jones's proximity made it difficult to think. "Show a little respect."

The silence lasted a few uncomfortable blocks before Dante said, "Jamal tells me you got your business degree from NYU."

"Uh-huh." Getting to know this man better was the last thing Phylicia wanted. "So who's Jason?"

Dante chuckled. "Jason Kouric was part of my unit in Afghanistan."

"He's rich and he enlisted in the Marines?" She couldn't keep the disbelief out of her voice.

"He was trying to prove something." Dante's teeth flashed white in the passing lights.

"How to get himself killed?"

"Money doesn't solve all your problems." His voice was low, soothing.

"It sure as hell makes things easier," she shot back.

"True," he conceded.

The repartee between them didn't block her sexual tension. It only heightened the desire plucking at her nerves. Damn, she didn't want to fall into this seductive spell he wove. Was that why she was picking fights?

She rubbed her palms against the folds of the cloak. What they needed was a different subject. Preferably one that didn't involve her. "Jamal says you're a resident advisor. Isn't that hard while trying to keep up with your own studies?"

"It does offer a different set of challenges." He ran his fingertips over a fold of the cloak between them on the seat, but didn't touch her directly. Still she shivered as if he'd stroked her skin.

It took a second to find her voice. "I take it you enjoy challenges."

He winked at her. "Definitely."

Chapter 3

Phylicia's sexual awareness of Dante Jones didn't abate during the ride to Long Island. And from the wicked grin on his face, he knew it too. Luckily, the kids kept up idle chatter about classes and neighborhood gossip. Otherwise, all she would have thought about was touching the man beside her.

The limo pulled into the driveway of an enormous cream brick mansion. White, purple and orange light strands wrapped around bare deciduous trees. More floods illuminated the yard. The drive was already lined with parked cars. Despite what Jamal had said, the party was already well under way.

Even with her unease concerning Dante Jones, Phylicia was glad for his steadying arm as they strode up the cobblestone walk. No doubt she would've broken her neck in Rain's insanely high heels.

A blond vampire opened the front door. "'Bout time you got here, Sarge." He pulled Dante into one of those manly, back-pounding hugs guys used to hide real emotion.

Dante introduced them to their host Jason, who in turn, waved them into the mansion.

Jason grinned around his fake fangs as he led them into the crowded living room. "Excuse me for not giving you the grand tour. I gotta keep on the move."

Dante gave his friend a shit-ass smirk. "Kelly's here?"

Jason rolled his eyes. "She finagled an invite out of my baby sister." His expression turned to horror. "Enemy at two o'clock." With a flap of his huge black cape, he dove through the crowd in the opposite direction.

"Shan and I are going to find drinks." Jamal and his girlfriend disappeared through another doorway.

Deliberately leaving Phylicia alone with Dante in a roomful of people she didn't know. The brat.

"Want to hang up your cloak?" Dante gestured back toward the entrance hall.

Phylicia nodded. She was used to the crowds of the city, but the mass of college students overwhelmed her.

Dante's hand at the small of her back radiated heat through her body. Maybe giving up her cloak was a bad idea. She could imagine what the feel of his skin on hers would do to overwrought nerves.

She undid the metal clasp, but before she could move, Dante's hands were on her shoulders. He slid the material off with a slow, sensual motion. One that sent a thrum low in her pelvis.

After carefully hanging the cloak in the closet, he stepped back. His eyes raked her form, his interest blatant. Obvious.

And his gaze, once again, had her nipples beaded underneath the sequined top.

Her breathing meshed with his, and time seemed to slow. His head dipped down, his lips millimeters from hers.

Laughter erupted behind them as party-goers spilled from the living area.

Dante pulled back, a slight smile on his face. "Would you like that tour?"

Phylicia nodded, not trusting herself to speak. She wanted him. Goddess, help her. She wanted Dante Jones. And for the life of her, she forgot why fucking him would be such a bad idea.

He took her hand and led her down the hall, giving cursory details. "There's the half-bath. Mr. Kouric's office. The sunroom for Grandma Kouric when she is in town."

She laughed. "You seem to know the house very well."

He tugged her further down the hall. "I practically grew up here. My parents used to work for the Kourics. And here we go. The library."

He guided her into the huge room. A quick flip of the lights showed that they were alone in an octagonal room with massive bookshelves on every other wall. Just as quickly, he flipped them off and shut the door.

"It's a little hard to see the architecture in the dark." She was delaying. The room had plenty of illumination from the outside floods. So why didn't she just walk right back out and join the rest of the partiers?

"What would you like to see?" His breath was hot on her neck. He was so close.

Phylicia backed up. Dante followed, stalking her. Her breath caught when her back ran into the wall between two of the bookcases. He pressed his body against hers, his hands planted on either side of her head. She should protest, complain, something . . .

Except the feel of his chest against her breasts, his erect cock nestled against her belly, his thigh shoved between hers made her want to weep with frustration. She'd relied on her vibrator for so long she'd forgotten what a real man felt like, smelled like.

And it was his smell that was so tantalizing. Clean. Fresh. Woodsy.

She grabbed the first distraction she could think of. "Your mom was the Kourics' housekeeper?"

Dante drew back, but only an inch. "Wow. That's racist. Didn't think you were that type."

Heat flooded her face. "I'm sorry. I didn't mean—"

"Yes, you did." That wicked smile of his was back. "My mom was the first African-American attorney at Mr. Kouric's law firm. And Dad was the architect they hired to restore this place. I have an honorable discharge from the Marines, plus a couple of medals for service in Afghanistan. Now that we've got my bona fides out of the way . . ." He leaned closer.

"I wasn't questioning . . ." She wanted to kiss him. She wanted to run. The conflicting desires had her knees quaking.

"Yes, you were." His dark eyes gleamed with pure lust. "Why are you so against being with me?" he whispered.

"I-it's not you." Sadness weighed in her heart. Why couldn't she have met Dante Jones before . . . everything else that happened? "I'm too old for you."

A soft, deep chuckle. He leaned closer and kissed her shoulder. "What makes you say that?"

"Because you're what? Twenty-five? Twenty-six? I'm not comfortable with our age difference." So why wasn't she pushing him away? It wasn't like he tied her to a chair.

This time he laughed in earnest. "Girl, you need to add five years. Besides you're only thirty-four. Neither of us are little kids here." He kissed her other shoulder.

"How did you—"

"I asked."

"I'm going to kill him," she muttered.

"Her," he corrected. "I asked Shan."

Phylicia gasped as Dante continued kissing a line up to her jaw. "But you're Jamal's RA." That protest sounded lame even in her ears.

"I'm not yours." His lips were so close to hers. "And I don't kiss and tell."

His hands moved then. Down to squeeze her ass, lifting and pressing his cock against her pussy. His kiss swallowed her moan.

Her arms encircled his neck, and she hung on for dear life. Their tongues tasted and explored. His fingers drifted between the gauze strips of her skirt and underneath the nylon bottoms, tracing the material from back to front. The rough texture of his skin against hers felt so good, so right. He brushed her slick, open folds.

She broke their kiss with a gasp. "Dante . . ." His name was half-protest and half-plea.

"Let me touch you," he whispered against her lips. "I've wanted to since I first saw you." Another soft stroke and she shuddered.

"Th-that was only yesterday."

Another chuckle. "No, baby. That was two months ago when you were unloading that cab in front of the dorm. Those tight shorts that hugged your perfect ass." His left hand massaged her ass cheek. "That bright orange t-shirt showing off the most perfect rack. All I could think was, 'Please, God, don't let her be assigned to my floor.'"

"What? Why?" After all his "perfect" bullshit, part of her was insulted.

"Because then it would be very unethical for me to want to do this . . ." Two of his fingers slid deep inside her pussy.

A whimper escaped her lips.

"And this." His thumb circled her clit.

Phylicia's hips thrust against his hand. She shouldn't. Morrigan knew she shouldn't, especially in the house of someone she just met, but she couldn't help herself.

Dante caught her mouth for another soul-searing kiss. Those fingers of his didn't stop their slow slide in and out of her wet passage. With each thrust in, his thumb came closer to that magic spot. And all the time, she shamelessly twisted and tilted her pelvis.

He was the one to break the second kiss. "Just let go, baby." The pressure of his hand against her clit launched every nerve in her body. She bit her lip to keep from screaming as she shuddered and panted in his arms to the waves rocking her body.

Another soft chuckle echoed in her ear as she tried to catch her breath. "Damn, girl. I'd like to think I'm all that, but when was the last time you were with a man?"

Phylicia couldn't help her own laugh. "Didn't your mama teach you not to ask a lady those kind of questions?"

"That long, huh?"

They both cracked up.

After a minute, Dante sobered and raised her hand to his lips. "I'd liked to do this properly in a proper bed. Stay with me tonight."

Phylicia blinked. He couldn't be serious. "In your dorm? Are you crazy?"

More laughter. Damn, she could get used to hearing his voice. "No. Here. In my bed. In my room."

Goosebumps raised along her skin where he stroked her back. "Your room?"

He shrugged. "My parents retired a couple of years ago. They moved to Atlanta to be closer to my grandparents. So the Kourics let me store my stuff here."

Her nerves were back in full force. "But I don't have anything with me."

"Oh, I think you have exactly what we need in your bag." His lips were back on her neck. Little tantalizing kisses left her mind clouded with desire. "And I don't mean the lipstick," he whispered in her ear.

As much as her conscience nagged that this was a stupid idea, Phylicia wanted to stay. "What about Jamal and Shan?"

One of his eyebrows quirked. "You do realize they're sleeping together, don't you?"

"Th-that wasn't—" She took a deep, calming breath. "I already know their relationship has become physical. Were they planning to spend the night here?"

"Their plans depended on you. Jason told them there was plenty of space if they didn't feel like driving back to the city tonight."

Guilt yanked at Phylicia. What kind of example was she setting for her son if she slept with a man she barely knew?

She opened her mouth to protest when Dante placed a finger under her chin. "No one's judging you here, Phylicia. Jamal and Rain care about your happiness. I'd like to be the one that makes you happy, but it's your choice."

A sinking feeling in her gut replaced the heated shivers from Dante's touch. "Rain? What the hell did she tell you?"

Another smile filled Dante's face. This one was warm, caring. "She only filled in the blanks that Jamal didn't know or wouldn't tell me out of loyalty to you."

Phylicia placed her face in her palms. The old witch had planned this from the beginning, and Phylicia had fallen right into the trap. Who needed love potions when one meddling biddy manipulated the entire island of Manhattan?

The laughter started deep inside her and came roaring out.

"What's so funny?" Dante watched her, a quizzical expression on his delectable face.

"We've both been pwned, sugar." She swiped the tears on her cheeks.

"We've been what?"

She grinned. "Not much of a gamer, are you?"

He shook his head. "After you live through the real thing, most of the FPS's lose their appeal."

It was her turn to shoot him a quizzical look.

He spread his fingers wide. "Just because I don't play doesn't mean I don't keep up on the slang. I am an R.A. after all."

She edged closer to him, touching him. "Well, if Mr. R.A. expects anything tonight, he'd better feed me."

"Your wish is my command."

The smile he gave her set off the butterflies in her stomach again. "Then you should have dressed as a genie. Pirates don't grant wishes."

"No, they don't." He cupped the back of her head. "They ravish their prisoners." And he preceded to do just that to her mouth.

Chapter 4

Phylicia tried not to comment on the size of the house as Dante guided her toward the kitchen. The man had been nothing but nice to her, and she'd stuck her foot in her mouth enough.

In the back of her head, a little voice whispered, *His kisses went way beyond nice. You want more orgasms.*

Well, hell, yeah! No one had taken her over the edge before with just a touch. She could only imagine what it would be like with his cock inside of her. *Incredible,* her little voice said. The hints through his pants had been enough to drive her crazy.

Dante led her into a kitchen that was a chef's wet dream. Stone counters lined most of the room, broken by stainless steel appliances. Over the center island, top-of-the-line pans and utensils hung from a copper display rack.

A half dozen people stood and chatted in the bright, airy kitchen. As quickly as Dante introduced them, Phylicia forgot their names, except for the petite white girl with the perfect highlights in her $500 haircut.

"Jason's Kelly?" she mouthed. His grin answered her question.

"Dante, you've got to try my punch." Kelly held out a plastic cup filled with purple liquid. Something about the girl sent a trill of unease through Phylicia. This was someone used to getting her way, and she didn't care who she stepped on to do so. No wonder Jason was avoiding her.

"No, thanks." Dante held up a hand. "I need something a little stronger." Everyone but Kelly laughed.

Phylicia didn't get the joke until he opened the refrigerator and pulled out a Red Bull. He looked at her. "What's your poison?"

His eye contact made her muscles clench in anticipation of later. "Any diet cola in there?"

"Phylicia?"

She whirled at the familiar voice. Behind her was the living embodiment of Tina Turner. If Tina were a six-foot-seven cross-dresser. "Rue!"

Rue, Phylicia's upstairs neighbor back in Manhattan, enveloped her in a massive hug. "How you doing, girl?" Then she caught sight of Dante and gave him a thorough up-and-down as he joined them. "And I approve of your accessory choice."

"Punch?" Kelly thrust the cup of purple liquid in Rue's face.

"Honey, I don't do no Kool-Aid." Rue deliberately turned her back on the girl who looked downright pissed.

"Rue, this is Dante—"

Dante pressed the can of diet soda in Phylicia's grip and held out his hand to Rue. "You probably don't remember me, Professor Adkins."

Rue grinned. "Fifth row, center. My two o'clock macroeconomics class last semester." She gave Dante another once over. "Though I like this outfit much better than your usual jeans, Mr. Jones."

Rue bent over Phylicia. "Though he does fill out those jeans damn well." She straightened and eyed Phylicia. "You still working for the witch in the Village?"

"Yes, ma'am." Phylicia grinned.

Rue shook her head. "What a waste of a perfectly good business degree."

Phylicia splayed a hand over her chest. "Excuse me? Do you have any idea what we pull in through online sales?"

Before their usual argument over internet retail could get started, a scream echoed through the house.

While everyone in the kitchen froze at the sound, Dante shoved his can on the center island and ran out the door. Another scream ripped the air.

The sheer terror in that cry tore through Phylicia's paralysis. She kicked off the stupid gold heels and raced after the pounding of Dante's boots up the staircase. By the time she reached the top, angry shouts filled the air to her right.

Phylicia ran toward the sounds coming from the third bedroom.

Inside, Shan knelt beside to a sobbing blond girl huddled next to the pink and purple bed. She draped her duster over the girl's ripped peasant blouse and exposed breast while she murmured comfort. The beginning of what was going to be a nasty bruise shone on the skin over the girl's cheekbone.

Meanwhile, Dante and Jamal held Jason, who kept lunging for a boy sitting on the other side of the bed. The boy's Darth Vader helmet lay on the floor, and blood gushed from the Sith wannabe's nose.

"I didud do nufing," the boy shouted. Or tried to while pressing his nostrils shut.

"You were on top of my sister!" Jason's face was bright red.

Phylicia crossed the room, dropped her purse and crouched next to Jason's sister. She took a good look at the girl. Her eyes were glassy. "What's your name, sweetie?"

"Brittany." Except the word came out more like "Britshneeeee."

A glance at the two plastic cups filled with purple liquid told Phylicia everything she needed to know. "Shan, run downstairs and fill a towel with ice while I help Brittany into the bathroom."

As Shan took off for the kitchen, Phylicia glanced at the men. Dante was whispering something in Jason's ear. Whatever he said must have been sinking into his friend's head. Jason was no longer trying to break free from Dante's grip.

They needed to resolve this before anyone did anything more stupid than they already had. She caught Jamal's eye. "Collect Vader's keys and call him a cab."

"I've already got the asshole's keys," Jason snarled. "He just needs a cab before I break other body parts."

Jamal shot a questioning look at Dante, but the ex-Marine nodded in agreement. After hoisting Vader to his feet, Jamal headed out the bedroom door with his charge. Phylicia bit her lip to keep from laughing when he not-so-accidentally guided Darth Wannabe nose-first into the door jamb.

Phylicia helped Brittany upright and got her into the adjoining bathroom. The leather duster slipped from the girl's shoulders as she rushed for the toilet. Phylicia winced at the volume of purple liquid the girl vomited. It triggered images from Phylicia's teen years that she'd much rather forget.

Pursing her lips, she grabbed a washcloth from the shelf next to the sink and ran it under cold water. When Brittany finally collapsed on the bathroom rug, Phylicia wiped the girl's mouth. By the time she rinsed the washcloth with cold water a second time, Shan appeared with ice in a Ziploc baggie and a dishtowel.

"Is she going to be okay?" Shan peered at Brittany.

Phylicia took the ice and towel from Shan and grinned. "Nothing that a hangover and a good pork breakfast won't cure." She knelt next to the semi-conscious girl and held the pack against the bruise on Brittany's cheek.

"She wasn't—"

It didn't take a genius to figure out Shan's concern, especially considering what her ex-boyfriend had tried back at their prom. Phylicia shook her head. "No, he didn't rape her."

Shan released a pent-up breath. "Good. I'd hate to have to track the asshat down and kick his keister to Brooklyn."

Phylicia chuckled. "Help me get Brittany into bed. The best thing we can do is let her sleep this off."

Dante and Jason had left the room as well when they half-carried, half-dragged Brittany to what was obviously her bed. Luckily, she was a stick figure. Otherwise, Phylicia and Shan would have needed one of the guys to help. The girl was dead-weight in their arms.

Or she was until they got near the nightstand. "Pu-u-unch—" Brittany grabbed for the cups.

Phylicia intercepted the girl's reaching palms. "No, Brittany. You've had enough for tonight." She looked at Shan as they maneuvered the drunk girl into her bed. "See if you can find some jammies or a nightshirt while I get rid of the crap she's been drinking."

Tingles rippled across Phylicia's skin the moment she touched the plastic. And definitely not good tingles. Both cups felt rank, disgusting. Swallowing her worry, she carefully carried the two cups into the bathroom. She dumped the contents of the first one into the toilet and flushed. The second one she held up to the light.

Something was in the punch. She closed her eyes and concentrated. When she opened her eyes, the faint swirls of black were more obvious in the deep purple. Not a drug or alcohol. A spell. One so subtle she hadn't detected it until she touched the container.

What in Morrigan's name was going on here?

She dumped the contents of the cup into the toilet and flushed again. Then she rinsed both cups in running water, making sure none of the contaminated punch residue touched her skin, before disposing of them.

When she returned to the bedroom, Shan had removed Brittany's jewelry and the remnants of her gypsy costume. Phylicia helped her wrestle a bright pink sleep tee on the girl, who mumbled about wanting more punch.

"No, Brittany. Time for sleep." Phylicia laid a palm on the girl's forehead. A little will and Brittany calmed down. By the time Phylicia pulled the comforter to the girl's chin, she was snoring.

Phylicia eyed Shan. "Did you or Jamal drink any of that punch?"

Shan shook her head.

"The truth, girl." Phylicia had never snapped at Shan before, but she couldn't take any chances. Not with someone playing games with the guests' lives.

Shan glared back. "Jamal wouldn't take any chances of losing his scholarship, Ms. Washington. And I don't drink."

Guilt over her own mistakes spilled through Phylicia's anxiety. "I'm sorry."

"It's okay." Shan's fine black eyebrows knitted into a frown. "Someone spiked the punch with something more than alcohol, didn't they?"

"Yeah. We need to get rid of it."

Shan rested her hands on her gun belt. "That may not be easy. Pretty much everyone here has had some."

The last thing Phylicia wanted to do was scare Shan, but if things were as hairy as she suspected, then she needed the kids out of the way and safe. "Find Jamal and see if you two can get the Kourics' chauffer to take you back to the Village."

"No." Shan shook her head so vigorously her cowgirl hat slid off. "That's how Jamal and I got into trouble last August. Mark and Bill got us to split up."

"Fine." Phylicia held up her hands in defeat. "But whatever you do, stay with me or Jamal."

Shan gave her a sharp nod. She retrieved her duster from the bathroom floor. As she came back out, she glanced at the sleeping Brittany. "What about her? We can't lock the door from the outside. What's to prevent some asshole from coming in and . . ."

Goddess, she hated lying, but the fewer people who knew what she could do, the better. "I'll jimmy the door."

Shan gave her a sly grin as she walked out of the bedroom. "There's a spell for that," she said, mimicking the announcer's voice of a popular commercial.

"I don't know what you're talking about." Phylicia followed and pulled the door shut. She traced a protection symbol on the door and enforced it with her will.

When she turned to face Shan, the girl shook her head. "You don't have to lie, Ms. Washington. Everyone on the block knows you're Rain's apprentice."

"That's a load of bullshit. I just work for her." Just how much had Jamal revealed to his girlfriend? They'd had several talks over the years about why her odd abilities needed to be kept secret.

"Ri-i-ight," Shan drawled. "Then why does my boyfriend carry around a magick sword?"

"It's not—"

"You forget who you're talking to." Shan jabbed a thumb at herself. "I'm the girl whose ex-boyfriend hung himself in order to become the living dead and kill me."

Phylicia's jaw snapped shut. Shan was right. She and Jamal were adults, had survived their own trial by fire. She held up her hands in surrender. "Fine. But so help me, I catch you gossiping . . ."

Shan giggled. "That's Rain and Grandmother Wong's department."

Phylicia rolled her eyes. The truly sad part was that Shan was right. Between the two old women, no one got away with anything in the Village. "C'mon. Let's find the guys."

They'd taken two steps toward the staircase when another scream rent the air. Then two loud *cracks*. Fear clenched Phylicia's stomach. It was the all-too-distinctive sound of gunfire.

Chapter 5

Instinctively, Phylicia and Shan dived for the floor. Someone shouted, then loud thumps and muffled grunts. Phylicia crawled to the banister and peered between the carved spindles.

Rue lay on the floor, crimson smeared on the hardwood. Dante had another guest dressed in a rabbit costume pinned underneath him.

Had everybody gone insane drinking the bespelled punch?

She climbed to her feet and raced down the stairs, Shan on her heels.

By the time Phylicia hit the bottom step, Jamal crouched next to Rue. He had pulled off his costume jacket and his t-shirt. Pressing the white cotton against the wound in Rue's shoulder, he looked up at Phylicia. "Mom, call 9-1-1."

Rue tried to bat Jamal away. "I'm fine. He just winged me."

Phylicia looked around, frantic. The ashy hue of Rue's face meant she was definitely not fine. "Where the hell's the phone in this castle?"

"I've got it, Ms. Washington." Shan pulled her hot pink smart phone out of her jeans' pocket, then frowned. "I'm not getting a signal."

Jason ran into the foyer, garbage bag zip strips in his hand. He knelt next to Dante, and the two men secured their rabbit gunman. The boy made the same odd slurring noises Brittany had uttered upstairs. Another punch victim.

"Dante, where's the phone?"

"Mr. Kouric's office." He pointed down the hall. Jason and Dante pulled Rabbit Gunman to his feet.

The boy caught sight of Rue and moaned. "Why doesn't she-e-e love me-e-e? I can't live wishout 'er." Then he started crying.

"I've got him." Dante tilted his head toward the corner by the closet. "Phylicia, would you grab that before someone else does something stupid?"

It was only then that Phylicia noticed the semi-automatic handgun lying on the floor. She crossed the foyer and, using a section of her gauze skirt, picked up the firearm. The metal was warm to her touch. "What should I do with this?"

"We'll lock it in Dad's safe while we call for the paramedics," Jason said.

Dante shot him a dirty look. "I just hope you have a good explanation for the police of how this kid ended up with your gun."

"It was locked up in my room," Jason said through gritted teeth. He led the way down the hall to his father's office.

They entered the office and Jason flicked on the lights. Phylicia covered her mouth at the sight that greeted them. Two guys and a girl were . . .

Crap on a cracker. Phylicia never thought of herself as naïve, but reading about certain activities and seeing them live were two different things.

The woman knelt before the first man, sucking his dick. The second man thrust his cock into the first man's ass. They were so involved they didn't so much as flinch when light flooded the room.

Phylicia glanced at Dante. He seemed as flabbergasted as she was. Even the Rabbit Gunman had stopped crying. On the other hand, Jason looked downright pissed.

He raised two fingers to his lips and blew a piercing whistle. The sound cut through the trance the three participants seemed to be in. They stopped and gave the unintentional spectators confused looks.

An icy ball centered in Phylicia's gut at their glazed eyes, an appearance all too similar to Brittany's. They needed to get Rue medical attention and get rid of the cursed punch in that order.

"You three, get dressed and get out," Jason barked.

When they remained frozen, Dante bellowed, "Now!"

Once the three cleared the room, Dante sat Rabbit Gunman on the burgundy leather couch. While Jason put the gun in the safe, Phylicia grabbed the receiver and punched in 9-1-1.

Nothing but static.

She cleared the number and listened. No dial tone at all. "We've got a problem."

Dante crossed the room and checked the set. His proximity soothed her nerves.

Dammit! I canNOT be thinking about sex now! The ball in her stomach wasn't just icy, it was a freaking glacier. Could she have accidentally touched the punch when she was disposing of it upstairs? She'd touched the semi-automatic after the Rabbit Gunman had shot Rue. Could the bespelled guests affect others through their sweat?

"Let's check the phone in the kitchen. The junction box is right outside." He looked at Jason and inclined his head toward the Rabbit Gunman, who was weeping again. "You got him?"

Jason gave a curt nod.

Dante strode out of the office and Phylicia followed him. Shan's warning about not splitting up echoed in her ears. Something was very, very wrong in this house.

"Shan!" Dante's yell brought her around the corner. "The phones are out. You and Jamal find our driver and get Professor Adkins to the hospital." He rattled off the directions for the closest one. "The ER docs have to call the police on a gunshot wound. Tell them we've got the shooter in custody."

Shan's eyes widened slightly. "Yes, sir." She pivoted and ran back to the foyer.

Phylicia jogged after Dante. "We have to get rid of that punch too. It's been spiked." She wasn't about to explain how. Shan's acceptance was gratifying, but a part of Phylicia wasn't about to spoil a potentially good thing by telling Dante the truth.

"Yeah, I kind of figured that one—"

She ran into his back when he stopped short. It took a second for her to realize what was happening in the main living room.

The trio in the office had nothing on the full-blown orgy occurring right in front of their faces. Underclassmen and grad students were engaging in every position and combination imaginable. And a couple of positions Phylicia honestly thought *Hustler* had lied about.

"Should we go back through the library hallway?" she whispered.

Dante held a finger to his lips and clasped her hand. Immediately, she understood. As long as they didn't attract anyone's attention, the college kids would remain in their sexual trance.

Slowly, they made their way around the perimeter of the room. Only one problem—the main living room was the size of half the old Giants Stadium.

They were two yards from the short hallway leading to the dining room. One black-haired naked man had been watching one woman eat out another, looking for his opening to join them when he caught sight of Phylicia and Dante. An ugly leer filled his face. He stalked toward them, his intent clear from his bobbing erection.

Dante moved faster than she thought possible. His comforting grip on her palm disappeared. He twisted the naked student's elbow in some martial arts hold. Before the student could protest or yell, Dante's other hand closed over the man's throat.

She glanced back. No one else noticed them.

Her heart raced. This wasn't the flirting student from the store or passionate lover from the library. This was a U.S. Marine in combat mode. The change excited and scared her at the same time.

Still silent, Dante dragged the student into the dining room. The man was semi-conscious from the lack of air when Dante laid him on the carpet. His body definitely decided his blood was needed elsewhere from his flagging dick.

Dante motioned her to follow him. She padded over to him, and once again, he held her hand. Together, they made their way the last few feet to the kitchen.

Another couple was on the floor, the girl riding the guy in a gyrating dance. Kelly stood by the punchbowl, an odd gleam in her eyes as she watched them.

She turned toward Dante and Phylicia, and a malicious smile twisted her lips. "Why, Dante, you're not having any fun."

The wrongness slammed into Phylicia. Kelly's presence had the same cloying rankness as the punch. Except she didn't have the drugged-out look of the kids who had drunk the spiked beverage. "Dante . . ."

He pulled loose from her and glared at Kelly. "What the hell did you put in that punch?"

She fluttered her eyelashes. "Interesting choice of words." Kelly snatched a cup of the vile liquid from the counter and flung it in Dante's face.

"Shit!" He wiped the stuff out of his eyes as purple drenched his white pants. "This is a rental."

"Oh, Dante." Kelly stepped closer to him. Black seeped across her blue irises and the whites of her eyes. "Your cleaning bill is the least of your problems."

Panic hit Phylicia's gut as if Kelly had actually punched her. Whatever Kelly was, she definitely wasn't human.

Phylicia yanked down a frying pan from its copper hook. Her swing caught Kelly in the temple, and the girl crumpled to the tile floor.

"Come on!" She grabbed Dante by the back of his vest, doing her best to pull him away from the nutcase and not touch the liquid coating his skin and clothes. The two kids on the floor didn't realize anything had happened. They kept screwing. The girl threw her head back and moaned.

"Dante." When he met her gaze, Phylicia felt a sliver of relief that sanity still lived in his eyes. "Is there a shower on the first floor?"

"Yeah, my room."

She followed as he charged down another corridor and raced into a bedroom. Unlike Brittany's pink and purple frilly décor, this one was decidedly masculine. Japanese-style prints decorated the walls. The bed was constructed of black lacquered wood, covered in a brilliant red bedspread.

"Lock the door," Dante ordered as he swiped off the stained red handkerchief and yanked off his vest. Purple spots hit the cream carpet, leaving ugly bruise-like stains.

Phylicia flipped the little switch on the knob. It wouldn't hold up if Kelly ordered the kids under her control to attack them. She was under no illusion that the crack on the head would put the—whatever Kelly was—out of commission long.

Desperate, she searched the room. The only thing heavy enough to block the door was the huge dresser that matched the bed. Phylicia ran to the other side of the monstrosity and pushed. It didn't budge.

Dante edged beside her, and together they shoved the black behemoth enough that it covered most of the bedroom door.

Phylicia tried to catch her breath and took a good look at him. Purple liquid still dripped from his chin and all-too-defined pecs. "In the shower. Now!"

He gave her a wicked grin. "I knew you wanted me out of my costume."

She planted her fists on her hips. "Whatever's in that damn punch may be absorbed through the skin." She pointed in the direction of the bathroom. "Shower."

Dante sobered at her assessment, pivoted and marched for the bathroom.

Or tried to march. He swayed, like he was drunk.

Phylicia rushed over and slung his arm over her shoulders. Sticky purple residue clung to her skin. *Morrigan, please let running water break the spell!*

She propped Dante against the wall. Screw the costumes. They needed to get this stuff off them, or . . .

Goddess, she couldn't think about the consequences, or she'd freeze.

No tub in the bathroom, just a stall bigger than her first apartment. She turned both handles until water blasted from the showerhead.

"You're sho beautiful." Dante's hands grabbed her shoulders, pulling her against his bare chest, naked stomach and very erect cock.

An hour ago, she wouldn't have protested, but dammit, she wasn't fucking someone under the influence. Considering how fast the punch affected him, she only had a minute or two before she'd forget her own freakin' name.

She took a step into the shower, but Dante pulled her back.

"Want you," he slurred and laid a trail of sloppy kisses along her neck.

"You can have me, baby." She turned to face him, forced a smile and prayed it was convincing. "In the shower."

His eyebrows twisted like he was trying to think through the spell's haze. "I shouldn't . . ."

"Let's get this sticky stuff off us so we don't mess up your sheets, Dante." Phylicia sucked in a deep breath, trying to concentrate.

"I need to be inshide you."

She could barely understand his words. His grip was so tight. The real Dante wouldn't hurt her. *That* she was positive of. But whatever was in the punch threw a person's morals to the four winds.

"I know, baby." She reached up and stroked his face, contaminating herself more in the process. "I want the first time to be special. Let's get clean."

"I don't . . . I . . . Phylicia . . ." His expression became one of pain.

"Come with me, Dante." She grasped his hands. They came loose from her shoulders, and she tugged him closer to the . . . to the . . .

It was getting hard to think, like her brain was mired in cotton candy.

He pulled himself from her grip.

She stepped under the running water. Like a crack of lightning, everything was illuminated. Close. Too. Damn. Close.

She let the spray soak her hair, caress her skin. Facing Dante, she reached for him. "Join me."

He shook his head, his expression a mixture of agony and confusion. "Don't want to hurt you."

She gave him a gentle smile. "You won't hurt me, baby. Please get in with me." The surety she felt under the running water almost scared her.

"Want choo too mush."

Dante stood outside of the stall, his fists pressed against his thighs. He was fighting the spell, coherent enough to realize his behavior was being manipulated. If he bolted through the window, he could get seriously hurt. Or hurt someone else under Kelly's influence.

Damn. There was only one way to get him in the shower.

Phylicia reached behind her back and unhooked the clasp of the bra masquerading as a costume top. Her breasts sprang free. She undid the clasp at her neck. The spangles made a funny tinkling sound as they hit the wet ceramic tiles. She kicked the top aside. Despite the warm spray, her nipples were at full attention, had been ever since yesterday when she first laid eyes on Dante Jones.

Her actions had the response she hoped. Dante's attention fixated on her naked torso. He stalked toward the stall.

She edged back, trying her best to make it appear she was giving him room. He needed to be under that showerhead.

Water hit the back of his head, but it didn't change his intent. The glazed look in his eyes made her want to cry and punch something at the same time. His mouth closed over hers.

There was none of the gentleness from their first kiss in the library. He was rough, brutal. This wasn't Dante, but something else using him. The rankness from the spell filled her head.

Everything hit Phylicia with a crystal clarity. The doctored punch was only the catalyst, not the actual plan. Kelly was being used as well. The entity inside her manipulated the poor girl through her unrequited crush on Jason. The thing inside Kelly was pulling the sexual energy from the drugged students to fuel something else.

Dante's lips left hers. He knelt and suckled on the tight, hot bead her right nipple had become. The sexual tension inside her rose, but it didn't cloud her mind. It made things even clearer.

She could see the energy being drained from Dante and the water pummeling that connection. He moved to the left breast, his lips raising energy that wavered between her and the spell. But the tangle surrounding Dante was dissolving under the shower. When the last black string severed, Dante looked up at her and blinked.

"Phylicia?" He blinked water from his eyes and rose. "What the hell—?"

Then panic and disgust filled his face. "Oh my god, I-I almost—" He turned away and covered his face with his hands.

"Dante." She laid a hand on his bicep. "It's all right. We're both all right."

"I—" His hands dropped. He twisted to stare at her, fury in his eyes. Fury at himself. "I almost raped you," he ground out.

"You didn't." She cupped his face. "You had the strength to fight a demon's spell." She shook her head in wonder. "You have no idea how special you are, Dante Jones."

"Demon?" The look he gave questioned her sanity and his hearing.

"Yes." With any luck, Jamal and Shan were well on their way to the hospital with Rue. Which meant Phylicia needed an ally and enough power to protect them both. Which meant Dante needed to know the truth.

She wiped water from her eyes and looked up at him. "There's something inside of Kelly, using her. From what you and Jason said, it may have bargained with her for Jason's affections, or it simply used her crush to gain access to her mind."

"That's imposs—"

"It doesn't matter whether or not you believe me, but if we don't stop it, things will get a lot worse. Right now, it's using sex to cement its hold over these kids. Next comes the killing."

Something flickered behind his eyes. He nodded. "I've got a pistol and some ammunition locked under my bed."

"No." At his incredulous expression, she quickly added, "These kids don't know what they're doing. Kelly herself may have been tricked by the demon. You start shooting, and you'll kill an innocent."

His face hardened as her words sank in. "Then what . . ."

Her blood raced. This was going to be the hard part. Rain made sure she knew the theory and mechanics, but she'd never actually tried it with anyone. "I need you to make love to me."

His jaw dropped. It took a couple of tries before he got the words out. "You want me to do what?"

"You're attracted to me, right?" Goddess, help her. Had the library been a joke? She looked at his package. Despite the water breaking the demon's spell, Dante still had a healthy erection.

"Yes, but—"

"Please, Dante."

"We're in the middle of a crisis, woman!"

"And if I had the time to prepare, to raise the power with another method, I'd do it!" She closed her eyes, leaned her head back and sought a modicum of patience. "Please." Tilting her head forward, she opened her eyes. "I wanted that perfect night in your bed, too. We will have it." She stepped closer to him. "Once we save these kids." Her breasts pressed against his hard chest as water sluiced over their heads and shoulders. "Dante." Her arms twined about his neck. "Please," she whispered.

His kiss was her answer. Not the exploration of the library. Nor the bruising punishment of the demon. This time, his kiss was a demand and a gift. His tongue invaded, probed, and her own tongue responded in kind.

Dante pulled back for an instant and tugged off his boots. He grimaced as he chivied out of his pants and underwear.

Things had been so tense between them, Phylicia hadn't noticed that the white breeches were smoking where the spiked punch had splattered on him.

"Oh, my Goddess! Are you all right?"

"Yeah. The spots are hot to the touch where the water's reacting with that damn punch." He ran his hands over his naked scalp. "I'm surprised I don't have chemical burns all over my head and chest." He smiled at her. "Now, where were we?"

Despite the situation, she couldn't help smiling back. "I believe we were taking off our clothes."

"Let me." Once again, he knelt before her. This time her muscles trembled in anticipation.

Her belt landed in the corner with a clatter. The soaked gauze skirt followed. He yanked the bikini bottoms down, and she stepped out of them.

His face was between her legs, his tongue lapping her folds. She braced her hands on his shoulders. He plunged two fingers inside her pussy.

Maybe it was the danger, the adrenaline heightening everything. Phylicia felt every nerve explode. The energy swirled around her, trying to race away, only to slingshot back in her cells, her mind, her soul as she pulled on it. The action made her hornier.

Damn. No wonder Rain was such an advocate of sex magick.

"Dante." She practically panted his name. "I need you inside of me. Now."

Not that he needed to be told twice.

He was already on his feet, his body pressing hers against the shower wall. His hands grabbed her ass and lifted her. She wrapped her legs around his waist. Her arms followed suit around his neck. He slid inside her pussy like the Goddess had made him just for her.

He took her hard. Fast. Her pussy clenched, trying to keep him buried deep in her. With a low guttural moan, he shivered against her. His energy and the throb of his cock released her own orgasm. The electricity of their desire filled her. His kiss swallowed her cries.

Slowly, her legs unlocked from his waist. If it wasn't for her arms around his neck and his hands on her ass, she might have fallen.

I'm punch-drunk on power. She giggled at the thought.

"What's so funny?" Even he was struggling to catch his breath.

Not wanting to scare him, she kissed him, then smiled. "I've had more orgasms with you in the last couple of hours, than I have since Jamal was born."

He leaned back, a wry smile on his face. "I find that hard to believe."

Her grin widened. "My vibrator doesn't count." She quickly sobered. The decorating style of his room gave her an idea. "Do you have a fighting staff?"

"Yeah. Why?"

"I need it." Reluctantly, she reached down and twisted the knobs. The shower sputtered to a halt. "I hope you don't mind if I carve it up."

Chapter 6

Five minutes later, Phylicia sat in the middle of Dante's rug and tried to ignore the scrabbling sounds on the bedroom door. She carved runes on his bo with meticulous precision using his Marine knife. The traditional Okinawan fighting staff wasn't her ceremonial wood at home, but it would have to do.

"As much as I like you naked, here's some shorts and a t-shirt that should fit you." Dante crouched and laid the clothes next to her. "Sorry, I don't have anything for your feet."

"We just have to get to the kitchen."

"Except we will have to go out the window to do it." Concern filled his face. He wore camouflage pants, an olive t-shirt and combat boots that had obviously seen their share of action.

"I'll be fine." She blew away dust and chips. "Give me a second."

Phylicia held the staff straight out in front of her and closed her eyes. The excess energy flowed from her palms and infused the spell carved into the wood. So much power lay at her fingertips. Far more than she'd ever gathered and controlled before. She prayed to Morrigan it would be enough to banish the demon and free the guests.

When she opened her eyes, she found Dante staring at her.

He shook his head in disbelief. "I saw some weird shit in the Corps, but you? Woman, you take the cake."

She rose to her feet and donned the shorts and Yankees t-shirt. Luckily, the knit shorts had a drawstring. They swept past her knees as it was, and at five-eight, she wasn't exactly short. She could have used the Yankees tee as a nightshirt.

Phylicia met Dante's eyes. "You remember what I told you?"

"We get to the kitchen. I dump salt into the punch. You'll take care of Kelly." He frowned. "I don't like it. Kelly could throw that crap in both of our faces." Dante laid his hands on her shoulders. "Let's face facts. I'm trained to take out the enemy. She won't take me by surprise again." From his grin, he was trying to take the sting out of his words.

She laid a hand on his forearm. "Dante, baby, you haven't been trained to deal with the thing inside of Kelly. I have."

He lifted an eyebrow. "And how many exorcisms have you performed?"

Phylicia didn't say anything. Couldn't. She'd be the first to admit theory and reality were two different things. She headed for the window.

After a moment of silence, Dante added, "Not to mention, you don't look like any Catholic priest I ever saw."

Phylicia looked over her shoulder as she strode toward their escape hatch. "Really? And exactly how many Catholic priests have you seen naked?"

He wiped a palm over his face. "That wasn't where I was going—"

A loud *thunk* made them both look at the bedroom door. Dante shoved past her to unlock and open the sash. "Time to go. That was an ax."

As if on cue, one of the top door panels split open. Sharp, shiny steel poked through.

Phylicia scrambled through the opening. The wood chips she landed on were only a couple of degrees warmer than the night air. Her breath misted in the frigid temperatures.

The second Dante was through, she turned and slammed the window shut. With a little concentration and the wave of two fingers, the lock clicked into place.

Dante blinked and shook his head. "It would have been nice to have you in our squad in Afghanistan." Once again, he took her hand.

The evergreen bushes snagged both skin and cotton knit when she pushed past them. Then they were on the icy flagstones of an enormous patio that surrounded the pool. They had taken only a couple of steps toward the kitchen when the outdoor floodlights cut out.

Phylicia whirled around. The house lights were gone as well.

"Your demon's cut the electricity." Dante's warm breath sent tingles through her body when he whispered in her ear. They both paused as their eyes adjusted to the darkness.

"We keep going." She tightened her grip on the staff. "It's trying to psych us out."

A screech came behind them. They both pivoted only to have a panther tackle Dante. Both figures crashed to the flagstones, but somehow Dante landed on top of the—

It was a girl in a black bodysuit Phylicia realized. Dante had her pinned, but she kept trying to bite him.

"Should I toss her in the pool?"

"No. We need running water."

"Well, I can't sit on her all night."

Rustling sounded behind them. Phylicia whirled to see shadows pouring around the corner of the house. More students in their costumes. Her heart froze. There was no way she and Dante could fight the twenty or so people and someone not get hurt.

Concentrating, she aimed the staff and sent a blast of frigid air at them. The students slowed a little at the gale force wind, but the demon clearly had its hooks deep in the kids. They struggled forward one halting step at a time.

"Mom, cut the wind!"

Phylicia's attention broke at the shout behind her. Jamal ran up to her, trailing a green hose behind him. He held out the sprayer in front of him, as if it were a weapon, and pressed the trigger. A stream arched out and hit the first boy in the face. The people behind him rushed forward.

"You need a wider angle."

Jamal twisted the nozzle and swept the sprayer back and forth. The front rank slowed. Both she and Jamal retreated a step. The first soaked students stumbled to a halt. As the other bespelled kids pushed past them, Jamal hit them with water. One by one, the bedraggled crowd stopped.

"Hey! Some help here!"

Phylicia whirled to find the girl in the cat costume fighting Dante in earnest. The ex-Marine was having a difficult time keeping her pinned to the patio.

With the other students no longer a threat, Jamal turned the hose on Dante's prisoner. In two seconds, she yelled, "Cut it out! Stop, dammit!"

Phylicia grabbed Jamal's arm. "Why the hell aren't you with Rue?"

He looked at her with an incredulous expression. "Because there wasn't enough room in the car. A couple of these bozos attacked three girls. Our driver Raoul held 'em off with a fire extinguisher until I could get the hose. Shan's with Rue. Raoul and I loaded everyone, and they're on the way to the hospital."

"That was stupid." She wanted to spit nails. He took a terrible risk. At the same time, pride filled her that he put the safety of others before his own.

"You're welcome for the save, Mom." Sarcasm dripped from his voice. He surveyed the dazed people standing there listening to them. "What's the plan? I don't think Jason's wannabe girlfriend is working on her own."

Dante clapped Jamal on the shoulder. "Get these kids to the pool house. There's plenty of towels." Dante lowered his voice. "Just one problem. Jason locked up the car keys to keep anyone from driving drunk. I'm not taking chances of anyone going back inside the house. You'll have to walk this group to the neighbors and call 9-1-1. Kelly and her friend have probably only cut the lines for this place."

"You and Mom will need backup." In the dark, Phylicia could still hear the concern in her son's voice. He dropped the nozzle.

Dante's white teeth shone under the starlight. "We'll be fine. You've taken out half the people who drank the punch. You did great, Jamal."

Guilt tinged Phylicia's emotions. Jamal *had* kept his cool and remembered Rain's lessons. Otherwise, she and Dante would be in real trouble right now.

She stood on her tiptoes and kissed her son's cheek. "Dante's right. I'm sorry I yelled at you."

He hugged her tight. "Please be careful, Mom."

He released her and stepped toward the drenched students. "You heard the man, people. Pool house, then the neighbors." Despite the confused murmurs, the kids followed Jamal.

Except the sword hanging at Jamal's side sang a protesting note.

"Fuck," he muttered. He turned back and pushed past the crowd. He then unhooked the scabbard and held it out to Dante. "She's insisting that she go with you."

Phylicia had to cover her mouth to keep from laughing at Dante's incredulous expression.

"Your sword talks?"

Jamal shrugged and shoved the sheathed weapon in Dante's hands. "It's more like music, but she usually gets her point across." He cocked his head as if listening to something. "Don't actually use her on any of the partiers. They're innocent. Just hold her up unsheathed and she can repel anyone who drank the punch. But whatever you do, don't let go of the scabbard."

Dante blinked. "Your talking sword has a built-in force field?"

"I promise to explain it later. She trusts you, and that's always a good sign."

Phylicia sobered. That last comment wasn't aimed at Dante so much as her. She glanced at the ex-Marine. "Your sword has good taste."

Jamal's shoulders eased a fraction. "Be careful," he repeated before he herded the freed kids toward the pool house.

Dante stared at Phylicia. "Next thing I know, you'll tell me I'm holding Excalibur or some other shit."

"Okay, I won't tell you." She pivoted, firmed her grip on the staff and marched toward the kitchen. Things had been going their way, but deep down, she knew the demon wouldn't be such an easy target.

The soles of Phylicia's feet burned as she crossed the patio. The water from the hose was already freezing on the flagstones. When she reached the sliding glass doors, she held up her hand. Dante halted, but the steam from his breath swirled around her.

Concentrating, she extended her senses, searching for any spell that may booby-trap the entrance to the kitchen. Her eyes locked with Dante's, and she shook her head.

At his nod, she stepped back. He ran his fingers along edges. Once satisfied, he held up three fingers. Phylicia readied the staff. Dante lowered each finger. When he reached "zero," he flipped the latch and carefully slid the glass open.

Phylicia tried to enter first. Dante grabbed her arm and shoved her behind him. He held the sheathed sword in front of them. She should've protested, would've protested, but the feel of his body against hers sent awareness cascading across her nerves.

Stop it! she told herself firmly. After the shower, she certainly couldn't blame her reactions on the damn punch. Tightening her grip on the staff, she pulled the door partly closed and examined the dark kitchen.

Starlight and the waning moon provided their only illumination. No one was in the room. The huge bowl of purple evil still sat on the table.

Moans and gasps filtered in from elsewhere in the house. The sounds set her teeth on edge. This demon would use the guests until they died of exhaustion.

Despite the freaking huge boots he wore, Dante moved in total silence toward a cabinet, then set the sword on the counter. He pulled out a small bottle and crossed back to the table. There was a soft hissing sound as he poured the contents into the punch.

He jumped back as the liquid bubbled with a fury. Clouds rose from the bowl. They both covered their noses and edged away from the table.

Goddess only knew what effect the fumes would have. With a little concentration, Phylicia directed the fumes toward the slight opening in the door.

The moaning grew louder.

Dante leaned close and whispered, "It sounds like everyone's in the front living—"

Crack!

He staggered and Phylicia reached for him. Sticky wetness coated the shoulder of his t-shirt. Dante started to crumple. She dropped the staff, trying to catch him. The ex-Marine was just too big. In the end, all she did was cushion his fall with her body.

A flutter of movement made her look up.

Jason stood over them, naked.

Phylicia didn't know what disturbed her more—the gun in Jason's hand, the dark substance smeared across his face and body, or his very erect cock.

Chapter 7

Phylicia stifled a scream as Jason reached for her. Trapped underneath Dante's muscular body, she couldn't evade him.

Jason yanked her roughly by her arm. For a split second, it felt like he would dislocate her shoulder. He kicked Dante's still form and freed her legs before dragging her upright. The setting moon through the glass doors lit his feral grin.

That look sent her survival instinct into overdrive. She stomped on his instep and lunged, her teeth digging into the wrist that held the gun. Jason grunted, but didn't release his grip on her.

Desperate for another tactic, she strained for the pot rack. Her fingers wrapped around the rim of a sauce pan. Not as good as the frying pan she left in Dante's room, but it would have to do.

Jason jerked on her arm. She used the whiplash and a quick pivot to smash the pan in his face. Blood poured from his nose. On the backswing, she nailed the hand holding the gun. The weapon clattered on the floor and slid out of sight.

He let go of her, but she couldn't take any chances. She slammed her knee into his groin. When he doubled over, she brought the pan down on his skull as hard as she could.

Before she could catch her breath, Jason was already using Dante's prone body to gain his knees.

Dammit to hell! Under normal circumstances, Phylicia knew she'd be no match for any ex-Marine. Right now, Jason was under the demon's spell and wouldn't hesitate to hurt her. She didn't have time to search for her staff. Probably couldn't reach it if she knew where it was. She raced for the sink.

Thank the Goddess, the Kourics had an industrial-style sprayer on their sink. She flipped on the cold-water spigot and pulled the sprayer loose. A quick whirl and she caught Jason in the face with the blast of icy water.

This close to the window she could see the dark splotches on his body were dried punch stains. Corded muscle wrapped around her, trying to wrestle the sprayer away from her.

With water pooling on the tile floor, Jason's feet slid out from under him. Phylicia tried to wrench free and keep the sprayer, but Jason's firm grip meant she went down as well. From the muffled *woof,* his chest cushioned her fall.

Phylicia twisted, keeping the flow on his face and chest.

After two seconds, he raised his hands to block the water. "You can stop now."

At the sanity in his tone, she sat up. Jason gave a half-screech, half-moan. Stifling her laugh, she whispered, "Sorry about that."

His body tensed under her in a different way. "Oh, God. Dante?"

"I'm still here."

Phylicia twisted to see Dante using the drawer handles of the island to pull himself into a sitting position.

"I'll have to kick your ass though for groping my woman." He grinned, but pain filled his voice.

Jason swiped at the bloody water dripping from his chin. "I think she already took care of that."

Phylicia scrambled over to Dante. Dark liquid glistened on the front of his t-shirt. "You're still bleeding."

"Is there an exit wound?"

"Yes."

Jason crouched on the other side of Dante. He handed Phylicia a couple of dish towels. Blood still trickled from his nose down over his lip. "Hold these over both wounds. Tight."

Dante grunted as she pressed them on each side of his damaged shoulder. She looked at Jason. "Now what?"

"Hold 'em in place while I tape him up."

With a start, she realized he held duct tape and scissors in his other hand. "You can't be serious?"

Jason ignored her and focused on his friend. "I'm sorry. I thought it was you and Phylicia knocking on the office door. Kelly threw a cupful of that punch in my face. I tried to fight the effects, but it was like she was in my head." He wrapped the silvery plastic adhesive around his friend's shoulder. "I'm pretty sure I missed anything vital when I shot you."

Dante winced as Phylicia pushed him upright so Jason could secure the tape around his chest. "You always did suck at target practice."

"Be glad I do, man, or you'd be—" Jason's voice broke, and he ducked his head to hide his emotions.

As much as she felt for him, they couldn't afford the time to wallow. "Jason, where's the car keys?"

"Dad's office. In the safe." He slung Dante's uninjured arm over his shoulder and helped him to his feet.

Phylicia spotted the staff under the table. She snatched it and stood. "Get Dante out of here—"

"No," both men said at the same time.

"You need backup," Jason added.

Phylicia jabbed a finger in his naked chest. "I got enough of that crap five minutes ago from my son. I'm not taking it from you. Dante's been shot, and you have a broken nose."

"Baby, the thing using Kelly has been picking us off in ones and twos all night." Determination lay under the pain in Dante's voice. "I'll carry the sword, Jason the gun and you the staff. This is going to take all three of us working together."

She pursed her lips. "You put the sword down for an instant, and look what happened."

He huffed in exasperation. "I won't put it down again—"

"Damn straight because you both are leaving. That thing in Kelly will be twice as dangerous now that it's lost a large chunk of its power source."

"We don't have time to fight about this," he snapped. "What's that demon going to do with those kids once it's done with them?"

Jason's gaze whipped back and forth between her and Dante. "Demon?"

A shudder ran up Phylicia's spine. There wouldn't be anything left but broken flesh and traumatized minds. And that's if they were lucky. She closed her eyes briefly, then opened them. Earnest, dark eyes stared back at her.

"All right. I need some more salt. And Jason needs some pants."

Less than a minute later, Jason had retrieved a pair of dirty jeans from the laundry room, and Phylicia had found a canister of table salt in the cupboard. In the meantime, Dante tried to wrestle the punchbowl to the sink with one arm.

Phylicia propped her fists on her hips. "What do you think you're doing? You neutralized it."

Jason collected his gun from where it slid between the refrigerator and the pantry. "So, we don't have to worry about getting drugged again?"

Phylicia shook her head. "There may be cups of punch in all the rooms. Do you have any plastic baggies?"

Jason fished three zippered bags from the pantry. A pantry nearly the size of Phylicia's bedroom in her apartment.

She tried not to let envy break her concentration as she divvied the salt between them. "If you see a cup, drop a pinch in to counteract the punch."

Then she helped Dante hook the sword and scabbard to his utility belt. He winced when she brushed against his injured arm.

Empathy tied her nerves into more knots. "You don't need to do this."

He reached for her, his rough fingertips brushing across her cheek. "Marines don't leave a man behind. And *we* need to finish this mission."

Dante leaned down. This time his kiss was soft and reassuring. Yet, it still left her gasping for breath when he eased away. "Time to do this, baby."

Phylicia took the lead as the three of them marched down the hallway. The moans and cries had dimmed while her focus was on the fight with Jason, then their preparations in the kitchen. Now, the sighs, the slide of skin over skin, the wet slapping came to the forefront of her consciousness.

Her steps slowed. A soft glow permeated the space ahead. Goddess, how she didn't want to walk into that room. What the demon forced those people to do was a perversion of everything she believed. But if she didn't do something soon, there wouldn't be anyone left for the authorities to save.

Assuming help is on the way, a little voice at the back of her mind mocked. No. She had to believe both Shan and Jamal got the groups they rescued to safety.

Digging her fingers into the wood shaft, she forced herself to make the last steps. The scene was nearly the same as the last time Phylicia and Dante had crossed the main living area. A fire had been lit in the massive brick fireplace, and a multitude of candles covered the surfaces that guests weren't having sex on. This time though, there were fewer people.

On a divan by the fireplace, Kelly gyrated on the lap of a naked young man while another woman kissed her and fondled her breasts. Her eyes were closed and her face contorted as ecstasy took her.

Or the thing inside Kelly did, Phylicia silently amended.

Demon Kelly turned toward them. Her eyes opened, both orbs entirely black. A glossy black that pulled Phylicia into their depths.

She blinked and broke the contact, careful to keep her attention on Demon Kelly's left knee. Damn, the demon didn't need the stupid punch anymore. If Phylicia wasn't more careful, she'd end up on the floor with the rest of the college students, literally fucking her brains out.

"Don't look into Kelly's eyes," she whispered over her shoulder.

Like a command had been given, all the party guests stopped what they were doing and stared at the trio with a glassy, drugged gaze.

Demon Kelly shoved the girl she'd been making out with off the divan. The girl landed on the hardwood floor with a thump and a whimper. "So you're the little witch causing me so much trouble."

Phylicia tightened her grip on the staff once more. "Leave this house, release these people and I won't cause you any more grief."

The low chuckle that issued from Demon Kelly's throat sounded like rattlesnakes thrashing in sulfuric acid.

Dante stepped to Phylicia's side. Metal whispered on leather as he drew the sword.

Jason eased forward on her right. "What the hell is that thing?" he whispered.

Demon Kelly rose with a fluid, serpentine motion that shouldn't have been possible with human joints and muscles. Fingers flicked at the fireplace then toward the trio.

Phylicia whipped the staff horizontally. The ball of fire flared around her air shield, singeing the floorboards and bubbling the paint on the ceiling.

Demon Kelly's eyes narrowed. Another gesture. Fluids from various cups and vases swirled into the air and formed a cobra-shaped series of bubbles. The liquid snake arrowed for Phylicia just as the fireball had.

A bit of concentration and the cobra splashed against her shield and dripped to the floor.

The instant she released the concentrated air, Dante and Jason sprinkled salt over the puddles. The reaction of the salt and liquid spat and hissed, but the fumes were nothing like the putrid gasses released when they neutralized the main punch bowl.

"*Striapach!*"

Demon Kelly's epithet and next gesture came so fast that Phylicia barely got her shield up in time. Objects in the room flew at them with hurricane force winds. Windows bent and cracked before smashing, becoming deadly projectiles. Glass and ceramics shattered against the shield. Heavier items bounced off, but the effort to keep herself and the ex-marines protected took its toll. Thank Morrigan, most of the candles blew out in the ferocious blast.

When the maelstrom died, Phylicia panted heavily. Steam rose from her nostrils as cold flooded in from the broken windows.

Around them, naked students lay cut and bruised with the occasional wax burn. As a single entity, the ones who could still move rose to their feet. Even those with obvious broken bones stalked toward them.

Anger welled up in Phylicia's gut. Someone was going to die at the rate things were going.

She slammed the end of her staff down on the floor. Hardwood rippled and heaved. A concentric wave spread across the sub-flooring, popping boards and nails. Party guests toppled.

Demon Kelly leapt and rode the divan like a surfboard, her disconcerting laugh rising above the snap and crackle of the wood. The leer on her face felt like tiny worms burrowing under Phylicia's skin.

"Well, well, well. You're not any old *striapach*. You're one of Her *striapachs*." Demon Kelly sprang, landing on all fours on the splintered planks. She shook her head, a mocking expression replacing the leer. "But you're sadly outclassed." She slammed a fist against the broken floor.

The entire house shook. This time the subflooring creaked and groaned before splitting open down the middle of the room to show the basement below. Cracks appeared in the walls and ceiling. Everything stilled for a moment.

Then from the broken plaster and shattered wood, wires and pipelines crawled out. In the light of the couple of remaining candles on the mantel and the fire, they looked like tiny snakes. Rotten egg smell filled the room. Dante and Jason dropped to crouching positions on each side of Phylicia.

She stared at the possessed young woman. "Are you insane? You'll destroy your host!" She jerked away from Dante's efforts to get her down too.

The ugly grin was back. "And?" Demon Kelly crawled toward Phylicia, her knees and elbows sticking out at odd angles.

With a roar, the thirty or so remaining guests charged Phylicia and the two ex-marines.

All of Tom's training sessions kicked into gear. Phylicia swung the staff into fighting position. A blow to a temple. A jab to the solar plexus. Anything to keep from the party guests off her.

The gun barked twice. Despite Dante's teasing, Jason obviously knew what he was doing. Two kids went down with leg injuries.

Dante had stood, was doing his best to keep the sword facing the crowd. Jamal had been right about its power repelling the possessed students. But it didn't protect Dante's back. One of the guest landed a blow on his injured shoulder and he cried out.

Then Phylicia realized what the demon was doing. Her minions were separating the three of them. And with every breath, the smell of rotten eggs was growing stronger. Once the natural gas hit the fireplace, everyone would die. And the energy released in the explosion and all those deaths would give the demon the power to physically manifest. Then there would be no stopping it.

The idea that sparked in her brain was nuts. It was idiotic. It was simply . . . insane.

And it might actually work.

She glanced back at the two ex-marines. Jason now had his back to Dante's. The men pivoted as one to keep their attackers at bay.

"Dante!"

"Yeah!"

"The second the spell breaks, get these people out of here!"

His eyes met hers for a split second, the realization of her craziness reflected in their depths.

She couldn't think about it any more. If she did, she'd chicken out.

Phylicia hefted the staff and took three running steps. Splinters and nails pierced her soles. Ignoring the pain, she planted the end of the staff and vaulted over the gap in the floor. She landed and rolled. More debris dug bloody furrows in her skin, but she kept a firm grip on the staff.

When she came to a stop, she looked up in time to see Demon Kelly leap across the giant crack. Delight flickered on the possessed girl's face as she scrabbled across the broken flooring like an insect.

Forcing herself upright, Phylicia planted the staff and braced her aching feet and arms. She closed her eyes and moved the top of the staff in tiny concentric circles. Air shifted around her, a slow, lazy swirl. Below and behind her to the right came the rushing charge of water. The sprinkler system.

"So weak you can't even produce a decent wind." The demon's sneer came through her words. "Pathetic, little *striapach*."

The threads of energy in the air moved over and around Demon Kelly. Phylicia suppressed a smile. The demon wasn't rushing her. Instead, she circled, attempting to analyze what Phylicia was doing.

Good. Phylicia fed more will and power into her little circle of wind, but kept the power leashed. She needed the demon a little closer.

"You can't stop me, you know. Your line has degenerated. Too much fucking with the humans." Arrogance flavored the demon's words.

What the hell was that thing talking about? *Ignore it*, Phylicia told herself firmly. *She's trying to mess with your head.*

The subtle change in air pressure said Demon Kelly inched closer. Phylicia twirled the top of the staff a little faster. She felt the energy of the remaining candles die as the moving air blew them out.

"Maybe I'll keep you alive. Let you watch me fuck your mate. Let my pets use you for my enjoyment—"

Phylicia sucked in a deep breath and held it. With a thought, she let go of the leash she held on the winds. The air itself screamed as it birthed a tornado in the middle of the Kouric's living room.

Demon Kelly shrieked in anger, tried to jump back, only to slam into a wall of air moving at incomprehensible speeds.

Slowly the vortex sucked anything breathable out of the tiny circle holding the two women. Demon Kelly twisted to glare at Phylicia, red sparks in her depthless black eyes.

The demon tackled Phylicia, driving precious air out of her lungs. Phylicia responded with a sharp crack of the staff on the possessed girl's head. The speed of the cyclone around them slowed allowing a little oxygen into the vacuum Phylicia had created.

Can't lose it. Not now. Phylicia dug into herself, fed more energy into the mini-tornado. The speed of the spinning air jumped. She couldn't breathe.

But neither could the demon. It gave up its assault on Phylicia, clawed at Kelly's throat, tried to crawl away only to be stopped by the damn-near solid wall of wind surrounding them. They both collapsed, gasping like beached fish.

Black spots danced before Phylicia's vision. She reached out with the tiny bit of energy she had left. The moan of stretching copper. Sealed joints snapped and cracked. Water arched through the broken window. Phylicia let go of the tornado, and icy spray soaked both her and Kelly.

Phylicia reached into her pocket. It took her precious seconds to open the zippered baggie with numb, shaking fingers. Too many crucial grains of salt fell to the damp, broken floor. More still stuck to her dripping palm. She flung the handful at the semi-conscious Kelly.

The girl screamed in agony. Despite her blurry vision, Phylicia would have sworn *something* crawled out of Kelly's mouth, its higher pitched shriek adding to the cacophony. Something black with glowing red eyes. Something that didn't belong to this world.

It glared at Phylicia with pure malice. Then it raced for the fireplace, disappearing up the chimney.

The remaining guests sprawled across the floor. Screaming and crying started as the pain of their injuries sank into their conscious brain. In the distance, sirens added to the noise.

Phylicia pushed herself upright. Across the room, Dante sat slumped against the wall, Jason crouched next to him. The firelight reflected his white grin. He raised his fist, his thumb upright.

She looked around. For the most part, everyone seemed intact. She closed her eyes, found the gas pipe and pinched the metal shut with her will. They'd beat the demon. Last thing they needed was a gas explosion on top of all the other damage.

Caw!

The noise drew her attention to the smashed window. Perched on the sill was her grizzled veteran. First the crow's good eye, then the blind eye turned toward her.

Caw! Caw! Caw!

His shrieks sounded like a claxon above the kids' moans and weeping. Underneath her hip, a subsonic vibration started. Phylicia reached out with her senses. Not the demon. The old house had simply had enough.

"Dante!"

The groan of support beams grew louder. Sharp snaps filled the air. A humungous wall of sound hit her as the damaged floor collapsed.

Then Phylicia was falling. Falling into the giant black hole beneath her.

Chapter 8

Dante tried to stand again, only to have the paramedic push him back down. Red and blue lights flickered around them, except where the halogen spotlights focused on the remains of the Kourics' front living room. The backhoe the rescue workers trucked over from a nearby construction site coughed to life.

"So help me, do that again, and I'll tranquilize you." She stared at him for a few seconds until reassured he wouldn't move. She went back to cutting off his duct-taped t-shirt, then said softly, "These guys know what they're doing. If she's alive, they'll find her."

He strained to peer around the ambulance door.

The paramedic laid a hand on his forearm. "The site's unstable. You won't be helping by bringing what's left down on her head, son."

Dante shot the paramedic a dirty look before he leaned back. As much as he hated to admit it, she was right. When the floor had opened up and swallowed Phylicia and Kelly, he thought his heart would stop.

Jamal appeared around the side of the ambulance, a worried expression etched in his dark skin. The neighbor he'd guided his group to happened to play for the Knicks. He'd let Jamal borrow his clothes, so the kid had jeans and a sweatshirt that fit.

"Anything?"

The freshman shook his head. "They won't let me help."

"Did you get the garment bags from the car?" Dante wasn't about to mention magic swords or demons in front of the paramedic, or she really would trank him.

Jamal nodded. "Raoul took Shan and our costumes back to the Village."

The pair had returned after they got Rue and the drugged grad students admitted to the hospital. Jamal gave Dante a rueful grin. "'Fraid you may be coughing up the cash for yours, man."

Dante said nothing, just went back to staring at the fire trucks and rescue vehicles blocking his view. He recognized Jamal's gallows humor all too well. The full price for the stupid pirate costume was nothing if Phylicia was—

No, he couldn't think like that. Especially not in front of her son.

The paramedic pulled one of the bloody towels from Dante's shoulder. He hissed at the wave of pain.

"Sorry," she murmured. "What the hell happened again?"

Dante chuckled, but kept his eye on Jamal. "Not much. Some douche spiked the punchbowl. Another asshole accidentally opened the fireplace gas line. Oh, and my best friend shot me after wrestling his sidearm away from a drunk party guest."

Relief flooded his system when Jamal gave an almost imperceptible nod. Good. He'd stick to the story Dante and Jason had worked out.

A flash of movement at the other ambulance drew his eye. Jason strode toward them, a blanket wrapped around his shoulders and his feet still bare.

"How's Brittany?"

Jason shook his head. "I don't know how, but she managed to sleep through everything. Not a mark on her. The firemen had to break down the door. Somehow, it was locked from the inside."

Dante pressed his lips together. Explaining Phylicia's talents wasn't going to help anyone, but it was good to know her first priority had been to protect Jason's little sister.

They watched the other ambulance head down the driveway. "I insisted she get checked at the hospital since she had some of that damn punch," Jason added.

"I'm sure she'll be fine." Jamal clapped a hand on the shorter man's shoulder. "Shan said according to Mom, Brittany puked everything up."

"Speaking of which . . ." Jason pulled a tiny gold bag from his back pocket. "I found this on the floor in Brittany's room. It's not hers, so I thought it might be . . ."

Jamal held out his hand and took the purse. "It's the one M-Mom brought—"

At the mention of Phylicia, all three men turned their attention back toward the house.

Dante clenched his good fist. The kid was trying so hard to keep it together, but it only added to the helplessness balled in his gut. "I can't just sit here." He started to rise again.

"Son . . ."

He glared at the paramedic. The silver liberally sprinkled through her dark hair shone in the flashing lights.

At his look, her face gentled. "At least let me pack your wound before you go charging over there." Then her stern expression returned. "And I won't be liable for your stupidity."

Dante gave her a sharp nod and sat down again. His left boot tapped an impatient rhythm while she did her job.

She was fitting him in a sling when some kind of commotion sounded off to the left, near the main road. A couple of police officers jogged by.

"Get out of my way!"

Dante stood. The voice sounded familiar.

"Ah, shit," Jamal muttered. "It's Rain."

A dark bird dive-bombed the ambulance before landing on someone's Porche nearby. It cocked its head in the direction of the raised voices.

"Ma'am, you need to stay behind—"

"Touch me again, young man, and I'll shove that nightstick up your ass!"

Yep, that was definitely the magic shop's owner.

Her distinctive silver hair reflected red and blue tints as she pushed past the officers without any regard for their "Do Not Cross" yellow tape. She spotted Jamal and strode toward them like she was the queen of Manhattan. Tom, the dark-haired white guy from the shop was tight on her heels.

"Where's your mom?"

For a split second, Jamal's face crumpled, but he caught himself. He waved at the wreckage. "She's somewhere under that mess."

Dante stepped forward and lowered his voice. "Can you find her?"

Rain met his eyes. Once again, it felt like her sharp blue gaze bore right through his skull and examined the individual brain cells. "Yes."

He grabbed her arm and together they raced toward the wreckage. He could feel Jason, Tom and Jamal pounding behind them. The minute he released Rain, she closed her eyes. He watched in amazement. Her steps were sure-footed, confident, despite the fact she couldn't see a damn thing.

"Hey, what do you think you're doing? Get back!" A fireman with "C-H-I-E-F" stamped on his helmet charged toward them. Red colored his face not covered by his bushy mustache.

"Here!" Rain pointed. Jamal, Jason and Tom jumped in and started digging through debris with their bare hands.

"I said, what the hell do you think you're doing!" The fire chief jabbed a finger in Rain's face.

Dante stepped between them, more to protect the chief than Rain. "Shut down that backhoe. You're digging in the wrong place."

"You have no idea what you're talking about—"

Dante ignored him and ran for the equipment. At his slicing motion, the operator turned off the engine. Everyone was silent and still except for the thrum of the generators.

Running back to Rain, he said, "Where?"

"Here." She pointed to a spot next to Jamal.

"You can't—" the chief spluttered.

Dante dropped to his knees. Together, he and Jamal tossed away brick, plasterboard, wood. A pipe appeared under the mess. There was a faint *bong*.

He held up a hand and Jamal froze. Behind them, rescue workers crowded around and muttered.

"Shut up, people!" The crowd stilled at Dante's order.

-boong-boong-boong. Bong-bong-bong. A pause. *Bong-bong-bong. Boong. Boong. Boong. Bong-bong-bong.*

Relief blurred Dante's vision. A cheer went up as the crowd recognized the code.

One of the firemen hit Dante's injured shoulder as he shoved past to start digging. The fire along his nerves made him gasp.

Rain grabbed Dante's good hand and tugged him back. He wanted to pull away, but she stood on her tiptoes, her lips close to his ear.

"It's okay, Sergeant. We did our jobs. Let them do theirs." She patted his chest. "Besides, you need your rest. Didn't you offer to do Phylicia in a proper bed?"

In his worry, it took a second for Rain's words to register. His lower jaw dropped, and he turned to stare at her. "H-How did you—"

Rain said nothing, just folded her arms and watched the men and women dig for Phylicia. The sly smile remained on her face the entire time.

Two hours later, Dante sat next to the gurney holding Phylicia as their ambulance pulled out of the Kouric's driveway. The lady paramedic, who'd originally treated him, checked Phylicia's blood pressure for the umpteenth time.

He twined the fingers of his good hand through Phylicia's dirty ones.

She smiled up at him and squeezed his hand. "I'm fine. Quit worrying."

Dante's heart ached. She wasn't fine. Cuts and scratches marred her beautiful skin. She couldn't walk from the damage to her bare feet. Dust filled her dreads. And he wanted nothing more than to take her home and care for her.

Except the authorities weren't about to let him, Jason or Brittany back into the house any time soon.

"When was the last time you had a tetanus shot?" The paramedic held a pen to her clipboard.

Phylicia sighed. "Jamal was two, so it's been sixteen years ago."

"Time for an update then." Concern etched her features. "Do you have insurance, honey?"

Phylicia shook her head, sending up a tiny cloud of dust that had all three of them sneezing. "My boss has a fund that we use for when any of us get sick or..."

At the odd expression on her face, Dante squeezed her hand again. "What's wrong, baby?"

"Except for Jamal's well-baby appointments and immunizations, we never had to use the medical fund until this year." She gave a rueful chuckle. "Now..."

Her eyes flicked toward the paramedic and back to him, the message loud and clear. Tonight's demon and whatever else she was thinking didn't need to be discussed in front of strangers.

"Just a little round of bad luck, baby." He brought her hand to his lips, and she laughed in earnest.

"Yuck! Don't do that!"

He raised an eyebrow. "I can't kiss you?"

"Not while I'm this filthy." She laughed again. "And there were rats in that basement. You *don't* want that kind of dirt in your mouth."

He leaned close to her ear. "Then we'll just have to take another shower together."

Unfortunately, a nurse, who bore more than a passing resemblance to Rosie O'Donnell than a certain sexy ex-marine, helped Phylicia bathe and wash her hair. And that didn't happen until hours after the ambulance arrived at the hospital. After the x-rays and MRI scans to make sure nothing was broken or hemorrhaging inside of her.

Phylicia blinked. Somehow, she'd fallen asleep. The bright morning sunshine that had filled her room had given way to deep shadows. She shifted to find Tessa reading in the chair beside the hospital bed.

The blonde closed her e-reader and reached for her hand. "How are you feeling? Do I need to get the nurse?"

Phylicia shook her head. "Just need a drink," she croaked.

Tessa helped her raise the bed and sip from a cup of ice water.

Damn, her muscles hadn't ached this much when she'd banged S-O-S on that pipe for hours. She leaned back against the pillows. "How's Jamal?"

Tessa laughed. "*He* came through this insanity without a scratch." She sobered. "Please don't be pissed, but he took Dante back to your place. Someone needed to watch Dante because he left the hospital against medical advice."

Everything ached and hurt, yet her pelvis twinged at the thought of Dante Jones sleeping in her bed. Then the rest of the crap rushed in.

"What about Rue Adkins?"

Tessa's curls flew as she shook her head. "Not as lucky as Dante. If Shan and the chauffer hadn't driven him—"

"Her," Phylicia corrected automatically.

"Her," Tessa repeated. "To the hospital in time . . ." She shrugged. "The good thing is nobody died. She's still in ICU last I heard. The girl in the basement with you . . ."

Phylicia could guess what Tessa's silence meant. "She's in the psych ward."

Tessa ran a hand through her curls. "Yeah. The doctors are chalking it up to an OD on a new designer drug."

Phylicia closed her eyes. That would be the safest explanation for everyone. Maybe death would have been better for Kelly. The girl had awoken in total darkness after being possessed by a demon, and something in her had shattered. Phylicia was no medical expert, but the girl would need some serious help. Assuming she'd ever be able to rejoin regular society. "Anything else?"

"Dante's Marine buddy is staying with Adrian, and his little sister is at Rain's since the authorities can't let them back into their house until it's stabilized."

Phylicia opened her eyes and smiled at Tessa. "So you drew the short straw and got stuck with me?"

Tessa's expression grew terribly still. "That's not funny. Do you realize how close we came to losing you?"

Moisture gathered in Phylicia's eyes. "All too well." It had taken all her remaining will to snap an air shield over her and Kelly as most of the first floor rained down on them. Then she used the last of her physical reserves to drag the unconscious girl to a more stable portion of the basement.

Sucking in a deep breath, she pushed the wayward emotions aside. She wanted, no, she needed to make sure Jamal and Dante were all right. "Any chance of getting out of here now?"

"Nope. The doc's keeping you overnight to make sure your toes still wiggle and your feet aren't infected." Tessa rattled the IV stand.

"Damn. I'd give anything just to brush my teeth." Good thing Dante wasn't here. Phylicia wouldn't want to kiss anyone with as much fuzz that had settled on the enamel in the last twenty-four hours.

Brushing curls out of her eyes, Tessa sighed. "I brought you some clothes and toiletries." She inclined her head toward the tiny closet under the TV. "Your purse is up there too."

"My purse?" The memory of the beginning of last night's insanity flashed to the front of Phylicia's brain. "Oh my goddess! I left Rain's cloak, shoes and clutch at the Kouric's."

Tessa stared at her with an incredulous expression. "Seriously? That's what you're worried about?"

It kept her from thinking about other things. Like her legs wrapped around Dante's waist in his shower. "Yes! I can't afford to pay Rain for that stuff. Not with my son in college."

"Well, you don't have to worry about replacing the bag. That's the one I was referring to. Jamal gave it to me before Adrian drove their collective asses back to Manhattan for some sleep this afternoon." A smirk filled Tessa's face. "You know, when Rain and I heard you had to drag Dante into a shower to sober him up, we were hoping for the best. But when I checked the bag, all the condoms were still there."

. . . all the condoms were still there . . . all the condoms were still there . . . all the condoms were still there . . .

Phylicia covered her face with her hands. The echoes of Tessa's words wouldn't stop. How could she have been so stupid? Hellfire! She hadn't been *that* stupid with Isaiah. It was simple bad luck that the rubber had torn and she became pregnant with Jamal.

But this time?

She'd dealt with gunshot wounds, drugged college students and a demon in the last twenty-four hours. Why the hell had she fucked Dante Jones without protection?

Because you wanted it, the nasty little voice in the back of her mind whispered. *You were so horny you didn't care.*

All the emotion she'd swallowed in the Halloween craziness erupted into sobs.

Chapter 9

A little over a week later, Phylicia sat on the balcony of Tessa's Central Park West apartment. The place would put anything on *Lives of the Rich and Famous* to shame. Granted, Tessa was only house-sitting for her business partner's parents, but still . . .

The temperature was in the low sixties, surprising as the calendar rolled into the second week of November. Autumn's last stab before giving in to snow and ice. From her view of the park, branches that had been full of color a few weeks ago were now naked and black.

She wiggled her toes under the bright Monday sun. It felt good to be free from the bandages, but her soles itched like crazy. The doctor said it was a good sign when he removed the stitches that morning.

The shrill ring of the phone sounded inside, followed by the muffled tone of Tessa's voice. Phylicia was grateful for everything Tessa had done over the last several days. She'd worked from home all week in order to take care of Phylicia. In the meantime, the rest of the staff at Morrigan's Cauldron, along with Shan, had covered her shifts.

And everything made guilt run thick under Phylicia's skin. She'd always found a way to take care of herself and Jamal.

On top of everything, her own son lectured her last night on how badly she was treating Dante. She deserved the tongue-lashing, but she couldn't tell Jamal the truth. She couldn't talk to Dante either. Not after screwing up so badly by having sex without protection. But that wasn't the worst. It was more than embarrassing. It was . . .

Reprehensible.

She'd used him while he was intoxicated. It made her no better than Shan's ex-boyfriend, and that kid had been slime when he was alive. It made her just like the demon who'd used poor Kelly.

"Enjoying your time off?"

Phylicia whipped her head around to find Rain standing in the patio doorway and glaring at her. Blue flames practically spat from the old woman's eyes. She marched the short distance and stopped next to the chaise, forcing Phylicia to shield her eyes from the sun's glare.

"I thought you understood that the doctor said I needed to be off my feet."

Thankfully, for Phylicia's retinas, Rain sat on the patio chair. "Physical healing's one thing. Dante's another. Why are you hiding?"

Can't think about what happened. She'll know. "This coming from the woman who can't see what's in front of her?"

Rain's silver eyebrows rose. "Excuse me?"

Phylicia folded her arms. Definitely time to go on the offensive. "Tom. He's got a thing for you, and you go out of your way to flaunt your boyfriends in front of him."

Rain matched her body language. "I don't dip company pens in my pot."

"Maybe you should."

"Really? How about I start with someone young enough to keep up with me?"

"You can try to seduce my son, but I heard Shan's pretty good at stabbing old corpses through their shriveled hearts!"

"At least, I'm not hiding from a man because I was too stupid to remember a condom!"

"You don't need a condom for your pruney, old—"

"Enough!"

They both turned toward the deep masculine voice. Dante stood in the same place Rain had been a moment ago.

Except for the sling, he looked almost the same as the first time Phylicia saw him. Dark blue denim hugging hips and thighs that da Vinci could have sculpted. The bright red Henley shirt. The small gold hoop flashing in his ear. But this time there was no flirtatious smile. Calling his expression furious would have been an understatement.

"Miz Rain, you need to leave, please." He jerked his free thumb toward the apartment.

The old woman stood. "Now just a minute—"

"I know you care about Phylicia, but this is between us."

Rain's eyes narrowed. "You don't order me—"

"Ma'am, with all due respect, I do agree with Phylicia on one point. Until you get your own house in order, stay out of our business."

Rain's jaw dropped. It had probably been decades since someone was that forceful with the old busybody. She stood and propped her fists on her hips.

Sharp blue eyes met Phylicia's. "I am *not* a busybody. And you're *not* pregnant, so get over yourself."

Rain stomped over to Dante. She shook an index finger under his nose. "Don't you *ever* take that tone with me again, young man."

Dante didn't look the least bit cowed. The fury in his expression eased, but his face still held a fierce determination. "Stay out of my personal affairs, and I won't."

Abrupt laughter spilled from Rain. "You just might survive living with her after all." She slapped the bicep of his injured arm. He grimaced in pain.

"Rain!" Phylicia raised a fist to her mouth. The old woman could be tough, but she'd never displayed such appalling behavior.

"Don't ever do that again," Dante said through gritted teeth.

"Then don't ever call me a bitch again."

This time Dante's jaw dropped as Rain marched past him and into the apartment. His attention remained on the patio doors while he walked to the chair Rain had vacated.

He finally looked down at Phylicia. "I didn't call her a bitch."

"Did you think it?"

His abashed look was an admission in itself.

She sighed and shaded her eyes again. "In case you didn't notice, I didn't call her a busybody out loud either. Sometimes, she just knows . . ."

They simply stared at each other for a long time.

Finally, he sat. "Is that why you were hiding from me? Because you might be pregnant?"

Once again, silence stretched between them.

Somehow, she found her voice after an eternity. "That's part of it. The other part—" She had to clear the growing lump in her throat. Uncomfortable meeting his steady gaze, she stared at her scarred feet. "I avoided you because I took advantage of you."

"Excuse me?"

Her head popped up. "You heard me. I-I—" She swallowed hard. "You were intoxicated from that punch, and I used you."

"Yeah, but I'm wondering if we were at the same party. The one where a demon-possessed bitch drugged me and I tried to force myself on you. Damn." He ran a hand over his scalp. "And here, I thought . . ." He looked out over the park. "I thought you were pissed at me about what happened in the shower."

Then he started laughing. Long. Hard.

"This isn't funny," she snapped.

"Yes, it is." The charming smile was back. "I guess I was being a bit of a tease in the library. And really, you couldn't help yourself with such—" He waved his free hand over his body. "—fine manly attributes."

"What!" She sat up straight. If there wasn't a chance of reopening one of the cuts on her feet, she'd kick him in the shins. Her fists clenched. If he got a little closer, she'd belt him. "Of all the conceited—"

Dante was faster than she thought. He was out of the chair, his lips on hers. She couldn't think, couldn't resist, didn't want to resist. His body slid onto the chaise, snug under the warm sunshine.

When they broke the kiss, he smiled at her. "Sure you don't want to take advantage of me again?"

Phylicia couldn't help herself. She smiled back. "Only if it's in a proper bed this time."

He pulled his arm from the sling. Fingers slid under her shirt and cupped her breast. His lips captured her moan of pleasure.

"Geez, you two! Get a room!" Tessa stood over them, hands on her hips.

Phylicia and Dante started laughing, but he removed his hand.

Tessa shook her head. "Keep that up, and Rain's prediction will come true."

She might as well have splashed cold water on Phylicia. "What prediction?"

Tessa grinned. "You'll be knocked up by Christmas."

Chapter 10

Five weeks later, Phylicia picked up her great-grandmother's locket from her jewelry box and fastened it around her neck. She had always believed it brought her luck.

Ironically, she'd put it on the day she found out she was pregnant with Jamal. The day her parents threw her out of the house.

"You ready, baby?" Dante leaned against the doorjamb. How long had he been watching her?

She wiped her palms against her skirt. Shan had helped her pick out the cream-colored suit. "Yeah, I just . . ."

Dante took two steps and pulled her into his arms. "Second thoughts about us getting married?"

"Goddess, no!" Even through his suit, his body felt so damn good.

"Then what? Worried that Rain will be running around at the party telling everyone she was right?"

Phylicia buried her face in his shoulder so he wouldn't see her embarrassment. They'd been putting up the tree last week. And forgot to use protection. Again. For all the lectures she'd given her son, she was a very poor example. "Not really . . ."

His fingers touched her chin and forced her to look up. "Our son isn't growing up without *both* parents."

"Daughter," she automatically amended.

"Hey, Mom! Tessa says Adrian's holding a cab for us!" Jamal's voice echoed through the tiny apartment.

Phylicia gave Dante a wry smile. "I'm more worried about how Jamal will react to having a sister."

"Don't sweat it, baby. We have his blessing." Dante's grin grew wider. "With the caveat that if I screw up with you, he has the right to behead me."

"Mom! Dante!"

Phylicia gripped his hand in hers. "I believe that's our cue."

Three hours later, the wedding party was in full swing. Shan's grandparents had closed their restaurant for the private celebration.

Phylicia had sworn off a couple of dances. The doctor had said her feet were totally healed, but her wedding shoes said something else. She, Shan and Tessa gossiped while their men filled dishes for them at the buffet.

Dante handed her a plate with a flourish. "There you are, Mrs. Jones."

"Thank you, Mr. Jones." She nibbled while Dante pulled her feet into his lap and gently massaged them. She would have relaxed if Adrian didn't keep staring at her chest.

Tessa waved a hand in front of his face. "Don't you know it's rude to stare at another woman's rack while your fiancée is sitting next to you?"

"Hey, that's my mom!" Jamal added.

Adrian shot Tessa a dirty look. "Ple-ease." He turned back to Phylicia. "Do you mind if I ask where you got your locket?"

Phylicia's hand rose to the etched silver. "It was my great-grandmother's. Why?"

The intense expression on Adrian's face didn't disappear. "Was her name Dunne?"

Something squirmed up Phylicia's spine. Even Dante paused at Adrian's odd question. "Yes."

"Virginia Dunne?"

The squirmy feeling froze with her shock. "How-how could you possibly know?"

Adrian looked at Tessa. "Sorry to spoil the surprise, but Phylicia's necklace . . ." He reached into his jacket pocket, pulled out a jewelry box and snapped it open.

Phylicia's breath caught. Inside lay a duplicate of her necklace. She looked up at Adrian. "Is there a picture?"

He nodded.

Her fingers trembled as she took the proffered box. Very carefully, she opened the antique locket. This couldn't be.

"Holy crap," Jamal whispered.

Phylicia reached to unhook her necklace, but her fingers shook so bad she couldn't make the clasp work.

Familiar hands touched hers. "Let me, baby." Dante worked the catch and handed the necklace to her. She clicked the release of the cover.

"Oh, my god," Tessa breathed as she leaned close to examine the pieces.

The women in the two pictures could have been the same person if it weren't for the beauty mark on the cheek of the one from Adrian's locket.

Phylicia looked up at Adrian. "We're related?"

"I think so." He pointed at the portrait from his locket. "My great-grandma Georgia had a twin sister, Virginia. Supposedly, she married someone their father didn't approve of, and he disowned her. According to my grandfather, she moved with her new husband to Paris. Despite the family disapproval, Great-grandma still wrote to her twin until the Nazi invasion. She never heard from her after that."

"Wait a minute."

Phylicia looked at Dante.

His face held an odd expression. He jabbed a finger at the two lockets. "Your great-granny is white?"

She arched an eyebrow. "Wow. That's racist. Didn't think you were that type."

He spread his fingers at her mocking. "Just surprising. That's all."

A smile tugged her lips. "Can't deal with a little milk in your coffee?"

He grinned back. "Just as long as there's plenty of sugar."

Jamal abruptly shoved his chair back. "Excuse me." He stalked into the crowd.

Phylicia caught Shan's eye. "What was that all about?"

She shrugged. "You got me."

Jamal made a beeline for Tom, who leaned against a wall, sipping a beer. The older man had been observing their table the entire time, and something about the way he watched Mom and Adrian set Jamal's teeth on edge.

Tom raised the bottle in a mock salute. "How's the new dad?"

In a split second, everything in Jamal rang with a crystal clarity, like it did when he held the Sword of Lugh. "You knew. You knew Mom and Adrian were related."

Tom said nothing, just took another swig of beer.

"Does Rain know?"

"Of course she does." An odd light sparked in Tom's eyes. "But she doesn't know that I know, and I'd appreciate it if you'd keep quiet for now."

For the first time ever, suspicion of the man flared in Jamal's heart. Tom had always been good people before, even if he was an odd duck. Everyone chalked it up to a bad experience during the first Gulf War, but now . . .

Jamal crossed his arms and glared at Tom. "Why?"

Tom faced him, his dark brown eyes deadly serious. "Because winter's coming, and I need everybody to think I'm a non-player in this game."

The same frisson of unease he'd felt at the Halloween party rippled across Jamal's nerves. "Mark last summer and the demon at Jason's. They're just the beginning, aren't they?"

Tom took another long swig before he answered. "Yes." This time his attention was solely fixed on the woman across the room, laughing with Grandmother Wong.

Rain Bean.

WINTER

Chapter 1

Another blast of frigid air whistled around the front doors of Morrigan's Cauldron, seeking and finding any egress into the store. The windowpanes rattled their displeasure at the late January storm trying to force its way past their guard. Even with the heat turned up, the draft raised gooseflesh along Tom Laoch's forearms.

Outside, a few pedestrians bent against the wind as they hurried to their destinations. It would be a quiet night if most of the street traffic consisted of the delivery kids from Wongs' Restaurant across the way.

Tom dipped his attention from the view as he cut open the box in front of him. With two blackouts hampering the city so far this winter, they couldn't seem to keep any candles in stock, much less the red and white tapers for Imbolc in two days.

"This doesn't feel right."

Tom looked up from where he knelt. Rain Bean, the owner of the Greenwich Village shop, watched as the wind dragged trash in its wake outside. "What do you mean?"

She rubbed her upper arms despite the heavy navy sweater she wore. "It doesn't feel natural."

"Winter rarely does."

Rain looked down at him. "Did you just make a joke?"

He couldn't resist a smile. "It's known to happen occasionally."

One of her fine dark eyebrows arched upward. "Be careful. You might hurt yourself. You'll definitely scare the children."

He placed the first box of votives on their display shelf. "They're not children any more, Rain," he said softly.

She made a disgusted noise in her throat and walked away.

His good humor faded. She couldn't see how much things had changed in the world. If they had lived centuries ago, Adrian and Phylicia would have been elders of their clan. At eighteen, Jamal was older than Tom had been in his first battle. Rain was simply too old to comprehend being young anymore, and despite his own centuries, he was a squawking infant himself in comparison.

She stomped back over to where he stocked candles, two twenties in her outstretched hand. "Go pick up our dinner."

"Don't you ever get tired of Chinese take-out?"

Anger sparked in her blue eyes. "I'm your boss, Laoch. Move it."

"Yes, ma'am." He stood, shoved the bills in the front pocket of his jeans, and stalked to the back room to grab his coat. Whatever the deal Rain had struck with the woman most folks in the Village knew as Grandmother Wong, he wasn't stupid enough to get in the middle of it. Pissing off one goddess in one lifetime had been enough.

By the same token, he didn't like leaving Rain alone in the store. She didn't have access to all her abilities while in human form. If a demon ate the portion of her soul housed in tender mortal flesh, it could increase its strength considerably.

Not to mention the possibility of sucking down the rest of her essence in the process if the demon was strong enough.

Luckily, the store manager Adrian Holloway hadn't questioned Tom when he requested that either he or Jamal Washington needed to be on duty when Rain was here through winter. The kid hadn't said a word about the changes in his schedule, but he made a point of bringing his sword with him when he worked. Of course, Tom's whole plan had gotten shot to the afterlife and back when Jamal's mother, Phylicia, came down with the nastiest case of morning sickness known to the human race three weeks ago.

But this week, Tom insisted he be the one to work the same shifts as Rain. Not that Jamal hadn't come a long way in his sword training over the last six months, but the attacks on him and Phylicia had come on Lughnasadh and Samhain, both High Sabbats. If Tom gambled, he would have laid everything that the next one would be on Imbolc.

"I'll be back," he said as he crossed to the front door.

Rain made some non-committal sound.

The wind nearly whipped the door from his grip and the bells jingled in alarm. He wrestled the heavy oak closed without breaking any glass and headed for the crosswalk. The first pricks of rain struck his face.

Great. Freezing rain on top of the plummeting temperatures. The entire island of Manhattan would look like a glazed wedding cake by morning, but a lot more dangerous.

Tom waited to make sure the traffic actually halted when the light changed. On the bus stop bench outside of Wongs' Restaurant, a line of crows huddled together against the freezing drizzle.

As he walked passed the birds, he said. "You guys better be keeping a close eye on her. You know an unfriendly is looking for her."

The matriarch on the end cocked her head, and a beady golden eye glared at him. *Caw!*

The entire murder took up her insult in a cacophony that echoed against the stone and bricks in this section of Greenwich Village. Tom smiled at them and plunged into the blessed warmth of the restaurant.

Of course, Grandmother Wong would be running the register tonight. She slammed Rain's order on the counter. Her grey hair frizzed in a halo from the humidity of the kitchen. "You don't come in here. You never come in here, Dog. You going to tell me what's going on?"

He handed the bills to her. "My boss told me to pick up her order."

Mrs. Wong snorted. "She ordered for two. I give you beef and broccoli." Her gnarled fingers jabbed at the buttons like the machine had personally insulted her.

Old suspicions arose. "Are you sure it's beef?"

Another snort, but her dark brown eyes twinkled. "Even I have to answer to a New York health inspector, Dog." She slapped the change into his hand, but when he went to pick up the bag, she grabbed his wrist. "Do you need help?" Her fingers were far stronger than the age-spotted skin and swollen knuckles would indicate.

"There's nothing in this matter that Compassion can offer that War does not herself possess."

"It is easier to destroy than to create. Preservation takes balance."

"If you two are finished trading Chinese proverbs, some of us would like our dinner now."

Tom turned to find a middle-aged man tapping his expensive leather shoe against the red and white floor tiles. "Just leaving." He grabbed the carryout bag and flashed Mrs. Wong a smile. "I've got it covered."

The middle-aged jerk shoved past him and gave his name.

Grandmother Wong's voice rose. "Don't have an order for Schwartz. You sure you're at the right restaurant?"

Tom snickered at her game as he headed back into the freezing rain. *Never, ever piss off a goddess.*

Tom waited as Rain locked the front door. Already, a thin glaze of ice lay over the streetlight's pole.

"Good night." She waved and headed down the street underneath her blood-red umbrella. He paced her, and her double-take would have been amusing under other circumstances.

"What are you doing?"

"I'm walking you home."

"I get that. The question is why you and Jamal have been doing it for the last two months."

"That's not the question you asked."

She grabbed his arm and dragged him to a halt. They both wobbled for a second on the slippery sidewalk. "You know what I mean. It was cute at first. Now, it's annoying."

He rubbed a hand over his lower jaw. Did he tell her what he suspected? Come clean with what he actually knew? That someone had ferreted her secret and she was a tempting target?

No. If he did, she would deny everything. He needed concrete evidence that someone was after her.

Tom looked up. Sure enough, dark birds lined the rooftops. "You need more of an escort than the murder."

She glanced up as well before she glared at him again. "What are you talking about? They're just birds."

Yeah, she was in total denial mode. "It's drizzling, and it's freezing, and I don't feel like getting pneumonia." He snatched her free hand and wrapped it around his elbow. "Come on."

"What's with the caveman routine?" she grumbled, but she walked along with him. He wasn't sure what she would have done if he picked her up and carried her. He wasn't sure he wanted to find out either.

"At the rate this crap is coming down, I want you home. I want to get back to my place without breaking several bones because I doubt if Henry would be happy if I spent the night on your couch."

"I'm not seeing him any more," she mumbled.

"Oh." The temptation to ask what happened lay on the tip of his tongue. *It's none of my business.*

Rain peeked up at him from under the umbrella. "'Oh.' That's all you have to say?"

He tore himself from those piercing eyes and focused on their footing. "What would you like me to say?"

Her posture became rigid. The anger flaring off her was a palpable thing. "Nothing," she muttered. "I don't want you to say a Mother-damned thing."

Father, help me. I will never understand the female side of the equation. He cleared his throat. "I'm sorry about Henry. What happened?"

Rain was silent for another half-block before she said, "The stuff at Samhain freaked him out."

Not the holiday itself, but Rain's mysterious knowledge that Phylicia was in danger. The desperate search after a demon pulled most of a Long Island mansion down on top of the young witch's head.

"Fuck him if he can't handle it."

A throaty chuckle came from Rain. "Well, that's not happening."

The implication settled in Tom's mind. "No sex for three months? Isn't that a record for you?"

She nudged him in the ribs. "You part of the contingent that thinks a woman over sixty shouldn't be doing the deed?"

He grimaced. "According to every commercial during a televised sporting event, a man my age needs chemical assistance to do the deed."

They both laughed. Probably for the same reason, he realized. Centuries later, their respective romantic exploits were a legendary part of human literature, even if things didn't quite work out between the two of them. A comfortable silence lay between them for the rest of the walk to Rain's building.

At the top of the steps to her apartment building, she paused with the key in the door. "You could stay the night. And not on the couch."

Damn, if his body didn't jump at the offer. He'd relied on cold showers and a lot of self-help to keep his libido in check since he entered this plane. He swallowed hard. "I work for you."

"So?"

"You've never gone after the men who work for you."

"Maybe I want one exception."

Tom stared at the street. Few cars passed now. The thin sheet of ice coated everything and shone under the street lamps. "If I say no, will you change shapes and try to kill me for rejecting you?"

She stiffened, and suspicion flared in her eyes. "What are you talking about?"

"Morrigan and Cu Chulainn."

Rain tried to cover, but her laugh was a little too forced. "That's just a story."

Her non-answer told him what he suspected. She thought he was one of his own descendants, like Adrian, Phylicia and Jamal. And yet, she adhered to her rule about not touching any of them. So why make a pass at him?

Unless his curse had followed him to the Summerlands and back.

Ironic that she appeared a sixty-something woman and he wanted her far more than when she'd appeared to him as a beautiful princess all those centuries ago. But back then, beautiful princesses were a sword blade a dozen.

The urge to kiss her became too much. He closed his eyes, bent and brushed her lips with his. The touch penetrated the illusion. Her skin was far softer than it appeared, tasted of honey and darkness and fresh water.

At first, she stiffened at his audacity, but her natural inclinations took over. She returned the kiss with a fervor he never imagined. His fingers twined through her hair, but instead of straight locks, curls met his touch.

She pulled away, and he opened his eyes. For an instant, she looked younger, much younger, with scarlet ringlets cascading down her back before the illusion dropped back into place.

A slight smile tilted her lips. "Does that mean you changed your mind?"

The old manners slipped into place. "Not tonight, m'lady." He lifted her gloved hand to his lips.

Her brows knitted into a frown. He hesitated, wondering if he'd screwed up again.

"Good night, Tom." She turned the key and slipped into the building.

Another urge hit him. He almost pressed the buzzer for her apartment. Squelching his hormones, he walked down the steps. A man, dressed in black clothing with his collar turned up against the freezing rain, brushed past him and jogged up to the building's main door.

High-pitched bird shrieks rent the air.

Tom whirled and slipped on the icy sidewalk. His knee slammed into the unforgiving concrete, and pain racked the joint.

A flurry of feathers charged for the entrance. Black bodies wedged themselves into the doorjamb to keep the door from locking behind the man. Tom scrambled up the steps on all fours, desperate to reach the heavy steel before the birds were crushed.

And before the stranger reached Rain.

Chapter 2

Tom shoved the door open as he climbed to his feet. "Stop him."

The freed birds spiraled up the open staircase in a cacophony of war cries. Tom raced up the three flights, his right knee screaming in protest at every step. He reached the fourth floor landing to find Rain on the floor wrestling her attacker while the crows dive-bombed him. Something metallic flashed in the assailant's hand.

Tom charged. He crashed into the man and knocked him off Rain, but kept his focus on the knife. He barely shifted his hip in time to avoid a knee to the groin. The asshole followed up with a head butt that left stars twirling in Tom's vision.

Ignoring the pain, he forced the attacker's hand into a locking hold, but his opponent knew the counter-move. Great. Just wonderful. Not only was this *not* a run-of-the-mill attack, but the jerk had martial arts and probably military training. Brute force would have to do.

The question was whether he could subdue Rain's attacker without killing him.

The stranger rolled to his feet in a smooth move. Steel flicked out, Tom automatically threw up an arm. Sharp burning traveled the length of wrist to elbow.

He kicked and the heel of his steel shod boot nailed the attacker's patella. He issued no sound, but his face paled. A sweep of the man's good leg brought him down.

Once again, Tom crashed into him. They tumbled across the floor. Somehow, Tom managed to end up on top. He slammed the hand holding the knife into the hardwood repeatedly until the weapon clattered away. A left cross nailed Tom's jaw, and the man bucked.

Through the wave of pain and dizziness, Tom grabbed the attacker's collar and beat his head against the floor until he stopped moving.

"Someone call 9-1-1."

Tom looked up at the strange voice. The birds formed a swirling curtain around Rain, but they were landing on the floor since the assailant was unconscious. The rest of the people in the hallway must be her neighbors. "We need to secure this asshole first."

Rain knelt next to him and ran fingers along his swelling jaw, but her words were addressed to a couple of the men watching them. "Derek, would you and Rory drag him into my apartment before we call the police? I've got handcuffs."

Tom winced as she helped him to his feet. "We need real handcuffs, not your plastic sex toy ones."

She shot him an evil grin. "Oh, they *are* real."

He would have shaken his head if he weren't damn sure he had a concussion, and he'd vomit in the process.

After improvising a pressure bandage for the cut on his arm out of a dishtowel and duct tape, Tom retrieved two more dishtowels and filled them with ice while Rain trotted to her bedroom. She came back out with three pairs of police-grade handcuffs and several yards of rope.

The crows fluttered in after the humans and perched on various bookcases. A couple landed on the kitchen table, guards for their prisoner.

Within seconds, Rain and her neighbors dragged him into the apartment and checked his pockets and clothing. Nothing. Not even another weapon. They securely cuffed her attacker to one of the heavy oak kitchen chairs they carried to the middle of her living room.

Her assailant looked to be in his late thirties. Short dark hair flashed a little silver in places. He was about five-ten, but definitely in superb physical condition. Tom's aching body could attest to that little fact.

One of the young neighbors took a plastic zippered baggie out in the hall.

"Don't touch the knife," Tom called after him.

"Don't worry, sweetheart." The one with the purple hair that stood straight up waved a manicured hand. "We watch all the crime shows. Derek won't leave any fingerprints." He faced Rain. "So is this the new boytoy, girl?"

Rain smiled as Tom limped over to her well-worn couch. "No. He works for me."

"Just as well." Rory flicked a couple of fingers. "He's a little too Neanderthal for my taste."

Derek sauntered back into Rain's apartment. The dark-haired boy in jeans and a Columbia sweatshirt held the baggie with the knife in front of him like it was a soiled diaper.

"Set it on the table." Tom lowered himself onto the cushions and placed one ice pack on his knee. He couldn't remember a time where he felt this bad after a brawl. But then, the last time he was alive, he hadn't made it past thirty, much less the forty years he was now. Alarm coursed through him when Rory pulled out his phone. "Rain . . ."

Her head jerked up from tying a noose. "Rory, it's okay. You don't need to call the police."

Tom recognized the thread of Suggestion in her voice.

"I don't?" Purple spikes wavered despite the bottle of hair products used to keep them in place.

She gave both young men a beatific smile. "Not yet. Why don't you and Derek finish your dinner first? You can come back here when you're done."

Derek's body quivered as he fought the glamour. "You sure about that?"

"I promise you can both be here when the police come to fetch our bad boy."

They pivoted without another word and left the apartment, closing the door behind them.

"Did he hurt you?" Tom eyed Rain.

"Only my pride at getting caught flat-footed." She retrieved the rope. With a few deft motions, she looped the noose around her attacker's neck and tied it around his wrists and ankles. When he gained consciousness, he couldn't free himself without strangling. "You clocked him pretty good. I hope he can be of use."

"Wake him up and let's see."

Rain walked to her windowsill and picked up a plant mister. She crossed back to their prisoner and squirted the man in the face. His eyes flashed open and lunged forward.

Or tried to. When the noose dug into his neck, he choked.

The demon was smart. Use a mortal, make it look like a random mugging, and no one would ever know . . .

Sweet Danu! Adrian's wife Jennifer and their unborn baby had been killed by a mugger. Maybe it wasn't a mugging after all, but deliberate murder. So what was the real plot? Take Rain's powers or kill the rest of Tom's family?

Rain's assailant tried to flex muscles and test his bounds.

Yeah, definitely ex-military. Tom flared at their prisoner. "Who hired you?"

From the corner of his eye, he saw Rain jerk. But the man was definitely a professional. He remained silent. His gaze was assessing, planning his escape. His eyes widened when they caught the crows decorating the bookcases

"Look, we can call the cops, but we both know that one way or another, you'll be out of custody in a few hours." The thug's lips twitched. Good. He was at least listening. Tom continued, "The way I see it you've got three choices. You can talk to me and disappear. You can take your chances with an employer who's pissed off that you failed to kill my friend here. Or you can be really stupid, protect your reputation and try to take her again."

Tom leaned forward. "But now she knows someone's gunning for her. Frankly, buddy, she's a lot more deadly than you realize. I saved your ass out in the hallway."

The man blinked and carefully turned his head to examine Rain. Tom could practically see the blur of brown fur in the hamster wheel of his mind.

"Helen Mirren in *Reds*?" Their prisoner's voice had a gravelly quality.

Tom smiled. "Something like that."

Rain's assailant grunted. "Knew something wasn't right about this job." He met Tom's gaze again. "No names. Woman approached my contact. He said she was a redhead. Unbelievable rack. Paid in full with cash." He smirked. "Fucked his brains out for the tip."

Tom ran his hand over his mouth. *Shit.* A demon used sex magic to get hooks into the guy's broker. He glanced at Rain. Her subtle nod confirmed his suspicions.

"Did you ever meet her?"

For the first time, the attacker looked worried. "Told you. Only my liaison."

Tom leaned forward. "Don't contact him. He's been compromised. You got a safe pack stashed?"

A slow nod.

"Run far. Run fast. Don't look back. You read me?"

"Five by five."

Tom let a sick smile twist his mouth. "Just remember. You decide to double-cross us I'm not the one you have to worry about. It's her and her friends."

One of the crows on the table screeched, and the rest of the birds echoed the sentiment. The assassin's face turned a new shade of greenish-white.

Good. If they freaked him out enough, he'd no longer be part of the danger equation.

There was a loud knock on the door before Derek and Rory burst into the room. "Ready to call the cops, yet?"

Tom looked at their prisoner. "Well?"

He shrugged, or tried to without throttling himself. "I'll take your deal."

"He's free to leave, boys," Rain said. She flashed him a grin that showed her eyeteeth. "For now."

Caw? The female crow on the table cocked her head and looked at Rain.

"Yes."

Their prisoner turned an even more pale shade of white. Did he realize Rain had just told the murder to keep an eye on him?

"Aw, man," Derek grumbled. "That's not fair. We wanted to see some hot cops tonight."

"Boys, would you be kind enough to unshackle our guest?"

Derek and Rory did as Rain asked.

Her attacker stood and stretched as he felt the lump he no doubt had at the base of his skull. His eyes met Tom's. "Any chance my contact—"

Tom shook his head. The guy was dead. Or worse.

The man blew out a deep breath. "He was good people." He shook his head. "Shame."

"Boys, please walk our guest and the murder down to the main doors," Rain said.

The assassin marched out of the apartment, not stupid enough to ask for his knife back. Derek and Rory followed him, and the crows took flight.

Tom watched Rain as she mulled over the information her attacker gave them. "Anybody pissed at you besides Mark Li and Bill Mailer's parents?"

A slim eyebrow lifted at the mention of the two boys in Jamal's class who had trashed the store last summer. "Not that I know of. Is our friend the reason you, Adrian and Jamal have conspired to walk me home every night?"

Time for some truth. "Actually, the demon Phylicia fought at Samhain is why I'm worried. It kept referring to her as 'Her *striapach*'."

Rain laughed. "A demon calling Phylicia a whore in Celtic isn't enough—"

Tom lifted the ice pack from his swelling jaw. "No, it's the capital 'H' in the 'Her' part. As in, it was interested in enslaving Phylicia because she's your apprentice."

Rain pivoted, her silver hair flying. She stalked to the tiny kitchen and started banging the measuring spoons, cups, anything she needed for coffee that would make a lot of noise. Her actions would be funny if the situation wasn't so damn serious.

He lifted both ice packs, pried himself off the couch and limped to the kitchen. She slammed the glass pot onto the burner. How it didn't shatter was beyond him. The glamour of an older woman fuzzed, and he caught a glimpse of the goddess in her full fury.

He set the ice packs on the counter and grabbed her hands to still them. "I'm spending the night here."

A sly smile spread across her features. "I guess I'm on top since you've been wounded in action."

"We're not having sex tonight, Rain." However, his cock had other ideas.

Her attention flicked from the fly of his jeans and back up. "I think I can persuade you otherwise."

Banging on the door saved him from the degenerating conversation. He motioned for her to stay put, but Derek and Rory burst in once again before Tom could answer it.

The grizzled veteran of a bird with a missing eye perched on Derek's shoulder, but it was the tiny mound of black feathers Rory cradled that caught Tom's attention. "One of your crows is hurt."

Tom's eyes narrowed. "Our friend?"

Derek shook his head. "No. He said good night and crossed the street. Most of the flock followed him. This guy—" he pointed at the crow on his shoulder "—started screeching, and we found the little one huddled under the mail boxes."

"Bring him over here." Tom hobbled over to the couch and lowered himself to the cushions.

Rory set the bird gently in his lap. A wing stuck out at an awkward angle. Tears smeared eyeliner down the boy's cheeks. "Is there anything we can do?"

Remorse oozed through Tom as he examined the crow. The entire murder had flung themselves between the heavy door and the jamb to keep it open for him.

The crow closed his eyes, his breathing labored. Tom carefully ran fingertips over his patient. In addition to the damaged wing, two ribs were broken. From the disjointed throbbing of the bird's pulse, the bones had punctured the lung, the pericardium or both. If they had pierced the heart itself, the poor little guy would already be dead.

Rain's warm palm touched his shoulder. "There's nothing you can do, Tom."

A familiar ache pressed against his heart. There had been a time, centuries ago, when he could heal with a blessing. How he'd wished for the old gift when Shan and her father had been attacked by a *kiang shi* last August. Then there had been the injuries Phylicia suffered when a house had literally collapsed on her while she battled a demon for the lives and souls of a group of students at Samhain.

But his wish had been selfish, and he knew it. Both women and Dr. Wong survived. The tiny form in his lap didn't have their luck. Blood bubbled from his airways.

"May the Tuatha de Danann be merciful and heal the wounds you acquired in their service," Tom whispered in Old Celtic. Tingling began in his fingertips.

With a gasp, Rain jerked her hand from his shoulder. The tingling spread, filling every nerve, every sinew. Beneath his hands, the crow stilled. Golden light danced between him and the bird.

When the light faded, the crow shook himself. *Caw?* He climbed to his feet and tested the previously broken wing, unfolding and folding it a couple of times. Satisfied, he leapt into the air. The powerful down stroke ruffled the stack of utility bills sitting on the trunk Rain used as a coffee table.

The crow circled the room twice before landing on the kitchen table. With a cry, the one-eyed bird glided over to join him. Both of them checked out the wing with a discussion of harsh caws. Black, glittering eyes settled on Tom. Their heads bobbed in unison.

An uncomfortable feeling tickled the back of Tom's neck, and he swung around to face Rain's neighbors. Derek's jaw hung open, his attention flitting between Tom and the healed crow. Rory crossed himself, a beatific smile on his face.

"You two should go home now." Tom didn't have Rain's touch though, and both boys shook their heads.

"Do you know what you just did?" Rory gave him an adoring look. "You performed a miracle, man."

"No, he didn't." This time, anger tinted Rain's Suggestion. "The crow's wing was only dislocated. Go home and go to bed. Fuck each other until you're exhausted. Tomorrow, you will not remember anything other than Tom popped the wing joint back in place and the bird was fine."

"Yes, ma'am." Derek's voice sounded distant, but there was no mistaking the lust in his eyes as he gazed at his partner.

"Good night, Rain," Rory said, the same disconnect in his tone. "Nice to meet you, Tom." The boys were kissing and fondling each other before they made it out of the apartment.

As soon as the door closed behind them, Tom looked up at Rain. "Wasn't that a little overboard?"

"How'd you do that?" She practically spat out the words. "That bird was on death's door." She jabbed an index finger in the direction of the once-injured crow. He made a nervous *cheep*.

Tom crossed his arms. "Truth for truth."

From the red that flared across her cheeks, that was the wrong thing to say. She stomped into her bedroom. A second later, she stomped back out and threw two blankets at his head. The old crow took off and managed to dart into her bedroom before she slammed the door.

The younger crow winged over the overstuffed chair between the couch and the bedroom. He cocked his head. His black eye glittered with a question.

"Guess I'm not sleeping in her bed after all."

The bird shook his head in a way that clearly said, "Idiot."

Only when Tom shifted to lay down did he realized his knee didn't hurt. The cut on his arm didn't burn anymore either. He climbed to his feet. No agony in the joint whatsoever. He bent it experimentally.

Nope. Not so much as a twinge.

His fingers ran over his jaw. The lump was gone. No tenderness either.

He walked to the kitchen and pulled a knife from Rain's butcher block. Carefully, he sliced through the duct tape and unwrapped the crusted towel. Only a faint pink scar showed through the tattered sleeves of his flannel shirt and thermal undershirt.

Well, that was a new twist to his ability.

Chapter 3

Tom tried not to smile as Rain stalked several paces ahead of him. She still had not said a word since last night. The morning had dawned bright and sunny, quickly dissolving yesterday's ice. By the time they headed for the store at eleven a.m., the sidewalks and streets were nearly dry.

The shadows of their aerial escort passed by as she stomped up the two steps to the door, unlocked it and charged inside. The deliberate *click* of the deadbolt shooting back into place drew a chuckle from him.

A flutter of black feathers pulled his attention away from the disgruntled woman. A third crow landed on the mail dropbox on the corner. He bobbed his head and waved his wing in an unmistakable *follow me* gesture.

Tom held up an index finger and pulled out his cell phone. He hated doing this to Phylicia, but Jamal was in class and Adrian had to get *some* sleep.

A quick glance confirmed the one-eyed crow perched on the tenement across the street where it would have a clear view of the front of the store. The bird he'd healed last night must be watching the back door.

A deep voice answered after the second ring. "Hello?"

"Dante, can Phylicia come in for an hour?"

The unmistakable sounds of someone worshipping the porcelain god echoed through the receiver. "What do you think?" There was a slight pause before Phylicia's husband added, "Is this about whatever's going on with Rain?"

Damn. Tom wasn't sure what was worse. The witch having an insane case of morning sickness or her ex-Marine husband who understood too much. "Never mind. I'll see if Mrs. Wong can stay for an hour." Putting two goddesses-in-human-form in the path of whatever was coming may not have been his best plan, but the odds of both of them getting nailed was a lot slimmer.

"Bullshit," Dante growled. "I was with Phylicia, facing that demon at Halloween. Not to mention Jamal's singing sword let me handle her. Give me a little credit and five minutes. I can babysit while you do whatever you have to."

Relief swept over Tom in a gentle wave. "Great. Get here as soon as you can."

Dante strode through the door ten minutes later. In one hand, he had a drink tray with green tea and coffee from the smell. In the other, he had a pastry bag.

Rain wasn't fooled. "What the hell are you doing here, Jones?" But her gaze immediately shot to the sweets.

Dante flashed her a white smile that shone against his dark skin. "I needed some breakfast with my second favorite girl in the world." He kissed her on the cheek, and Rain preened under the attention. "Besides, I heard Laoch was a total asshole last night, and you know I'm much better company."

Tom hid his smile. He'd underestimated Dante. Again. He grabbed his coat. "Thanks, man. I owe you."

Dante saluted him. "No prob. Take all the time you need. We'll talk when you get back."

Something told Tom that Dante wanted to talk about more than the Rain situation. Had something happened at his and Phylicia's apartment as well? If so, Phylicia was better protected in her warded home than being on the streets. Tom hadn't missed the slight bulge at the back of Dante's waist.

He plunged back into the cold. The crow took off and he followed. A twinge of unease tickled his spine as the bird led him in the general direction of the NYU campus. The crow veered south and dove through the stone arch of Washington Square Park.

No, no, no. Tom yanked his phone out of his pocket as he walked and thumbed Jamal's number. No answer, but he didn't expect one if Jamal was truly at class. "Jamal, it's Tom. Call me when you get this."

The crow back-winged to land on a park bench. He pointed toward the naked forsythia bushes behind the forest green slats where he perched.

Tom approached what appeared to be a mass of black rags. The smell gagged him first, but it was the sight that churned his battle-hardened stomach. He knelt beside the body. There was very little blood considering the corpse's entrails had been pulled from the abdomen and arranged in the form of a pentagram. An arm covered the face, but a small patch of pale blue-ish skin at the wrist confirmed the dead man wasn't Jamal. Then he recognized the clothes.

Rain's assailant.

"Hey, what are you doing to that guy—" An ear-splitting scream rent the air.

Tom looked over his shoulder. The girl kept screaming. Her companion had raced to the nearby garbage can and proceeded to lose her breakfast. He pulled the screaming girl away from the corpse and handed her off to someone in the gathering crowd.

He punched 9-1-1 into the phone still in his hand. He was explaining his discovery to the dispatcher when a mounted NYPD officer rode up.

Tom rolled his neck as he sat in the police station's interrogation room. It was nearly four in the afternoon, way past the hour he'd promised Dante. "For the last time, I was walking through the park when I saw this crow staring at a bundle of rags."

"And why would you care about what a freakin' bird finds fascinating?" The detective with the crew cut and the bulldog jowls asked for the umpteenth time.

"Crows are carrion eaters, sir." It didn't hurt to be a little polite. The detective was only doing his job after all. It didn't mean Tom had to like it. "Most of the wildlife in Washington Square don't wear clothes."

The female detective, Rodriguez, inclined her head toward the door. "Go get a cuppa joe, Ron."

Her partner snorted and stomped to the only exit of the room. "This ain't over, asshole."

Once he slammed the door behind him, the female detective leaning against the wall shot Tom a wry smile. "Sorry about that. Detective Simmons has a tendency to get caught up in a case." She crossed the room and sat down in the chair closest to him. "Can I show you something?"

Despite the frisson of unease that crawled up his spine, Tom nodded.

The detective pulled four photographs from her manila folder and spread them out in front of him. "Do you recognize any of these people?"

He leaned forward and examined the pictures. There didn't seem to be any connection between the three men and the one woman he could see. Except that these were crime scene photos and each of the subjects was dead.

He raised his head. "No, ma'am. I don't. Should I?"

"And you're sure you didn't recognize the dead man at the park?" Dark eyes stared into his.

Tom shrugged. "Like I told the officer at the scene, he looked vaguely familiar, but I could have sat next to him on the subway for all I can remember."

"Did you touch the body?"

"No, ma'am."

She went through all the questions her partner had hammered at for the last few hours.

"Do you drink blood?"

The new inquiry threw Tom. He blinked. "No." So, it wasn't his imagination. The corpse was missing its blood.

"Have you ever used it in Wiccan rituals?"

The reason for the extended questioning clicked. *Sweet Danu! They think I did it.* "Not in this lifetime." He pasted on a frown. He couldn't laugh at the absurdity of the situation no matter how ludicrous the accusations.

"So you used blood in previous lives?"

He kept his gaze on her steady. "Detective, the only blood I've spilled in this life and my previous ones was my enemies' on the battlefield."

"Did you consider these people your enemies?"

Tom tapped the closest photo. "I would have to know these people before I considered them anything. The man I found? I considered him a bunch of rags until I noticed the crow's interest. My guess? So did every other person that walked by the body this morning."

Her eyes flicked toward the one-way glass before she changed tactics. The next question must have made her uncomfortable because she dropped her attention to the photographs on the table. "Have you ever had black-outs before, Mr. Laoch?"

This time, Tom couldn't resist a chuckle. "Only after really great sex, Detective."

"I-I-I'm talking about your PTSD." Rodriguez's cheeks bloomed dark rose under her dusky skin.

"That was the Army's official diagnosis ten years ago because my C.O. thought he was trying to help me." Crap. They'd already done a background check. He couldn't explain the berserker rage that had happened when his unit was under fire in Kuwait. The detective wouldn't believe him.

He needed to change subjects. Fast. He grinned. "If you want to know my whereabouts, I was with my boss last night. All night. We were trying to keep it quiet from the rest of the staff, but I suppose it had to come out sometime."

His effort worked. Once again, her eyes couldn't meet his. "B-but Ms. Bean's sixty-eight."

Tom leaned back in his chair. "Have you ever read Ben Franklin's essay 'Advice to a Young Man on the Choice of a Mistress,' Detective?"

She shook her head.

"To paraphrase Mr. Franklin, in the dark, all pussies are the same."

"I see." Rodriguez collected the photos and stuffed them in her folder, her motions stiff. "Well then—" She cleared her throat. "It goes without saying that we'll need to confirm your story with Ms. Bean."

Tom rose, but he couldn't resist the last jab. "And don't leave the city?"

"And don't leave the city." She rifled through her suit pocket and pulled out a card. "Here's my number if you think of anything else that might help us."

He made a point of stroking her fingers as he took the white slip. She shivered at his touch before she caught herself. Good to know some of his old charm existed.

"I definitely will, Detective." He pivoted and sauntered out the door.

When Tom swung the front door of the store open, it wasn't just Dante waiting for him. Adrian and Jamal were with him. Adrian looked up from a pile of paperwork on the counter, but Jamal halted in mid-pace, the broadsword in his hand.

The kid marched over to him, his expression too stern for an eighteen-year-old. "What did you buy me the first time you took me to the Museum of Natural Science?"

"A cheap plastic velociraptor because I made the mistake of letting you watch *Jurassic Park*." Tom eyed the weapon. "It was yellow and green."

"Where the hell have you been?" Jamal blurted.

"Being entertained my New York's finest." Tom scanned the store. "Where's Rain?"

Dante laid a hand on his stepson's shoulder. "Calm down." His eyes met Tom's. "Phylicia and Tessa took her across the street for dinner about five minutes ago. The girls will keep her there while we talk. Why the hell did the NYPD question you for so long?"

Tom pulled off his coat and tossed it across the counter. Adrian reached for the mini-fridge underneath and pulled out a bottle of water. Tom accepted it with a nod, unscrewed the cap and took a grateful swig before he said, "Whoever hired Rain's attacker murdered him last night along with four other people."

Dante and Adrian's mouths fell open. Jamal yelled, "What the fuck!"

Tom filled in the other three men on the events of last night. Well, everything except the crows' role, Rain bespelling her neighbors and his healing of the injured bird.

"Apparently, our mercenary didn't get out of the city fast enough. The other four murders happened within the last twenty-four hours. From the way the police are acting, the blood was missing from the corpse and the entrails arranged in the shape of a pentagram on the other four bodies as well."

"Shit," Adrian muttered. "NYPD thinks they've got a serial killer on their hands."

"And a mental-case Army discharge who works at an occult store in the Village found the last body." Tom slammed the plastic bottle on the scarred countertop. "It would be a crappy horror B-movie if this wasn't my life."

"You're not a headcase," Jamal said. The look in his dark eyes was fierce.

Dante leaned on the countertop. "The truth doesn't matter. Only the official report." He turned his attention to Tom. "There's more. Someone's been following Phylicia and me. All she sees are shadows though."

Adrian quirked a blond eyebrow. "You haven't seen them?"

Dante shook his head, then shrugged. "I don't think she's lying to protect me if that's what you're asking, but I trust her instincts. But there's more. While you were gone, Tom, a woman was standing on the sidewalk looking into the store. I would have sworn it was Kelly."

"The girl from Jason's Halloween party that was possessed?" Jamal asked.

Again, Dante nodded. "Once she knew I saw her, this odd smile appeared on her face. It gave me the willies. Then she turned and walked away."

Tom's mouth grew dry. "You didn't follow her, did you?" Jamal's personal question when he entered the store now made sense.

A wry smile tilted Dante's mouth. "And leave Rain alone? Hell, no. But I did make some phone calls. The real Kelly is still locked up in a private psychiatric hospital in Connecticut. I don't know who was standing outside the store, but it wasn't her." For a moment, he looked out at the neon lights shining from the restaurant across the street. "I think it may have been the demon who possessed her."

"Sounds more like a Kelpie," Jamal muttered. When Dante gave him a funny look, he said, "A shapeshifting water fae. They lure you to drown by appearing as a beautiful woman."

Dante rolled his eyes. "It would have been smarter to disguise herself as my wife instead of the possessed nutcase who drugged my best friend and got him to shoot me."

Blood. Sacrificial victims. Dark magick. Demons. Shapeshifters. Tom tapped his fingertips on the countertop. Somehow this all fit together, but how?

When his brain hit the answer, his blood turned to ice. "Abhartach."

Jamal stared at him, eyes wide. "Oh, fucking 'A,' we are in deep shit."

Chapter 4

Dante and Adrian looked at each other, then at Tom again, total confusion written on their faces. "Who?" Dante asked.

Tom ran a hand over his face. "A very dangerous 6th-century sorcerer. Jamal—"

"Any disturbance at Slaghtaverty Dolmen. On it." The eighteen-year-old already had his smart phone in hand and tapped in the inquiry.

Tom whirled and raced for the back room. It was a long-shot that Rain kept her real books here at the store. But letting her go back to her apartment now was unthinkable. He opened the half-door to the dumbwaiter.

"What the hell are you doing, Tom?" Adrian stood behind him, his head tilted in askance.

"Checking for Rain's grimoires." Tom raised the carriage until it cleared the opening and locked it. "Her books of magick."

"I know what a grimoire is. I do manage an occult store." Adrian's dry comment hung in the air. "I mean, why do you think they're here?"

Tom probed the back panel until the secret compartment popped open. "She kept the sword here."

"The antique hunk of steel Jamal's been carrying around?"

"Uh-huh." His finger found leather and parchment and . . .

He pulled out the tiny hunk of plastic. A crow's head topped the thin black casing. "Well, what do you know? Witchcraft for the twenty-first century." He handed the USB drive to Adrian and retrieved the two huge traditional tomes from the compartment.

As Tom shoved the cover back into place, Adrian's words sunk into the whirlwind of his thoughts. He looked at the other man. "You can see the sword?"

"An English broadsword is a little hard to miss." Adrian smirked.

"Celtic," Tom automatically corrected. Dammit it to hell, should he have been training Adrian all along too? He hefted the huge books and headed for the storefront. "You can see it though?"

"Is it supposed to be invisible?" Adrian asked as they pushed through the bead curtain separating the areas.

Dante looked up from where he peered over Jamal's arm at the phone's screen. "Is what supposed to be invisible?"

"Jamal's sword," Adrian said. He stepped behind the counter and popped the drive into a USB port on the store's computer. His blond head bent over the screen as he examined the files. "How do you spell Abhartach?"

"Depends on the source," Jamal absently answered as he thumbed through his own search. "Use the keywords: 'dwarf,' 'blood,' and 'sorcerer.' Bingo!"

Tom glanced up from the pages he was carefully flipping through. "What'd you find?"

"The mother lode in *The Irish Times*." Jamal glanced at him before he began reading out loud. "'Four American college students were arrested after they were found intoxicated by the side of the road near The Giant's Grave, known locally as Slaghtaverty Dolmen. The stones of the landmark, the alleged grave of an evil sorcerer, had been disturbed. Blood was also found on the bare earth under the hawthorn tree which shades the stones, but it matched the blood type of one of the students. Authorities chose not to file charges and remanded the students to the custody of the American Embassy after they were treated at a local hospital. According to a source, who asked not to be named since he was not authorised to speak on behalf of the hospital, all the student had cuts on their wrists.'"

He held up the phone for Dante to see. "Girl in the middle look familiar?"

"Kelly." Disgust painted Dante's voice. He ran a hand over his shaved head. "Let me guess. Your evil sorcerer is who possessed her last Halloween?"

Tom shrugged. "I doubt it. Probably something he summoned once the idiots freed him." He looked back to Jamal. "When did this happen?"

The kid swiped the screen of his phone. "Fuck. It happened on Litha."

Dante waved a hand. "Plain American English for the non-Wiccan present?"

"Summer Solstice," Adrian said.

"Right before all the shit started," Jamal added.

Tom stared out the window. Five forms huddled at the bus stop. Beyond them, the neon sign at the restaurant winked "Open." Somewhere, out there, an undead sorcerer sought the magickal score of a lifetime.

He was so lost in thought when a black shadow came out of nowhere and crashed into the huge plate glass, he jumped.

Chapter 5

The crow fluttered to the window ledge. It alternated between raucous caws and banging on the window with its beak.

Tom raced for the door. Across the street, the murder dive-bombed the five people waiting at the bus stop. The crows wouldn't have gone insane unless . . .

Pow! Pow! Pow! Cracks spread across the glass front door of the Wong's restaurant.

Instinctively, the pedestrians on the street dove for cover.

Tom ran for the restaurant, Dante and Jamal tight on his heels.

One of the men smashed the cracked glass with the butt of his gun, but he couldn't get through the door, like an invisible shield stood in the way. He flew backward as if someone had shoved him.

Phylicia stood in the empty doorway, her hands raised, palms toward the men outside. "Don't shoot them, baby! They're possessed!"

Dante growled an obscenity under his breath, but tucked his sidearm back in his waistband.

Great. Tom ducked the roundhouse one of the men threw at his head and swept his assailant's leg. *Not only are we outnumbered, these idiots don't know what they're doing.* His assailant looked up at him. Tom wasn't sure what was worse, the sick grin on the man's face or the solid black covering his eyes.

A heavy weight landed on his back, and a forearm wrapped around his throat. Tom flipped forward, and the second attacker tumbled over his shoulder. They needed to end this quick before someone got killed.

"Phylicia, we need salt!"

"On its way," she yelled back. The man with the gun threw his body at the doorway over and over despite the crows pecking at his exposed skin. By some small grace, he wasn't shooting at the young witch. Tom didn't think Phylicia could deflect a point blank bullet with her wall of air.

He raced to help Jamal, who was pinned by two of the men. The kid hadn't pulled out the sword slung across his back, but his efforts not to harm an innocent were going to get him killed.

Adrian appeared at Tom's side, and together they yanked one of Jamal's attackers off the kid. "Cops on their way," Adrian muttered as they struggled with their captive.

"Won't do us much good if we're dead before they get here." Tom clipped the attacker in the temple with his knuckles. He staggered and collapsed to his knees.

"Guys, get them as close together as you can!"

"You're crazy, baby!" Dante shouted back, but he delivered a movie-worthy backspin kick that drove his attacker away a couple of steps. He tripped over the first assailant's body and flailed a moment before he landed on his ass on the sidewalk.

Jamal pulled the sword from the bag slung over his shoulder. The sheathed steel repelled the kid's opponent and forced him to back toward his buddies.

Tom snatched the fourth man by the collar as he started to flee and wrestled him toward his the growing pile of bodies. At the same moment, Phylicia rammed the one with the gun toward his compatriots.

Tom shoved his prisoner on top of the heap and leapt backward. "Clear." The crows scattered.

A mini-tornado enveloped the five possessed men. They were so far gone, they didn't even look surprised at the odd event in the middle of winter.

Phylicia stepped through the shattered door, her beautiful face scrunched in concentration. Behind her, Tessa and Shan lugged a huge steaming pot. Rain followed, her hands waving gracefully and the ancient language pouring from her lips. Streamers of hot water rose into the air and danced over the men caught in the tornado.

"Get back," Tom ordered Dante, Adrian and Jamal. Even Adrian obeyed without question.

Phylicia dropped her hands, the whirlwind died, and hot water splashed over their assailants.

Swear words and shouts of pain echoed down the street only to be drowned by the approaching sirens.

Chapter 6

In Adrian's office, Tom kept his gaze level as Detective Rodriguez repeated her questions for the third time. At least, she hadn't dragged him down to the Village precinct for questioning.

Finally, she closed her notebook and slapped it repeatedly against her other palm. "Mr. Laoch, I believe you know more about the last twenty-four hours' events than you've told me."

"Detective, I've told you everything I can."

Anger flickered in her dark eyes though her expression remained impassive. "You should have let NYPD take care of the situation at the restaurant. You put yourself and your friends in danger needlessly."

Irritation flared inside him. "Maybe that's the problem in this culture. Everyone waits for someone else to 'take care of the situation.'"

Rodriguez smirked. "Oh, yeah. I forgot your girlfriend was having dinner across the street. Guess you decided to play hero before she tossed you aside for someone else?"

"That's not funny."

"Neither are the things I've learned about the people who are employed at Morrigan's Cauldron."

His fingers dug into his damp jeans as he struggled to remain calm. "What do you mean?"

Rodriguez rested her elbows on her knees, her gaze intense. "Average kinky stuff like Bean changing boyfriends faster than I change clothes is one thing. Then there's the not-so-average weirdness. Things like a recent high school graduate dragging the corpse of his best friend to this store. Or that a couple of your co-workers attended a Halloween party in Long Island where the house exploded."

His lungs started expanding again. All she had were police reports. "Bill Mailer is a very sick boy who couldn't deal with Mark Li's suicide. He blamed Shan and Jamal. As for the house, the fire chief at the scene said there was an undetected natural gas leak in the basement, which resulted in the explosion. Everyone at that party is damn lucky to be alive."

"According to the neighbors, your girlfriend's a witch."

Tom leaned back and folded his arms over his chest. "By that token, so am I. It's a colloquial term for any member of our religion."

"You're avoiding my question."

"You didn't ask a question, Detective. I have no problem answering your questions concerning any criminal activities I may have witnessed, but you're treading the edge of religious harassment."

She held her hands up in surrender. "My apologies, Mr. Laoch." She rose. "If you remember anything else, you have my number."

Rodriquez paused with her hand on the door. "Tom, those men at the restaurant . . ." Her eyes closed and opened as if she were choosing her words carefully. "They all have rap sheets that include felony assault and battery along with manslaughter. If anyone here is involved in something, I can help you."

His attitude toward her softened. She would have been a fine spearsister at his side centuries ago. "I appreciate your offer, Detective, but we can take care of ourselves."

She shook her head and opened the door. "Maybe, but at the rate you're going, you'll be dead by the end of the week."

Tom knew the real fight lay ahead. Once the police were gone and they helped the Wongs board up their missing front door, the eight of them gathered in Adrian's loft apartment above the store.

"Rain can sleep here. I'll stay at Tessa's for a while," Adrian said.

"No." Rain's voice was calm, but lightning sparked in her eyes.

"This place is warded and easier to defend physically," Tom said. "I'll stay and guard." She glared at him. "On the couch," he finished and glared right back.

"Dante and I can make the run to her apartment and pick up anything she needs," Phylicia said.

"Excuse me," Rain bit out. "I'm sitting right here."

Tom rubbed his forehead. "I don't think that's a good idea."

Rain huffed and crossed her arms. He continued to ignore the ugly looks she gave him.

Dante chuckled. "You think some evil sorcerer's minions can take out a witch and a Marine?"

Tom shook his head. "He won't stick to hired or possessed help since they've failed. You're making an assumption you can stand up to Abhartach himself."

"So far, he hasn't done anything except on your major Sabbats, right?" At Tom's nod, Dante continued. "Even then, it's never been direct. Whatever you guys call Groundhog's Day, it isn't until tomorrow. Since he needed to murder five people to possess these thugs, I'm guessing he probably shot his load on tonight's attempt. We'll be fine for an hour or two."

"Phylicia," Adrian started. "Can you swing by Tessa's place and lay some protective wards?"

Her dreads bounced. "No sweat. I'll grab what I need downstairs before we leave."

Jamal waved a hand for attention. "We've got another potential problem, folks. There's a nor'easter off the coast and a cold front sweeping in from up-state. They're supposed to clash right on top of us. Weatherman's predicting blizzard conditions by tomorrow evening, and NYU is already cancelling classes for the afternoon. Abhartach doesn't have to use just magick. He could use this storm against you. Collapse the roof with snow or some other shit."

Tom ran a hand through his hair. It was free. He'd lost the leather tie that kept it out of his face in the fight. "Great. This is getting better and better."

In the silence, Tessa piped up for the first time. "Is one of you going to explain to me what's going on, who's after Rain, and why?"

Rain speared each of them with her gaze, daring them to tell Tessa the truth.

Tom rubbed a hand across his stubbly jaw. While there were secrets that were not his to reveal, knowledge was power and the poor woman was in the middle of this mess, like it or not. She needed to know. All of them needed to know.

"Abhartach avoided death through his magick by drinking the blood of his subjects. The only way for him to become invincible is to drink the blood of the Tuatha de Danann, one of the Celtic gods. The next best thing would be someone imbued with the power of a Tuatha. He's after Rain because she's the manifestation of Morrigan's power on earth."

Chapter 7

Tom felt for Tessa as shock, disbelief and amazement chased each other across her face. Her jaw dropped, and she looked at each person in the room before she faced her former neighbor. "You're a fucking goddess?"

The question had Adrian, Jamal and Phylicia laughing hysterically.

Even Tom had to smile. "In Morrigan's case, that's literal. Anyone she had sex with became invincible on the battlefield."

Tessa rolled her eyes. "I guess it explains a lot."

"What's that supposed to mean?" Rain scowled.

Tessa wasn't intimidated one bit. "I lived across the hall from you for how many years? You needed to install a revolving door." She faced Tom again. "Why her blood to become superman? Why not, um—" Her pale skin burned bright red.

Tom gave her a reassuring smile. "Because the sex aspect only works if she's willing."

Dante shook his head. "Man, that only explains why this douche bag is after Rain. It doesn't clarify Zombie Mark coming after Jamal and Shan last summer. Or the shit that went down at my buddy Jason's Halloween party."

For the first time, Jamal's girlfriend Shan Wong spoke up. "Someone had to teach Mark Li the spell to turn himself into a *kiang shi*." She studied Tom. "This has something to do with Phylicia and Adrian being cousins, doesn't it?"

"Yeah, Tom." Rain sneered. "Why don't you tell them *everything*?"

In that instant, he was reminded of why he found her unattractive all those centuries ago. "You're still pissed because I was faithful to my wife and refused to sleep with you. Let it go."

"You were married?" Adrian blinked.

"Oh, don't let him give you the innocent act," Rain purred. "He wasn't exactly faithful to the missus. Or did you forget about your little tryst with—" She put a hand to her face in mock horror. "Oh, wait, you did. Your mistress's husband wiped your memory."

Boom!

The building shook from the sonic detonation, and everyone clapped their hands over their ears.

Everyone except Phylicia, who was on her feet. "That's enough from both of you!"

Even Rain looked at the young witch in surprise.

"I don't care what went down between the two of you in the past." Phylicia jabbed index fingers at Tom and Rain. "But if this asshole is why my kids are in danger, he's going down. And you two are going to stop fighting, or so help me, Abhartach won't be your real problem. You feel me?"

Tom swallowed air to get his ears to pop after the sonic boom Phylicia launched on top of them. "Yes, ma'am. No more arguing."

"Rain?" The threatening look Phylicia shot her mentor would have scared the shit out of any reasonable person.

"Fine," the older woman muttered.

"All right, then." Phylicia's attention turned to Jamal and Shan. "You kids are spending the next couple of nights at our apartment." Shan opened her mouth, but Phylicia wagged an index finger. "No arguments. You two are staying here until Dante and I get back, and you're skipping any classes tomorrow that haven't been cancelled."

"Yes, Mom," Jamal said, sounding like he was twelve again.

With the nasty look on Phylicia's face, Tom resisted the urge to laugh.

Tom closed and locked the door behind the other three couples. He watched them pile into a limo. Tessa had insisted on calling her business partner's car service. Tom had to admit she was being sensible. It was a credit to that sensibility that she had taken the entire craziness of Abhartach in stride.

Adrian had been practical as well. He and Tessa stayed at the store until Phylicia and Dante returned from Rain's place. They headed out together so Phylicia could lay down protection spells at Tessa's apartment. Between Dante,

Jamal and Shan, the witch had three warriors to back her up if they were wrong about Abhartach laying low until tomorrow.

Tom glanced at the antique clock on the shelf behind the register. Well after midnight. No wonder his eyeballs felt so scratchy. He hit the light switches and headed for the staircase.

When he reached the loft, Rain was curled up in a corner of the couch, a mug of tea gripped between both hands. On the glass and steel coffee table, another cup sat. Steam wafted from the surface.

A peace offering.

He eased onto the black leather cushion on the opposite end, reached for the tea and took a sip. One of Mrs. Wong's herbal blends.

"How long have you known?"

Rain's question shouldn't have surprised him, but it did. He leaned back, kicked off his boots and put his feet up on the coffee table. "Since the beginning of this lifetime." He grinned. "Of course, the store name doesn't exactly hide you."

"They sent *you*. Why?"

He met her steady gaze. "When The Dagda, Brigit and Father have the same vision that your powers are in danger of being stolen, it's best to heed such signs." He shrugged. "I can't tell you their reasoning of why I was the best choice."

"Like I couldn't take care of—"

"You can't. Not by yourself. Not in human form."

Her mouth pursed for a moment. "Dr. Wong is going to be pissed that you sent Shan into danger. You should have sent her home."

Tom swallowed a second smile. She changed the subject because she knew he was right, and it ticked her off. "I doubt it. He knows Shan's been coming to the gym with Jamal since August." Tom sipped his tea before continuing. "She's catching up to his skill level. Fast." He shrugged. "Considering her grandmother, I'm not surprised."

"Grandmother Wong knows who you are?" Rain practically spat the words.

Again, he shrugged. The fact that Rain didn't say old woman's true name meant she didn't want the Chinese goddess's attention. "I'm more surprised you didn't figure out my identity earlier."

She couldn't meet his gaze any more. Tracing a finger around the rim of her mug, she said, "I thought you were one of the children of the prophecy."

Air whistle between his lips. "That's why you're here? You think the Fomorians are forcing the prophecy into reality?" The Tuatha de Danann had driven the demonic race from this plane after his death with the help of his children. But his experiences with them in his first life had given him the chills, and more than a couple of nightmares.

Sharp blue eyes met his again. "Your father isn't the only one who can see the future, and frankly, I don't need foresight when simple deductive reasoning will do. They need all of your descendants dead to return to this plane, Cu Chulainn. Why else murder Jennifer Holloway?"

Adrian's wife, Jennifer. She was pregnant when she was stabbed to death in what the police thought was a mugging gone bad three years ago. Stabbed just like the five people yesterday. Innocent victims in the millennia-old battle between the Tuatha de Danann and their enemies. The possibility of Abhartach working with a Fomorian agent didn't bode well. The sorcerer may be a twisted, nasty character, but selling out his own race?

Tom wiped a hand over his face. Even if he told Detective Rodriguez the truth, she would never believe him. Not that he wanted to involve the NYPD in this mess.

Rain cleared her throat. "Look, um, I'm sorry . . . about what I said." She leaned forward, set her mug on the table and twined her fingers. "Earlier. I shouldn't have brought up—" She breathed deeply. "I shouldn't have brought up the past." Her laser-like gaze shot to him. "But you really pissed me off."

He set his empty cup down as well. "I know, and I'm sorry for spilling your secrets, but the kids need to understand what they're up against. Tessa and Adrian are the least prepared of all, and that's as much my fault."

A soft smile tilted her lips, made her look decades younger. "'The kids'? They are all adults even by the old standards, Cu Chulainn. Or that's what you told *me* yesterday." She leaned toward him. "Tell me something. Why didn't you use a proper Tuathan first name?"

He chuckled. "What do you know of the Christians' mythology? Of the disciple Thomas?

Understanding flitted across her features. "Do you still doubt me, Thomas Laoch?"

"No." He inhaled, trying to clear his mind. She didn't smell of vanilla or Chinese tea. Instead, sea grass and wild bog filled his head. "You don't have to use magick, Badb."

She quirked a silver eyebrow. Fresh straw and the clean smell of a good horse came next.

"Enough, Macha." Once again, the spell faded. He was ready when rich, dark loam came. "You cannot control me this way, Anand."

She pulled back, surprise on her features. She hadn't believed him when he said he remembered everything.

"I've said the three names of the Morrigan. Show your true self."

Dark red spread from the roots of her hair. Wrinkles smoothed into flawless alabaster skin. Blue darkened as green spilled into the irises. This time a blood red eyebrow rose. "Happy now?"

He took her hand between both of his own. "Has it ever occurred to you that if you'd come to me as yourself all those centuries ago, I wouldn't have said no?"

She gave a very unladylike snort. "Now, where would the fun be in making things easy? Besides, you had no problem deflowering the virginal daughters of all the local kings back then. I figured if you thought I was just another one, it wouldn't have been an issue."

He chuckled. "I was also a horny teenager at the time. Then—" He hadn't exactly been faithful to Emer. Emer, his wife from that lifetime, who long ago passed into other lives between her times at Tir na Nog. "Things changed."

Morrigan laughed as well. "Is that the reason you kept telling Jamal to keep his pants zipped?"

"I'm not the one who gave him three boxes of condoms."

"You know Phylicia was ready to kill you and Adrian for the boxes you each gave him." She sobered and leaned even closer. Her other hand folded over his. "Would it be such a bad thing if you unzipped your pants now?" Earnest green eyes stared into his.

He shook his head. "You simply will not give up, will you?"

She trailed fingers along his arm, and the hand still between his palms grew hot. "It's the act of life, Cu Chulainn. If it gives our mortal bodies the power to see to Abhartach's defeat and save the lives of your grandchildren, what is the harm?"

Still he hesitated. He'd never had a problem accepting a woman's offer before. His rejection of Morrigan centuries ago had more to do with his *geas*, his curse, his doom, for the sins of that lifetime. The only difference here was that he remembered that life, the recollections necessary to understand his purpose in this existence.

There was *nothing* to hold them back in this lifetime.

Tom lifted her hand and kissed the delicate skin inside the wrist. Rain's intake of breath said he hadn't lost his touch. He scooped his hands under her ass and pulled until she lay on the couch. Her legs spread in invitation.

Instead, he removed her boots and peeled off her socks.

She propped herself on her elbows and tilted her head as he massaged her soles. "Seriously? This is your idea of foreplay?"

A wry smile twisted his mouth. "Since that comment's coming from a woman whose idea of foreplay involves threats and bodily harm, excuse me if I don't follow your advice."

Rain glared at him. "What's that supposed to mean?"

He reached for the button of her jeans. "Queen Medb invaded Ulster. I was in the middle of fighting one of her champions when you tried to drown me."

"Medb's army wouldn't have gotten as far as it did if you hadn't been screwing some farm girl." She tore at her denim overshirt, the snaps popping like firecrackers.

"You cursed the Ulster army, which is why I was the only one guarding the border." He dragged her jeans over her hips. His erection pressed painfully against his own fly.

"I wouldn't have cursed the army if your king hadn't been an asshole and used my names to make me race while I was pregnant!" For an instant, her eyes literally burned red.

For some strange reason, her ire only amused him. Even with her abilities limited in her human shell, she could definitely boil his brains in his skull or rip his heart out with a thought. But their bickering increased his desire, and from her panting, it was having the same effect on her.

He traced the dark red curls through her translucent white cotton panties. "So what you're saying is that none of what happened in Ulster was your fault?"

Breath hissed out of Rain and her hips lifted to meet his touch, demanding more. "That's exactly what I'm saying."

He dragged her underwear down her thighs. Her muscles twitched under his hands from her impatience. "Then it goes back to our original problem. Why do you feel you have to trick me into your bed?"

"I never invited you into my bed." She yanked at the sleeves of her shirt, wrestling it off from her awkward position. The white long-sleeved tee underneath rode up, showing an expanse of creamy skin. It teased him when the hem stopped short of her ample breasts.

"Not true." His hands slid under the infuriating hem. Upon investigation, he found the front clasp. Pushing bra and shirt up revealed areolas nearly as red as her hair. It took him a few seconds to unglue his tongue from the roof of his mouth. "You did last night."

"Well, we're not in my apartment tonight, are we?" She swung her legs around and stood up in one smooth motion. The heavy tee and the bra joined the rest of her clothes on the floor. Morrigan posed before him in all her glory. "But I suppose any bed will do."

She sauntered toward Adrian's bedroom but paused in the doorway, a coy expression on her face. "Are you coming?"

So many smart aleck comments filtered through his head, but in the end, wisdom prevailed. Or maybe it was his dick that won. He rose and walked slowly over to her. His fingers caressed her cheek before he bent and took her mouth.

The kiss turned torrid. All of his carnal needs in this lifetime exploded in that melding of their lips and tongue. It wasn't the tentative exploration of new lovers, but raw passion of two people who'd known each other a very long time even if they hadn't acted on their physical attraction.

He picked her up and carried her to the bed. She sat up though and undid his jeans as he pulled off the layers of sweatshirt and dark navy t-shirt. Faster than he thought possible, he was naked and on top of her, licking and nibbling on her magnificent breasts.

Her hand reached for him, stroking the shaft, and he grabbed her wrist. "Don't. I won't last."

"Then let's get the first time out of the way, so we can take forever the next." That sultry smile promised more than the two rounds. She wrapped her legs around his waist.

His dick knew what it wanted. He plunged into her hot, willing passage, and it took every ounce of control not to explode then and there.

Her hips rocked against his, and he picked up the rhythm that was old when Mother Danu came into existence. Nails dug into his back, urging him faster. He didn't think he could stop if he wanted to, swallowed by her green eyes.

He blinked. Something shifted, and golden ribbons of light danced around him. Where he touched Morrigan, they peeled from him and twined around the deep red streamers that waltzed around her. "What the hell?"

Her hands cupped his face. "I told you before. It's the act of life. Of creation. Of the first magick."

He didn't feel like anything drained from him by the lights' strange dance. In fact, he felt stronger, more powerful, like he could take on an entire army again. Their connection took on a new urgency. He pumped into her, let the delicious friction envelope him.

The familiar tightening of his sac took him by surprise. He moaned, and his cock pulsed.

Embarrassment quickly followed his release. Dammit. In the past, he'd made sure his partner was satisfied.

But Morrigan's legs tightened around his waist, and the squeeze of her pussy said she reached her own passion. The contractions sent more ripples through his cock.

They lay there for a moment. Her satisfied smile told him more than any words.

He withdrew and rolled on his side, head propped on his fist as he regarded her. "Happy now?" he said, repeating her earlier words.

Confusion knitted her fine brows. "What do you mean?"

He grinned. "You've deflowered a virgin."

Her eyes widened. "You must be joking? You're over forty!"

Tom looked up at the ceiling. "Hmmm. I'm probably the inspiration for that silly movie."

"Never in this lifetime?"

He looked back in time to see a skeptical eyebrow rise. "Not unless you count—" He pumped his fist.

She laughed and pushed him flat on his back before she straddled his hips. Damp curls tickled his dick. "Then you've got some catching up to do. And we have all night to do it."

Chapter 8

Tom awoke to fingers stroking his chest hair. He turned his head to find Morrigan cuddled against his side, but she stared at the ceiling, unaware of the patterns she traced on him.

"The flurries have started," she whispered.

"Should we even bother opening the store today?"

She sighed. "Might as well. The neighborhood will want candles for the storm. Plus, Adrian's coming in this morning to do payroll and go over some orders he needs to place."

Tom sat abruptly. "By himself?" Chill prickled his skin. He wasn't sure if it was the building's century-old furnace not keeping up or a touch of foreboding.

"No." She rolled onto her back, her hair a glorious spill of red against the white cotton sheets. Maybe the problem was the temperature of the room by the way her areolas tightened.

Or it could have been the fact he couldn't take his eyes off them.

He couldn't blame his erection on magick. His fingers reached for one of the hard tips and rolled it between his thumb and forefinger. Her gasp of breath told him this was something far more primal.

"Is the murder going to be sufficient?" He leaned over the breast he played with and traced a circle with his tongue.

Her back arched, offering him more. "They're watching all three places, and there are scouts at both my apartment and your efficiency."

He gently bit the nipple before he moved to its twin. Her fingers threaded through his hair, encouraging him.

Kissing his way down her stomach drew a sigh of anticipation from her. He sprawled between her legs and hoisted her thighs over his shoulders. The petals of her labia parted as he watched. He blew gently to encourage them. The pale pink lips darkened and the bud of her clitoris peeped from its hood.

The first stroke of his tongue drew a moan from her. She tasted of sea salt and honey. He couldn't resist it. He licked and sucked her sweet juices, enjoying her reactions as her muscles trembled.

His fingers sought her passage as his lips massaged her clit. She cried out when he entered her. Maybe there was some good from having his old memories after all.

Her internal muscles contracted around his fingers. She was so close. He released her clit. When he blew over the swollen bud, her mew of protest turned into a scream of release. Spasms squeezed his fingers and her pussy quivered.

He circled her clit a final time with his tongue and sat up. "I want you on top."

Her eyes remained closed. "Why?"

"I want to see your face when you come this time." He lay next to her and tweaked the plump nipples.

A sly smile spread across her features, and her eyes fluttered open. Not wasting any time, she straddled his hips and slid over his cock.

Danu, help him. She felt so hot, so right, as her pussy surrounded him. She brushed her dark red waves over her shoulders and arched her back.

He reached up and cupped her full breasts. Her skin was so damn soft, except for her tight nipples. His thumbs brushed the buds, and they hardened even more under his touch.

She started rocking, a slow easy rhythm. He nearly swallowed his tongue when her hips shifted into a figure-eight motion. The friction on his cock was delicious.

His hands dropped from her breasts and grabbed her ass, spreading her cheeks so he could plunge deeper into her wetness. Her internal muscles squeezed him, and it all he could do not to flip her over and pump into her pussy.

Her eyes closed and her hands braced on his chest as she continued her erotic dance. He gritted his teeth against the heavenly torture. *Need to think about something else before I lose it. Dinosaurs. Yeah, dinosaurs are good. Tyrannosaurus rex, velociraptor, triceratops—*

Pain shot through his forehead. "What the fuck?" He glared at Morrigan.

She leaned back, but her thumb and middle finger were poised to flick him again. "You are *not* thinking about dinosaurs in the middle of sex."

"I was doing it for your benefit."

A wicked smile filled her face. "I don't need that kind of help, Hound." Her fingers flashed and nails dug into his nipples.

He reacted without thinking and shoved her off him. She didn't look a bit surprised or shocked when he pinned her wrists above her head and kneed her thighs apart.

"Is this what you want?"

"Yes," she hissed.

He rammed into her, but she was so slick from before, it felt . . . perfect. Her legs wrapped around him and her hips lifted to meet his thrusts. *All right. If that's the way she wants it.* Instinct took over and he pumped into her.

Her smile became feral, her cries animalistic. And she literally howled in his ear when her pussy convulsed around him. His own throat emitted a low growl when his balls tightened and his cock throbbed. Elbows shook as he kept from crushing her while his body emptied into hers.

She shrugged her wrists loose from his hold, and her laugh had a maniacal sound. "That's the way sex should be. Wild. Untamed."

Tom chuckled. "You're crazy, you know that?"

"And that's my advantage."

They ended up taking a shower together. To save hot water, Morrigan teased. It turned into another session of Tom burying himself in her sweet pussy until the shower turned cold.

Once they dried each other, Tom borrowed an old pair of jeans, a clean t-shirt and sweater from Adrian's closet.

He couldn't help watching the woman next to him. It felt unnatural to ask, but he said, "Might be best if Rain were here in case Adrian comes up without knocking."

She shrugged the illusion on as if it were a cloak. Color leached from her hair until it was once again silver. Green bled from her irises, turning sharp blue. Lines of experience darted from the corners of her eyes and spread across her skin.

Rain reached into the bag Phylicia had packed for her and pulled on jeans and a sweater, completing the transformation. When she reached for her brush, his hand closed over hers.

"Allow me."

She gave him a quizzical look but relinquished the wooden handle. He gently ran the bristles through her hair. As he suspected, the tresses felt as soft as last night despite their appearance. She stood patiently, watching him in the mirror, while he braided a single plait.

"Up or down?"

"Down," she whispered. She pivoted and pulled his head to her for another heated kiss.

When their lips parted, he leaned his forehead against hers. "We can't. Adrian—"

"Hey, you guys decent?" Adrian's voice echoed up the narrow staircase.

They both chuckled at the interruption.

Tom walked into the living room and leaned over the railing. "Yeah. We were about to raid your fridge for breakfast."

Adrian jogged up the steps. Damp spots dotted the shoulders of his gray parka, and droplets sparkled against his blond hair. He held up two bulging reusable grocery bags. "I've got plenty of eggs in there, and I picked up some non-perishables for you. Snow's started. Not sticking yet." He crossed to the kitchen, set the bags on the table, and unzipped his coat. "I don't know if this registers on your weird-o-meter, but a flock of crows followed me here."

Rain flashed a smile at Tom. "Told you we had back-up."

While Rain appropriated the back office and phoned the members of the local coven to cancel the evening's Imbolc bonfire due to the impending storm, Adrian focused on paperwork at the counter, which left the customers to Tom.

Not that he had a whole lot to do. A few of their regulars came in for supplies for their private holiday celebrations. A handful more stopped in for candles in case they lost power in tonight's predicted blizzard.

A little after one p.m., Rain ran into the showroom. "Something's happened."

Before she finished her sentence, the phone rang. Adrian spoke quietly before he looked up at Tom. "It's Manuel at Faraday's Gym. He said someone broke into your apartment. He's called the police, but he needs you down there now."

The same suspicion Tom felt was reflected in Adrian's face. He took the receiver. "What's going on, Manuel?"

"There was this godawful smell coming from your room this morning. When I saw the dead bird and those terrible symbols on the walls, I called the police. Tom, I didn't know what else to do." Someone was talking to Manuel in the background. "I didn't mean to get you in trouble, but the lady police, she wants to talk to you."

Shuffling sounds echoed in the receiver, then a feminine voice said, "Mr. Laoch?"

Tom closed his eyes at the all-too-familiar voice. "Yes, Detective Rodriguez."

"We need to talk."

The little crow Tom had healed perched on his shoulder during the walk to Faraday's. Two others flew escort as the bird briefed him.

Manuel and a uniformed officer waited for him on the sidewalk.

"I locked this place tight last night, and it was locked this morning." Crimson tinged Manuel's face. "I don't know how someone got in here."

"I know you did, man." Tom tried to give the gym's manager a reassuring smile. "I don't blame you."

The uniform gestured toward the door. "Detective Rodriguez is inside, sir."

Tom climbed the two flights of stairs, Manuel and the cop following. At the third floor landing, a crime scene technician was taking pictures of his apartment from the door. Detective Rodriguez caught sight of him. A puzzled frown knitted her eyebrows as she took in the crow perched on his shoulder.

They sized up each other for a long moment before Tom said, "Aren't you going to ask about my whereabouts last night, Detective?"

"My partner already checked with the neighbors. You didn't come home. Ms. Bean didn't go home. The Wongs said you and she stayed at Morrigan's Cauldron last night while Mr. Holloway, who actually lives in the apartment above the store, left with his fiancée around midnight along with the rest of the staff and their significant others." Rodriguez gave him a vicious smile. "Anything you want to add?"

"Has anyone gone into my apartment?"

"Not yet." Her eyes narrowed. "Why?"

"May I look? I promise not to touch anything."

She motioned for the technician to back away.

Tom approached but made sure not to cross the threshold. The metaphysical protections inherent in any home had been shattered. He may not be able to see them, but he could definitely feel them.

Furniture and rugs had been shoved aside to reveal the building's original hardwood floors. In the center of the living area, the grizzled, one-eyed crow, who'd been watching Tom's apartment, had been sacrificed, his entrails removed to form a pentacle. Just like the human victims. Symbols had been painted on the walls. From the color and smell, it wasn't Sherwin-Williams.

Thankfully, neither Manuel nor the police had set off the trap.

The crow on his shoulder gave a mournful peep.

Tom reached up and stroked the little guy's head. "I'm sorry. I can't raise the dead," he said in Old Gaelic.

"Excuse me?" Rodriguez sounded more than a little spooked.

He turned to the detective and switched back to English. "There's too much blood on the walls, more than could have come from the bird. He's left another body somewhere."

She wiped away the shock that flashed on her face. "Can we talk privately?"

"Just a moment." He motioned to Manuel. "Go down to my pick-up. There's a white sage stick in the glove compartment. Light it and set it in one of your ashtrays. Place the ashtray in the doorway, but don't cross the threshold yourself. Otherwise, you'll set off the trap. Got that?"

"Yeah." Manuel glanced inside, crossed himself, and took off down the stairs.

"Trap? What trap?" Rodriguez openly glared at him. The uniformed officer tried to hide his smile of disbelief. The technician glanced nervously between the three of them before he surreptitiously crossed himself as well.

"Something that would have killed whoever stepped into the apartment first," Tom said. "Our killer decided to make his warning about my involvement permanent."

From the detective's expression, she believed him and wasn't real happy that she did.

They borrowed Manuel's office downstairs while the gym's manager disabled the killing spell with the smoldering sage. The little crow hopped onto the desk and tucked his head under his wing while Tom and Detective Rodriguez talked. He leaned back in the desk chair once he finished his statement.

Detective Rodriguez's expression hadn't changed in the last ten minutes. "Why would this mercenary—" She glanced at her notes. "—Abhartach care about the American side of your family?"

"We believe he was hired by a third party to wipe out our clan. He's simply being thorough."

She cocked her head. "The Troubles are supposed to be over in Ireland."

"This goes back before the English took over. Centuries even." Tom waited a few heartbeats before he added. "Are you going to tell me whose blood he painted on my walls, or do I find out on the five o'clock local news?"

Rodriguez blew out a deep breath. "What the hell? Jamal Washington's roommate was attacked in their dorm room at NYU. Your story kind of explains why the kid's still alive. Your mercenary realized he had the wrong person."

"Will he be all right?"

"He's still in the hospital from blood loss, but yeah. His girlfriend found him in time. At first, the paramedics thought it was an attempted suicide from the cuts in his wrists. But that didn't jive with the rope burns on his arms and ankles."

She leaned her elbows on the desk. "Let me get all of you into a safe house. We can protect your family, Mr. Laoch."

He rose. "With all due respect, Detective, no, you can't."

She shook her head. "Jensen said you people were stubborn as hell."

"Jensen?"

"Detective Todd Jensen." Her tired smile didn't reach her eyes. "He's the officer who had to deal with the body of Mark Li in the middle of your store's floor last August."

Tom nodded at the reminder. "I remember now. Tall with sandy hair."

She stood as well. "Look, I can't force you, but you have my number if you change your mind."

"I'll keep that in mind, Detective." He didn't think she'd appreciate it if he told her either Abhartach would be dead, again, by the end of the day. Or he would be.

Chapter 9

Snow was coming down harder and sticking to every surface. Inexperienced drivers made the six-block trip back to the store even more treacherous, but something told Tom he'd need his pick-up before the night was over. The little crow hadn't left him since he headed for Faraday's. Tom had to insist that the bird crouch on the passenger floorboard while he was driving. The seatbelt would do more harm than good for the crow if another vehicle hit the truck.

When Tom strode into the store, he stopped short. Adrian sat on the floor. Grandmother Wong knelt on one side of him. Her eldest son, Chen, crouched before him. The surgeon was checking Adrian's pupils with a penlight. The serious lump at the temple would no doubt leave the store manager with a black eye by tomorrow morning.

Grandmother Wong looked up at Tom. "The sorcerer and his demon took her."

Adrian batted the penlight away. "I'm sorry, Tom. When she walked in, I thought she was Tessa." He started to shake his head and thought better of it. "The bitch tossed me around like a rag doll." He didn't seem to notice the crow sitting on Tom's shoulder.

On the other hand, Tom had the distinct impression that Grandmother Wong and Chen deliberately chose to ignore the bird while in front of a mortal.

"You've definitely got a concussion," Chen said to Adrian. His voice was gravelly thanks to the scars on his vocal cords. When the *kiang shi* slashed his throat last August, his smooth tenor disappeared forever. "We should perform a CAT scan."

"Fuck the CAT scan," Adrian growled.

Grandmother Wong patted his shoulder. "I came in before the kelpie could kill him. Her allies drugged Rain and took her out the back. They had a vehicle waiting and killed the bodyguards."

Tom scowled. "So there's three of them?"

The smile on Grandmother Wong's face was awful to behold. "Two. The kelpie that attacked Adrian is the greasy smear by the back door." She sobered. "You will need your father's help, Dog."

"Do you know where Abhartach took her?"

"No. He masks their location with spells. You have until midnight. I will guard Adrian and Tessa until your task is complete."

He bowed deeply. "Thank you, my lady."

She pointed a gnarled finger at the door. "Go."

Tom hammered on Phylicia's door for the third time. *Danu, please don't let any of them be foolish enough to leave this sanctuary tonight.*

A shadow drifted over the peephole. The apartment door swung open. The barrel of a handgun aimed straight at his left eye, Dante's steady hand on the trigger.

"What costume did I wear at Halloween?" The ex-Marine's deep voice said he was a hairsbreadth from pulling the trigger.

Despite the ludicrousness of the question, relief seeped into Tom that Dante took the danger seriously. "You were a pirate. And I'd like to point out I had to listen to Rain comment on your tight white pants for the next three weeks after Jason's party."

Dante lowered the weapon. "TMI, man." Behind him, Phylicia lowered her staff and Jamal his sword.

"Adrian called ahead and told us what happened at the store," Dante added.

The crow peeped from under Tom's coat.

"Who's your friend?" Phylicia nodded to the bird.

Tom grinned. "My back-up."

"You can't be serious?" Dante gave the crow a skeptical look.

Caw! He tilted his head, a bright yellow eye glared at the ex-Marine.

Tom wasn't about to translate the name the crow called Dante.

Shan stepped forward, a Louisville slugger in her tiny hands. "Why are my grandmother and father involved in this?" Her fingers gripped the handle so tightly that her knuckle bones shone white through her skin.

Too many secrets around here. Tom raked a hand through his damp hair. "Your father's keeping an eye on Adrian because the idiot has a concussion and refuses to go to the hospital. As for your grandmother, she's a nosy old biddy. Always has been since the day I met her. Anything else, you need to ask her." He turned to Phylicia. "Any way you can do a tracking spell?"

She shook her head, dreads flying. "Mrs. Wong asked me to, but nothing's worked so far."

Think, man. "He's a sixth century sorcerer. He may be able to block spells, but what about the GPS in her smart phone? She always keeps it in her back pocket."

A wide grin split Jamal's face. "On it."

Tom caught the kid's arm before he took a step. "Jamal, I need to borrow her, if she's willing." He inclined his head toward the broadsword. The metal rang out an enthusiastic peal.

Jamal looked at the sword in his hand. "Fickle, aren't we?"

It gave a long moan that sounded suspiciously like a teenager saying, "Ple-e-e-e-ease."

Jamal sheathed the sword and handed it to Tom.

"Got it," Shan called from the claustrophobic kitchen. She had the neon pink clamshell of her notebook open. "Rain, or Rain's phone at least, is in the New York City Marble Cemetery in the East Village."

"It's not New York Marble?" Tom said. Apparently the city fathers couldn't come up with more imaginative names for the island's graveyards. Last thing he needed was to go to the wrong one.

"Definitely New York City. The signal's coming from a group of mausoleums to the left of the main entrance," Shan confirmed.

"All of you need to stay inside until you hear from me. Definitely don't leave the apartment before dawn." Tom pivoted for the front door.

Dante grabbed his elbow, his dark brown gaze deadly serious. "You don't go into a combat situation without support."

"I have support." Tom took Dante's arm in a warrior's clasp. "Keep my grandchildren safe." He released Dante and jogged for the staircase before the ex-Marine could puzzle out Tom's slip of the tongue.

The storm had turned into a white-out, made eerie by the reflected glow from windows and streetlights. The truck crept slowly down the deserted streets, its headlights barely able to penetrate the curtain of snow. Even with the heat turned up full blast, the crows, huddled in the passenger footwell, shivered violently. Thankfully, people heeded the mayor's warning to "hunker down." No one was out, not even the NYPD.

Tom glanced at the clock on the dashboard. It was taking him too damn long to cross Manhattan. While midnight would be the ideal time to sacrifice Rain and drink her blood, Abhartach was known to be a greedy bastard back in his day. He had no reason to wait. Who could possibly interfere in this storm?

They were a block from the main gate when the truck fishtailed wildly. Tom struggled to control the slide. "Hang on!" The crows started shrieking.

He turned into the skid, but the snow was too wet. The pick-up plowed nose-first into a snow bank. The collision was slow enough that the air bags weren't triggered.

Tom looked down at the crows. "Everyone okay?"

At the chorus of affirmatives, he unbuckled his seatbelt and popped open the door. The wind blasted into the compartment. Icy particles whipped inside and made his face feel like it was being power-sanded. There was no way the murder could fly in this storm.

His little buddy clambered over the transmission hump. Tiny claws dug into Tom's jeans. The bird worked his way to the right coat pocket and climbed inside.

In a chorus, the other crows called him an idiot. He poked his head past the pocket flap. His rejoinder suggested the rest of the murder do something that was anatomically impossible even for birds.

Apparently, the little one's taunt worked. The next thing Tom knew he was climbing out of the truck with a murder of living crows attached to his coat. He grabbed the sword, and ducking his head against the storm's fury, he followed the wrought iron fence to the cemetery's main entrance. The normally locked gates swung wildly in the wind.

Tom caught one and walked through. The abrupt silence inside the cemetery's walls left his ears ringing. No wind. Snowflakes drifted through the air, not the slashing ice particles that they encountered out on the street. Only a couple inches covered the ground, a white blanket that reflected the ambient light from the street. Two of the crows whispered between themselves. Tom had to agree with their assessment. It *was* pretty freaky.

As one, the crows release their hold on his coat and started scouting. All except the little one. He flung himself from the coat pocket and circled Tom once before he settled back on Tom's right shoulder.

Tom pulled the sword from her scabbard and aimed for the left path. She hummed softly for a second in acknowledgement. A couple of the crows remained near the gate as a rear guard. The rest fanned out in front of him and to the sides.

Tom walked past three of the mausoleums when the crow at point dove for the ground. The rest of the murder followed suit. Tom ducked and crawled to where the crows peered around their cover.

Rain lay on a pile of dead leaves and snow underneath the outstretched arms of a headless stone angel. She didn't move. Only a faint mist from her nose told him she still breathed. A weathered leather bag sat next to her.

Nearby, a dwarf dressed in an odd mix of furs and Gore-tex sang to himself. He danced around the bare patch of earth as the unearthly lyrics spilled from his lips. No dormant grass covered the sterile soil. No snow either. The flakes seemed to slide away from the circle Abhartach formed with his jig. His steps were similar to an Imbolc celebration, but *wrong*. Not life affirming at all.

Tom scanned the clearing. The problem would be getting to Rain. None of the monuments or headstones near her prone body were large enough to use as cover. He needed a diversion.

Through hand gestures, he conveyed his plan to the crows. Their heads bobbed. Thankfully, the sword had the sense to remain quiet.

His thighs tensed, ready to spring, when his buddy screeched in his ear before the crow launched himself into the air.

As Tom started to dive, fire seared his back. He rolled and leapt to his feet.

Behind him stood something out of a nightmare.

Chapter 10

The creature before Tom was solid black except for the burning red eyes. Crimson drops fell from one set of its talons, turning the pristine snow coal-dark. A demon that looked just like the one Phylicia encountered at the Long Island Halloween party.

Except this time, it was solid.

Now, the deaths made sense. While Abhartach drank their blood to restore himself, he used the energy from each victim's demise to give his pet demon substance in the mortal world.

Holding the scabbard along his left forearm as a shield, Tom slashed at the demon with the sword. The creature nimbly danced out of the way.

Both the sword and the crows cried out in warning. Tom jumped back as a sickly greenish ball of energy hit the monument he'd been hiding behind. Shards of marble erupted in the deafening crack.

Abhartach gestured with his fingers and muttered under his breath. Tom's attention flicked over the scene. Two birds down. No cover. Only one decision that gave him a chance of surviving the murderous sorcerer.

Tom charged Abhartach.

The undead dwarf dodged, but his concentration was disrupted. Not giving him a chance to marshal his magick, Tom swung the sword. She hummed a gleeful tune as he hacked and slashed at the nimble sorcerer.

Since their rescue plan was shot to the Summerlands, the crows had adapted. From the corner of his eye, Tom could see the murder dive-bomb the demon, keeping it off-balance and out of his way.

Abhartach dodged another swing that should have taken off the bastard's head. "Can't hit me." Abhartach's high-pitched laugh grated on Tom's ears. "Where did you learn such pitiful swordsmanship?"

Tom blinked. Rain's hand moved toward the bag. Was she conscious? Yes, she definitely drew something from the leather case. One blue eye winked and closed.

Tom shifted to keep between the sorcerer and Rain. He grinned. "The court of the King of Ulster," he said in Old Gaelic.

The dwarf froze, staring at Tom for a moment before he rolled over the bare dirt and snatched up his bag. Tom surged forward more intent on slicing the strap than cutting off Abhartach's head. The last thing he needed was the sorcerer to pull out some monstrosity he wouldn't have a prayer of defeating in his human form.

"*Leave him.*" The sibilant words came from the demon.

Tom whirled to find its arm wrapped around Rain's chest, her body dead weight. The demon pushed Rain's head to the side, exposing her pale skin and blue veins. Talons rose for the killing strike.

"*Surrender now, or she dies.*"

"I don't think so," Rain said. Her eyes were still closed, but a terrible smile bared her teeth.

"*Why not, fleshling?*" it taunted.

"Because I am *the Morrigan*!" She plunged a copper knife into the demon.

It shrieked. The unholy sound shattered the three closest gravestones and cracked others. Red eyes faded like dying coals. The black form sizzled and bubbled, shrinking in on itself until it was nothing more than a steaming black puddle.

"Noooo!" Abhartach's scream echoed among the mausoleums.

All energy fled from Rain and she collapsed in an unmoving pile.

The smoke from the demon's remains rose into the cold air. It seemed to coalesce and aimed straight for Abhartach.

Even as the sorcerer's hands rose to form a warding spell, Tom jumped and swung with all his strength. The sword squealed and struck true. Abhartach's head bounced a few feet before rolling to a stop in the middle of the circle of dirt. The body toppled forward.

The smoke form of the demon shrieked as the crows tore through its wisps with wings and claws. Within seconds, it was gone.

Instead of triumph, fatigue claimed Tom with a vengeance. Not even after his berserker rampage during the first Gulf War had he felt this kind of exhaustion. He stumbled over to Rain and collapsed beside her. This time she wasn't feigning unconsciousness.

He set aside the sword, before he managed to sit and pull her into his lap. The surviving crows crowded around them. He scanned the area, and his heart sank. Nearly half the flock lay dead around them.

"Rain? Rain? Come on. Wake up. We've got to bury Abhartach's body before someone finds us, or he'll be revived tomorrow night."

Nothing. No stirring. No fluttering of the lashes.

The wind picked up and snow fell more heavily within the cemetery now that Abhartach's magicks no longer warded the place. Tom placed two fingers on her neck. The pulse was still there, but very weak.

He didn't exactly feel like a million gold pieces either. The cuts on his back burned and everything ached. "Rain?" He sucked in a deep breath. "Badb. Macha. Anand. I've said the three names of Morrigan. Answer my call."

Rain groaned. "Anybody get the number of that bus?"

Tom pulled her close and laid a gentle kiss on her lips. "You'll be fine. I just have to get you to a hospital."

She stared up at him, but the glazed look in her eyes said something was terribly wrong. "I've been poisoned. The only reason I lasted this long is because of what we shared last night." She cupped his cheek. "The demon poisoned you as well. If you go now—"

"I'm not leaving you." Tom checked the sorcerer's body, half-afraid it would spring up any minute. A fine layer of white flakes covered the headless corpse. "And I damn well can't leave him lying there. What do you—"

Rain had passed out again. She must have used the last of her strength to destroy the demon's physical form.

He placed his hands over her heart as he had for the bird he healed. No tingling in his head or fingers. No welling of energy. Simply nothing.

The same little crow hopped closer to him. *Caw.*

Tom leaned back against the monument. He hated to admit the bird was right. No one else who understood this insanity could reach them in time. He took a deep breath. Steam wreathed his face as he said, "Kwan Yin, I respectfully ask for your help."

A tiny whirlwind started near a naked bent oak. Warm air burst from the wind, and the snowflakes transformed into lotus petals. A woman, dressed in silk robes of pink and pale blue, stepped out of the mini-maelstrom. Her glossy black hair was piled on her head, held in place with jade and gold combs. Dr. Chen Wong, dressed in a red parka and heavy boots, followed behind her, two shovels over his shoulder.

"I have come as you requested, Dog."

Tom shook his head and smiled as he looked up at her. "You knew I'd need help."

"I suspected my assistance might be necessary." Her porcelain skin didn't hold the wrinkles it usually did, but the twinkle in her brown eyes was the same. "I will care for her. You must dig."

Once Tom settled Rain in Kwan Yin's arms, Chen tossed him a shovel. The surgeon shook his head and glared at his mother. "How are we supposed to dig frozen ground?"

She bowed her head. "It is no longer frozen."

Tom plunged his shovel into the soil. She was right. It was soft, like a field after the first rains of spring.

"How deep do we need to go?" Chen asked.

Tom eyed the body for a moment. "Four feet to play it safe."

They dug for the next couple of hours. Like it had with Abhartach, the snow avoided them with Kwan Yin there, though it was progressively getting deeper around the clearing.

Finally, Tom tossed the severed head into the hole. Together, he and Chen lowered the dwarf's body in with his feet pointing up.

Refilling the hole shouldn't have taken so long, but the poison was having its effect. His arms shook, and he dropped almost as much dirt as he tossed over the body.

"Wait."

Tom glared at Kwan Yin. "We don't have that much time."

She looked at the little crow, and he bobbed his head. "Place his companions in the grave with the sorcerer. Finish covering them. Then find three pebbles."

Tom looked at Chen, who shrugged. It took them a couple of precious minutes to collect the bodies of the crows and carefully place them inside the grave. While Chen shoveled in the last of the dirt, Tom combed the fence line for three appropriate rocks.

Once Chen packed down the earth and Tom placed the stones on top of the grave, Kwan Yin brushed Rain's face with her fingers. "Wake up, old friend. You have one more task."

Rain batted weakly at Kwan Yin's hand. "So tired."

"I know, but your magick must seal the grave."

Rain needed Kwan Yin's help to sit. She closed her eyes, and for an instant, Tom feared she'd passed out again. But she started singing.

The pebbles grew until they were nearly boulder-size. Nine ghostly crows with piercing gold eyes emerged from under the rocks. They circled the boulders three times before they settled on the stones. This time, the sorcerer wasn't crawling out of his grave.

Tom crossed the little clearing and sat next to her, but the light in her eyes was already gone. It took all his strength to reach out and gently push down her lids. A lump formed in his throat. "It shouldn't have ended like this." He slumped against the monument.

"It ended as it should have, Cu Chulainn."

At the familiar voice, he raised his head. Morrigan stood before him in her armor, spear in hand and red hair flowing. She held out her other hand. "It's time for us to go home, my love."

He took her hand and everything grew whiter and whiter until there was nothing to see but her emerald eyes.

Chapter 11

The harsh ring of the landline woke Jamal out of a sound sleep. Beside him, Shan stirred under their nest of blankets. He lifted his smart phone from the nightstand and glanced at the time. Seven-oh-four a.m.

Dawn.

The steady rhythm of Mom's voice came from the hallway. The cry of shock. Then Dante's deeper tones.

Out of instinct, he slid from his bed. Cold burned through his socks. He knelt and reached for the sword under the frame. Even as he remembered Tom had borrowed it, his hand found the smooth pommel. He dragged out the scabbard. Stared at it for a long moment before he pulled the steel free from the leather sheath.

Impossible.

As the thought raced through his brain, she gave a low mournful moan.

Shan bolted upright at the sword's sound. "What's wrong?" Steam clouded around her face. For a split second, he saw a dragon, not his girlfriend.

At the same time, a knock rattled the door. "Jamal, baby, wake up. That was Detective Rodriguez. Something's happened." His mom's voice. Pained and broken.

He knew. Rain and Tom weren't coming back. At least, not in his lifetime.

What should have been a ten-minute walk to Morrigan's Cauldron took the four of them nearly an hour trudging through the two feet of snow the nor'easter had dumped on the city. No one said anything over the steady roar of ploughs and the scrape of snow shovels. Sunlight bounced off the pristine drifts making Jamal wish he'd brought a pair of shades.

Unlike Mom's apartment, the store was warm and cozy when they stepped inside. Mom rushed into Tessa's arms and both of them started crying. Red rimmed Adrian's eyes as well, but he said nothing, just handed out mugs of strong black tea.

Jamal nodded his thanks and accepted the hot ceramic. The whole thing seemed surreal. He couldn't imagine the store without Rain's laughter or her sharp eyes that missed nothing. Or Tom's quiet certitude while training. The athletic bag that held the sword shuffled restlessly on his shoulder.

The bells on the door rang, but instead of their joyful tinkle, the sound was dull, hollow. The man who stepped through seemed the opposite. He was about Dante's six feet in height, much slimmer though, with pale blonde hair and the type of white skin that burned instead of tanned. His clothing screamed money, from the cashmere coat and tailored suit underneath to the sharp, conservative haircut.

"Good, you're all here." A Rolex flashed on his wrist when he removed his coat and tossed it on the counter before setting his briefcase on top of the scarred oak. Like this was his home. "I'm Luke Fairhaven. I represent Ms. Bean and Mr. Laoch in their earthly matters. Let's get down to business, shall we?" He started pulling folders and stacks of paper from his briefcase.

"Wait a minute." Adrian set his mug down with a harsh *clink.* "I want some details about this accident they were in. Rain doesn't—" He drew a harsh breath. "Didn't have a car."

Fairhaven stared at the contents he'd pulled from his briefcase. "Mr. Laoch's truck was stuck in a snow bank near Chinatown. Their bodies were found some distance from the truck, frozen. Obviously, when the truck ran out of gas, they tried to seek shelter from the storm and didn't make it."

He's lying. Jamal never dreamed he'd use something from the lame communications class NYU freshmen were forced to take, but the man's body language matched that of someone avoiding the truth.

Fairhaven shuffled paperwork and pulled out a sheaf. "I've already made arrangements for Mr. Laoch's truck to be released from the police impound lot." He met Jamal's gaze. "Per his last will and testament, all worldly goods go to Mr. Jamal Washington."

Jamal automatically held out his hand for the first set of papers. A brand-new title sat on top of the sheaf, his name clearly typed on the line for the owner's name. But it was the look on Fairhaven's face that unnerved him. The one that said the attorney knew exactly what Jamal was thinking.

He stared at the paperwork to break the eye contact. Not even Rain's freaky mind-reading trick bothered him this much.

"As for the gym—" the attorney began.

"Wait." Jamal looked up at Fairhaven. "What about Tom's family? Shouldn't they get his stuff?"

Fairhaven blew out a breath and stared out the large front window for a moment. "Ms. Bean was his closest relative here, Mr. Washington."

"Rain?" It didn't make sense. Tom admitted at Mom and Dante's wedding that he and Rain knew Adrian and Mom were third cousins. So why would he hide his and Rain's relationship?

A wry smile quirked the attorney's lips. "She was his aunt." A collective set of gasps came from the rest of their group.

"What are you talking about?" Mom asked. "Neither of them said anything of the sort."

"Not to mention, they were . . ." Tessa's face flamed bright pink as she realized the implication of Tom and Rain's romantic relationship. "It's not true. It can't be." She buried her face in Adrian's chest, and he wrapped his arms around his fiancée.

Fairhaven had the audacity to snicker. "If it makes you feel better, Ms. Mc-Clain, she was his aunt by marriage. Not to mention his father was adopted, so there's nothing untoward about whatever sexual relationship they had."

Dante surged forward. "You may think this is funny, asshole, but they were our friends."

Jamal grabbed his stepfather's shoulder. "Let it go, man. There's nothing we can do. They're gone."

The ex-marine whirled and glared at Jamal. "I don't care. He's *not* insulting our friends."

Fairhaven waved his hand over the stack of papers. "Can we please get through this? I do have a flight to catch."

"The airports are closed because of last night's snow storm," Tessa blurted.

Fairhaven drummed his finger on the counter, a perturbed expression on his face.

When everyone stayed silent, he continued. "As I was saying Faraday's—"

"Tom doesn't own Faraday's gym," Jamal said.

Fairhaven rolled his eyes. "Please?" He waved a hand at the pile again.

"Sorry," Jamal murmured.

"The gym is now Jamal's as well." He looked Jamal in the eye. "I suggest you keep Manuel Garcia as manager. He's done an excellent job, and it's been profitable despite the recent recession. However, he'll be looking to retire in seven years. You might want to consider making Mr. Jones a co-manager."

Jamal nodded and accepted the next pile of paperwork the lawyer handed him.

Fairhaven spent another half-hour going over the division of the store's business and building between Mom and Adrian.

Then the attorney pulled out a sealed envelope. He handed it to Mom. "This is Ms. Bean's private instructions concerning the training of yours and Ms. McClain's daughters." He stared Mom in the eye. "They will be like you, you know."

"My daughter?" Tessa squeaked.

Fairhaven smirked. "You and Mr. Holloway forgot to use secondary protection while you were on antibiotics for your sinus infection last week. She will be born on Samhain."

Everyone remained silent and stared at each other for a long moment. This was too much like the crap Rain pulled, always knowing things she shouldn't.

"Mr. Fairhaven?" Shan looked nervous addressing him, which was weird since her mom was an attorney, too, though this guy could have given Rain a run in the freaky department. "Wh-what about their bodies? Or a funeral?"

A shiver ran through Jamal. Despite what the lawyer said, there was no way Rain and Tom had simply frozen to death.

"It's already been taken care of," Fairhaven answered. He started shoving the remaining folders into his briefcase.

"When?" Mom asked. "Where?"

Fairhaven clicked his briefcase shut and grabbed his coat. "If you wish to arrange a memorial service here in New York for their acquaintances, that's your prerogative. I've done my job by following their instructions to the letter."

Thoughts raced through Jamal's head. Rain had always said the six people in the room and Tom were her family. Maybe she hadn't been speaking figuratively.

And if everyone in their family were *special*, it would explain the zombie last summer and the demon at the Halloween party. But if the demon that had been after Rain had killed her and Tom, there would have been some evidence. Did Fairhaven know about the demon? What was he hiding?

"Good day, ladies and gentlemen." Fairhaven stalked across the floor and yanked open the door. A blast of frigid wind hit the pile of remaining Imbolc flyers on the counter. The red papers flew in all directions.

All except the gold one on the bottom. A flyer accidentally left over from the Lughnasadh celebration six months ago. The beginning of all the monsters coming out of the woodwork.

Lugh.

Luke.

Everything clicked in Jamal's head, and he raced for the door.

Pedestrians were venturing out on the sidewalks. The figure of the tall blonde man bobbed nearly a block away.

"Mr. Fairhaven!" Jamal jogged after the fake attorney.

The man ignored him and headed for the crosswalk.

"Lugh!"

The light turned green, and the Tuatha stepped onto the snow-covered blacktop.

"Grandfather!"

Lugh paused in the middle of the street and slowly turned. He no longer looked quite human. His pale blonde hair was shaggy. His eyes were set wider apart, and were a more intense blue than they appeared before. His skin wasn't just pale. It looked like the fine bone china cups Mom used for the holidays.

"It's a dangerous thing you claim, child." The quiet voice cut through the sounds of the city coming out after the storm.

Jamal slowed to a halt in front of Lugh. "But it's the truth, isn't it?"

Everything ground to a stop around them. The handful of trucks on the street paused. No honking, no obscene gestures at the two of them standing in the crosswalk. The outlines of people fuzzed. Even the pigeons paused in mid-flight.

The smile Lugh gave him held teeth far sharper than a human's. "Truth is a relative term."

Jamal pulled the bag from his shoulder. "I believe this belongs to you."

Laughter echoed from the buildings, bright and sharp despite the blanket of snow. "Not any more. She has chosen, and chosen wisely I suspect."

The old stories ran through Jamal's head. "Is everything okay between Tom and Rain? I mean, I know they forgave each other before he died . . . the first time. But I don't get why they came back."

Lugh looked toward the ice blue sky for a long moment before his attention returned to Jamal. "Things are coming. The mortals need champions. The champions needed to be taught. There are . . . limits to what we can do here and now." He turned to walk away.

Desperation and grief gripped Jamal. "Will we see any of you again?"

Lugh peered at him over his shoulder. "You already know the answer to that, grandson."

"Then tell Tom . . . tell my grandfather . . ." Jamal fumbled in his coat pockets. Lugh turned and waited with an impatient expression.

Dammit, I can't say thank you, not to a Tuatha. But what the hell could he give? His fingers closed around a tiny plastic figure. His lucky dinosaur.

Mom couldn't afford a babysitter when he was little. When Tom watched him, they almost always went to the Museum of Natural Science. The little yellow and green velociraptor Tom bought for him had been his first toy.

He held out the little dinosaur. "Give this to him. Tell him he's the best teacher I ever had."

Lugh accepted the brightly colored bit of plastic and inclined his head. He lifted his foot.

Jamal blinked in the bright sunshine. The Tuatha disappeared between one step and the next. Not fading, just simply not there.

A horn blared. Jamal whirled to find a four-wheel drive SUV, the man behind the wheel gesticulating wildly. He jogged back to the sidewalk, and the driver gunned his engine. The SUV fishtailed for a second before the tires gripped the icy slush that covered the pavement.

Jamal tried to wrestle the implications as he walked. He approached the store when something on the opposite side of the street caught his eye. A dog sat next to the bus stop bench in front of the Wongs' restaurant. The mutt was freakin' huge. Next to the dog, a crow perched on the back of the bench.

The two animals looked at each other. Six months ago, if someone had told him the dog and the bird were talking, he would have thought that person needed a trip to Bellevue. But after he'd dealt with a *kiang shi*, a Celtic demon and finding out he was related to a god in the last year, reality was up for grabs.

The dog rose and shook himself. He walked to the crosswalk and looked both ways before he trotted across the street. His tags jingled, a cheery sound.

Huge wasn't the word to describe the mutt. Maybe ginormous. His shoulder easily reached past Shan's waist. Automatically, Jamal slung the sword bag over his shoulder and held out his right hand. The dog approached cautiously and sniffed. Once he finished his inspection, he wagged his tail so hard he nearly tipped himself over.

Jamal laughed and petted the mutt. The canine patiently waited while he checked the tags. Current shots. New York County dog license. When he saw the dog's name on the front and "Jamal Washington" printed on the back of the nametag, he wasn't a bit surprised.

"Come on, Hound." He waved and the dog followed him into the store.

"What the hell is that?" Tessa took a wary step away from the two of them.

Jamal grinned. "This is Cu Chulainn. Another one of my inheritances."

Mom stood frozen at the counter. "Names have power, Jamal. You know that. Maybe you should give him another name."

"What's wrong with Cu Chulainn?" Dante interjected. "He was the greatest hero in Irish mythology." He flashed Jamal a startling white grin that said, "See? I'm doing my homework."

"He does look like he's part Irish wolfhound," Adrian commented.

Hound trotted over to Shan and started sniffing her. When she giggled, he sat and wagged his tail.

Mom closed the distance between her and Jamal. "Maybe you should find another home for him, baby. He's too big for a New York apartment, and you definitely can't keep him in your dorm room."

He sucked in a deep breath. "I was thinking about that. What if I move into the loft apartment? That way one of us can keep an eye on the shop, we'll save on my room and board at NYU, and Hound can stay here."

Mom gave him the skeptical eye. "I don't know—"

"Look, you and Dante are going to need more room when my baby sis is born." Jamal waved a hand toward the other couple. "Same with Adrian and Tessa."

Tessa's pale cheeks turned hot pink at the suggestion. "We don't know that I'm pregnant yet."

Both Jamal and Mom faced her. "You are," they said at the same time.

Mom turned back to him, her expression sad and lost. "This is all too fast. We don't have any answers . . ."

"They've been in front of us all along, Mom," he said softly. He drew her to the window. "Read the words, then look across the street."

Her lips mouthed the sign. Her body went rigid at the crow still perched on the back of the bus stop bench. Her hand went to her mouth, and her gaze shot to the dog, who happily sat next to Shan.

The huge mutt rose and padded over to Mom. Clear, expressive eyes looked up at her.

"It can't be," she whispered. Her eyes widened until white shone around the glittering brown irises.

"Cu Chulainn wasn't just a legend. Great-grandma Virginia and Great-aunt Georgia were descended from him." He laid a hand on Mom's shoulder. "Rain and Tom sacrificed their mortal bodies to keep Abhartach from obtaining the Morrigan's power to murder the last of Cu Chulainn's line. We're the only ones who can wield the Sword of Lugh. Keep the human race safe." The rest of what Lugh had said could wait until later, once everyone absorbed the events of the last couple of days.

The bells on the door rang, this time with a little jingle of hope. A woman poked her head into the store. "Are you open?"

Inside the store, the wave of relief at the interruption was almost palpable. Adrian waved her inside. "Of course. How can we help you?"

The woman stepped inside. "Praise the Lady. I just need some candles. We've got heat." She grinned. "Thank the gods for good old-fashioned steam power. But our electricity's out."

Within five minutes, more people poured into the little shop. The business helped keep Mom and the older folks' minds off their loss. Hound didn't leave Shan's side. Adrian assigned her to ringing up people in order to keep the huge dog behind the counter so he wouldn't alarm the customers.

Jamal glanced out the window as he helped an elderly lady pick out some novels from the used paperback shelves. He would have sworn the little crow on the bench across the street knew he was looking at it. The ebony bird bobbed its head once before it flew away.

Acknowledgments

Without the following people, this book would not be in your hands . . .

To Jaye Manus of QA Productions for dealing with my perfectionist streak with grace and to Elaina Lee of For the Muse Design for figuring out what I want despite haphazard descriptions.

Much love to Genius Kid, who is off in the world, adulting now, and to Darling Husband, who only smirked when I demanded we fill our empty nest.

Suzan Harden is a recovering attorney who writes fiction to regain her sanity. She currently lives in the Great Lakes region with a husband who believes writing is a practical career option and a kid who thinks she's too enamored with superheroes.

Visit her webiste: www.suzanharden.com. Or check her out on Twitter (twitter.com/Suzan_Harden) or Facebook (facebook.com/SuzanHardenWriter)